TUNNELS

E. A. Padilla

David,

I hope you enjoy the book!

Sincerely,

E. A. Padilla (aka Andre)

Tunnels
E. A. Padilla

EAP Publishing

eappublishing.com

Copyright © 2017 E. A. Padilla

ISBN 978-09964818-5-4

First Edition 2017

PUBLISHER'S NOTE

Also by E. A. Padilla

RULE ONE TWENTY

MICHASO

Dedication

I want to extend a shout out of gratitude to my friends, family and loyal readers.

Thanks to those who volunteered the use of their names for characters in the book: my friends Peter Davies, Doug Elliott, Carla Hutchison, and James Newland; and my family Kyle B. Blair, Shelby "Angelie" Blair, and Nena Valdez.

Also, a special thanks to Tony Yoder for his insight as a military pilot; to Tony Castro for his insights into the Marine Corps; and to my mother, Clara Neebling, for her artwork on the cover.

1

The satellite tech's eyes were tired and dry and became scratchier with each blink. His vision began to blur. Without looking at the clock, he could sense that his ten-hour shift was about to end. Unlike his pilot friends, his acceptance into this elite Satellite Intel position did not require 20/20 vision. In fact, one hundred percent of his team, from the lowly filing clerks to his commanding officer, all wore prescription reading glasses. The glasses were their distinguishing feature. Like a long distant runner from Kenya with a thin sleek physique, so it was the SIGINT'S SAT INT (Signal Intelligence-Satellite Intelligence) Unit. The SAT INT's distinguishing characteristic was prescription glasses.

The selection process for SAT INT centered on one's ability to remain focused. One exam required candidates to search, for long periods of time, for slight variations in colors and topographical anomalies. It was a skill that most of the general population considered irrelevant. It came as no surprise that his co-workers, since childhood, enjoyed solving jigsaw and Sudoku puzzles, and loved astronomy. It was probably the overuse of their eyes that caused the fatigue and need for prescription glasses.

"So, anything new?" asked the X.O. (Executive Officer).

Blinking his eyes, Lt. Doug Elliott, known as Moon Dog to his friends, turned his head away from his oversized HD color monitor and faced the X.O.

"No sir," Moon Dog replied as he stretched his arms above his head and released a big exhale. "I've been waiting for Labor Camp 101 to perform their monthly execution. I've got a feeling it's about that time again."

The X.O. glanced at the wall calendar. "The DPRK (Democratic People's Republic of Korea) tends to perform their executions on Fridays, although in April and December they preferred Wednesdays. I wonder why?" X.O. Newland mused out loud to no one in particular. "How's that new GSP (Geothermal Subterranean Program) working?"

With excitement, Moon Dog explained, "It came online early last night. It took a while to dial it in. During our initial briefing with the Development Department geeks, we decided to divvy up the area around each labor camp into one-hundred-meter-square quadrants. Each team member was assigned one hundred sub-quadrants. If we can perform a cursory scan, we should be able to process at least two quadrants a night. Based on those estimates, we will complete the cursory evaluation within fifty days. From there, we can identify areas that warrant more scrutiny."

Nodding his head, the X.O. listened. "Go on, Lieutenant."

Grateful the X.O. wanted more detail, Moon Dog continued. "We learned something already, not that it should have been a surprise. This region has countless larger-than-normal underground lava tube formations. It's smart that the DPRK chose to modify their existing geology. It makes sense. These guys are very resourceful. Smart. Much of their work has been done for them by Mother Nature. If they're lucky, the lava tubes are going the direction that they want."

Images from Labor Camp 101 were picking up movement. The X.O. and Lt. Elliott exchanged glances. The X.O. raised his chin, directing Lt. Elliott's attention back to the large screen. The satellite transmitted its data down to the Agency's secure top secret building inside of Camp Bonifas along the DMZ (Demilitarized Zone) just four hundred meters from the border separating Korea along the 38th parallel. Lt. Elliott turned his attention back to the screen. It was clear that the occupants of Labor Camp 101 were beginning to gather outside of the barracks.

One of the other Surveillance Techs commented, "Looks like it's going to be a communal stoning today. Guess they got tired of the standard bullet to the head. This poor guy must have tried to escape."

"It's been a while since they've used stones," the X.O. interjected. "Poor bastard," he added in a soft whisper loud enough for Moon Dog to hear.

Lt. Elliott magnified the view inside the compound. Modern technology had changed the way data was collected. In the past, surveillance required the use of cameras, film drops, and high flying jets. Back then, the U2s and SR-71s ruled supreme. Today, the satellites were the workhorses. They represented the bread and butter of the Agency's SIGINT. Technology allowed for super high definition and super high-speed filming. Now, videos could be slowed down, making it possible to watch the fluttering of a bumblebee's wings. Other videos could freeze the wings still during their inflight hover. Video clips could be broken down to individual photos without blurring. Images were clear, focused, and capable of four hundred eighty distinct colors.

Moon Dog's monitor displayed close-up images in the crowd. As all twenty-two Surveillance Techs directed their attention to Lt. Elliott's monitor, the room became still. To be present in the room, one had to have the highest security clearance. Everyone held a key-coded secure card and had the clearance to see what was about to be shown. Everyone present had witnessed a DPRK execution. The most novice tech in the room had already witnessed four. Everyone present knew this one wouldn't be their last.

The X.O. understood human curiosity. The reaction seemed universal. The entire SAT INT unit watched in silence. One could feel the vibe of the room change. There was something about witnessing the final moments of a person's life. Although morbid, it was spellbinding. No one offered commentary. They each went through their own internal processing. The initial disgust was followed by self-reflection, then sadness. For this unit, it was part of the job. Life in the military inevitably involved witnessing the death of others. Unlike the combat units, it had been a rare occurrence that members of SIG INT had, with such regular frequency, been exposed to executions. The DMZ was no ordinary place. The border between North and South Korea was considered by many to be the most dangerous place on earth.

The SIG INT unit had no control over what it witnessed, documented, or reported on. Its role was to capture data, organize it, and forward it. There were others at different pay grades and different skill sets. These people were the analysts. They made the recommendations. Hangings and public executions were still performed the world over. During America's recent past, photographic images were circulated. It was human curiosity. Watching an execution came with the understanding that one was about to witness the last moments of another person's life. From the moment of death, everyone present understood that the person was gone. That person had no more tomorrows. The finality and frailty of life was never better understood than when one watched a person die. The absolute empathy, the universal understanding of death, was something every human would someday face personally. Those present were forced to contemplate their own mortality right then and there.

Most people accept that their life is finite; they acknowledge that one day, we each in our own set of unique circumstances will cease to exist. But witnessing an execution forces the onlooker to think it through. It no longer represents an intellectual matter to contemplate at some future time. Being in this SAT INT Unit provided each member a steady, in-your-face event that challenged each person to reach his or her own conclusion about life after death.

The irony of the situation was that the Agency knew exactly where these atrocities were taking place. They knew exactly who was in authority and who participated. However, they could do nothing about it. It didn't take long before the more senior technicians had seen enough. They were no longer intrigued. The fascination that had drawn their attention to the macabre scene began to wane. Their morbid curiosity had diminished. Heads began to turn away from the monitor.

The hum of the computer fans was the only noise in the surveillance room. Waiting, everyone sat motionless. Moon Dog's monitor flashed the images of at least fifty DPRK camp laborers. They were walking toward the center of the clearing. They gathered around rocks stacked up in a pile. The blank expressionless faces were framed by the edge of the monitor screen. The group of laborers parted, making way for two fellow laborers. Holding the man's arms, they escorted him toward a large pole buried into the ground. It was clear what was about to take place.

At that moment, a loud electronic buzzing sound cut through the silence of the room. The oversized red light that was mounted to the center of the ceiling panels began blinking. Everyone in the room looked up at the light, then back down toward the X.O.

"What is that noise?" asked the newest Surveillance Tech.

In unison they looked up, rotating their swivel chairs toward the center of the room. Staring away from the monitors, they waited for the X.O. to speak.

"It's the new GSP (Geothermal Subterranean Program). It just picked up something." Following protocol, the X.O. barked out his orders. "Lt. Elliott, have you been recording Labor Camp 101 activities?"

"Yes, sir!"

"Good. Everyone, redirect your individual monitors. Check your assigned quadrants." The X.O. looked up at the main system Admin Monitor. He located the flashing numbers 830, then continued. "Go to quadrant 830. The surveillance system will continue to save images of all surveillance activity on the bird."

In unison, the Surveillance Techs switched their monitors to quadrant 830. They had trained for this moment. It was their first non-training event. It was happening live.

"Everyone, focus on your assigned sub-quadrants."

Everyone began recalibrating their computers and went to their preassigned sub-quadrants. The GSP booted up and began searching through each quadrant for any underground anomaly. It was designed to locate any movement other than a natural geological phenomenon. It didn't take long. Within minutes, Lt. Elliott's computer terminal began chirping a high-pitched ping. It sounded like those used with submarine sonar systems. Everyone turned and looked at Moon Dog.

"I've got it, X.O.! It's sub-quadrant 64!"

"Holy shit, Moon Dog!" replied the X.O. "Here we go! Re-task Satellite 7. I want a redundant bird lined up to takes this one's place if we need to desynchronize the orbit. We want those coordinates isolated and the subterranean mapping started ASAP. After the back-up bird is programmed and tasked to this new location, I want to begin to un-sync and rendezvous to the West Coast drop site. This matter is now Top Level clearance and "hands-on only" security protocol. No email or transmission of this data in any format. Understood?" The X.O. shot a stern face toward each member of the team, making eye contact with each member, daring someone to speak.

The X.O. reached across his Admin console and pushed the red toggle switch, deactivating the recording program that forced an erasure of the data fifteen minutes pre-location of the sub-quadrant. This prevented any other computer in their surveillance systems to store this data. Now, the data was only being stored on the satellite flying 22,236 miles above. After erasing the data, the program began overlaying that memory with the general surveillance of the labor camps, rendering it irretrievable. For all intents and purposes, it was now up to the bird in the sky to capture and deliver the data. Nothing was saved inside Camp Bonifas' top security facility.

Now, the Agency was dependent upon the satellite's capabilities. From that moment forward, only the satellite recorded the images. For the time being, the satellite's ability to transmit surveillance data had been cut. The only open lines of communication the satellite had to earth were directional and maintenance commands; all other communications had been disabled. The surveillance system and the communication systems were designed as separate standalone systems. Nothing was shared, not even their power supplies. In fact, the research and development had been provided by separate companies and then assembled together in a plug-and-play scenario. The developers were unaware that their systems were operational. The Agency led the developers to believe that the project had been shelved. It would take a complete rebooting of the program to delete and scrape all prior data. It was a real deletion and scraping, not like the way commercial PCs delete programs.

Going forward, the satellite data would be exchanged the "old school" way, from hand to hand. To prevent any unauthorized dissemination or alteration of this information, every person in the chain of command would now be under strict surveillance to assure that protocol was maintained.

"We're opening a project name for this intel," explained the X.O. He opened a separate random-name-generating program. He entered his security clearance code and pressed enter. The system selected the project name: *Hummingbird.*

"Okay people, the code word for this data is now called *Hummingbird.* Lt. Elliott, because your assigned quadrant was where the anomaly was found, you'll need to sign the witness form confirming the decision to cease all local recording of data. Are we in agreement, Moon Dog?"

"Yes, sir, X.O.!" barked Lt. Elliott.

The X.O. exited the room to retrieve the form that was printing in the outer room on the main floor. As the door to the Surveillance room slammed shut, the newest Surveillance Tech broke the silence as he walked toward Moon Dog. "Lt. Elliott, I don't understand. What just happened?"

"The goddamned North Koreans are digging another tunnel!" Moon Dog replied.

*   *   *   *   *

Angelie just completed the required one hundred hours of international teaching credential program studies and had received her certification. She had been raised in the United States, adopted at five years of age from Korea. Her goal was to return to South Korea and teach.

Like most Korean Americans, her family ate only Korean food, watched Korean dramas, and watched only Korean network news. To do this, they had installed a specialized internet receiver with a separate subscription that allowed them to get every major South Korean network, in real time, while living in the US. Her family attended an international Christian Church made up of many biracial couples. Most couples had met while the husband served in the military in South Korea. A fair number of Korean families lived near Kansas City, Missouri.

There was even a small Koreatown, an area that catered to Koreans, with restaurants, grocery stores, and countless other services that one would need to survive in the modern twenty-first century world. In the unique style particular to the Korean Culture, beauty shops, travel agents, insurance and real estate agencies, cell phone shops, cosmetics boutiques, and natural health food stores all crowded inside an oversized grocery store that had once housed a Kmart store.

Similar to other ethnic mega stores, Koreans followed this shopping mall concept. After finishing with their shopping, many patrons ended the experience with a visit to the food court that provided authentic Korean cuisine.

An American unaccustomed to this type of shopping environment would have felt somewhat out of place. Because these mega stores catered to Koreans, Hangul (Korean language) was the predominate spoken language. The cashiers spoke English. Within the community, these cashiers maintained an elevated status compared to the non-English-speaking customers who assumed these cashiers could speak perfect English. In reality, not so much. For American-born patrons, no such accolades were given. It was a struggle to understand some of the cashiers with their heavy accents.

Ju Hee had taken on an Americanized name Angelie. She had heard the name during the playing of an old subtitled American Western movie. She pleaded with her adoptive parents to be called Angelie, and they finally agreed. It was printed on her first communion and baptismal ceremony notification.

Most people who knew her family would have described them as an ordinary immigrant family, chasing the American dream. Angelie's parents ran a dry-cleaning business that employed only her parents. No one outside their family unit was hired. On rare occasions, one parent would travel back to Korea while the other parent stayed behind, tending to their business.

Her parents had lived in the US for over thirty years. Their conversations with other merchants in Koreatown helped soften their accent. Even within a small country like Korea, there were subtle regional accents, and sayings that suggested where a person had learned to speak, just as in the US, where the distinct pronunciation in New England stood in deep contrast to the drawl of the deep South. Her parents had attended night school and hired a private tutor. They wanted to become more proficient with the English language. Their goal was to use English as their principal language, but not for the reasons one would expect. From time to time, her parents relaxed. They would forget their mission and let their guard down. Whenever this happened, their old speaking styles reappeared.

These lapses never lasted through an entire conversation. Rather, it happened while pronouncing a word or using a phrase. On those rare occasions, their so-called Korean friends never mentioned it. The reaction might be a raised eyebrow, knowing that they must have been from the north. It was understood that some immigrants came from the northern territory. Unless they chose to share their background, it was left alone and never brought up or discussed. Unlike Americans, most Koreans would not mention such things. It was none of their business. The Koreans held in high esteem others who had a "heavy mouth."

Both of her parents claimed to have been born and raised in Seoul. Given their declarations, no one mentioned anything—at least not to their face. Their friends had their reservations. It was understood that people had their own reasons for leaving their homeland. Korean immigrants were not motivated to dig deeper to prove anything to the contrary. If people chose to twist their story, who were they to question their reasoning? Most people hid from a past. For Koreans, it was no one else's business. In their eyes, omitting things wasn't deceitful; it was their choice. No one questioned it. Angelie's parents had lived in the US for many years. Those who noticed the accent chose not to mention it.

Both of Angelie's parents had jumped into the US from Vancouver, British Columbia. They came across under the cover of a Canadian winter storm. Unknown to their smugglers, the DPRK government had made all the arrangements, using a Chinese associate who helped them with these cases. The associate had been paid in Chinese currency. When a job was paid with crisp, clean, fresh, uncirculated bills that appeared to have come straight from a bank's vault, it always got his attention. Being a professional smuggler, he was experienced in dealing with many types of currency. He understood how to detect counterfeit bills. Not once had the DPRK ever passed him bad money. Ever.

Without fail, the people he transported for the DPRK were serious. Without exception, those travelers were determined, prepared, and unfazed by their long, dangerous journey to the US. And the hardships where many. Her parents started their journey hidden inside the deep bowels of a Chinese cargo ship. For weeks, it cruised over the Pacific Ocean. During the entire six-week voyage, they never saw natural sunlight.

After arriving in Canada, they faced even more isolation. They were hidden inside a steel freight-train boxcar dropped off along an isolated road next to a train track along the US-Canadian border. The smugglers tried to calm the stowaways hidden in the containers. They would be locked away for two days. The only available food was stored inside several plastic grocery bags. They contained cold packets of stale vegetables and rice. The fifteen stowaways shared several oversized plastic buckets to relieve themselves. To keep warm, each person was provided a thin dirty sleeping bag, blankets, and pillows. Then they were forced to wait for the smugglers' return. This was the most dangerous part of the journey. Fearing fire, no heaters were provided, and there was a finite amount of air as well as food. The smugglers had learned these lessons the hard way. The current process, was the true, tested, and safest way.

Over the years, the smugglers noticed that the stowaways who paid with crisp uncirculated bills were different. Unlike the others, these people exited those stuffy foul smelling metal containers without any reaction. They were the only ones who never complained. Unlike the others, they never smiled as they emerged into the fresh Canadian mountain air. They never raised their arms in a celebratory victory. Instead, these stowaways just marched along, crossing the snow-covered pathway and jumped over the railroad tracks. Out of habit, the smugglers studied the individual stowaways as they struggled up the embankment on the opposite side of the railroad tracks and then descended to the waiting cargo van on the dirt highway. Sometimes, a few of the stowaways projected an image of physical strength and endurance.

Once the stowaways were safe inside the van, most flashed a huge ear-to-ear grin. Not these stowaways who paid with the uncirculated bills, though. The smuggler looked out over the dirty faces stuffed inside the van. As they traveled over the dirt, driving toward a snow covered paved road, everyone bounced on the bench seats. Once they reached the United States, those special few remained stoic. Their facial expression remained calm and determined. The smuggler knew from their reactions which travelers were truly from South Korea.

The smuggler watched the stowaways walk through the doors of the Denny's restaurant. It was easy to separate the members of this this ragtag bunch. Unlike the others, the journey for these special few was far from over. It was just beginning. The smuggler could sense that they were grateful to eat a warm meal. Watching them drink their strong black coffee and eat stacks of pancakes and slices of greasy bacon, he noticed slight differences. Watching them sit in the booth eating, he surveyed their faces. His gaze migrated toward the last two sitting in the far corner of the oversized booth. He had no doubt that these were the two. They were the ones. Someone else had paid their fee with three hundred thirty-four thousand Chinese Yuan, equivalent to $50,000 US dollars each. All the bills were crisp, clean and appeared to be uncirculated. The bills were bundled in official bank currency bands grouped into one-hundred-thousand stacks. These two travelers were different, he was certain. They weren't from Seoul. They were from the DPRK.

*   *   *   *   *

2

Nena had been promoted to her current position as the Korean Director of Intelligence's Satellite Surveillance Division. Her formal title acronym was KDI-SSD. Everyone referred to her as the Director.

She had risen through the ranks in her cultural homeland of the Philippines. Like the highest-ranking position in the US Government, the Agency had decided long ago that only "American" born citizens qualified to raise to the level of director and above. At that pay grade, the person had access to top secret materials. Due to the sensitive nature of the information, the Agency required some other intrinsic level with which to measure a person's loyalty. Presumably, being born in the US made a person more loyal. Therefore, it was somehow factored in. Given the thin veil of distinction between military and the civilian-based Agency, it was understood that the children of US officials and military personnel born abroad were automatically considered to be American citizens by birth, the overriding factor being that at least one of the parents was a citizen.

Nena Valdez had been born an only child. She was raised on one of the most important military bases in Southeast Asia. It was the home to the famous Seventh Fleet's forward maintenance station for the US Navy.

Nena's father had received his Master's degree in History from UC San Diego while assigned to the San Diego Navy Yard. His next assignment was to Subic Bay, in the Philippines. It was on that assignment that her father had followed the footsteps of many other military personnel, finding love and marrying a beautiful Filipina.

She happened to be the daughter of a prominent Philippine government representative. For several tours, her father was assigned to the Philippines. During that time, he sharpened his language skills, And this was the main reason his attention to language caught the eye of the Agency. Unknown to Nena, while still working for the Navy her father had been recruited into the Intelligence Division. Once Nena was recruited into the Agency, she became privy to this information, and learning this secret was more than a shock. She had thought she knew her father, yet he had been living a double life.

In hindsight, she recalled a subtle twinkle in his eye, like he was hiding something. Learning her father's secret, Nena revisited and analyzed those memories. She recalled conversations of a type that most typical young children have with their parents. With this new insight about him, she now recognized that her father always had the right answers. He provided unique points of view, providing detailed analytical responses to her innocent questions. He seemed to have input on any subject and was able to expound upon the how's and why's of the world. Rather than giving her the typical "because" or "I don't know" answers, for each question she asked, her father instead provided concise, well-thought-out responses. The information was presented so even a child could understand. Each reply included enough detail and background. It wasn't until she attended middle school that she noticed her father provided better answers than her teachers.

Nena's father was promoted within the Agency based on his outstanding work ethic and copious attention to detail. His field reports became the standard, and he received special attention from his superiors. As the political and military climate in Southeast Asia changed, his unique language aptitude was flagged by the Agency. He was approached with other opportunities that allowed him to stay in Southeast Asia. He was an American born citizen with Korean blood lines, he spoke advanced Korean and Spanish, and through his marriage he became proficient in Tagalog (the predominant language of the Philippines).

Language skills normally took years to acquire. The fact that he was a natural, having learned two of the languages from an early age, in a natural home setting as opposed to a structured artificial educational environment, was the key. His word usage, street vernacular, and subtle authentic and original sentence structures were what made him, and other people like him, valuable assets. From a language perspective, they could pass as locals. Maybe it was these same reasons that the Agency had kept their eye on Nena. She had been raised under a similar set of circumstances. Her father had proven his loyalty. He also demonstrated his ability to keep his occupation off everyone's radar. In this particular case, the old adage, that the apple doesn't fall too far from the tree, was accurate.

Nena was working behind her closed office doors, reviewing another intelligence briefing, when her secretary knocked on her solid oak double office doors. Hearing his knock, she raised her head from her desk.

"Enter."

"Director. We have a situation in the Surveillance Room. The new GSP found something. They've already disabled the bird and have submitted the required form for your signature."

Taking the printout, Nena read the authorization form. It was a new process, a new system, and this was the first time it had been used. The form was signed by a Lt. Douglas Elliott. The Authorization Form confirmed that Lt. Elliott was the agent assigned. He was the one who detected the presence of what appeared to be the construction of a new underground structure inside quadrant 830, grid 64. The form had also been signed off by the X.O., James Newland, and time stamped. It now awaited her signature and *red*-inked thumb-print. As she opened the top draw to her oak desk, she found her ink blot.

Like everything in the intelligence world, this ink blot was anything but ordinary. It had been engineered specific for Director Valdez. Each ink vessel had a unique composition, designed for each director. It was possible to duplicate a fingerprint, and even the retina of an eye, but not this chemical signature. Each blot was purposely created with slight variations in its composition. It was catalogued and microscopically coded. Only so many of these ink blots were created. The catalog was kept in the central archive, protected under layers of encoded electronic storage folders that could be accessed only through password firewalls. There were no hidden programs. No back door to infiltrate. All documents requiring this type of stamping authentication were placed in a vacuum-sealed envelope. A chemical reacting sealant was used that was designed to decompose over the next fifty years. This process was implemented so that an Archive Specialist could determine exactly how many hours earlier the authorization had been sealed. The process had been developed by the Agency and was similar to carbon dating analysis. Only the most sensitive and top secret issues utilized this form of authentication.

This Korean Surveillance Team was designed as an early warning process. By all means possible, its principal function was to predict and avoid a DPRK invasion into South Korea. There was evidence to support the belief that the discovery of tunnels created for that purpose could lead to another full-scale war. Such a discovery would be unlike the modern military campaigns in the Middle East. The Agency analysts understood the paranoia that existed in the DMZ; it was unlike any other spot on the globe. Finding an invasion tunnel could require the US to take a pre-emptive strike to destroy the tunnel. That action, in and of itself, would be an act of war. It would require the US to take the fight to them, inside their borders, and initiate an offensive maneuver. It would not be a retaliatory response to a DPRK attack.

Unlike Iraq, Libya, Afghanistan, Somalia, Vietnam, and the countless other countries in which the US had been militarily involved before, this was different. The DPRK possessed nuclear weapons. It had the fourth largest standing army in the world. What made the situation more dangerous was that the DPRK was isolated and paranoid, maintaining a serious belief that the US was bent on seeing them destroyed. This combination of factors was a recipe for a global disaster. What they had uncovered could be the spark to a powder keg that could not only lead to the destruction of both sides of the DMZ but escalate into a global conflict.

As Director Valdez inserted the fully executed authorization form into the clear plastic vacuum-sealed folder, she opened the expandable binder folder titled *"Hummingbird."* She snapped the ring binders shut, and the sound reverberated through her office. She punched the intercom.

"I need an encrypted message sent to our contact on the West Coast."

*　*　*　*　*

Walking through her kitchen, Carla Jo looked up at her laptop sitting on the countertop. It was open to her Gmail account. She had never given her email address out to anyone except her employer. She was working as a special independent contractor and maintained a low public profile. She was single; no children, no boyfriend, just her golden retriever Prince. Whenever she had to go on long assignments, she dropped Prince off at the local Veterinary Clinic. They were the only ones she trusted with him. Of course, he always got the VIP treatment; daily walks, special thirty-minute playtime, and a bath before he came home. Prince was ten years old and was known by everyone there. He really seemed to be royalty of some sort.

After getting a cold can of Mug Root Beer from her refrigerator, she glanced back at her laptop. Still no messages. She strolled back into the living room and rolled out her workout matt. It was her daily ritual. She planned to do an hour of crunches while she watched TV. Before turning on the television, she tilted her computer tablet, positioned it so it faced her, and leaned it against the couch. Carla Jo made sure to check her email. As a test, her employer would send her an email at varying times during the day. The employer timed the number of seconds it took each contractor to reply. She was told five years ago that the contactor with the best response time got the first opportunity on the next assignment.

When these contractors were on assignment, the daily emails were suspended. Upon the completion of an assignment, the email status checks would commence on the fourteenth day following the conclusion of their last assignment. The employer forced a two-week break. If they didn't, they knew most of the contractors would put themselves immediately back in rotation. It was like a forced unpaid vacation. Carla Jo's last assignment had concluded eighty-two days prior. She was getting a little antsy.

Like most of these special contractors, Carla Jo had an abundant supply of computer devices in which to keep in touch. She had a laptop, desktop, tablet, and two smart phones; an extra one in case her main one somehow broke or was rendered inoperable. Assignments were doled out only during a typical nine-to-five window. During those times, each device was opened to her Gmail account, the volumes set to max, and plugged into an electrical outlet to assure that each device remained fully charged. She was focused, prepared, and ready for her next assignment. She was "Good to go! Yes, sir!"

Carla Jo lived in a high-end apartment complex that looked more like a condominium unit with large oversized rooms and attaching two-car garages. Her place was located just off Highway 78, which ran east and west in the northern section of North San Diego County. She had selected her residence based on its strategic location. Ten minutes to the north was Camp Pendleton Marine Base, and thirty minutes to the south was Miramar Naval Air Station. Another fifteen minutes south was the Naval Base in San Diego and the Navy Seal Training facility on Coronado Island.

She was ex-military. Her claim to fame was being one of the first female combat-trained marines who was subjected to the same standards as her male counterparts. She had been recruited into a special elite program designed to work in conjunction with the Agency during covert civilian missions. In order to work in this capacity, she, like her other independent contractors, was assigned a civilian cover and had to work outside the normal confines of the military structure. For all intents and purposes, these people were ordinary citizens. But there was nothing ordinary about any of them. Like the other contractors, Carla Jo was an excellent marksman and swimmer.

At thirty-two years old, she was beyond fit and blended in, matching the Southern California stereotypical lifestyle. She surfed and was a certified scuba diver. From a distance, many disappointed young men, had unwisely approached her during her ocean swim training sessions. They had proceeded with the misguided belief that she was just another "So-Cal babe." The few men who got close enough got the message she wasn't interested from her stern, serious expression; she never smiled and remained stoic. Without pretense, she walked toward the shoreline, concentrating on the task ahead. Every day, she plunged into the breaking surf for a two-mile ocean swim. Without trying, she exhibited her physical strength and prowess. She exuded self-confidence and projected an absolute, undeniable confidence; a power to be reckoned with. She rarely noticed the presence of immature boys who approached her. They were invisible blips, brief nuisances soon to be dismissed. Her military training reduced others to inconsequential nothings that warranted no attention or concern.

Carla Jo's daily routine involved an early rise at five thirty. Dressed in sweat pants, she stretched out before stepping out for a quick five-mile warm-up jog before breakfast. She avoided caffeine and alcohol and participated in such distractions only when she was off the clock, which was almost never. Twice a week, she went to the shooting range, keeping her weapons skills sharp. One never knew when the situation would call for close, hand-to-hand combat to include her standard-issue Berretta M9 double-action sidearm, considered an effective weapon up to fifty meters. On the other hand, the contract situations she was tasked with had to be able to handle long distance shots as well. Like every one of her counterparts, she was a trained marksman with the Remington M40A5 rifle, better known as an A5. It was deadly accurate to one thousand meters. For a few elite special-ops personnel, a more beefed-up caliber, .338 Lapua Magnum, could reach out to one thousand, six hundred meters (equivalent to a mile). She was proficient with them all.

She lifted weights on Mondays, Wednesdays, and Fridays. Tuesdays and Thursdays were MMA (Mixed Martial Arts) training. Carla Jo had the physique of a person who had committed herself to be literally the best she could be. She was the result of years of drive, dedication, commitment, and perseverance.

Getting ready to watch her favorite movie, she slid the DVD of *The Shooter* into her Blu-ray player. She stretched out on her black exercise matt to perform a nonstop set of crunches. As she cupped both of her hands behind her head, lying on her back with her legs slightly bent at the knees, she heard a distinct tone. The noise blasted at full volume from each of her devices strategically located throughout her apartment. The sounds bounced off the walls to create an unusual synchronized electronic symphony. Directing her attention to the closest device, Carla Jo flipped onto her stomach and belly-crawled her way to her tablet.

Staring at the screen, she could tell that a message had just been delivered to her Gmail account. She was frantic as she pounded the display to access the message. When the message did finally display on the screen, she tapped the reply button and hurriedly typed "I am ready" and clicked Send. She watched the screen change as a prompt came back confirming that the message was sent. Carla Jo remained frozen, staring at the screen, her eyes unblinking. She was waiting for a reply. As she waited, she relived the time it took for her to reply. Wanting to get an exact time span, she accessed her sent messages. There was only a ten-second difference in the time stamp from when she had received and replied to the message. As she contemplated this time, she got an automated encrypted message. The caption read "I'm coming in at 7:14 a.m. PST." As her pulse began to race, she tapped the screen and opened the message.

Based on the day of the week, she would need her code book. To an ordinary person, it looked like a Sudoku Puzzle page. But embedded under the squares of the puzzle were small graphic icons. Only after the puzzle board was moved off the page could they be seen. However, even if this message had been intercepted, it had to be deciphered. The hidden message required that once it was accessed, a unique code had to be entered within ten seconds from the time the message was opened. The person had only one chance to enter the correct code word. If the wrong word was entered or the time limit had expired, the message would be permanently erased. In combination with the unique password, she would need to enter her code name,

SPARTAN. She loved the sound of it. She had no idea whether these code names were randomly assigned or picked. Either way, Carla Jo thought it fit her personality and lifestyle to a "t."

Carrying her computer tablet to her office, she set it down on her desk. Then she scurried into her master closet, turned the light on, and closed the door. Kneeling, she pushed against the drywall panel just behind the closet door. That section of drywall held a secret nondescript hollow pocket within the wall. As she pushed on the drywall, the magnetic latches, similar to those used in bathroom medicine cabinets, detached and a small drywall door swung open. Reaching into the opening, Carla Jo pulled out a small black book. Closing the panel firmly, she returned to her desk where she had left her computer tablet. She sat down and began looking for the code inside her black book. She had created a cheat sheet so she could locate the code with ease.

The code had two meanings that required Carla Jo to decipher the date as well, as if the code were flipped. Every day of the year was broken down into the number. It was either a regular year or a leap year. For example, the list started with 1-365, 2-364 and so forth. The numbers represented the day of the year with three hundred sixty-five days; 1-365 represented January 1. But because that was too simple, there was another factor which would determine if the date was to be flipped to its mirror opposite. Instead of the first day of the year, it represented just the opposite—the last day of the year, December 31. Carla Jo's cheat sheet broke down four sets of codes: a regular non-leap year, a regular leap year, a flipped opposite non-leap year, and a flipped opposite leap year. For a leap year, the code for January 1 read 1-366.

Using this decipher-code cheat-sheet reference, Carla Jo looked up at the message. A date determined whether the code would be flipped. Every message included a date. In reality, that date had nothing whatsoever to do with the actual date. It represented yet another code. The code would have a redundant meaning. An even month would have an even day. Or it would be an odd month with an odd day. An even date code meant that the decipher code would not be flipped to its opposite. If an odd month and date was used, then the message was flipped.

Once Carla Jo had her lists set out in front of her, with the top portions of the papers weighted down by heavy commercial staplers to prevent the papers from accidentally moving, she was ready to begin. She slid the cursor over the message icon and double clicked. The screen then flashed an overlapping screen with a blank input prompt. She typed her code name "Spartan" and punched enter. A date appeared: August 30, an even month and even day. Carla Jo now knew the code would not be flipped. This year was not a leap year, so she knew which decipher code sheet to use. She glanced across the dates on her cheat sheet and saw that August 30 was the 242nd day. So for a non-leap year, she would enter "242-365." She entered the deciphered code and pressed enter. Another email message opened.

Had she entered an incorrect code, or exceeded the allotted ten-second time limit, the message would have appeared as garbled gibberish. But she had processed the message perfectly, no mistakes. The message flashed onto the screen. As the message appeared, Carla Jo leaned forward, studying the Sudoku puzzle that appeared on the screen. The puzzle was titled *Hummingbird*. The puzzle configuration was always the same. A unique puzzle pattern had been created specifically for each contractor. Although the configurations were always the same, the data used inside of each puzzle was different. In addition, the underlying sections that hid the data fields was always hidden in the same locations. Carla Jo's puzzle configuration had six hidden fields.

During her training, she had been forced to learn the order in which she had to access all her messages. If a contractor opened the hidden fields in the incorrect order, the hidden data would be erased. The purpose for such elaborate codes, passwords, and failsafe measurements was twofold. The most obvious was to prevent unauthorized access. But the other, more sinister, reason was it gave the contractors several opportunities to purposely enter a wrong code and destroy the sensitive and secret information. It was understood that this information was never to be divulged voluntarily; it could not be compromised for any reason, even if it meant sacrificing their life or the lives of others. It was the cost of playing the game. The information the contractors received was beyond Top Secret. In every instance, the information they possessed was much more valuable than all the contractors' lives combined. At least that's what they had been told.

After accessing the fields in the correct order, she began to extract the information. Carla Jo copied all the data and pasted it into an extraction program. Once all the data was transferred into the program, she printed the data. Once she checked the printouts, certain that all six pages printed correctly, she moved the cursor up to the title and double clicked over the H. Another input prompt displayed. She entered her code name in reverse, "natrapS," and hit enter. The program erased all the data with a permanent hard scrub and began reformatting the hard drive to overlay the area with multiple layers of Whitney Houston's mpeg soundtrack of the national anthem during the 1991 Super Bowl. The program was designed to write, erase, and rewrite that mpeg, ten different times, over the portion of the hard drive that had been used to process this message, making sure that the data was permanently erased, incapable of being extracted even by the grunts back at Langley. The programmers thought that using that mpeg was fitting symbol. It was a hacker thing.

As the erasure program booted, a final important documented began printing. It was designed not to be shown on the monitor. The single page read "Congratulations! You've answered the puzzle correctly. Your prize can be found in the 33rd Catalog Edition, page 2078, paragraph 117, item 3950W." This print out was a simple code. It was the GPS location 33.2078, 117.3950 W. Carla Jo was very familiar with that location. It was somewhere in the Oceanside Harbor.

Carla Jo closed her tablet as well as the other devices in her apartment. She kept only her desktop computer open and began scanning the pages. The pages looked almost blank; at least, that's what anyone else would have thought. But the data had been printed on the back side of the page and was extremely small. She laid each page onto the scanner and began expanding the images to the maximum magnification. The image was still very small. She printed the magnified images and then went back into her master bedroom closet. She closed the door, opened the hidden wall access and returned the code book. After closing the secret access door, she walked to the other end of the closet and reached into the far corner of the upper shelf. On top, she pulled out what looked like an ordinary golf ball range finder. It wasn't.

Still inside the closet, she bent down and plugged the device into a Commodore Amiga Computer. This vintage machine had no modem connections and was hidden beneath her shoe rack. It was plugged into the only outlet that had been added to the closet and was hidden behind the rack. This obsolete computer had a sophisticated graphic card, however. The Agency had modified it to magnify these messages and then save the image on old-school floppy discs that had been enhanced with modern technology. Although the discs looked like the old plastic floppy discs that only had 1.2 megabyte storage, in reality they could store up to 1 terabyte; one million times more data. It was constructed with plastics and had no metal components. It could be hidden inside a book and pass through any international commercial airport without fear of detection or damage. The saved data could only be opened by another program designed by the Agency and using the same variable password and failsafe measures Carla Jo had used to access the original message.

Carla Jo appreciated that this assignment was going to be all about intelligence information. She was probably assigned this case because of her geographical location. Her intuition told her that the GPS coordinates most likely meant she would be picking something up from a satellite drop. This was a step back in time to the art of "old school" espionage. This assignment would involve a lot of hand-to-hand exchanges and face-to-face meetings. This was an art that only serious-minded intelligence agencies dared play; those unworthy or incapable of adhering to the rules need not apply nor participate. Only the foolish would enter this game, this arena, without appreciating the inherent risks. To be captured trying to compromise such data, or to vet human assets, would result in only one consequence. The Agency didn't care who such a person worked for. They had learned the hard way. The decision to extend a potential asset's life in hopes of determining who they worked for had proved a risk that failed more times than it worked.

The Agency changed its procedures when it came to security breaches. If a breach was confirmed, like a dam that had sprung a leak, the most immediate goal was to plug it. Once a spy was located, the risk that the person could escape and divulge any secrets was unacceptable. The new protocol was immediate termination. The priority was not to interrogate the mole. To have access to this level of information was in itself, an indication that others already knew too much. The first order of business was to eliminate the mole. Only after such a leak had been resolved would the Agency begin an investigation. The assumption was that the enemy now had the information. Two teams would be assigned to the same tasks; one assuming no compromise while the other one assumed they had the information. Two separate contingency plans were played out based on two very different sets of circumstances.

Espionage was a game of cat and mouse in which the Agency had been invited late to the party and was working hard to catch up. It had done a good job. Now, most other countries considered the US to be the gold standard of espionage. It had cut its teeth honing its skills dealing with the Germans, Soviets, Chinese, Cubans, Iranians, Israelis, and Koreans. In recent times, the Agency had been learning how to deal with most of the Middle Eastern countries. For the time being, it looked like it was again Korea's turn. Since 1954, the Democratic People's Republic of Korea (DPRK), better known as North Korea, had always remained on the

Agency's radar. After the passing of Kim Jong Il and the rising of his son, the Agency had taken an accelerated interest in the DPRK, as well as in the Middle East.

As Carla Jo began to piece together the cryptic message, she had a feeling that she would be making a trip to the Oceanside Harbor. Turning off the Amiga computer, she went straight to the desktop and rebooted it. She googled the GPS coordinates. Yup, she was correct. It was the Oceanside Pier.

3

Nena opened the sealed envelope. It confirmed that Satellite 7 had been released from its geostationary synchronized orbit and dropped into a low Earth orbit. It circled the globe every ninety minutes and was making its descent toward the West Coast of the United States. Nine revolutions around the earth would be required before it could drop its small encrypted payload. Unlike a standard communications satellite that was parked 22,300 miles above the earth, where the force of gravity is cancelled, military intelligence satellites were mobile with advanced and sophisticated propulsion systems. It could arrive at its destination within thirty-six hours.

Looking away from her report, Korean Director of Intelligence Valdez thought back to her prior briefings. She had been shown what a satellite package looked like. It looked almost like a bowling ball case, without handles. She was impressed by its light weight and strange texture. It wasn't metallic. It seemed to have a blended texture almost like a rock. When the designers explained the design and capabilities, she was impressed. The satellite was designed to not only evade and maneuver around commercial air traffic but to avoid civil and military authorities as it maneuvered toward a specific earth location using a specialized parachute system. To avoid detection, it could delay its parachute deployment as low as one thousand feet above sea level. Upon entry into the ocean, the package would disconnect its chute and submerge at a depth of two feet. The package was designed to maintain a distance no more than one hundred feet from its GPS target and maintain its location for up to seventy-two hours.

The delivery was timed to enter the water in the evening. An extraction contractor would be assigned to pick it up using an audio frequency receiver that was synchronized with the receiver that would be controlled by the contractor. When the package received the frequency emitted by the contractor's synchronized device, like a dog that runs back to its master, the package would rise to the surface of the water, making a beeline toward the device.

Closing the envelope, the Director hole-punched the message and placed it in the folder titled *"Hummingbird."* Glancing at the accordion-bunched folder spine, she contemplated how long it would take to fill it up to its maximum thickness of four inches. Valdez knew that she needed to start looking ahead to when the package would be processed and delivered to her in Camp Bonifas. The intercom buzzed, interrupting her thoughts.

"Excuse me, Director Valdez. X.O. Newland is here."

"Send him in."

The X.O. had been pulling an all-nighter, making sure that sub-quadrant 64, grid 830, had his full attention. Even with the sophisticated satellite images, he knew they'd need some feet on the ground. After saluting and waiting to be told to take a seat, X.O. Newland was eager and prepared to give the Director his report.

"So, X.O., what do you have for me?"

"Well, Director, here are the mapping images." The X.O. opened his working folder and handed the Director color copies. Newland knew she would be adding these documents to her folder. He pulled out several pages and handed them to her as he spoke.

"We're certain that some form of underground work is being performed. We've pulled in the Audio Bird from Vandenberg and are leaning into the sounds as best we can with the micro-narrowing software. The thing that makes the sounds so interesting is the lack of metallic and combustion engine noises that are typically associated with tunnel digging. Combine that with the lack of obvious roads to and from anywhere near the area we monitored, and it supports the notion that they are purposely hiding their efforts," the X.O. explained.

Raising his eyes from the colorful mapping diagrams, he paused until the Director's gaze broke away from the maps. As they made eye contact, he continued, "I'm sure you've considered the fact that we're gonna need boots on the ground?"

"Yes. Who were you thinking about bringing in?" the Director asked.

"How about Gibby?"

"Is he still active? Wow, that guy is a legend in his own right." After some contemplation, the Director nodded her head in agreement. "It makes sense. Right up his alley, really." Anyone else?"

"We're gonna need a newbie for the DMZ. Our prior local on-sight asset just punched his ticket and went Stateside. The other one took a pot shot to his shoulder while walking the DMZ from an overanxious DPRK border guard. He's still considered unfit for active duty until further notice; he'll be in rehab for the next six months. Go figure. After all these years without needing to utilize these assets for their intended purpose, now, with the shit hitting the fan, we're left empty."

Listening to the X.O., the Director opened one of the lower filing cabinet drawers and pulled out a thin folder. Glancing at the single sheet of paper inside, she contemplated the possibility of using a newbie that was landing later the next day. Looking up, she spoke.

"I've got a greenhorn flying in tomorrow. He's got military experience and even has some official political kill shots under his belt from Afghanistan. He has never been on a formal Agency assignment. He was just tapped during his last tour. All he knows is that sometime during this assignment, he will be posing as a regular DMZ grunt. Officially, he will be part of our detail. He's been briefed. He knows he will most likely be sitting on the bench waiting for some playing time."

"Well, Director, it's all about timing. Looks like this new guy will get a chance to show how prepared he is in terms of handling this opportunity. This is one hell of an opportunity, and I'm hoping he has a long list of skills ready to be put to work."

The Director punched up Lt. Kyle Benjamin's online personnel shield. Although he had entered the Marine Corps hoping to get his wings, he washed out due to an unusual medical situation that popped up during flight school. The kid didn't want to fly props, so he asked to go on the ground as a sharpshooter, something his father apparently did with the Corps. The Director liked what she was reading and felt optimistic. She knew this assignment would involve more than just taking pot shots from the DMZ guards.

"It's his third tour," she said. "He's twenty-seven years old, recently divorced, no kids. He's biracial, Caucasian-Filipino. Likes to work out in his spare time.

He's just under six foot and weighs in at one hundred seventy-five pounds.

"He's perfect. What's his cover assignment?"

"He's already slotted for the DMZ patrols for his first six months," replied the Director. Looking up and making eye contact, the X.O. and Director exchanged smiles.

"He sounds like our guy," said the X.O. "I'll drop by Gibby's tonight. What type of contract do you want me to offer him?"

"Standard twelve month. This assignment is dicey. Put a carrot of $100,000 at the end. If shit hits the fan, let him know his boots may be needed a little north of the 38th." The Director raised her eyes as if to measure the X.O.'s opinion on how the contractor would feel about it. Without hesitation, the X.O. replied.

"Oh, he's good to go. Gibby's an adrenaline junky. He'd probably love the chance to walk on the wild side," smiled the X.O.

"Be careful what you wish for. Make it happen," ordered the Director.

*   *   *   *   *

Carla Jo had been sitting in her car parked along the Oceanside Harbor. Her 4x4 Toyota 4Runner was parked in one of the oversized boat-trailer parking spaces. Given the easy access of the coastal beaches along all of San Diego County, no particular beach dominated in popularity. The entire thirty-plus-mile stretch of golden sand provided exceptional places for surfing, boogie boarding, and sunbathing. The locals had access to a resort lifestyle. Other than during the peak summer months, when a percentage of the 3.3 million county residents flooded to the beaches, followed by vacationers and the weekenders from nearby LA and

Orange Counties, this beach was for the most part, sparsely populated.

The monitor light bounced its reflection off the front windshield. She had been waiting until midnight before she ventured out into the Pacific Ocean. She had been tracking the package for the last twenty minutes. Her computer was pinging out the GPS coordinates of the floating buoy that she had placed out earlier in the day. Carla Jo had completed her preliminary reconnaissance of the area. No sailboats or other vessels had anchored in the area. The night was moonless and the water was flat.

She closed and slid her laptop under the driver's seat. Before she locked the car doors, she stepped out of the car with her bare feet and slid her full-body wetsuit over her one-piece swimsuit. She walked around to the back hitch and dislodged the kayak from the trailer. After dragging the kayak over the concrete walkway and onto the beach, she placed the car keys into a customized wetsuit pocket. She had already prepared and rehearsed her cover story. She planned on telling anyone who approached her that she was out on her weekly midnight kayak run.

As she paddled out toward the buoy, the satellite package hovered two feet under the surface of the water. She pulled out a duffle bag from inside the kayak. The ocean was calm, almost no waves. As she continued paddling out, an infrequent wave lapped up against the side of her boat. She continued paddling. Carla Jo glanced up, searching the horizon. No other boats had taken up position near the buoy.

Carla Jo had participated in similar retrievals. Through much practice, she had mastered the ability to spin the kayak in a full three-hundred-sixty-degree turn. With ease, she checked her surroundings. The last thing she wanted was to struggle retrieving the package and then be surprised; caught off guard by an unexpected boat. She was certain that no other vessel of any type was in the vicinity.

When she was within four hundred meters of the buoy, she opened the bag and pulled out the retrieval device, nicknamed "the dog whistle," and attached the long strap that was permanently attached to her wetsuit. She pushed a button and the device booted up. A small fluorescent screen wired to the device was stored in the bag. It lit up the interior of the kayak with a soft, mint-green glow. Fifty-two minutes had passed since she entered the water.

The strap and latches had been battle tested. It could withstand being run over by a sixteen-wheeler's fully loaded tractor trailer; it had survived being dropped from two thousand feet onto hard rock. Through it all, it still functioned properly submerged three-thousand meters under the ocean. She double-checked that the fastener was secure before she pulled it out of the safety of the kayak. Leaning out of the kayak, she stuck the dog whistle into the water. Using both hands, she had a firm grip onto both sides of the device. Using her thumbs, she depressed the toggle switch. Carla Jo scanned the ocean, looking for the package to break the water's surface.

The package had hovered without incident. When it received the high frequency message, the programing switched from its hibernation hover program and began to surface. The package began sending its reply to the dog whistle. Once the package surfaced, a red neon light began blinking and a high frequency tone began chirping out from the package. As the package ping sounded, a confirmation electric chirp was emitted from the dog whistle, almost as if each of these devices were calling back and forth between one another. As Carla Jo held the dog whistle underwater, she could see a small wake approaching the kayak. She tightened her grip on the dog whistle, anticipating the impact from the package.

The package was designed to react as it came into physical contact with another floating object. Once contact was made, the package would float stationary in the same location for twenty seconds. If the package wasn't retrieved by then, it would sink back under the surface of the water. Once submerged, it would revert to its automated circular hover, waiting to receive another high frequency message from the dog whistle. This process would repeat until the package was retrieved or the battery died, at which point, the package would sink to the bottom of the ocean.

As the package approached the kayak, the repeating tone increased in frequency until the sound reached a constant solid tone. As the package touched the dog whistle, Carla Jo's forearms absorbed the inertia of the impact. She glanced down into the water. She could see the package floating to a stop. Before reaching back into the ocean to retrieve the package, she lifted the dog whistle back into the interior of the kayak. She ran her hand over the top of the floating package to locate the handle. It felt similar to a suitcase handle. She gripped the handle and hoisted it into the kayak. Then she depressed a button initiating the transmission message back to the satellite. Thousands of miles above, a message was received, confirming that the package had been retrieved.

Carla Jo pulled a towel from inside the bag and wrapped it around the device. When it was safely wrapped, its size allowed it to be placed into the bottom of the kayak. Then she disconnected the dog whistle's leash and strung it through the package's handle several times and then reconnected the leash to her wetsuit. She was positive everything was secure. Now, she knew even if the kayak accidentally capsized, both the dog whistle and the package would remain attached to her wetsuit. It had only taken sixty seconds from the time the first high frequency message was sent out to the time the package was secured.

She glanced back and located the buoy she had placed out earlier in the day. She unharnessed it from a cord that was anchored to the bottom of the ocean. Once it was freed, she pulled the buoy toward the kayak. A thick, four-foot-long cord was attached to the kayak, and she attached the other end of it to the buoy, before dropping it and letting it float behind. She began paddling back to shore. Glancing around, she saw no one present. As she approached shore, she thought about her next move. She would need to take the package to the safe house, and she wasn't looking forward to the drive to Salton Sea. That's where the real work would be done.

4

Gibby sat in his office. His large, industrial sized metal doors were shut tight and locked. His encrypted laptop was open, sitting in the middle of his desk. He had already received confirmation through the satellite feed that the package had been safely acquired. Gibby was an eyes-on-target kind of guy. Using a satellite, he spied on Carla Jo from above, preferring to watch the action in real time. Gibby was assigned as the local lead agent. He had some skin in the game should anything go wrong. It was his decision to hire Carla Jo. He liked calling her CJ. Once this ball got rolling, he knew that as the lead agent out, posing as a regular non-affiliated Agency geek, Gibby was expendable. If things didn't go right, he'd be hung out to dry. Whenever he had an option, he had made a habit of going old school, eyeball to eyeball, hand to hand.

After Gibby saw CJ's vehicle drive away with the kayak in tow, he continued to watch her travel the surface streets toward Interstate 5. He kept her in view until she made the connection to Highway 78 East, at which point he closed the program and re-tasked the satellite to begin its climb back to 22,300 miles where it would escape earth's gravity. Once there, it was programmed to go into a geostationary orbit, posing as a communications satellite until it was needed again. The Agency had one of these parked satellites in every time zone around the globe. This made it very easy to reposition their birds to see anything, anywhere they needed, without losing their global capabilities. In those cases, they would pull down one of these parked satellites to replace the one that had to be re-tasked. Closing his laptop, Gibby placed it back into its carrying case and laid it on his oversized leather chair. Glancing up at his wall-mounted clock, he noticed that it was almost 4:00 p.m. local Seoul time. There was a sixteen-hour time difference between his location and CJ's.

Gibby stared down from his third-floor office window, watching the mass of humanity below. The official name was Seoul Special City, home to 9.98 million residents; the eighteenth largest city in the world. Gibby watched the pedestrians scurry below and dodge between the traffic. It was a typical day. Cars at a standstill; bumper to bumper traffic jam. The streets were full, overflowing with buses, taxicabs, and other cars. Staring out the window, he was on his tenth cup of strong American coffee of the day. He reminisced how he had come to work for the Agency.

Gibby had been born and raised in the small town of Red Bluff, located in Northern California. His legal name was Michael Gibson. After receiving his high school diploma, he had moved to Southern California and attended UC Irvine. There, he received his undergraduate degree in Physics. He had been in the NROTC and after graduation was assigned to the Home Port of the Pacific Fleet.

Like most navy guys in the late '80s, the smash-hit movie *Top Gun* had made a huge impact on the Navy's ability to recruit. It seemed that watching Tom Cruise's character Maverick had been more than a box office hit.

It had literally changed the way the Navy was seen by young males. Since that decade following the movie's release in 1986, the Navy's recruitment efforts had never been so successful. Unfortunately, like so many other young men, flying jets wasn't in the cards for Gibby. However, while stationed there, he took full advantage and received a PhD in Computer Science from UC San Diego. He had been assigned to the Intelligence Unit straightaway, and he took to it with abandon.

Gibby had a very competitive nature. Being stationed in San Diego exposed him to some of the most elite forces in the US armed services. He was grateful for his gift of brains, but he also felt the need to prove to himself and others that he had what it took to be a battle-qualified sharpshooter. He made it a point to seek out the highest rated Navy Seal snipers for the year. With much finagling and the greasing of many palms, Gibby would inevitably get the opportunity to shoot side by side and match bullet for bullet against the best of the best. Prior to his reassignment to Seoul, South Korea, the rumor mill had gone wild as Gibby was purported to have shot out the target of the adjacent shooters target. When the target was retrieved, it reportedly contained shots in the pattern of a makeshift happy face, with two eyes and the nose located in the dead-center bullseye.

Even with such antics, his drive and ambition, combined with his educational achievements, took Gibby down a different path. He had come under the Agency's radar. They had been looking at him with a different set of lenses.

He had been at the right place at the right time. His skill set had developed during a time when computer technology was in its infancy. It was a perfect storm that carried Gibby far away from the civilian dream job he aspired to, at the Los Alamos Jet Propulsion Laboratory in Pasadena. He had spent the last twenty years in the military building his resume, and he had promised himself he would punch out only after he had acquired the mandatory twenty years' active service, as his goal was to retire with a full military pension.

At the early age of forty-two, just as he was ready to punch his ticket, the unthinkable happened: He was lured away from his dream career by the fringe benefits that the Agency could offer him. Unlike the scientific world at Los Alamos, the Agency dangled the opportunity for him to become a full Agency operative, with the full weight and backing of the United States of America. He would have unlimited access to, and cooperation with, all branches of the military. He would also have access to cutting-edge technologies. Although the monetary compensation working for the Agency would never even approach what he could earn as a civilian, many seasoned Agency veterans told him that, as an operative, there were other legitimate and not-so-legitimate ways to supplement his income.

It hadn't taken Gibby long to realize that, by working on the front line of the Agency, he was in a unique set of circumstances. He had access to state-of-the-art technologies that were just coming out of development, and he would have the advantage of testing and using these new devices decades before they became available to the public. It didn't take a genius to recognize which upcoming products and devices were destined to become overnight sensations. Armed with this information, he could make some wise investment decisions that could build his retirement portfolio—probably more than he could by earning higher wages combined with corporate-sponsored retirement-contribution–matching plans. It was the excitement of being on the cutting edge of the military industrial complex, combined with the intrigue of espionage and covert operations, that won the day. Gibby had become an adrenaline junkie, hiding in plain sight.

The ultimate carrot. He wasn't required to constantly move. The Agency wanted to keep an eye on the DPRK. He would be assigned as part of the covert Agency network surrounding the DMZ. He would be able to work in one of the most dangerous areas in the world, where two opposing ideologies had been in a quasi-state of war for decades. The DMZ was still protected by NATO forces. It was littered with barbed wire fences and land mines. Politicians were constantly rattling their sabers. The ongoing drama of missiles being tossed into the south and the nonstop declarations of war dominated the media. In Gibby's mind, there was no other place than the DMZ; he was hooked. His biggest challenge involved the local language, food, and overcrowding. Otherwise, Gibby was all in.

Gibby reached for his keyboard and pressed the "enter" key. After closing the satellite link, he checked the time. He picked up his phone and dialed his unofficial contact inside the Agency.

"Hey, Moon Dog. It's Gibby."

"Well, well, well. Long time, no see, my friend," replied Lt. Elliott. "What's cooking, buddy?"

"It's that time again."

"I was wondering if I'd be hearing from you."

"Why don't you swing by the Korean BBQ around 5:30 today? It's been too long, my friend. "It's time we got caught up."

"I'll see you there," replied Moon Dog. After ending the call, Moon Dog stuffed his cell phone back into his pocket. Lt. Elliott glanced up across his desk at X.O. Newland. With a nod of his head, Moon Dog spoke. "Contact has been made, sir. I'm set to meet with the local asset today at seventeen hundred thirty."

The X.O. reached across his desk and grabbed a thin folder. He handed it to Lt. Elliott. "Your contact will need to get this greenhorn up to speed. He's been on the Agency payroll for several months. He's just been waiting for his assignment. He's set to arrive later today on a flight from Pearl." X.O. Newland kept a firm hold on the folder. He waited until Lt. Elliott stared into his eyes. Only then, did he release his grip.

"This is his first assignment."

Pursing his lips, Lt. Elliott nodded his head. After saluting, Moon Dog exited, closing the X.O.'s office doors. He couldn't help but contemplate how this poor bastard was going to break his cherry on an assignment in the DMZ. What an assignment! Not many Agency guys could make that claim. Assuming he survived, those were some serious bragging rights. It was hard enough for those poor DPRK peasants to stay alive. Moon Dog thought he would hate to see what they'd do to the greenhorn if they found out what he was up to.

Lt. Elliott walked back through the secure surveillance room and shut down his computer. As he sat in his government issued ergonomically adjustable rolling chair, he opened the thin folder and read the greenhorn's bio. His name was Benjamin. Kyle Benjamin. Inside was a color photo. The greenhorn had a typical jarhead crewcut. Moon Dog closed the folder and stuffed it into his laptop bag. Cracking a smile, Lt. Elliott whispered, "Welcome to the DMZ."

*   *   *   *   *

The flight over the Pacific Ocean was uneventful. His first hop landed him in the jump seat of a C-130 heading to Tokyo. He switched planes and took a small supply flight to Seoul. His back felt fair, given his twenty-two-hour journey from Los Angeles. The layover in Seoul left him unprepared for what he would find at the DMZ (Demilitarized Zone). It was hard to believe that these countries had been one. The differences were unimaginable. One would never guess that the culture, passions and prejudices of each country had at one time stemmed from the same history—a common beginning. The same Korean bloodlines flowed through the veins of citizens on both sides of the border, but those bloodlines were their only similarity. Each country evolved along divergent paths with different mindsets, cultures, and belief systems.

* * * * *

Tae had been lying on his side the last hour. He had stepped too close to a sensor. He knew that in no time, guards would be by to check what had caused the disturbance. He didn't want to be found, so he crawled under a fallen tree. For decades, this tree had been growing in an unusual position. It had become a landmark on the trail. Standing among the other mature trees, its presence had become commonplace. It had become invisible, while still being out in the open. The tree was just two years shy of reaching its two-hundred-year anniversary. The northern guards had come to recognize it as part of the landscape. They rarely examined it in any detail. The guards had become complacent. Besides, it had been years since anyone attempting to defect had been caught passing through this part of the DMZ. There were easier ways.

Tae's calf had been pressed up against the tree limb so long that the ridges from the bark had caused temporary indentations on his skin. Hanging onto a limb, his fingertips felt the circular patterns on the surface of the bark. Tae assumed they had been caused by old AK-47 rifle shots; wounds that had been fired years prior. Tae occupied his thoughts thinking about his route home, a journey he'd made once a month over the last ten years. If a person wanted to make it through the DMZ undetected, he zigzagged along following the animal trails. If he could walk in a straight line, it was only be a two-mile barrier. But that was not the case. This was the DMZ, and the journey was long and time consuming.

During Bill Clinton's presidency, the north softened its stance with the south. There was hope of making real progress toward reunification. Most defectors traveled through China in the north, or by sea through Thailand or Japan. Over the years, Tae used different surface trails. He was careful, always timing his return. He did not want to be late for work the following Monday. Due to these time restrictions, Tae had to take chances. Unlike others, he wasn't fleeing never to return. He would be coming right back.

Tae's visits had a different purpose. His family had lived above the 38th parallel their entire lives. He had been born, raised and still lived in the same home. His brother had moved south to Busan, where the fishing industry had been promising. However, because of the Japanese occupation before World War II, his family had been split, separated by the DMZ. His father was uninterested in defecting; he refused to abandon their homeland in the north. He maintained a personal belief that his family line came from the original dynastic blood line. Regardless, to defect south would be a slap in the face of his ancestors who fought to preserve the nation.

Each year, there was a tradition. At least one male family member would secretly trek up an old mountainside to their hidden family shrine, which was hidden in a deep ravine. Once, during an evening of the new lunar year, his father took him and his brother together. He waited until they were both ten years old. It was a reminder of what Korea and their ancestors had endured, and it was like a small secret family holiday, a personal celebration acknowledging Korea's stamina and endurance; a reminder of how they'd survived constant attacks from both China and Japan. This journey was their way of honoring the sacrifices that so many Koreans had endured.

The cave entrance was camouflaged by a rock that, to most people, appeared to be a huge, immoveable object. Unless you knew the rock's purpose, it would never have crossed one's mind to consider rolling it back. In fact, this rock was the entrance to their family shrine, and only fathers and sons knew about it. For centuries, it had remained hidden, and, for generations, Tae's ancestors had taken this same trip, performed the same ritual, and paid their respects in similar ways to what they did that day.

As Tae clutched the massive tree limbs, hiding from the coming soldiers, his thoughts drifted back to his first visit to their family shrine. As the large boulder was rolled back, he could smell the stagnant air escaping from the cave. The floor was dirt, a mixture of fine powdery composition. He could imagine the sound as his father struck the match. A vivid memory came forward of his hearing the distinctive sound echo inside the cave. He could almost see his father lighting the old oil lamps that hung at the entrance. He remembered the sour smell, a pungent odor, as the lamps burned. He recalled the light reflecting off the wall. Then, he remembered crawling through the deep cavern, and his father's describing what they were about to see. It was their family secret. They couldn't tell anyone about this place.

His father explained that when they were grown, they too would share this secret with their sons. They could describe everything, just as their father had done. Until that moment, they had known nothing of its existence. Their father had made them promise to keep this secret. Only after Tae and his brother had made their pledge did his father push open the wooden door located in the back of the cave.

With vivid clarity, Tae remembered that first visit. Tae had grabbed his younger brother's hand and squeezed it tight. Walking through the doorway, his father had raised the lantern. Using his free hand, he'd pointed. In the middle of the room sat a wooden table. An object wrapped in a silk tapestry was mounted on the wall above. The table had detailed carvings along its legs. Following his lead, they knelt on the ground and bowed their heads. The traditional bowing ritual was something that all Koreans learned at a very early age. In unison, they bent their arms at the elbow, with their palms facing forward. Then, kneeling on the cave floor, with legs bent at the knee, they extended their arms out to their full length. Then, they leaned forward, bending at the waist. They bowed forward until their outstretched arms and hands rested flat on the ground. With their faces pressed against their biceps, they remained in this position, paying their respects. Tae recalled suppressing the urge to look up at an object that was mounted on the wall above the wooden table. He remained still, waiting for his father.

After untold minutes, their father rose and walked toward the wooden table. With his chest puffed up with pride, his father reached up toward the wall. With care, he unfastened the tattered bindings that kept the object attached to the wall. His father's body obscured most of Tae's view. Tae waited as his father removed it from its casing. He could see puffs of dust form as his father peeled it from its confines. With patience and care, he tugged at the worn string. As it unraveled, he laid the metal object onto the wooden table. His father turned. In his outstretched arms, Tae could see the light from the lantern ricochet off a shining metal sword. Staring at the sword, he noticed intricate markings. Time seemed to stand still.

As Tae studied the sword further, he noticed a thin wooden marker hanging from its hilt. From watching historical dramas, Tae understood the significance of the marker. For thousands of years, when Korea had become a nation, a wooden pass was issued to those venturing outside the Royal Palace. The wooden marker signified status and prestige. Only a select few possessed these passes.

The marker was dusty, dull, and faded. With the leather wrap encasing the sword, his father wiped it clean. Clear of debris, his father tilted the sword and wooden marker toward he boys. Trying to read the markings, their eyes strained. It was written in Chinese characters, not modern Hangul. It took a moment as they translated the ancient markings. Once they finished, their mouths dropped open. The name "Bojang Chang" was written on the ID; it was "his" sword. They knew that name; he had been a famous monarch of Korea.

Their father explained that Bojang Chang was more than that. He was one of their direct ancestors. Bojang had been one of Korea's last rulers. He was the twenty-eighth monarch of the northernmost region Goguryeo; one of the Three Kingdoms of Korea. The formal beginning of Korea took place in Goguryeo, established by the famous King Chumo in 37 BC.

In 668 AD, almost exactly seven hundred years later, the Chinese Tang had surrounded forty castles near the border. That was where Bojang had been captured. But Bojang was not put to death. The Tang chose to dishonor him by placing him in charge of the Liaodong commandery. During this occupation, Bojang continued to stage small rebellions using refugees and other allied tribes. Because of his continued retaliation, Bojang was banished in 681 to Szechuan and died the following year.

After learning about Bojang, Tae was taken aback. This great man was one of their family members. Later, he learned that inside family circles, Bojang was called by his birth name Chang.

The family felt slighted by the way he had been treated. Since he was the last ruler of Goguryeo, the insult cut deep. He was the last ruler of one of the three original provinces of Korea, yet, no temple had ever been constructed in his name. No other prior monarch had been so mistreated. Over time, Bojang's legacy drifted into obscurity. Through this annual pilgrimage to the family shrine, Tae's family continued to honor one of its own.

*   *   *   *   *

Regardless of their bloodline, Tae's father was just a common person. He had no power and received no special privileges. His familial association with Korea's past was of no consequence. It held only a personal sense of pride and satisfaction. a secret they had guarded for generations. To understand their bloodline was to understand the reason Tae's father remained loyal to the DPRK. This was his homeland. It made sense. He knew his father would never defect south. In his mind, there was only one Korea—a unified one. Likewise, most DPRK residents, would never turn their backs on their heritage. Countless times, Tae had pleaded his case, arguing the logic in leaving. He pointed out that going south was not an act of treason but an act of survival. Regardless of the current political differences, it was the arbitrary boundary that created and perpetuated their differences.

The north and south still maintained similar core values, as well as the same language, history, and bloodlines. In current times, it was still common for family members to be separated by the DMZ. After all, this forced separation was caused by other, more powerful nations. These superpowers focused on their own self-interests. They were more interested in Korea's geographical location. It gave the superpowers a military and political presence in Asia.

Survival in the north was difficult. The weather was extreme and resources were scarce. Tae would trek south to secure medicine and food for his parents, wife, and two children. As the oldest son, he was responsible to care for his parents, not just his wife and children. His youngest brother, on the other hand, had decided to remain in the South, for, by comparison, the south was rich. The average lifestyle of a South Korean was one that only the elite and powerful enjoyed in the north.

Tae felt at peace in the DMZ. It had been isolated for many years. Because of the isolation, small strips of land became sanctuaries for the wildlife and vegetation. These isolated areas reverted to their original pre-civilian state. No roads, no construction, no cultivation of any kind took place there. This isolation resulted in utopian areas that *National Geographic* longed to investigate. They stood in deep contrast to the militarized areas inside the DMZ. The DMZ was a death trap dominated by land minds, barbed wire, and hidden gun turrets.

Through Tae's frequent trips through the DMZ, he developed an animal instinct. He could predict the coming of the patrol by the reduction in wildlife activity. The bird cries disappeared. There were no animals along the trail. It was like a ripple on the surface of a pond. The wildlife moved away from the soldiers. As they walked along the outer woods, they could hear the sentries' footfalls.

Peering through the branches, Tae turned his head and saw a group of soldiers. He hid beneath the fallen tree branch. The guards paused and inspected the sensor before marching back to the border. They wanted to get back before nightfall. The guards assumed that a deer had set off the motion detector.

The north spent a large percentage of its annual budget waging war against the south, and war had taken its toll. The north's lack of resources made its actions predictable. Night patrols took more resources, flashlights required batteries, and soldiers on patrol required more meals. These limitations were never openly discussed. The DPRK used this scarcity mindset to emphasize the use of daytime patrols. However, the officers knew it also reduced the temptation of soldiers' defecting under the cover of night.

Tae waited an hour before coming out of his hiding place. He gathered his homemade oversized hemp bag, being careful not to damage the medicine or expose the food inside. He'd wrapped each item in newspaper to prevent their jostling against one other. It also prevented the smell from escaping and attracting unwanted attention from the wildlife. Tae slung the bag over his shoulder and sneaked back through the overgrown vegetation. He couldn't wait to get back to his family.

He had been gone twenty hours, and he was still expected at the factory the next day. In thirty years, he had never been late. He had never taken a vacation. He held no hope of a better life. His goal was to take care of his parents, wife, and two children, and he prayed for reunification with the south.

Tae paused, waiting for the trail sounds to return to normal. Without notice, everything went silent. The crickets even stopped chirping. During the silence, Tae heard the snapping of sticks. A skinny young man jogged through the meadow. He stopped and turned back before shuffling through the high grasses. His head darted from side to side. Tae recognized him. He was one of the young homeless teens who begged in the plaza. His shirt was worn thin, his pants were tattered, and he wore open toed sandals. Tae sat motionless behind the thick vegetation, watching the boy make his escape.

Tae was saddened as he watched the boy enter the forest. It was obvious that he had no plans, no help, no provisions, and no chance. Even if he made it through the DMZ and somehow into the south without being detected, his attire, his lack of resources, and even his speech would give him away. He might be viewed as a spy by the south. Would he know where to go? If the boy had family in the south, maybe. They could help him make a transition. Without sponsorship, many defectors faced prosecution as a spy, or else incarceration. Many defectors made a conscious decision to choose incarceration in South Korea versus the life as a peasant in the DPRK. At least the south consistently fed its prisoners; there was no fear of starvation, whereas starvation was an ever-present fear for peasants in the north. It was an accepted belief that being a prisoner in South Korea was a better life than most peasants had in the north.

As Tae waited for the natural sounds of the forest to return, he turned his thoughts toward his journey home. He crouched down and scurried back across the same field, going the opposite direction from what the boy had traveled only moments earlier. Tae would be in his home in less than an hour.

5

Lieutenant Kyle Benjamin had been briefed on the conflict. Most non-Korean persons had little understanding about the conflict and customs surrounding the region. To most, it was just a country divided, with extreme communism to the north and a liberalized, Americanized society to the south. To truly understand Korea, though, one needed to look back to its very beginning. From the beginning of its existence over two thousand years ago, Korea had struggled to survive, sandwiched geographically between the giant China to the north and the warring, aggressive Japanese to the southeast. These other two countries took turns dominating, conquering, and abusing little Korea. Without Korea's innate ability to survive, it would have long ago ceased to exist. Before World War II, Japan once again invaded Korea, stole Korea's treasures, and enslaved hundreds of thousands of women and young girls to pleasure and service their military. To survive, Korea chose to look past its grim history. Against all odds, this collective mindset, its culture, was its biggest resource. The Koreans did more than just survive; they thrived.

Looking down through the jet window, watching the military vessels cruise out of Seoul Harbor toward the Sea of Japan, Lt. Benjamin recalled what he'd learned during a briefing. How could this small country have survived the Japanese naval onslaught? On May 2, 1592, with a total of only ninety-one ships—a combination of advanced Panokseon (more commonly known as turtle ships), small warships, and fishing boats—Korea successfully defend an invasion of its homeland by 1,700 ships of the Japanese navy.

A successful military was one that understood its enemies. Success depended on exploiting another's weaknesses. This formula, more times than not, translated into success on the battlefield. Before Lt. Benjamin left for his new post, the Agency had required every agent assigned to Korea to study the history of Yi Sun Sin. He was a real-life war hero and legend. Yi Sun Sin remained undefeated in battle.

His most famous victory came at the Battle of Myeongnyang in 1597. Knowing that Japan held a superior number of solders and warships, and anticipating another invasion, Yi Sun Sin worked with his team to develop a revolutionary new ship, "the Panokseon." It had thick heavy walls, was armed with twenty heavy artillery cannons, and was protected by a unique roof covering with large metal spikes to prevent boarding. This advanced design was an innovation that the Japanese had yet to encounter. In contrast, although the Japanese had superior numbers, they had no mounted cannons and relied on close-range, ship-to-ship exchanges, fighting with bows and muskets. Yi Sun Sin's small band of thirteen Panokseon "turtle ships," combined with his superior knowledge of the area, currents, and formation-attack tactics, had the home field advantage in repelling three hundred thirty-three invading Japanese warships. The Battle of Myeongnyang stands as one of the most impressive naval victories to date.

Yi Sun Sin personified the Korean culture. His dedication and sacrifice helped outsiders understand the reality of Korea's past and what they did to survive. Indeed, there is no better way to predict others' actions than by studying their past successes and failures.

As the jet began to descend into South Korea, Lt. Benjamin couldn't help but admire the country for its rich heritage, and he looked forward to learning more about its culture and military challenges. The US had existed as a country for less than 300 years, whereas Korea evolved from Three Kingdoms in 57 BC., and had been existence for over 2,000 years.

Unlike the US, the country of Korea had not been created on a foreign land. Nor were they the aggressors taking the land from less developed people. In comparison, Koreans were more similar to a particular American Indian nation. Like the Indians, Koreans already existed in their country and had come under constant attack by more developed, wealthy, and aggressive nations. However, unlike Native American Indians, Mexicans, and French, who were forced from what is now US states or territories, Koreans, through their sheer will and determination, survived. Against all odds, Korea had remained an independent nation, controlling its own destiny. Prior to World War II, Korea had once again been dominated by Japan. At the end of the war, rather than allowing Korea to return to its independent status as a unified country, it was divided by the USSR, China, the US, and the United Kingdom. It was arbitrarily divided along the 38th parallel. This border became known as the DMZ.

This trip was very special to Kyle. He'd been on several other tours of duty, but this one was different.

He had been recruited into the Agency just the year before. His Top-Secret security clearance background check had been completed before he had even been approached. The Agency had a unique situation that required an expedited processing. Although he had been on their payroll for over a month, this was going to be his first assignment. Although his paycheck would be processed by the Department of Defense, the essential codes were changed; he was assigned to a new department.

Exiting the plane, Lt. Benjamin felt the unbearable humidity push against his senses. As he walked across the tarmac, he struggled to carry his duffle bag over his shoulder. He pushed the door open, hoping to feel the rush of air conditioned air wash over his body. Instead, he was disappointed to be met with damp cool air provided by the swamp coolers. He planned to get some grub and then catch the military shuttle to the DMZ, where he was expected at twelve hundred hours. He had two hours to kill and was starved.

"Where's chow?"

"The O-Club is down the hill to the right. You can't miss it, sir," replied one of the MPs standing guard at the air terminal arrival gate. "Don't worry, sir, the O-club has real AC," nodded the grunt. With a sigh of relief, Lt. Benjamin continued his walk down the road. He needed to freshen up before he met his new C.O.

*　*　*　*　*

He had counted seventy-one such hideouts along his journeys south. Although these DPRK soldiers were skilled at remaining concealed, like all Koreans it was their addiction to eating kimchi that gave their presence away. The distinct garlic, sour cabbage delicacy emitted a strong pungent odor that could be   detected for hundreds of meters. Knowing where the bunkers were located, Tae could cross the DMZ through the safety and cover of the night. He never relaxed. Still fresh on his mind was the memory of seeing three of his friends publicly executed for being caught in the DMZ.

*   *   *   *   *

Lt. Benjamin had recently entered his living quarters and had prepared to meet his new commanding officer. Stretched out on his bed, looking up at the ceiling, he heard a loud knock on his door. Immediately he barked out "Enter!"

A tall thin man with round rimmed glasses opened the door. He was carrying a thin, sealed envelope and a plastic bottle of what looked like water. After saluting and waiting for Lt. Benjamin's response, the man spoke.

"Sir! We've been waiting for your arrival. Something happened on your hop over from Pearl, sir. I've been instructed to hand deliver this to you ASAP, sir! May I please see your dog tag?"

Taken aback, Lt. Benjamin stood, reached inside his shirt, and pulled out the tags that hung around his neck and held them up to the man. The man reached out and pinched them between his left thumb and index finger, then lifted a digital camera. Lt. Benjamin heard the internal mechanism buzz as the image was captured. The man then held the device horizontally on his palm. As Kyle looked down, he could see that the opposite side of the camera was a miniature scanner.

"Sir. If I could have you press your right thumb on the screen, please."

Kyle held his thumb out and pressed it on the device. He heard a slight hum, and a bright light flashed under his thumb. Kyle watched his thumb glow red from the bright light inside of the scanner. After a moment, the light stopped. The tall thin man turned the device over and depressed a button. Within seconds, the device emitted a high-pitched electronic tone. Then a fluorescent green light turned on.

"Your identity has been confirmed. I have a Top Secret message for you Lieutenant. I need you to open the envelope in my presence. But before you do, please step back and face away. I am not authorized to see the contents inside. When you're ready, I am required to turn my back away from you as well. Then, when you read the message, you are to commit it to memory."

With a puzzled look on his face, Kyle held the thin sealed envelope and stepped back away from the tall thin man. "I'm about to open the package," Kyle told the man. On cue, the tall thin man turned his back to Lt. Benjamin and looked at the floor.

Kyle followed his instructions and tore open the sealed envelope. Inside, there was one single page of paper. It contained two sentences and read:

"You will be approached by your contact. The code word is *Hummingbird*."

Kyle read the message three times, committing it to memory. The tall thin man spoke, breaking the silence. "Have you read the message and committed it to your memory, sir?" He remained facing down, looking at his feet.

"Yes."

Without raising his head, the tall thin man handed Kyle a plastic bottle of what looked like water. It was only half full. "Now, sir, you'll need to roll the paper into a tube and insert it into this bottle of liquid. When the paper is inside the bottle, reseal the cap and twist the cap tight. When you're sure it is tight, shake the plastic bottle several times. The note will dissolve. Let me know when you've inserted the paper and closed the plastic bottle."

Again, Kyle followed his instructions. He rolled the paper and shoved it into the bottle and closed the lid. Holding the clear plastic bottle up in front of him, Kyle spoke.

"I'm done. It's ready." Kyle raised the clear plastic bottle up for the tall thin man to verify. The man looked up from the ground.

"Sir, if you could please shake the bottle up and down. It will take about twenty seconds for the note to dissolve.

Kyle began to shake it. They both watched the rolled-up piece of paper dissolve before their eyes. The once-clear liquid turned cloudy. Within seconds, it cleared.

"Now what?"

"I wouldn't drink it. But theoretically, if you were in a tough situation and were dying of thirst, you could. I wouldn't advise it otherwise. When you get a chance, you can just dump the water in the toilet." Turning to go, the tall thin man stopped at the doorframe, with his back to Lt. Benjamin. Speaking in a hushed voice, "I've been told this is your first assignment. Do not mention anything you do with anyone else unless they give you the code word, sir." Just before he opened the door, the tall thin man turned his head. Again, in a muffled whisper, he said "Welcome to the Agency." The man then opened the door and left. The entire encounter had lasted less than two minutes.

Still standing, Kyle felt stunned. He wasn't expecting such an unusual meeting. It had happened so quickly. He sat back down and stretched back out, lifting his feet onto the bed, and thought, *"Hummingbird?"*

6

The sun just peeked over the horizon. The man liked his job assignment. It beat his very first one, repairing potholes on the outer country roads. He didn't miss those subzero winters, with wind chill dropping the temperature an additional twenty degrees. Down in the tunnels, it was peaceful. Compared to the surface, it was warm. The goal here was to dig without being detected. Speed wasn't an issue. With this goal in mind, working in the tunnels was one of the quietest job assignments around.

The tunnels constructed in prior years were crude modification of existing caverns. This one was different. It was the longest of its kind, running twenty-four kilometers (about fifteen miles), and it was about a hundred meters wide. They were fortunate to find an existing network of cave systems. Much of their work involved reinforcing the ceilings and expanding the existing tunnel. If it had been located in the United States, this section would have been wide enough to hold one side of the famous 405 Freeway in Southern California. If the DPRK wanted, they could create four car lanes with shoulders on both sides. However, this wasn't the goal. The tunnel had been designed to facilitate a sneak attack into the Republic of Korea.

Much effort had been placed on reducing the sound. Only electric vehicles were used, for example. Every vehicle in the tunnel had padded frames. The forklifts' metal tongs had been covered with foam secured by heavy-duty tape. When the vehicles moved inside the tunnel, it was reminiscent of a bumper-car ride at an amusement park. During the most extreme winter months, the DPRK workers filled thick rubber tubes with water. The tubes were then inserted into cracks inside the rock walls. At night, Mother Nature assisted in the soil removal process. The frozen water expanded, helping t break up sections of earth.

Working in the tunnels took a certain personality; it wasn't' for everyone. The slow pace, quiet environment, and isolation underground for long periods of time were hard to get used to. Over decades, the DPRK learned the skill sets needed to excel in this place. The government officials in charge of constructing the tunnel learned that forcing people to adapt to these conditions was not the answer. The tactics used elsewhere in the DPRK did not apply here. Using their standard tactics was not effective. The principal concern in the tunnels was to remain stealthy. This focus prevented them from yelling at and shooting guns over the heads of the laborers. To discipline and intimidate the laborers, the supervisors were forced to remove the workers who required an attitude adjustment from the job and taken above ground. Away from the tunnel, they could discipline and reprimand the laborers. Over time, this process was found to be inefficient.

Even in the DPRK, human nature found a way. Like a Darwinian experiment of survival of the fittest, combined with the human tendency to create efficient processes, the selection process for Tunnel Projects evolved. The successful supervisors, laborers and engineers began to show consistent traits; they were people with methodical, patient, soft spoken, easy mannered personalities. The overseeing of the Tunnel Projects fell under the purview of the military; consequently, military personnel and resources were used. Most heavily bureaucratic systems typically boiled down to statistical analysis and comparative data to evaluate success. Through this evaluation process, it became clear that focusing on personality traits was just as important as hiring only those who possessed a particular skillset. Like any other organization, teams that possessed the highest production levels attracted attention and were studied. Over time, the DPRK identified these characteristics and incorporated them into the selection process for all underground Tunnel Projects.

The Tunnel Projects became specialized, growing into a cottage industry. Due to the military involvement, it remained a secret. Those involved were isolated and controlled by a select few. Those working on the Tunnel Projects held special status. The DPRK's focus was on reunification. The Tunnel Project exemplified its ongoing effort to reunify the nation. Not only did these workers receive special social recognition, but they also had the privilege to work in pleasant conditions. They enjoyed a much different environment than that of most other military units. Those in charge wanted to make sure that this positive environment was kept a secret from the other sectors of the government and labor pools.

The Tunnel Projects managers discouraged anyone from discussing the pleasant, peaceful working conditions. In fact, they urged everyone to express opposite feelings; to emphasize the isolation, fear, and danger of being underground. After the newcomers had experienced the work, it didn't take long for the them to realize that the rumors were false. Working in the tunnels was the best labor job available in the DPRK.

*   *   *   *   *

As one of the most experienced tunnel workers, he was promoted to his current position, where he supervised a crew of twenty men. His team's principal task was to secure the ceiling and walls in the tunnel, as there was a constant fear that the cave would collapse and trap the workers. Through his years of working as one of the common laborers, he had helped excavate and construct seven other tunnels. His superiors were all formally educated. They held official titles and certifications. He, on the other hand, had come from the school of hard knocks, learning the trade of tunnel building on the job.

There was something to be said about real-world experience, especially regarding the skills needed for underground tunneling. Without the benefit of high-tech heavy machinery, the best advice came from those who did the work. Most academic intellectual types were good with hypothetical situations only; statisticians relied on their equations and theoretical scenarios. But those working underground trusted the experience of those with whom they worked side by side. Everyone depended on these decisions and recommendations.

During his twenty-year tenure, the supervisor had earned the trust of his peers. On his watch, only three people had ever died because of a collapse, and never had his crew's actions been to blame. Equally important, in not a single case had the south discovered the existence of these tunnels. Other crews and supervisors had not been so lucky. To date, only four of the tunnels had been discovered by the Republic of Korea. Due to their discovery, the efforts to continue working those particular tunnels were abandoned. Ultimately, the South plugged the holes. These few discoveries did not deter the DPRK.

With such an impressive record of achievement, it had become traditional to rub the supervisor's safety helmet. As was true of most Asians, the workers were superstitious. Like a group huddle before the start of a game, rubbing his helmet for good luck had become a ritual. It was something every member of his crew did before entering and exiting the tunnel. If he had worked anywhere else other than North Korea, he would have been famous, and undoubtedly his story would have been told in a documentary film. However, the DPRK wasn't like the rest of the world. The supervisor's success was appreciated only by those lucky enough to work with him in the tunnels, and they were sworn to secrecy. No one outside of this tight-knit community had any clue about what they did.

As they entered the newest cut, the supervisor spoke in a whispered voice.

"I've already double checked the caissons and the overhead braces. Everything checks out fine. Remember, like the turtle, slow and steady. This isn't a race. We don't get a prize for finishing early. My goal is ten meters over the next seven days."

His team had just finished their afternoon break. Before allowing his men back into the tunnel, part of his job was to double-check the area, and he took this responsibility seriously. He never delegated that task. His workers appreciated that about him. Unlike some other supervisors, he never took advantage of his position and power. He had never asked for special treatment. He never abused his authority. When things went bad, other supervisors argued that delegating the inspections allowed them a buffer with the government officials. He deemed this process was destined to fail. He reasoned that, in the long run, subordinates did not have the experience needed to succeed. Over time, supervisors who delegated the responsibility sustained more delays. Over time, those crews following this process were involved in more accidents. Because of these issues, the government and military "bean counters" inevitably noticed the poor results, and these delegators were required to explain their results.

During an internal investigation, upper management uncovered the practice of the supervisor's delegating this responsibility. Depending on the severity of the accidents that preceded the investigation, it could cost the supervisor his life. Unlike other parts of the world, the DPRK didn't use demotions. Here, what other countries would classify as a procedural infraction could result in an execution.

The supervisor understood why he had been promoted. It was because of his experience, which allowed his team to work in relative safety. In the long run, imparting his experience was more efficient. He understood that shirking that responsibility put others in danger. This supervisor was one of the most respected among his peers. Inside the tunnel community, he was a legend and hero.

The part of the job he detested most was dealing with defectors. From time to time, as a supervisor, he had unfettered access to the tunnel. On occasion, he would find a civilian who somehow found his way into the labyrinth and was trying to escape to the south. The party line required him to notify the military attaché assigned to his crew. It would be up to that officer to decide how to proceed. In each of the nine cases that this had happened, the defectors were taken above ground and never seen again. He speculated that they were taken to one of the labor camps. The supervisor never asked what happened to them. He guessed that the defectors wanted a more comfortable lifestyle available in the south. He was critical of these people. He considered them weak and defective.

Like many citizens inside the DPRK, the supervisor yearned for better lifestyle. He wished for wider varieties of resources. However, he viewed their hardships as challenges they were destined to face. He reasoned that many other cultures had their own similar challenges. The isolation and extreme winters that the people living in the Arctic and Antarctic regions faced were similar; those people were forced to endure extreme temperatures and scarce resources. He guessed that those areas were even more harsh than what those living inside the DPRK faced. It was where they were born and raised; where their parents and grandparents had been born. Their ancestors had adapted; facing those challenges was a way of life for them. Still, he had never considered abandoning his homeland.

The supervisor's thoughts returned to the challenges of today. He needed to focus on the tasks at hand that assured his own safety and that of his crew. His eyes watered as the miniature electric tram's motor hummed through the deep tunnel, carrying his crew to the fair depths of the newest tunnel. Each car carried two men. He always traveled in the last car. From there, he could look over his crew and get a sense of their moods and concerns. Before they started, he inspected each man, making sure they had each wrapped their boots with the thick cotton fabric sleeves. His visual inspections were a habit, performed in the caring way a parent makes sure the children are ready for school. As the rush of air splashed against his face, he could see his crew relaxing, with their boots propped up on the sides of the open-faced transport compartments. Once they disembarked, they would begin another grueling ten hours of labor to extend the tunnel. They used electric-battery–charged expansion jacks and shovels.

It was a long process, and it seemed their work never stopped. The tunnel crews worked every day, rotating so that each crew received a day off each week. Although these types of crews had existed since the end of World War II, the effort to construct an oversized tunnel had never been proposed until now. The prior ones had been small, designed to transport small numbers of foot soldiers through narrow openings. This one was different. It was tall, wide and long, designed so that entire regiments, complemented with tanks and other transport vehicles, could travel undetected.

For the safety of the men, no fueled vehicles were allowed inside. It was bad enough having exhaust systems throughout the structure to extract the fumes of the combustible engines. It was too risky. During the construction phase, miles of soft-hosed piping ran along the tunnel where outside filtered air was pumped into the tunnel. There was no concern that CO_2 from combustion engines would occur; everything inside the tunnel was electric. Later, large compaction trucks would be used. For now, the only concern was over the available oxygen in the tunnel. As the men breathed, they expelled carbon dioxide and nitrogen. Over time, it had the same effect.

The electric tram continued into the newest section of tunnel, and the high-pitched electric hum echoed against the tunnel walls. As they traveled down the tunnel, the supervisor stared at the battery-powered sensors along the air tubes. Seeing neon green light, he was confident that the air flow was working. It was their lifeline pumping valuable air into the tunnel. For the last six months, they had been digging inside the Republic of Korea's territory. They passed another battery-powered lantern. Other than the flashlights that each man carried, these lanterns were the only light available. The electric tram slowed and the crew stirred, preparing to disembark and begin work.

The front end of the tram held empty containers that would carry the dirt, rocks, and other debris out of the tunnel. Each container held approximately 1,000 kg; about 2,200 pounds. The daily goal was to fill all the containers before heading back. After the electric train stopped, the crew climbed out. The supervisor carried two portable lanterns while leading the crew down to the end of the tunnel. After setting down the lanterns, the supervisor paused to listen for any unusual noises. He was about to instruct his crew to commence digging when a low rumble echoed. From the side of the tunnel, a section of wall crumbled inward. Startled, all the workers turned their attention toward the noise. Fearing a complete collapse of the structure, they were relieved to see a small opening into an adjacent natural cave formation. The supervisor walked over to inspect the opening. The small amount of earth that tumbled inward calmed their nerves. It wasn't a full collapse. The newly excavated tunnel was located next to a lava tube, that's all. The crew waited for the supervisor to decide on the next move. He had the experience, and they trusted him with their lives.

Many times before, the supervisor had seen this type of collapse. For now, they were safe. He needed to determine the size of the adjacent formation. He was more excited about the possibility that the adjacent area could expedite their progress. It all depended on the layout of the lava tube; if it went in the wrong direction, or the formation presented an increased risk of collapse due to the composition of this newly exposed space. A decision would need to be made; perhaps the lava tube ran in the direction they were digging, or perhaps they would be required to backfill the tunnel and begin digging in a different direction; away from this newly discovered formation.

The supervisor raised his hand. "Men, return to the tram while I investigate the collapse."

The supervisor walked toward the collapse and pointed his flashlight into the opening in the wall. The light from his flashlight illuminated a natural cavern. It appeared to angle away from the direction they were digging. Disappointed, he concluded that even if the area was deemed safe, it did not offer any advantage. The direction of the adjacent tunnel was unusable. At best, they would be delayed bracing and reinforcing the area. He glanced up and down through the opening. He couldn't help but wonder if people from the Republic of Korea were using this adjacent tunnel. As he backed away from the opening, he knew he would have to advise his manager, who in turn would send a geological engineer down to make a formal determination. Until that was done, it was too dangerous. He instructed the crew to return to the train. He wanted to get out of the tunnel to report the incident.

As the crew re-boarded, they each had a sense of gratitude for being on his crew And appreciated the decision he had just made. Other supervisors would have instructed their crew to continue digging without knowing for sure if the tunnel was safe. The supervisor walked back to the last open-faced compartment. He made sure all his crew were accounted for, and all their equipment was onboard, before he directed the driver to begin. His crew's safety was his responsibility and priority.

*   *   *   *   *

Tae froze. He heard the side wall give way and watched the earth crumble inward falling back into the tunnel. He was close enough to the newly created opening that he could feel the air pressure change. He felt his ears pop and a soft breeze rush pass his cheek. Concentrating, Tae could hear the distinct sound of footfalls approaching the opening. With a rush of adrenaline, his heart began pounding in his chest. Fighting to keep control of his senses, Tae dropped to the ground. He turned, facing away from the new opening in lava tube wall. Tae forced himself to remain as motionless as possible, and waited.

Within seconds, he heard a muffled conversation. He could just make out the words. They were speaking Korean. By the accents, he could tell they were from the north. He correctly assumed that they were tunnel diggers. Concentrating on every sound, Tae heard a metallic click. The noise echoed between the tunnels. Tae glanced upward toward the opening. A bright light beam cut through the darkness. The light beam scanned his side of the cave. The light moved from one side to the other side of the cavern. Lying below the collapsed opening, Tae could listen to the conversation.

"What do you see?"

"It's a lava tube. It is very long." Pausing, a man stuck his arm through the opening. The man pointed the flashlight inside the cavity. "The lava tube meets our tunnel here." Tae could see the man tilting his head up and down to inspect the area. From below the opening, Tae could see the man's lips moving as he continued speaking. "The lava tube continues down the opposite direction. I don't think we can use it."

After a brief pause, contemplating the situation, the Supervisor continued. "I'm not confident about this area. I don't want anyone in this area until I know for sure that it's safe. For now, let's go back. I want an engineer to evaluate its condition."

With a sigh of disappointment, the supervisor turned off the flashlight and pulled his arm back through the opening. As the crew walked back away from the opening, Tae heard what sounded like many boots. He remained motionless, lying on the ground of the lava tube. After hearing a distinctive electrical whine as the tram pulled away, he finally moved. Crawling along the ground, Tae muscled his backpack over his shoulder. Then he ran along the lava tube, down the worn path, away from the collapsed section. Although his eyes had become adapted to the darkness, he used his flashlight to avoid falling. The last thing he wanted to do was stumble and create an unnatural noise from inside the lava tube.

Tae knew from experience that any noise in the tunnel was amplified and would echo throughout the cave system. Fear of discovery overtook his emotions. He began running away from the collapsed opening to put as much distance as possible between him and the tunnel diggers. He scurried up toward the opposite end of the large open lava tube structure. Feeling he had no choice, he turned on his flashlight.

Meanwhile, as the motion of the tram settled into a steady rhythm, the supervisor relaxed. Sitting in the last compartment, he glanced back toward the collapsed section and something caught his attention. He could swear he saw a light shine through the tunnel. Blinking back in shock, he concentrated on peering into the tunnel, trying to determine if the shaking of the tram or the lanterns were affecting his vision. He continued staring back toward the collapsed opening. There. He saw it again. He was certain. A bright beam of light bounced around erratically. What shocked him most was that the light appeared to be coming through the opening from inside the natural lava tube.

The tram entered a large open area inside the tunnel. The lighting changed, ruining everyone's night vision. In unison, the crew blinked their eyes. Some men raised a hand to shade their eyes from the overhead lighting. The supervisor turned away from the collapsed section of tunnel and began questioning what he had seen. He leaned against the handrail, bracing himself as the tram accelerated up an incline. As the steady forward motion of the tram rocked him back and forth, he began contemplating what he would tell his manager. He soon forgot about the light.

7

Angelie had been preparing for the first assignment of her life. She had been adopted at the very young age of four and raised in the American Midwest. Her upbringing behind the closed doors of her home was anything but a typical US experience. As she sat through the last course of the day, her mind drifted. She dreamt about how it all started.

Unlike her classmates, Angelie had been trained in Korean martial arts of Tae Kwon Do, in golf, and in archery. She was also schooled in languages and covert surveillance skills. Being a Korean, it wasn't unusual for her to be a student of Tae Kwon Do. However, she had been taught to avoid attracting attention to herself. She was forbidden from participating in soccer, volleyball, and softball. They were deemed too popular and could attract the attention of unwanted eyes. In addition, the skills acquired to succeed in these sports would did not enhance her skillset; at least in terms of what were considered skills that would enhance her future as an operative. She purposely avoided mainstream activities. Few of her classmates had any clue of her highly developed skills. She flew under the radar.

As a Korean, Angelie had the advantage of being raised truly bilingual. Her adoptive parents went to great lengths to formally teach her all aspects of the Korean Language, Hangul. Their household was like a learning exchange. Her parents taught her Hangul. In return, she taught her parents English.

The DPRK had understood the importance of developing these skills. Before immigrating to the US, both parents were recruited from the most prestigious learning institution in North Korea, Pyongyang University. All universities there were state funded and controlled. Her parents' ultimate assignment was to establish a training center for other future infiltrators who would learn what it would take to "pass" as American. Their first and most important pupil was their adopted daughter.

To accomplish this goal, they were instructed to learn everything they could about what really made a person an American. They needed to get inside the psyche and uncover what made Americans tick. Again, their daughter Angelie was recruited as a bridge for her parents to reach this understanding. In pursuit of this goal, Angelie selected courses that helped with this understanding, choosing elective coursework that would shed light on this subject. Armed with this knowledge, Angelie could pinpoint habits, insights, and attitudes that contrasted with the beliefs and attitudes her parents held. Throughout her formal education, beginning with elementary school and continuing through middle school, high school, and college, she used her parents as sounding boards to compare these differences. She yearned to communicate what she learned and uncovered. Their evening dinner discussions became philosophical debates on the subject.

To further enhance those nightly discussions, they practiced their language skills on each other, through the unavoidable stops and starts between each other to correct a pronunciation, to explain why a word choice was most appropriate to be used in that particular sentence, or define a slang term that would best describe something. Those discussions required Angelie to speak in Korean and for her parents to respond in English. Neither side could use their preferred language to further the conversation. These nightly conversations advanced everyone's skill levels. Their biggest breakthrough took place during her second year in college when Angelie took an American-Korean History course. Through that course, she felt she finally uncovered the truth, the real differences. This form of training would be used to help future waves of infiltrators.

The DPRK's challenge had always been to establish a process that reduced the likelihood that their human assets would be enticed and lured away by the luxuries and freedoms available in the West. Initially, a lot of effort went into understanding why so many candidates chose to abandon their assignments and defect to the US. The DPRK lacked the ability to accurately predict the likelihood of defection. For a brief period, they resorted to kidnapping outsiders and forcing these captives to teach their operatives about western society. During that era, kidnappings in South Korea, Japan and even America had become commonplace. This process had the desired effect. It exposed their recruits to a foreign way of life, to that language and culture. However, over time, this approach failed.

In years, past, the emphasis had been more about recruiting only those having the mental and intellectual capacity to acquire information, as opposed to selecting candidates who had possessed the mindset dedicated to the DPRK's culture and committed to its continued survival. This was the key concept. It was imperative that the DPRK choose individuals who had this concept firmly planted in their psyche. Only when this distinction in *emphasis had been uncovered, where the culture of their true homeland had been nurtured did the DPRK begin to see progress. With this understanding, the DPRK began to honestly present its vision for the future by analyzing and glorifying Korea's unique mental and historical perspective. That perspective had a filter that was overly critical of imperial domination by foreigners. Through this honest approach with itself, the DPRK intelligence community began to make real progress.*

At every education level, Angelie pursued clarity about the separation of Korea. From the answers to a never-ending stream of questions she posed to her teachers and university professors over a decade's time, she constructed her own interpretation. She concluded that the biggest factors were how each country was created as well as the philosophical differences between the US and Korea.

Korea's organic evolution over two thousand years, struggling to survive multiple invasions by both China and Japan, was the biggest factor in its development. Through those ongoing conflicts, Korea learned to rely on its ability of self-reliance.

In contrast, the US evolved over time, as the unification of a multitude of immigrants who joined together based on a common goal yet were separated by their ethnic and cultural differences. What mainly kept the American people unified were the concepts of fairness and equality. Over a comparatively short period of time, the US revolted from its sponsoring country, Great Britain, to form the United States of America.

Through a long string of wars, as the aggressors, the US, captured territories previously held not just by Great Britain but by France, Spain, Mexico, and many North American Indian tribes. This conquest continued until the

US physical boundaries extended from coast to coast, crossing the entire North American Continent.

Angelie believed the US was so motivated by the concepts of fairness and equality that it jeopardized its own existence through a civil war, and later through the Civil Rights movement in the 1960s. During each internal conflict, its leaders were assassinated. Society's desire for fairness and equality resulted in the literal human sacrifice of its leaders. History proved that such sacrifices were a worthy exchange in pursuit of these ideals.

This distinct understanding about Korea's past provided an insight into why the DPRK could reach the hearts of its people. Unlike other failed communist countries, other than Cuba, the DPRK remained one of the last few extreme forms of communistic governments. However, unlike prior communist nations, the DPRK had remained focused on one simple goal: to survive. This survival instinct was like the Jewish State. Unlike the Native American Indians, who had lost their land and much of their culture,. the DPRK remained focused on a single purpose: to reunify and re-establish itself, once again, as a single unified Korea.

One could argue that the motivation for reunification came from the fear of separation. In their minds, their past existence over thousands of years seemed to be contingent upon their ability to exist as a single undivided country. Now, being separated jeopardized their long-term existence. The DPRK appeared to be fearful that accepting a state of separation could represent the beginning of the end. Throughout Korea's history, China and Japan had invaded and occupied Korea in attempts to divide it into different geographical factions. Once these invading nations were repelled, Korea's geographical boundaries and culture were reassembled, restored to their prior state.

From the Koreans' point of view, the issue centered on the artificial separation imposed by meddling outsiders. It was difficult for the DPRK to understand how the US could not see that their situation paralleled what the US also faced during its own civil war. The United States did not permit the southern Confederate States to secede to create a separate nation. The DPRK saw itself in a similar light. It was difficult for them to understand why the US in particular, given how it handled its own "artificial separation," was unable to see the situation from the DPRK's point of view.

Likewise, the DPRK failed to appreciate the most fundamental aspect of the conflict from the United States' point of view; the fact that the US remained committed to the concept of fairness and the pursuit of happiness. The US appreciated its apparent hypocritical position when it considered how it resolved its own artificial separation during the Civil War and seemed to justify the hypocrisy based on the distinction that its separation was based on a universal human right, a belief that slavery was evil. Because the motivation was to destroy slavery, purportedly an evil concept, a division based on this evil concept could not be justified or permitted. Allowing the US to remain separated based solely on possessing different opinions, under these circumstances, was logically unworthy of support

Angelie concluded that the main point was the difference in core values. The DPRK had a single-minded goal of surviving. In contrast, the US could not imagine survival if it did not also include equality and fairness. To survive without adhering to these concepts was, to the US, unacceptable, as its core value was in jeopardy. The US, therefore, was motivated to make it fair, no matter what; whereas the DPRK saw survival of the Korean culture and its boundaries as the most important issues, regardless of the presence of equality. Through the eyes of the DPRK, the concept of survival was what mattered. The fact that Korea had existed for thousands of years supported their belief that being a single unified nation was the key to their survival. They believed that the common denominator in their survival had been the fact that they had remained intact. The longer they remain a separated country, the more likely their future existence was jeopardized.

Furthermore, it was difficult for the DPRK to understand why its southern relative, The Republic of Korea, was unable to see this dilemma. Regardless of the freedoms and abundant resources that they received by maintaining an alliance with the US, how could those fleeting comforts outweigh the importance of reunification? The DPRK remained incredulous as to why the Republic of Korea continued to choose these comforts, as opposed to demanding reunification knowing that the continued separation would jeopardize the continued existence of their culture. The fact that the US had only existed for a relatively short period further supported the belief that the Republic of Korea was making a mistake. Until the US could attest to being a country of long standing, with at least one thousand years of existence, the DPRK took the position that the US was unqualified to manipulate and coerce its brethren to remain separated.

Angelie likened the situation to a mother who felt that her child had been wrongfully taken from her, in that the DPRK continued to do everything in its power to bring the abducted child back to the safety of its home. To accept the separation would have been as if the DPRK had voluntarily abandoned its southern territory and accepted the reduction of its geographical boundaries. What made this separation more tragic was the reason for its division. It wasn't divided because of Korea's inability to withstand the atrocities of an invading nation. In this case, an arbitrary decision had been made by its allies: the United States and the USSR. A decision was made on their behalf, dividing the territory that was being illegally held by the Japanese. Prior to World War II, Korea had been a single intact sovereign nation. However, this fact had been ignored. Instead, it was divided along the 38th parallel among the superpowers. Korea was treated like a spoil of war, rather than an independent sovereign nation.

Angelie shook her head, trying to redirect her thoughts away from the philosophical discussions she shared with her parents; those long evening discussions that formulated her opinion of why the Korean Conflict continued. She had always appreciated the ingenuity, entrepreneurial spirit, and strong opinions in the United States. But through her eyes, through the filter from where she had been raised, the United States remained naïve. Maybe inside the border of segments of the US, the concept of fairness existed. But overall, it was difficult to argue that even behind the great ivory-tower walls of the United States, inequality and unfairness abounded. From the negligent infrastructure provided in Detroit, to the apparent unjust treatment between the police and ethnic minorities, as well as the preferential treatment of the elite and large corporations, the obvious disparities could not be ignored.

As her professor continued lecturing, Angelie's thoughts drifted away once again.

She began to think back to the many times that she watched the other merchant friends talk about the struggles of homeownership. The excessive taxes; sales tax, income tax; federal tax, social security tax; workers' compensation tax; use tax, etc. The complex and apparent addiction to money and consumption was something the DPRK had warned her parents about. They were counseled on the need to avoid being preoccupied with money. Her parents were coached to create their operation so that it could remain agile, able to alter course and change directions. Other than the minimal requirements of society, they were to avoid scrutiny by the federal government. No one in their household had ever received any form of governmental citation. Not a parking or speeding ticket. Nothing.

They had no credit cards and paid for everything with cash or money orders. They rented a modest two-bedroom apartment and their separate business location. Their business was not intended to become a thriving financial enterprise. It was only a means to support their personal lives, and to provide a realistic cover for their main objective. They had never been intoxicated by the need for recognition based on power or wealth. Angelie's parents had prevented her from competing in any of her extracurricular activities; unwanted attention was to be avoided. Many of her coaches were perplexed as to why Angelie showed no interest in participating in any of the formal competition events. It was common knowledge that she possessed the highest skill level in archery, chess, and Tae Kwon Do. After failed attempts at convincing her to compete, some coaches had visited her home in a vain attempt to convince her parents. Her coaches gave up their efforts, as their attempts were politely rejected. Each coach walked away confused over her parents' apparent lack of support for Angelie's natural gifts, and left frustrated by the idea that her talents would go to waste.

On the contrary, from her parents' point of view, the archery, chess, and Tae Kwon Do had a different purpose.

They provided a training ground preparing her for her first assignment. The DPRK had instructed her parents to develop her skills to become a full-blown international covert operative with the cover as an International Teacher of English. This occupation was in high demand throughout many developed nations. The wealthy elite and developing countries wanted their children to be taught English from citizens born and schooled in the United States. Angelie's first assignment would be in the Republic of Korea. Although she was fully bilingual in Korean Hangul, no one except her parents knew. As far as anyone else was concerned, she was capable of only basic conversational exchanges. Her life was a constant charade, trying to appear unable to understand in-depth Korean. She had been forbidden from ever speaking Hangul with anyone outside of the home.

To help achieve this charade, she had been taught at an early age that she needed to help her parents learn English, and this was the best way. On one occasion, Angelie was beaten by her parents for her misstep. She had mistakenly assumed that it was safe to speak Hangul in her parents' shop, when others were not present. Her parents explained to her that, to prevent someone else from listening in and finding out their secret, she could never assume others weren't present. There was always a chance that if she spoke Korean outside the home, someone could overhear. They took no pleasure in what they did. The look in their eyes said it all. When she was being punished, Angelie could see the sadness on their faces. She understood that there was no enjoyment in having to treat her this way. That lesson had been a powerful one that would later save her life. They had prepared her well.

8

Carla Jo stretched her arms and yawned as she turned the steering wheel, maneuvering her SUV down a neglected asphalt road. The Agency used this isolated safe house near the Salton Sea for many reasons. It had a small population, making it easy to maintain surveillance. Its isolation reduced the likelihood that a neighbor would drop by for an unanticipated visit. It just wasn't a place that attracted marketers or Jehovah's Witnesses wandering door to door.

Back when the waters teamed with fish, the Salton Sea was in its heyday. But those days were long gone. The area no longer sponsored lavish parties thrown by Hollywood celebrities. The shoreline maintained a steady retreat as annual droughts extended into decades. As the water evaporated, the lake's salinity increased. The toxins drained from the suburbs hundreds of miles upstream and settled to the bottom of the stagnant, shrinking sea. Abandoned buildings now dotted the horizon, standing askew as the extreme desert heat advanced the deterioration of their concrete foundations. Unable to maintain their structural integrity, walls leaned and ceilings crumbled in on themselves. The worst areas of town looked like an apocalyptic movie set.

Even with the economic challenges that the community faced, there still existed a small number of houses clustered in sparse, grassless neighborhoods. Unlike a typical subdivision, these subdivisions consisted of ten homes sharing the same street. They were not constructed based on a master plan or a single developer. Rather, these neighborhoods seemed to spawn up individually, built by different contractors. The landscaping was designed to suit the extreme temperatures and complement the encroaching desert sand banks. The landscaped yards include boxed shrubs and cactus plants. The dirt and street met without benefit of concrete curbs. Visitors from outside the area would be shocked at the condition of the asphalt roads. The extreme temperature fluctuations caused the roads to buckle. The constant rippling effect had damaged the roads' surfaces to the point that driving on them was like traveling over a sea of raised paver markers. Driving on the warped surface was so extreme that even the most luxurious vehicles experienced abrupt jolts with every rotation of their tires.

The Agency couldn't have designed a better location. The safe house was centrally located in Southern California: east, yet far removed from the major metropolitan cities. There was easy freeway access from the four major interstate freeways 5, 15, 10 and 8. The small population, combined with the dry atmosphere, made it a perfect location to synchronize satellite surveillance over the safe house. The Agency provided immediate real-time surveillance. The extreme environment reduced the presence of wandering pets left outside to fend for themselves. The yards didn't even have any water sprinklers. The Agency learned that this neighborhood had no children. During Halloween, no one went door to door playing trick or treat. Other than the isolated few retired neighbors that lived in the neighborhood, everyone minded their own business. For the Agency, this location was a dream come true.

As Carla Jo approached the house, she recognized that this part of the mission came with dire consequences. Before she turned down the street that led to the safe house, she took several deep breaths. She ran through the scenario. She mentally rehearsed the order in which she had to proceed. Only after she was one hundred percent confident that she knew what to do did she proceed. She had been here several times before. She knew that once she started the process, there was no turning back.

This safe house was used for only the highest level of security missions. Here, the standard operating procedure was unique. Carla Jo stopped her vehicle just in front of the driveway, letting the vehicle idle in park. She then depressed the custom toggle switch inside of her car. The toggle had been designed to look like a cigarette lighter. In reality, the device initiated an electronic signature burst that was decoded inside the safe house. A surveillance Satellite Tech was watching her. Once her vehicle approached the home, a sensor outside the safe house triggered. The vehicle's movement triggered an automated notification. The notification was relayed to a twenty-four/seven/three-sixty-five live surveillance team. In turn, they would verify the target in real time.

The tech waited to receive the e-sig (electronic signature) data burst. The vehicle's VIN (vehicle identification number) and odometer reading were received. The VIN was a match. The odometer reading was within the parameters of what would be expected based on her driving habits. There hadn't been a large variance of miles driven since her last visit. The Satellite Tech adjusted the angle of the overhead satellite image. He then activated its infrared heat sensors. The only heat signatures present were in the driver's front seat and the front engine compartment. He glanced around the interior of the vehicle and no other heat signatures were present. He was confident that the driver was not accompanied by another person, nor was someone hiding in the vehicle. He now needed to verify the identity of the driver. While still in infrared mode, the Satellite Tech pushed the magnification view back enough to verify that no other persons or vehicles were present. He then rotated the view of the general area. He was confident that no aerial drones were present. Only a lost sea gull crossed his field of vision.

Carla Jo waited in front of the driveway. She knew the drill. Like every contractor before her, she knew that this location provided a lethal all destruct failsafe protocol. Should the need arise, the garage and driveway were designed to explode with enough force to destroy the entire house and vehicle in the driveway. She had been told that it was designed to mimic a gas-line leak that had exploded. As she waited to be cleared and given access to the safe house, she held her cell phone, pretending to be on a call.

The Satellite Tech was confident that the person inside the vehicle was the independent contractor listed on his computer screen. She had followed protocol by informing the Agency of her intent to enter the safe house and had arrived within her expected arrival timeframe. The Tech flicked the mouse on his computer and activated a split screen. He continued looking down on the vehicle. He opened another satellite feed to capture a horizontal view of the vehicle. This satellite was located five hundred miles away and maintained a

LEO (Low Earth Orbit) synchronization over the San Diego corridor, keeping an eye on Camp Pendleton, Coronado, and the San Diego Bay. That satellite specialized in live camera shots and was equipped with an abundance of independent cameras. Three such satellites hovered over the San Diego Area. This area was one of the United States' most important military sites. It was located not only within a largely populated area but also next to an international border. The Satellite Tech activated the satellite camera and zoomed in for a high definition facial recognition. Once he had the driver's head in his view, he initiated the program.

Carla Jo was looking out of the front windshield waiting for the signal. She took a deep breath and exhaled. She concentrated on what was about to take place. She closed her eyes and continued her wait.

The two exterior wall-mounted garage lights turned on. Within seconds, the lights began blinking. As her adrenaline kicked in, Carla Jo's pulse quickened. She tried to relax her facial muscles, as she knew a satellite was about to begin the facial recognition. This was the final critical procedure. There was a zero-failure tolerance. As expected, the garage lights turned off. After a brief pause, the right light began blinking. She powered down the passenger window, placed her cell phone on the passenger seat, and removed her sunglasses. Then, she turned her head. She understood that under no circumstance could she turn away from the open window. To do so would be a signal to the Satellite Tech that she was being forced to enter the safe house under duress. If that was the case, the gas-line–explosion scenario would be initiated.

The horizon-based satellite waited for the window glass to fully drop before beginning the scan. Past experiences had proved that any glint of sunlight or peripheral reflections off the glass window, would hinder the facial recognition program. The tech saw that the driver's face was now in clear view and was about to start the program. As Carla Jo waited, she heard something off to her left. Although her face remained facing forward, her eyes rolled upward as her brain tried to recognize what was making the sound. Her mind associated the noise with some form of large hollow object. Her mind continued trying to decipher the sound, trying to catalog it into something that made sense. It was a natural human reflex. She regained her concentration and forced her eyes forward, waiting for the scan to be completed. She remained distracted by the unusual sound, though. It continued nonstop, getting louder. She heard a distinct crunching sound as if rocks were being crushed under the weight of a rolling object.

Without warning, a sudden noise reverberated from the street. It sounded like the commotion took place very close to her SUV. Startled, without thinking, she instinctively turned her head. Out of the corner of her eye, she saw someone pushing a large, plastic-wheeled garbage can across the neighboring driveway. One of the wheels had dropped into a dirt hole. The force of the neighbor man's arms and legs pushing against the garbage can, while the wheel was trapped in the hole, caused the can to topple forward. The hinged garbage can lid fell open. With a loud hollow sounding crash, the can tipped over on its side, dumping all its contents onto the roadway. Recognizing her mistake, Carla Jo tried to turn her head back toward the open window.

As she realized what she had just done, her pulse quickened and her heart seemed to jump into her throat. In that split second, she chastised herself for not timing her arrival during the early morning. As she jerked her head back to the right, she hoped that the program had already completed the scan. She held her breath, hoping that the garage door would open. She tried to regain control of her emotions and push back the fear that was rushing into her mind. She fought back the urge to slam the car into reverse and accelerate backwards off the driveway. Her mind screamed at her to do something, anything. It took every ounce of courage to try to remain calm and in control. She was like a duck paddling across the water. On the surface, the duck looked calm and relaxed, while under the water line the duck's legs pumped vigorously to propel its body across the top of the water.

Carla Jo continued holding her breath. As each millisecond passed, she found herself praying "my soul to keep." Unable to bear the agony of waiting, she closed her eyes.

*   *   *   *   *

Riding a civilian cab from the Camp, Lt. Benjamin was going to see his contact. His first introduction was unannounced and unorthodox. As his cab traveled down the road, blurry images of Korean storefronts passed by his field of vision. His mind wandered as he recalled meeting Gibby.

Earlier that day, he had been at the rifle range shooting targets. Camp Bonifas had one of the few long-distance shooting ranges outside of the States. Lying on his stomach and after unleashing his first round, Lt. Benjamin was surprised to see what appeared to be a stray bullet hit his target. Given the distance below the center bullseye, Kyle thought that it had to be an errant deflection by one of the other shooters.

Kyle lifted his head away from his scope and glanced up and down the line of shooters. There were five other shooters; three to his right and two to his left. They were all dressed in green fatigues, lying down in similar prone positions, their eyes staring through their scopes focusing on their targets. He waited to see if any one looked up. No one did. All the others continued to shoot at their targets. With a shrug of his shoulders, Kyle returned his attention to his target. He blinked his eye to adjust looking through the scope. Looking at the target, he discovered there were now three new hits. This time, Kyle knew it was no accident. Although each hit was well below the bullseye, each impact lined up in a distinct rounded oval pattern, like a curved line bowing in the middle.

Rather than rise up again, Kyle decided to remain still to examine his target. In quick successive bursts, his target took six more rounds. As the last bullet penetrated his target, he realized what was happening. Whoever it was, the shooter had skills. The impact marks had been placed to form a smiley face. The shooter's last shot hit the center bullseye. Kyle studied the impact marks and couldn't help but smile. There were two rounds representing the eyes, six impact rounds for the curved smile, and the last one a dead center bullseye for the nose. Kyle couldn't help but respect the shooter's skills. That was some impressive shooting.

Kyle rolled over away from his weapon. After he discharged the metal-jacket bullet, he cleared the chamber. Then, he stood up from his crouched position. He couldn't miss the shooter to his far left. The man stood and cradled his weapon. With a huge ear-to-ear grin, like a politician driving a convertible acknowledging the crowd during an election year parade, the man waved. Lt. Benjamin was taken aback and burst out a sincere heart felt chuckle.

Kyle's thoughts were interrupted as a city bus passed by his cab. The roar of its diesel engine pushed the huge bus forward as it accelerated away from the curb. As he settled back into the well-worn bench seat of the cab, he let his mind wander. His thoughts returned to the shooting range.

The man who had been shooting at his target looked back before walking toward Kyle and out of the shooting range. The man stretched out his hand and curled his index finger toward himself in successive motions. Like a pet owner using sign language, he called Kyle over to him. Being the new guy to the DMZ, Kyle thought he would play along. In elaborate fashion, this man had gotten his attention. Kyle followed the man and lost sight of him as the man exited the enclosed shooting area. Once outside, Kyle saw him sitting down at the outside patio of an adjacent food shack. In the States, the military would never allow alcohol to be served so close to a shooting range. But this wasn't the States. Everything was different near the DMZ. And things here were run by the locals, not within the confines of the military compound.

As Kyle approached the table, he saw two large frosty mugs of beer collecting condensation from the humidity. He could see circular stains on the worn table cloth covering the cheap wooden table. Flashing that same ear-to-ear smile, the man picked up where he had left off earlier and cranked up that politician's wave before breaking the silence.

"How'd you like my picture?"

With a pleasant but inquisitive smile, Kyle approached the table. Reaching out his right hand, he exchanged a solid firm handshake before replying. "You definitely got my attention. Is this some kind of hazing ritual you old guys do to new recruits, or what?"

"Ouch. 'Old guy.' It shows that much, huh?" he replied, as if Kyle's comment had affronted the man's ego. Kyle looked at his body, which showed obvious signs of middle age. The man stretched his arms out, extending them away from his body and turning his head downward, as if examining his not-so-firm midsection. After a brief pose, the man looked back up at Kyle. Flashing that same politician's smile, he chuckled.

"You should've seen me in the day, Kyle. My body was a sight to behold." Noticing the confused look on Lt. Benjamin's face, the man continued speaking. "I'm guessing you're wondering how I know your first name and why I would try and get your attention." Kyle looked like a deer caught in the headlights. Without delay, the man continued speaking. "Take a seat, young man. I've been instructed to take you under my wing, so to speak."

The man paused, allowing Lt. Benjamin time to absorb everything. Recognizing that he had been having too much fun with the newbie, he changed his demeanor. Without fanfare, as if a switch had been thrown, Kyle watched this man's facial expression somehow change before his eyes. In that split second, the man's expressions no longer depicted a pleasant, happy-go-lucky attitude. In that moment, Kyle recognized something only seasoned military personnel acquire. Kyle knew his kind: a person who, when called upon to take extreme measures, wouldn't bat an eyelash. A person who recognized that if he didn't do it, someone else would. A person who understood that it wouldn't be his first and it wouldn't be his last. Kyle stared into the man's eyes, and the façade that had been propped up earlier melted away. During that brief pause, Kyle sensed he was being sized up. As the silence was about to become awkward, the man finally spoke.

"My name is Michael Gibson. I'm retired military. People call me Gibby. I'm here to introduce you to Hummingbird."

As Kyle heard the words, it hit him. This was it. His first real Agency assignment. As his mind made sense of what was happening, he felt a cold sweat run down the back of his neck. This guy was his contact. It was starting. He didn't know it yet, but in the very near future, Gibby would save his life.

9

Tae waited across the street, sitting on the dirt bank of a drainage canal. The canal encircled a neighborhood that housed common laborers. His humble attire and downtrodden gait seemed to blend in with the other working class people who walked along its streets. Tae had been waiting over an hour before he saw the door open. Craning his neck, he waited to see if he recognized the person opening the door before he stood. As the door opened, a face hidden in the shadows stared out across the street, as if searching the crowd. As the man's face turned in Tae's direction, they made eye contact. A bright smile flashed from the shadow of the doorway. Tae watched as the man closed the door. He waited for the window shade in the living room window to open. This was their sign. It meant that the coast was clear.

When Tae saw the shade open, his tired face relaxed. Like one of Pavlov's experiments, his body subconsciously responded as if had been trained to react on cue. He looked up and down the street. Convinced that he wasn't being watched, Tae began walking away in the opposite direction and then crossed the street, being careful to use the crosswalk. He made a conscious effort to appear to be confident. He had become a creature of habit, purposely taking a precarious route to his destination, just in case he was being watched. Unlike his first journey to this location, when he had been on the brink of hysteria, he no longer found the urge to make a beeline to his destination. He was no longer afraid to walk in the open.

Over the last decade, he had made this journey once a month. Only during the extreme winter months did they alter their schedule. After the first snowfall, Tae prepared for a final visit, one that would not be repeated until the brutal winter weather subsided. Those final winter visits were always a challenge. Tae would need to carry back twice the amount of provisions as he normally carried. That trip also signaled the time for his family to begin rationing what few surplus items they had been able to accumulate over the prior months.

Those journeys across the DMZ involved a fifteen-mile, one-way trek. If it weren't for the need to stop and start to remain hidden from the DPRK soldiers, the trip could be done in as little as four hours. Being unable to walk in a straight line, and depending on the presence of people, though, it took up to nine hours. The return trip was always easier. Being freshly showered and rested and having a full stomach enhanced his physical and mental condition. His fresh, clean clothes contrasted with his appearance when he had emerged from the thirty-kilometer journey south after treading through the damp, dusty underground caverns. After he cleaned up, he would finally feel like he fit in.

That hadn't been the case during those first few crossings. Back then, he had been lucky. As he reached the opposite street corner, Tae doubled back along the concrete paved walkway that ran along countless storefronts. As he glanced through the window of a postal store, he thought back to the time he received the package. If it hadn't been for that package, he never would have considered making these journeys. It had changed his and his family's lives forever.

There was a time when the DPRK had softened its stance toward the west, and there was a true sense of optimism that unification was possible. During the Clinton Administration, Secretary of State Madeline Albright had been sent to Pyongyang, where she met with the Supreme Imminence Kim Jung Il. The US and the DPRK had made huge headway toward peace, cooperation, and mutual respect. Their relationships had improved to the point that families who had remained separated since the Korean Conflict could travel between the countries to re-establish contact. It was during that time when packages could be exchanged, most going northward to help families living in the north. Everyone understood that all packages would be opened and scrutinized. Anything that the government deemed unacceptable would be removed and disposed of. When Tae received that first large package, he felt an unaccustomed sense of excitement, an emotion that most North Koreans seldom experienced.

The package had obvious signs of being opened. The contents inside had been shuffled, no longer neatly organized. Only later did he learn that one of the packages of sweet brown rice and several of the multi-vitamin containers had been confiscated. Apparently, the first waves of goodwill packages received by the DPRK had been misappropriated by the government postal workers. But over a brief period, the constant and increased amount of care packages that poured across the border was overwhelming. The government postal districts became concerned that if the workers continued to pilfer these humanitarian gifts, it could jeopardize the newfound friendship and trust that was developing with the US and the Republic of Korea. More important than the international political fears, the postal workers expressed concerns over the practical matter of transporting and possessing items that had obviously been manufactured abroad.

The top government officials thought long and hard about how to handle the predicament and made a decision: They ordered all postal workers to refrain from any additional pilfering and directed all efforts toward appropriate censorship searches. However, under no circumstance were entire packages to be confiscated. Rather, they would be delivered to the rightful recipients. Most of the correspondence was sent to family members living in the remote villages outside of the cities. It was reasoned that there was a high likelihood that these people had a long lineage and deep attachment to those properties. The senders understood this and assumed that, if their relatives were still alive, they would still be living there. However, for some transient citizens, there was a limited understanding of the exact address and location of certain loved ones. Consequently, it became a challenge to locate everyone. For those whom the postal service was unable to locate, there was a high likelihood, that many of them had either passed away or had been banished to labor camps.

When all efforts to locate the recipients had been exhausted, the packages were classified as undeliverable. All personal letters that accompanied the undeliverable packages were destroyed. The contents were then divided up and delivered to the labor camps. Otherwise, the clear majority of those later packages with known addresses were delivered.

Tae changed directions after crossing the street and now made his way back to the downstairs apartment with the open blinds. With each step closer, his thoughts returned to his memories about that first package.

He had just arrived home after a long day at work. As he climbed the front porch steps, he saw an oversized cardboard box. A memo was taped to the top. The notice informed the recipient that the package had been sent from his brother who lived in Seoul. The memo stated that in the spirit of reconciliation and as a sign of friendship, the Postal Authority had inspected this package and deemed its contents to be acceptable for use and consumption. The recipient must understand that any items deemed inappropriate had been confiscated and properly destroyed.

After reading the notice, Tae glanced up and down the road. He couldn't help but question the validity of the entire situation. He was skeptical. After making sure no one was watching him, he opened the door and pushed the box into the house. As he closed the door, he called out to his family, "Look what I found on the porch!"

Receiving a postal delivery in the DPRK was an event. All their relations lived together under the same roof. There was no Home Shopping Network or Amazon Home Delivery in the DPRK. Everyone came running into the front room. After everyone was present, his ailing father broke the silence.

"What is it?"

Everyone stared at Tae. He was the one who had found it. He was the one who had decided to bring it into the house. No one spoke. During the silence, the other family members stepped backward away from the box. One could sense fear building up. Everyone continued staring at the box. A sense of dread seemed to settle across everyone's faces. After several moments, they each began to voice their concerns.

"It's probably a trick," said Tae's mother.

"Did you see who delivered it?" asked his wife.

"I don't like this. We can only get into trouble for having anything to do with this thing," his father added. After a brief pause, Tae's father stood on his toes to peer inside the top of the oversized box. A hush filled the room. Everyone's eyes darted between their father and the box. Their facial muscles twitched with anxiety as they tried to interpret the father's expressions. After leaning forward, he let his leg muscles relax as his feet returned to a normal standing position on the worn wooden floor. Looking back at his eldest son Tae, his father spoke.

"We should hide this thing until we know what it's all about." Looking into Tae's eyes, he asked, "Where's it from?"

"It's from Seoul."

In unison, all the family members, even his two young children, raised their hands up to their mouths and took a deep inhale in disbelief. Nodding his head up and down, his father pointed his index finger toward the front closet. Tae understood what he wanted and began pushing the box down the hall. No one offered any assistance. In fact, they did just the opposite. Everyone stepped back, giving Tae room to push the box down the hallway. No one even touched it. Once the box was hidden out of sight, no further discussions occurred. Out of sight, out of mind. Everyone moved toward the kitchen to eat dinner.

During dinner, no one spoke. It was as if everyone was preoccupied, trapped in their thoughts contemplating the box. Dinner went by quickly. No one seemed to have an appetite. Afterward, Tae's mother cleared the dishes while everyone else wandered back to their bedrooms. A sense of fear had settled into their little home. No one knew how this would affect their future. Tae's wife patted his forearm in a reassuring manner before speaking.

"You'll need to go to the Postal Authority tomorrow morning to see what we should do."

After exchanging sad and fearful expressions, she turned out the light. They each lay down onto their padded floor blanket. Tae reached across to turn on their electric blanket. Neither spoke as they stared up through the darkness at the ceiling, uncertain what their future held. Sleep came late into the night for everyone in the household.

Early the next morning, Tae walked alone to the regional postal authority office. He had no idea when it opened. Although he'd seen the building many times before, he had never had an occasion to visit until today. Tae was the first to arrive. He had arrived at 6:00 a.m. sharp. Typical in a farming agricultural community, day started before sunrise. But with a bureaucratic office, it wouldn't open until 7:00 a.m. Tae positioned himself outside of the office doors, waiting for the postal authority office to open.

As Tae stood outside the doors, he watched other men walk up. As they approached the sign, they avoided eye contact. The hours of operation were posted on the wall. Realizing that they had made the same mistake by arriving too early, an internal sense of embarrassment and fear seemed to escalate. Tae began to wonder if these men had also received a similar package.

For decades, the citizens of the DPRK had been conditioned to be fearful. This fear created the natural tendency to avoid deciding and acting out without permission, questioning themselves whether they had done anything wrong. The men's body language suggested that everyone present was outside of his comfort zone.

Over the next hour, the line of men grew to thirty-one persons. Tae had been keeping count. He was first in line and had somehow been unofficially designated as the most senior person present, a position he had hoped to avoid. During their wait, idle conversations were nonexistent. No one had the courage to speak out. During his wait, Tae had been thinking through his situation and was certain that this was some form of test in loyalty. He had convinced himself that he was doing the right thing by coming down to the postal authority office. He felt good about not opening the box. It was in the same condition as it had been discovered. Because it hadn't been opened, no one in his family had any idea as to what was inside.

At exactly 7:00 a.m., the large wooden door opened. A small elderly man with deep facial lines pushed the door open. As the door opened out from the building, the old man came into full view. He paused, taken aback by the presence of so many people waiting outside. After propping a worn wooden doorstop under the door, he turned and faced the men. Waiting with bated breath, the men concentrated, paying close attention to everything the old man did. With a self-conscious expression, the old man looked up and down the line just before he bowed with a deep bend forward from the waist, the type of bow typically saved for people in high authority. It was obvious that the old man felt compelled to offer a sincere acknowledgement toward the waiting crowd. As if on cue, the line of men bowed in unison. The old man waited for the men to rise back up into an upright position, before he spoke.

"I'm certain most, if not all of you are here because you have each received a package." The old man paused, looking up and down the line, waiting for a reply. No one moved or spoke. It was beyond quiet. The old man closed his eyes, pursed his lips, and nodded his head, as if he recognized their apprehension. Of course, it was a natural reaction. Until now, no one in the DPRK had ever received anything sent directly from South Korea, especially with the consent and assistance of their own government. In fact, many citizens believed that having any direct contact from the south warranted a visit from the military intelligence, if not a trip to a labor camp. The old man opened his eyes. With great effort, he flashed the sincerest friendly expression while clasping his hands together in front of his stomach before speaking.

"Comrades, the world is changing. The Supreme Excellence has been working with the Imperialist Americans. In an act of support, to develop trust, with the hope of establishing a peaceful reunification with the south, a softening of certain restrictions regarding the exchange of communications between our borders has been encouraged. To that end, let me assure you that the packages that you may have received," The old man again paused, looking up and down the line of men to see if anyone would acknowledge his assumption. It was to no avail. Once more, no one moved. Not even a casual nod of a head. You could hear a cricket chirp, it was so quiet. After a brief pause, the old man continued to speak.

"...the packages are rightfully yours. No one will be punished for accepting whatever gifts are inside of the boxes. Each box has been opened, searched, and evaluated. If an object was found that was deemed inappropriate, it has been removed and properly disposed." The old man looked out across the crowd. Like a slow warm breeze that passed over a frozen arctic valley during the first moments indicating that spring had arrived, the old man watched as the expressions on the gathered men's faces began to thaw. He watched their facial expressions soften as their clenched teeth and jaw muscles began to relax. He could detect a subtle twinkle in the corner of some of their eyes, as they suppressed a broad smile behind their normal day-to-day façade. Several men began turning their heads, searching the faces of the others. Trying to capture some recognition, some acknowledgement about what this elder government employee was saying.

As quickly as that minute flash of group optimism appeared, it remained hidden under the surface of their outward emotions. Due to the decades of conditioning, isolation, fear, and overwhelming demand for absolute dedication and discipline to the cause, no one allowed those feelings to surface. The men remained in control of their emotions, choosing to remain silent and skeptical.

During that brief silence, the old man recognized their disbelief. He broke the silence. He turned his head toward the open postal building doors. He yelled instructions to someone inside to bring out the official memos that had been prepared for this eventuality. The government had anticipated something like this would happen. A memo had been drafted.

A young postal employee exited the building carrying a stack of paper. He handed the old man half of the stack. They both began distributing the memorandums to the group of waiting men.

"Please take one of these memos. It is on official government letterhead and signed by his Supreme Eminence Kim Jung Il himself. This document is your express written permission to have in your possession the package. A similar memo should also be attached to the box that you received."

Each man reached out his hands to receive the memo and began reading. They each studied the paper, reading every word. In short order, the thirty-one men who had been waiting all morning began to disburse. Some went away on foot, while others climbed onto their parked bicycles and rode away. Others walked toward the nearby bus stop. In no time, the postal line disappeared. Not a single person had verbally admitted to having received a package. Yet, everyone waiting had accepted and read the memo. Not a single person had entered the building. As the old man watched the men disperse, he wasn't surprised. Most citizens in the DPRK avoided going into any government building. It was understood that many who did were never seen again.

Tae began walking back home. With a sense of purpose and pep in his step, he quickened his pace. Once he arrived home, a thirty-minute debate ensued. After reading the memo, they discovered the exact same one taped to the box. But this one seemed to carry more weight. It had been hand delivered to Tae by a postal employee, as opposed to its having been attached to a mysterious package that somehow appeared on their doorstep. After a unanimous vote, his family permitted Tae to remove the hidden box from the closet. Like a kid opening his first Christmas present, Tae tore open the box.

With delight, he found four large bags of rice on the very top. A mish-mash of other bags of dried seaweed, squid, bottles of multivitamins, two large sealed packages of red pepper, salts and spices. There were boxes of Chocolate bars, expensive flavored vinegars, and a variety of pastry cookies that were individually wrapped in beautiful red foil. Their faces were alight, as they flashed the biggest smiles any of them could remember. Just when Tae thought things couldn't get any better, near the bottom, he found two large cartons of Marlboro Reds. It was as if Tae had just hit the lottery. He frantically dug the cartons out and hugged them both with his forearms. Everyone laughed. His wife saw a large cellophane shrink-wrapped box of dried instant noodle soup packages of varying flavors and name brands. As she *picked them up out of the box, she saw a plane white envelope and handed it to her husband.*

Tae noticed that the envelope had already been opened. He shook the envelope to see if the censors had allowed the letter to be delivered. To everyone's surprise, he found a four-page handwritten letter from his brother. Just before the formal division of the country along the 38th parallel, he had been fighting in the south, hiding with a few of the remaining Korean bands of resistance against the Japanese before their departure. On September 7, 1945, following the devastation and chaos at the close of World War II, the United States' famous Douglas MacArthur had appointed John Hodge to administer Korean Affairs.

Initially, the USSR, US, China and Great Britain were to oversee the redevelopment of Korea. The Chinese and USSR tried to establish their own provisional government and sent representatives to discuss how Korea was going to be handled. Hodge refused to meet with them.

Tae's brother had been in Busan, a coastal fishing community at the time. No one expected what happened. His brother was trapped in the south. Like others, he expected the separation to be temporary so he decided to wait it out. But reunification never materialized.

They ate like royalty that night. He had read the letter aloud, nonstop, several times. Listening to the words was like getting reacquainted with a family member they hadn't seen for decades.

*   *   *   *   *

As Tae stepped up onto the curb, he turned toward a large, plate-glass window. It was his personal sign that the journey was almost done. He strode heavily past this window. His weary legs felt like mush. The joints in his knees and hips were stiff, almost locking into place.

Peering through the other thick, plate-glass windows, he watched several families seated around beautiful wooden tables, each table having its own individual barbecue grill and exhaust hoods. The people held shiny metal chopsticks and drank from porcelain teacups. The restaurant was spotless. As they enjoyed their meal, the patrons smiled.

Turning his head away, he leaned forward and mustered his last bits of strength. He could almost smell the meal that he was certain his brother had prepared just for him. He could almost imagine its aroma. It had become their ritual during the past ten years. As Tae's legs stopped on the cement sidewalk, he looked up at the door. It had taken him a little less than nine hours. Stepping onto the threshold, Tae looked up at the keyhole. Then, he depressed the doorbell. His heart began to race, and his pulse quickened.

As the door opened, tears leaked out of the corners of his eyes. He couldn't help it. It seemed to happen every time. As the door swung open, Tae could just see his brother's face. His brother bowed. Tae returned the bow and waited for his brother's eyes to raise up and make eye contact before he walked inside. Before the door could swing shut, Tae wrapped his arms around his brother, extending a frail hug, and buried his face against his shoulder.

The wonderful smell of soup broke his trance. Tae felt the hunger pangs he had been suppressing rumble from his empty stomach. His brother stepped away. He tilted his head down, staring at Tae's stomach. With a big smile on his face, he finally spoke.

"Let's get some food!" Tae's face lit, flashing a jagged-tooth grin. They stepped forward into the dining room. His brother had the table covered with small hors d'oeuvres with a multitude of fresh vegetables and kimchi dishes, a large fried fish, barbecued pork ribs, rice, and hot soup. It always reminded Tae of the meals he had with his family to the north; but those meals were only for special occasions. Tae couldn't help but feel bewildered at the concept that people in the south ate like this every day.

10

"Hey Moon Dog!"

"Yes, sir!" replied Lt. Elliott.

"Are we ready for the briefing with the Director?" asked X.O. Newland.

"Sir! Yes, sir!"

"Then let's get it going."

The X.O. and Lt. Elliott exited the secure Surveillance Room and walked toward the Director's office. They turned down the hall and waited in front of a white line painted on the concrete hallway floor. Further down the hall stood two armed guards positioned in front of the entrance to the Director's sanctum. These guards rotated out every sixty minutes. An entire detail of twenty men was assigned on this detail throughout the day. When not guarding the Director's office, they were assigned other duties inside the camp.

Lt. Elliott had heard others talk about what the Director's area was like. X.O. Newland had been down here many times, stretching back through two prior directors. Those past visits had been because of numerous DPRK missile launches and the downing of a Korean Airlines commercial passenger plane. Today's visit would be much different. The wall speaker blared, breaking the silence. The voice of a male boomed, bouncing off the walls as it ricocheted off the corridor passageway. "Lt. Elliott and X.O. Newland, you may both enter now."

The two guards turned toward the large metal double doors, and each opened a door. Then, they walked through and paused on the other side. Waiting, they held one of the doors open. The guards' faces were fiercely intense. They stared down the two guests as they waited for them to pass through the open doors. As Lt. Elliott walked through the doorway, he glanced up toward the ceiling. Until then, he hadn't noticed the cameras mounted above. Upon entering the doorway, they discovered another longer corridor with another identical set of metal double doors. No pictures or other personnel were present; it was literally empty. On the ground were four sets of painted foot impressions painted on the concrete floor. A circle was painted around each pair of impressions. That same voice called down from the speakers.

"If you could each stand on one set of footprints and hold your arms above your head, please."

X.O. Newland knew the drill and stepped forward to take his position on one set of painted footprints. In a hushed voice, he asked Moon Dog, "You're not packing heat, right?"

Lt. Elliott had already raised his arms above his head and was frozen in position. As he processed the question, his eyes rolled up toward the right. He had to think about it. Normally, Surveillance Techs wouldn't be carrying a sidearm with them into the Surveillance Room, but the DMZ wasn't like a typical stateside assignment. It was a standing order that all personnel, military and civilian, whether combatant or noncombatant, while moving around the base, were to be armed. The Surveillance Techs, upon entering the Surveillance Area, would stow their weapons in the Sectional locker room. At the end of their shift, they would retrieve them. Only in secure areas where VIPs were located were firearms prohibited. Only the VIP's protective details could carry weapons. Much thought had gone into this protocol. The last thing the US Military and US Intelligence community wanted was for someone with a loose screw to try to whack a VIP.

Everywhere else on Camp Bonifas, aside from the VIP areas, was simply too dangerous. The entire camp location was a literal stone's throw away from the enemy. From a certain location, one could glance down and see the unmistakable light blue building that straddled the borderline between the north and south. Across that painted line on the asphalt road, only inches away, stood DPRK soldiers. The DPRK soldiers stood on their side of the building, trying to ignore the Republic of Korea's sentries standing meters away, separated only by air. In this location, there were no physical barriers.

After a quick glance, Moon Dog was one hundred percent certain that he wasn't armed. Looking into the X.O.'s eyes, Moon Dog shook his head, confirming that he wasn't packing. With a quick nod of his head, the X.O. acknowledged his understanding. It was as if Moon Dog could hear the X.O. saying, "Good to go!"

"Please remain still," one of the guards said, as he backed down the hallway while the other guard pushed a black button on the wall. In unison, the guards stepped back behind the doors, out of sight. After a brief pause, the silence was broken by another voice, this one coming from a different intercom originating further down the hallway. The new voice instructed them to proceed toward the doors ahead.

As they began walking, Lt. Elliott whispered, "Hey, X.O., what if we were packing?"

"There's a solid metal wall that would drop between us and both sets of doors. We'd be trapped like mice in a maze. If someone had entered the Director's area with other ideas on their mind, 'their emotions would have gotten the best of them,' know what I mean?" the X.O. replied. Lt. Elliott pursed his lips and nodded his head. Lt. Elliott was reminded that working for the Agency was never cut and dried; they were always several steps ahead of you.

Before they reached the end of the hallway, the double doors opened, and a different set of guards peered out. One guard waved them inside. Lt. Elliott recognized one of the men. He had heard that the Director hand-picked her personal security detail, which consisted of six men. While in the DMZ, at no time was the Director left alone. She could be separated by only one door. It was protocol until she returned to the US mainland, which did not include Hawaii, Alaska, nor the other territories. No Agency director traveling abroad was ever left unguarded. All were valuable United States assets that warranted twenty-four/seven/three-sixty-five protection. Every Agency director was a legitimate VIP.

In a deep baritone voice, one of the guards said, "Come this way, gentlemen. The Director has been waiting."

*   *   *   *   *

"So how are father and mother?"

Tae turned his gaze away from the food. He'd had his fill of galbi, kimchi soup, rice, and fried fish and was sipping the sweet chilled cinnamon ginger tea. Tae set down the delicate ceramic cup on the wooden table before replying.

"They are fine. He looks forward to the day we are no longer separated. This year's rice crop has been a blessing. We have also been able to purchase more items imported from China. I'm worried about this coming winter, though. They're both getting older. I'm grateful they've remained healthy all of these years, thanks to the medicines you get for us." Tae paused as he smiled before continuing. "The snow has started to fall in the mountain ranges last week. It won't be long before we must take another break from my visits here. We should be good next month, but that may be the last visit until spring."

The brother nodded his head. He understood that this next trip would require a bigger supply of food and medicine. "I have an oversized tan backpack you can take back next time. It will be able to hold more than last year. Are the tablets helping with Abogi's (Father's) arthritis?"

"They've been a lifesaver. Whatever they are, they are dong the trick. The puin (my wife) was wondering if you could refill the cosmetics you provided last year as well." Tae asked as he glanced away from his brother, avoiding eye contact. He felt guilty asking for such frivolous items. Lipsticks, eyeliners, and makeup powders were not essential items. However, his wife had been so surprised. He knew how much enjoyment they brought her and couldn't resist asking. Not knowing the cost, Tae was uncomfortable making such a request. His guilt was further exacerbated, given he was in no position to repay his brother.

His brother watched as Tae's shoulders slumped forward and his head bent down, avoiding eye contact. It broke his heart to see his older brother like this. He felt guilt living in the plentiful south, while the rest of his family remained north. Many times, when his mind was clear of any concern, his thoughts would drift back to the time following the Great War, when the superpowers decided the fate of Korea, dividing it at the 38th parallel. He was one of the lucky ones. Two years before the countries were officially established, it had become illegal to cross over between the countries. Most people had thought that the separation would be brief. But as years turned into decades, it became clear that reunification was not going to be a simple matter.

When he thought about his standard of living compared to his family trapped in the north, he felt a constant sense of shame. The fact that he had refused to sneak back north during those initial years to be with his family made it worse. He knew his father would never leave the north. That was his father's home, the land where his father's family had died to protect and preserve it; a place that hid his family shrine deep inside the mountain cave. Unlike his family resigned to living in the north, the brother had learned to appreciate a simpler way of life that offered true enjoyment, freedoms, and a deep inner sense of happiness, things he had never experienced in the north. He never told Tae, but he loved life in the south. He accepted the fact that the United States held a great deal of power and influence over them. But at the same time, accepting this new way of thinking brought an inner personal, individual sense of opportunity and freedom.

Over the years, the brother watched the southern area transform into thriving cities with towering skyscrapers, efficient, high-speed subways, bus lines, highways, and airports. He enjoyed the prosperity of his newfound friends in the south. Everyone seemed to ride the success that capitalism and a free economy provided. He knew he could never return, even if the decision meant being separated from his family. The brother had found love, married, and had two children. He kept the part of his life about his family in the north a secret from everyone, including his wife and children. While they lived in a luxurious condominium in downtown Seoul, he had secretly rented out this dilapidated two-bedroom flat on the outskirts of a rural township. He feared that if anyone found out he had been providing supplies to the north, he would be labeled a spy. The fact that they were his blood relatives made no difference. The line had been drawn in the sand. No one could be entrusted with this secret, not even his wife.

The economic differences between these two countries was difficult to fathom. On the surface, South Korea had the feel of the United States, but in some ways was better. It had expanded its manufacturing into a giant international player. Hyundai and Samsung had become internationally recognized brands of the highest quality. Even the elite sport of professional golf had been taken to the highest level as the South Koreans dominated the LPGA. It was as if South Korea had taken advantage of its opportunities when given the chance to participate in international affairs. Even in their eyes, they had exceeded their own expectations. South Korea had transformed its subsistence-farming community into a prosperous global leader, moving from dirt roads and rice paddies to high-speed trains, airports, and international manufacturing in less than three decades. In comparison, the north hadn't fared so well.

It hurt Tae's brother to see how his mother, father, Tae, Tae's wife, and two children were living. But what could he do? His father refused to leave. His mother was unwilling to abandon his father. Tae, the older brother, had the obligation to take care of his parents. Over the decades, he could see it in Tae's eyes: Visiting the south was like visiting another planet. It no longer resembled anything he understood, having lived his entire life in the hermit country to the north.

To sit across the table from Tae and recognize what looked to be shame for simply asking for ordinary cosmetics for his wife pained him to the core of his soul. A luxury in the north, makeup something most high school girls owned by the pound, stuffed away in their oversized cosmetic bags. The brother had planned to give Tae a special present so that Tae could present it to his wife in the north. Smiling, he walked over to the hall closet and took out a dark brown, thin leather purse. As he carried it to Tae, he opened the top of this expensive designer tote and handed it to him.

Tae took the tote and reverently inspected it. The strap was still covered with brown paper wrap to protect it from being scuffed. It had golden connecting clasps that had nothing to do with the efficiency but everything to do with appearance. As Tae pulled the sides of the bag open to look inside, he saw that it had been stuffed full of eye shadows, makeup foundation containers, powder blushes, fake eyelashes, lipsticks of varying shades, lip glosses, and an eyelash curler. There were even a compact hair straightener and several large glass vials of perfume. Tae couldn't believe what he was seeing and was frozen in shock. He didn't know what most of the items were for, but he knew his wife would. And if she didn't know, she would figure it out.

Tae's brother could sense the deep appreciation for the items. Before Tae could reject the gift, his brother spoke. "Let's be sure to wrap all of the breakable glass bottles in paper. The last thing we want is for a guard to hear the clanking of the glass as you go through the tunnel."

They looked away from the purse. Tae nodded his head and exhaled. As he looked up, they stared into each other's eyes. Like brothers the world over, they could communicate with facial expressions. Nothing more needed to be said. Tae's brother broke the awkward pause, flashing a heartfelt smile. It was the least he could do. Tae recognized the guilt his brother must feel, living in the south while they struggled to survive in the extreme north.

Tae never viewed their situation as anything except that this was their life. Their hardships were accepted as the circumstances of their life—nothing more, nothing less—like the Eskimos who had lived in the extreme conditions above the Arctic Circle region, struggling with the elements and scratching out a meager existence. The Eskimos, like many other indigenous people across the globe, were free to relocate to a less challenging climate. Some did, but many didn't. Humans tended to form a fundamental attachment to their own culture. The fact that their circumstances offered extreme challenges wasn't necessarily an issue. They were like a special fraternal organization, unwilling to abandon traditions. A way of life developed, passed down from their ancestors. Outsiders need to see other people from this perspective. With this insight, one began to recognize and understand the solidarity and satisfaction that a culture had achieved from being self-reliant. One began to appreciate and respect the tenacity that such cultures possess as they battle to survive.

Unfortunately, most outsiders were incapable of seeing this point of view. Some outsiders could neither understand nor appreciate the sacrifice, the sheer struggle all those individuals had overcome. Most outsiders hadn't considered the number of people who died protecting and preserving their way of life. For these people, it was incomprehensible why such cultures didn't choose to submit to a new, foreign point of view. Why didn't they abandon their old way of doing things and accept a more sophisticated and easier way? To outsiders, making this choice seemed to be the only rational choice.

Across the globe, historians had seen Native Americans, Australian Aborigines, the Indians in the rain forests of the Amazon basin, and the Eskimos of the Arctic Region. It was impossible for some to abandon their unique heritage and culture. They were unable to accept the foreign, modern ways of living. Thus, it was no surprise that the North Koreans, like those other cultures facing similar circumstances, refused to accept and submit to a foreign way of life. It was part of the human condition.

Breaking the silence, Tae's brother walked over to his desk and opened the top drawer. He pulled out a fresh set of batteries, a new flashlight, and two cartons of Marlboro Red cigarettes. He turned and handed them to Tae. Tae tore into one of the cigarette cartons before his eyes settled on the flashlight. It reminded him of what had happened in the tunnel.

"That reminds me. Something happened."

Tae's brother froze with a blank stare before he replied, "What happened?"

"As I was coming through the tunnel, near the underground water spring, the wall caved in." Tae paused and looked his brother dead in the eye. All their pleasant feelings evaporated. "I saw workers with flashlights and tools, and I could hear an electrical transport vehicle."

"Did any one see you?"

"No."

"Are you certain? You must be absolutely certain."

"I am. I waited lying down for thirty minutes. A man stuck his arm through the wall opening and pointed a high beam flashlight into the cave area. After looking around, he left."

Tae's brother walked back to the dining room and sat down. Tae had been using a natural lava tube cave system for the last ten years. While in the tunnel, no one had ever crossed his path until today. The realization began to sink in, and Tae's brother began to contemplate why the north was building another tunnel. As they sat thinking in silence, this discovery seemed to suggest something else. It wasn't so much a concern about being discovered. There was a bigger issue. Why were they digging another tunnel into the southern territory?

"Were any of the men armed?"

"I don't think so. But," the brothers' eyes locked onto each other with an intense stare, "they were being extremely quiet. Not just the men who came into the opening to look around. As I sat waiting, there wasn't a sound. Only soft shuffling of feet and subtle crumbling noises and the sound of scraping hand shovels. There were no power tools; no jack hammers; no supervisors shouting out orders. Everyone was whispering."

11

Kyle had just returned from this first introductory briefing at the DMZ. Everyone went through it. He pulled his boots off and jumped on his bunk to take a brief rest before hitting the mess hall. His thoughts drifted back to his most recent meeting with his Agency contact, Gibby.

"So, Kyle, you landed yourself in one hell of a first assignment," Gibby said as he tossed back his first shot of Soju (Korean rice wine). After swallowing all the clear liquid from a shot glass, he continued. "Man, I love those! Nice and tasty, with some serious kick later."

Kyle waited for Gibby to finish chewing a sliced piece of barbecued pork rib. He couldn't help but notice how proficient Gibby was with chopsticks.

"Why do you say that?" Kyle asked.

"Well, normally, a greenhorn's first assignment is just watching our good buddies to the north from the safety of the Surveillance Room. Not this time." Gibby paused as he reached out across the table and maneuvered the wooden sticks, sandwiching minute pieces of sweet, marinated, sliced octopus legs and tossing them into his gaping mouth.

"What do you mean?" Kyle asked, doing his best to control his voice. He didn't want to let on how anxious he was becoming.

"Well, let's put it this way. Are you afraid of the dark?"

"Not particularly. I guess it would depend on the circumstances. I would be a terrible Marine if I did get afraid of anything, really," Kyle offered, hoping to bolster his macho persona.

"Well, let me restate my question. Are you comfortable functioning in the dark for extended periods of time?" Gibby pressed.

"I've trained in isolation. Also, did some time in a sensory deprivation tank. Even attended a survival-capture training scenario."

"Why'd you go through that training?"

"I had originally been slotted as a pilot. I went all the way through flight school for F-18s in El Toro. I washed out," Kyle said with an intense stare down, as if daring Gibby to make a wisecrack. Gibby knew better and leaned forward, glancing around the room to make sure no one else was close enough to hear what he was about to say. It was probably unnecessary.

This restaurant was Agency controlled. Although it was a legitimate restaurant, the place was swept daily for all electronic surveillance devices. The Agency understood that there needed to be places other than the government military bases in which to meet their agents. Through years of hide-and-seek espionage games, they recognized that if an agent were being followed, it wouldn't take their counterparts long to figure out which service members were Agency operatives. Having their agents meeting in the same nondescript government-looking buildings would be dead giveaways. Restaurants were a perfect cover. After all, everyone needed to eat. Many Agency meetings were held in the open, in front of the *public. It was extremely difficult for agents to completely avoid meeting their handlers in a well-known agency hangout. All efforts were made to make such meetings few and far between.*

Comfortable that they were alone, Gibby whispered, "You're going to be assigned to the night watch. You'll be walking the DMZ perimeter, solo." Gibby raised both of his eyebrows, scrunching the muscles in his forehead. Kyle sat still, showing no reaction.

Gibby was impressed. Making a mental note to himself never to play poker with this greenhorn. Gibby reached into his jacket pocket and pulled out a small box. It was slightly bigger than a typical case used to hold a necklace. Placing the box on the table, he slid it in front of Kyle.

"Just put it in your pocket. Open it when you get back to your room. I'll send you an encrypted email. It explains what it is. We'll talk tomorrow, here for lunch."

Gibby wiped his mouth on the cloth napkin and stood. After tossing the napkin on the table, he pulled his dark Ray-Ban sunglasses out of his front pocket and slid them over his eyes. With a quick flipping of his head from side to side, his shoulder-length hair waved back and forth. Gibby walked toward the front door. He glanced back. Kyle remained in his seat, contemplating the information.

Gibby reached the glass double doors before turning back toward Kyle. Before speaking, he waited until Kyle looked up and made eye contact. "Later, dude," mimicking Jeff Spicoli from the movie Fast Times at Ridgemont High. *Then, he turned and walked out.*

Back in his room, Kyle reached into his pocket and grabbed the object Gibby gave him. It was a small metallic device that looked like a small bird. It was about three inches tall and two inches wide. There were equal-length indentations on both sides. Hidden under the device were five small metallic spheres that looked like ball bearings. The metal orbs were a dull gray color with a porous texture, not smooth. He'd been studying the objects for the last hour, contemplating what they were. Then, an electronic tone emanated from his laptop computer, interrupting his concentration. He recognized the sound well: He'd just received an email. Kyle placed the items on his bedstand and walked toward his desk. Using a special encryption program, he opened the email and began reading.

"While I was tossing your room, I took the liberty of leaving you a little something in your top dresser drawer. Oh, by the way, nice boxers, dude. Aren't you a little too old for Scooby Doo shorts?"

The message had been sent from a random-generated non-military email address. If another agency tried to locate the physical IP address of the email sender, they would be led on a wild goose chase around the globe. Kyle was curious. How did Gibby get access into his room? How could a long-haired civilian get access to an officer's room on one of the most secure bases on the globe? Reading the message, he was a little embarrassed about the "boxers" remark. They were a gift from an ex-girlfriend. It had been a running joke between Kyle and her. For some reason, he found it difficult to discard them. Now, he made a mental note to discard them the next morning.

Kyle stood and locked his door and jammed a wooden chair under the doorknob. After jiggling the chair from side to side, he was confident that only through great effort was anyone coming through that door. Walking back to his dresser drawer, Kyle opened the top drawer and saw that his bright blue Scooby Doo boxers were spread out, covering something. Lifting the boxers, Kyle found a rectangular box about six inches deep and eight inches long.

He removed the box from the drawer and carried it to his bed. He pulled off the top and discovered what looked like an electric portable cooktop. He'd seen similar devices plugged in within the rooms of other personnel on base. He'd assumed they were used to boil water to prepare a popular instant noodle soup. As he pulled the cooktop out of the box, he noticed that the weight seemed off somehow; it was too heavy. Kyle examined the other objects inside the box. He found loose cables and a plain white unsealed envelope. Inside the envelope, he discovered a handwritten note.

It was from Gibby. The scribbled writing explained that although the device worked perfectly well as a portable electrical cooktop, it was a concealed DVD player that could read only customized encryption discs. The note explained that the back side of the burner plate contained an external port. It included instructions on how to use the enclosed cable to jack the cooktop to any computer laptop. The portable cooktop would act as a standalone processor, with all the necessary hardware and programing to bypass the laptop's internal computer system. The only part of the laptop computer to be used was its monitor screen. The Agency could have included a monitor, but to do so would have defeated the purpose of the disguise and been a dead giveaway as to what it really was. The cooktop also contained a small, nondescript hole, designed to look like a screw fitting; in fact, it was a slot. When pushed, it pivoted inward, exposing a standard receptacle that could accommodate standard headset prong fittings.

The Agency had designed this device so that it processed everything except the image. This innovation prevented the laptop from utilizing any of its internal components. When in use, the laptop was tricked into believing that only the screensaver was being activated. The goal was to prevent any agent's personal computer from leaving any footprints that could later be viewed. Only the screen from the computer was used, like a standalone monitor. The computer's processors, short-term RAM, and hard drive programs were never accessed. It was perfect disguise. Only a trained eye would notice the subtle cosmetic differences between this portable cooktop and the millions that were found throughout Korea.

Kyle examined the DVD. It looked like any plain generic blank DVD disc—no logo, label, or artistic image. It had double-sided, shiny, silver-colored discs with circular grooves. Hidden in the bottom were two small, handheld controllers. Each included a small, high-resolution built-in monitor. One controller had cords, and the other was cordless. Other than this difference, they were identical.

There was also a simple, easy-to-understand schematic that explained how to hook up the device to his laptop. In no time, Kyle had the cords attached and had inserted the DVD disc. He glanced back at the door one last time before beginning. Following the instructions, he depressed the on-off button. Kyle heard a soft humming sound. Then an image displayed through the laptop. Leaning toward the screen, Kyle studied the images. After adjusting his headphones, he listened to the narrative.

12

Director Valdez gestured toward the two chairs in front of her large oak desk. "James and Doug, please sit down. It's nice to see you both again," she said with a confident smile.

Doug couldn't help being both intimidated and impressed. Just getting through the security to her office spoke volumes about her power and importance to the Agency. The hallway approaching her office, had a slight downward slope and was constructed with thick, reinforced concrete steel. It didn't go unnoticed. No doubt the double doors were reinforced steel, capable of taking a direct hit from a mortar round. Moon Dog also noticed that the temperature in her office was cooler. Then it hit him. They were in an underground structure, probably the first level of a bunker complex.

Director Valdez studied the men. She had a longtime working relationship with X.O. Newland. In contrast, other than reading the information inside of Lt. Elliott's personnel shield, this was her first face-to-face meeting with the lieutenant.

"Did either of you need anything to drink?"

"I'm fine," replied X.O. Newland. Moon Dog just nodded his head in agreement. Folding her hands across her desk, she looked them both straight in the eye before speaking.

"Gentlemen, as you're aware, we're working on a highly sensitive Top Secret mission, code word *Hummingbird*. What makes this situation so sensitive is that we have been tasked with a preset of conditions that require a specific response. Since the time the DPRK was placed under an embargo and cataloged under the infamous "axis of evil label," the powers that be developed a detailed pre-determined response plan."

In an intense, unflinching cadence, Director Valdez continued to stare-down the men. Prior to this meeting, neither man had any reason to question her credentials or question her rise to this position. With each word that she spoke, with each gaze she flashed, the respect these men held for her increased.

"I know you're aware of the re-tasking of the satellite because you were both on duty when the new advanced programming detected the alleged tunnel-construction activities. I use the word "alleged" because this is the US of A. And as you're aware, we never rely on possibilities and suppositions. So, until we get direct, non-inferential data, eyeball-on-target specific confirmation, we must remember that our degree of certainty is limited. For now, we are relying on satellite surveillance feeds and suppositions. We just don't know one hundred percent. We're relying on our SAT birds as our only means of intelligence on the matter. However, this type of data is inadequate to make a formal recommendation.

"And yes, gentlemen, I said 'our' recommendations." With a slight grin forming in the corner of her mouth, she paused. These few moments of silence gave Lt. Elliott and X.O. Newland time for her words to soak in. Moon Dog and X.O. Newland exchanged quick sideways glances. They couldn't believe their ears. Was the Director issuing field promotions? They returned all their attention back to the Director, concentrating on her every word, ready to dissect every syllable.

She was enjoying the moment. She studied Lt. Elliott and X.O. Newland's faces. She couldn't help but derive a personal sense of satisfaction. This was her first one. She could only hope that there would be many more such opportunities. As in any important endeavor worth pursuing, she felt a sense of excitement as she handpicked her team. Unlike her current team, the Surveillance Unit consisted of a never-ending stream of bright intelligent people whom she inherited. They were transferred, selected by a computer algorithm that routed new assignments after people concluded their tour of duty. Careers in the military evolved over years, like a connected train of assignments destined for future assignments until, one day, a person reached the age when either the government or they elected retirement. From that moment, the train simply stopped.

Today, other than her personal security detail, her team was expanding. The first member she had selected was Carla Jo Hutchison, an independent contractor from San Diego. Carla Jo oversaw dispatching the surveillance evidence that would be used to justify the onset of the mission. The strict adherence to the chain-of-evidence protocol had been established to prevent the Agency's inability to address public concerns that arose. They had learned this lesson during the September 11th fiasco. The Agency's inability to present untainted evidence to the public sparked countless conspiracy theories where unscrupulous videos were shared over the internet, deepening the apparent cover-up. The Agency had evolved and understood that they needed to be in front of that curve. As such, the Agency had adopted a strict, verifiable chain of evidence to support all missions that had global significance.

With this understanding, the Director fully appreciated the possibility that, should the powers that be choose to alter the facts, well, that was their prerogative. It was her responsibility to answer to her immediate supervisors and follow the chain of command. It was not her place to question orders. The ultimate decision on how to proceed in such important decisions was well above her pay grade and beyond her control.

It was a requirement to be one hundred percent confident that the evidence acquired was not tainted, fabricated, or manipulated to achieve a goal or objective. To achieve this goal, they were forced to revert to old-school tactics. Everything would be exchanged face to face. Any evidence obtained would be processed and transported from one hand to another hand. There would be no break in the chain of custody of the evidence. Only trusted assets and personnel would be used. The reliability and loyalty of these select few must be considered unquestionable. This strict protocol was the reason the satellite had been untethered. This process was implemented to prevent the satellite image data from being transmitted to multiple sources on earth. Protocol dictated that under this situation, only her team could have access to the data.

"As we speak, the physical surveillance video is on its way to us. Until the closing of this file, the only other location with a copy of that tape is stored in a safe house that has twenty-four/seven/three-sixty-five immediate-tasked human-eye surveillance. My asset should be on the way to us as we speak."

"The other piece of the puzzle is our local asset. He has already contacted our in-house Agent operative, Kyle Benjamin. This poor bastard doesn't know it, for his first assignment, he has landed in a hornet's nest.

"Gentlemen, don't let the number of days he's booked for the Agency fool you. This guy is tough as nails. He had almost finished Naval Flight School in the F-18 until for some unknown reason, his body started having physical complications with G forces. It's very unusual. Not the first time it's happened, and probably won't be the last. It came out of nowhere. He had already passed Survival Training. I know you both can appreciate what that entails. Believe you me, not too many of your Surveillance Techs have ever been dropped off in the forest alone, in an undisclosed area, and told to hide from an enemy, with the understanding that, even if you were good enough to evade detection for forty-eight hours, you still had to turn yourself in to the enemy so you could be mistreated, interrogated, stripped, dumped in a hole, given no food, water boarded, and left to sleep in cold wet hole in the ground, and forced to use a plastic bucket to relieve yourself.

"I've been told that throughout the entire scenario, the enemy force speaks only a foreign language. The entire ordeal lasts seventy-two hours. It's designed to break the pilots. And it works. There is a percentage of pilots that, even after going through the strict competition to get jets, are broken at the realization that their job isn't some glorified movie depicted in *Top Gun*. Our guy, Lt. Kyle Benjamin, had avoided detection and was forced to turn himself in."

After a brief pause, the Director continued. "Benjamin was given many options. Everyone was shocked when he chose sharpshooting rather than take another pilot slot flying props. He ended up pulling a tour in Afghanistan and notched six confirmed kills all of the political persuasion. He's the real deal, boys."

"Now here's the next stage. We need real U.S. eyeballs down in that tunnel. Our buddy Benjamin doesn't know it yet, but we're going to have him literally take a walk on the wild side. He's been assigned to a solo walk detail along the DMZ. It's nothing unusual. We send our personnel on this duty every so often. But this is the first time it's an Agency guy from the Surveillance Unit. Also, no one from our team will be able to directly help him out. We will not have any face-to-face meetings until after he gets back. And that's only if the assignment goes as planned.

"I have other local assets on Benjamin, doing a little visual babysitting. Under no circumstances, and I mean none—zero, nada—are either of you allowed to approach him. Kyle's gonna get some tough love right now."

The Director paused and stared down both men. Nothing needed to be said. They both got it. Lt. Benjamin was disposable. If the shit hit the fan, they'd cut him loose and throw him to the wolves. Everyone knew that going across the DMZ border and entering the DPRK was an act of war. But in the Agency's eyes, when the DPRK began building another advancing tunnel that had only an offensive-first-strike implication, they started it. The DPRK was foolish to believe that the US wouldn't find out.

"Lt. Elliott."

"Yes, ma'am?"

"Congratulations on your promotion to Surveillance Analyst-5. You just jumped five pay grades from technician class to analyst class. But you need to be at level five to be able to participate in this type of stuff. It comes with retroactive pay to boot."

Moon Dog couldn't help but flash a huge ear-to-ear grin. His chest even puffed out slightly as adrenalin flushed through his body. He couldn't hide his excitement. His energy was contagious and seemed to infect the X.O. The Director flashed a matching wide smile.

"You will report directly to X.O. Newland. But through the duration of this *Hummingbird* assignment, you now have direct access to me as well."

The Director reached into her desk, produced a new security badge, and handed it to Moon Dog, shaking his hand. "Congratulations."

Lt. Elliott looked at the badge. He examined it closely. He couldn't detect any difference from the one he had. His facial expression gave away his confusion.

"Lieutenant, the badge looks the same. However, it is now magnetically coded and has an embedded GPS tracker. Until this assignment concludes, you are on a very short list of people who have access to the elevator outside that door." After a brief pause, she continued, "It will take you one thousand feet underground to a shelter complex."

Nodding his head, Lt. Elliott detached his old badge from his belt loop and switched out his badge. He then dropped the old one on the Director's desk.

"Lieutenant, your new assignment is an isolated surveillance room. You will now have two dedicated satellites at your disposal to do with as you please. As this assignment progresses, you will inevitably need assistance. At that time, approach the X.O. and inform him of your needs. Again, keep in mind you are not to divulge anything about this conversation with anyone else. Do not share your new security clearance, the badge, or the existence of the underground bunker. For now, it's just you, me, and the X.O. If you need to speak to me about something directly, you are hereby ordered to do so straightaway, without delay. There is no formality in terms of chain of command, as we currently have only three players.

"Lieutenant, for all intents and purposes, your control over the satellites represents the single most important protection Benjamin has at his disposal. You will be his eyes and ears while he is on the other side. You will be the ultimate authority in terms of relaying the data to any of our other assets on the ground."

The room fell silent. The Director nodded her head and explained, "I'm going to keep the X.O. here to go over some more details. Do you have any questions, Lieutenant?"

Moon Dog's mind was racing. He had tons of questions, but nothing that was pressing. He knew he could discuss the fine details with the X.O. later. With that, Moon Dog stood.

"No, Ma'am."

He was just about to exit the room when the Director added one more item.

"Oh, by the way, your room has been fitted with surveillance, visual and audio. I'd suggest refraining from any embarrassing activities that you don't want others to see on a big screen back in Washington."

"Yes, ma'am!" replied Lt. Elliott. As he exited the office, he saluted the Director and the X.O. When Moon Dog turned down the hallway, he heard a loud electronic beep as he passed under the main corridor archway. That hadn't happened on his way into her office. He also noticed the light indicators flash a steady green light. He hadn't noticed their presence before. He thought it was probably the GPS tracking and magnetic coding causing the response.

As he walked back toward the final corridor, he glanced down the opposite end. He could just make out the elevator. She wasn't kidding.

13

The supervisor had been making progress. The collapsed section of tunnel had been examined by one of the geological engineers. After much disappointment, they had all agreed that the natural lava tube wasn't going to help; it continued in the wrong direction. His manager had gone as far as to request portable, above-ground sonar imaging until they realized that they were well outside of the DPRK, making that examination impossible. Everyone had appreciated the advantages of utilizing the lava tube; it could have saved much time and resources. But It just wasn't going to work.

The supervisor had been adamant that no one was to enter the opening. All investigations and tests were to be performed from their side of the opening. There was no telling if anyone from the other side had been using that section. The last thing anyone wanted was for the DPRK workers to be discovered by the south or, worse yet, the Imperialist Americans. His biggest fear was for the lava tube to collapse.

They had not expected this section to have any lava formations. But then no one had any experience this far into the Republic of Korea. For the last year, they had been digging well past the DMZ boundary. Everyone involved understood they were deep inside the South Korean side of the border.

The supervisor had ordered his crew to reinforce the collapsed section. He alone would be responsible for going into the discovered cavern area to determine how best to conceal the opening. Throughout the previous twenty kilometers of construction, they had four similar situations, but those occasions had taken place on their side of the DMZ. This was different. They were over the border and no longer had the luxury of simply boarding it up and reinforcing the area. If this collapsed section was later discovered by the Republic of Korea, the tunnel crew wanted it to appear as if it had collapsed naturally.

They waited to disguise the surrounding area to prevent further investigations into the site. They were ordered to prevent, with absolute certainty, the discovery of the excavation tunnel. The supervisor understood that there was no way to prevent the discovery with one hundred percent certainty. But the meaning of the order, the intent, was understood. Failure in this regard came with severe penalties; penalties that would affect not just the workers but family members as well. Discovery by South Korea was not on option.

As the supervisor walked back toward the collapsed section, he was confident that no one in his crew had been on the other side. For weeks, he had questioned everyone on his crew, as well as other engineers sent in from the capital. He had been adamant about everyone staying on this side of the collapse. He required even the outside investigation team to sign a notice confirming their understanding of this requirement. He disliked the extra effort it required to secure the signatures and schedule individual, face-to-face interviews. However, he also knew that this extra layer of written evidence set the tone in terms of the seriousness of the situation. If things went wrong, this paper trail would be available to help point the blame.

This tunnel project was unlike the others. It was their most ambitious. The ultimate destination was not just inside of the Republic of Korea. The goal was for the tunnel to open just outside the capital, Seoul. This project was the first time that such a large tunnel had been excavated. Unlike prior attempts, this tunnel had the capacity for two-way traffic that stretched nearly one hundred kilometers (62 miles). In short, it was a game changer. There was no doubt in anyone's mind that if you were involved in something that jeopardized the project in any way, there were going to be serious consequences. The supervisor was confident that no one had disobeyed the order.

The tunnel had progressed several hundred meters beyond the collapsed area. The section had been temporarily isolated. A makeshift artificial landscape had been created around their side of the opening. Designed to look natural, it created a barrier that prevented anyone from the other side from either seeing anything man made or easily entering their excavated tunnel. Before the section was to be permanently sealed with concrete footings, the supervisor had to enter the opposite chamber area of the lava tube and determine the likelihood of discovery. It would be his call. It would be his decision whether to abandon this section. If it were abandoned, it would require that much of the freshly excavated area would have to be back filled. To do so would set the project back by a year or more.

The supervisor hoped to proceed without abandoning this section. He paused. At the opening, he listened for any internal noises. He heard nothing. It was silent.

He crouched down in a sitting position and peered over the top of the opening and waited ten minutes. There were no sounds. He turned on his flashlight, which ruined his night vision. He placed his hand over the flashlight. As the light rays penetrated through his skin, the color of his hand turned a bright pink. He kept the flashlight covered as he stretched his arms through the opening, directing the beam of light toward the ground on the other side of the opening. Again, he paused and listened. He was reluctant to uncover the flashlight. After a brief pause, he was certain that everything was quiet. Finally, he removed his hand and directed the beam of light into the other side.

The flashlight beam lit up the opposite wall. As his eyes adjusted, he directed the beam up and down the cavern. It was a massive cave. Several lava tubes seemed to converge from several directions. It almost looked like a switching yard in a subway station. Certain that no one was there, the supervisor stood up from his crouched position and directed the flashlight toward the ground. He was interested in what lay directly beneath the collapsed area. He didn't want to climb through the opening and fall through a sinkhole on the other side. Just as he was about to step through the opening, something caught his attention. Trying to stop his momentum, he almost fell through the collapsed section in the wall. Leaning forward, bending at the waist, he pointed the flashlight along the wall between the tunnel they had excavated and the natural lava tube. What he saw was unmistakable.

It looked like a trail, like a path walkway worn from constant use. it had overlapping impressions. He studied their shapes. They were long and oval with crisp edges. His mind searched for any other explanation. He could come up with no rational alternative; they were footprints.

The supervisor held his breath, shining the flashlight beam up and down in both directions. He saw no one. Quickly he backed away from the opening and ducked back through the collapsed hole. He had changed his mind; he would not be going inside now. He turned away from the opening and sat on the ground, leaning back against the wall and contemplating what to do. He turned off the flashlight and sat alone in the dark. Inside, this artificial camouflaged area created a hidden space so small that only one person could fit. He was hidden from view by either side. He remained seated, waiting for his eyes to readjust to the darkness. The isolation was a place for him to think. What would he do? Who would he tell? Lost in thought, the supervisor found the darkness and quietness relaxing and became mesmerized by his isolation.

Then he heard something. It was like small pebbles falling away, rolling off the cavity walls, tumbling downward and impacting the ground. His senses refocused all his concentration toward his hearing. What was that? His crew was on a break, huddled several thousand meters back down the tunnel. It couldn't be them.

Then he heard it again. This time, it was a little louder, like something impacting the ground, combined with crunching sounds as if something were compressing rocks. He concentrated harder. Closing his eyes, urging his ears to their maximum hearing capability. Willing them to pick up the faintest disturbance. He heard it again. This time, the sound was measurably louder. He was certain that the noise was coming from inside the lava tube section. The natural sound of the underground cavern seemed to amplify the sound, like a speaker. The supervisor closed his eyes, concentrating on the sound. He noticed that it was occurring in a consistent rhythm. There was no doubt in his mind. As each noise increased in volume, he recognized it. They were footsteps. With his back against the common wall, the supervisor rolled his eyes up in his head toward the direction of the noise. From the other side, someone was walking toward the opening. The supervisor sat frozen, listening to the steady footfalls getting louder and louder. Whoever it was, he was almost in front of the opening. Instinctively, the supervisor held his breath and waited. Without warning, he could see a beam of light shine through the opening. It lit up the wall just above the supervisor's head.

*   *   *   *   *

Tae was at the halfway point. He had walked through this section of tunnel for almost ten years, once a month, except during the extreme winter months. The flashlight was much brighter with the fresh new batteries. As he rounded the corner, he slowed his pace. On his earlier trip going to his brother's, he had almost been seen. He knew each corner and every formation. He'd been thinking about it since he started back north. What were his comrades up to? Digging another tunnel into the south was a dangerous game.

Tae could see the last turn before he arrived at a long straight path that ran next to the excavation tunnel. He was disappointed that the tunnel had caved in at that section. It was his favorite place. He thought of it as his own personal sanctuary. It was a section where several tunnels came together, forming an expansive cavern opening. It looked like a cathedral. At the upper section, there was a small underground spring that pooled before percolating through several large fissure cracks as it trickled somewhere deep underground. This was Tae's break area. He would stop, remove his shoes, soak his feet and get a bite to eat. Of course, he would smoke a cigarette.

These breaks seemed to be much more enjoyable on the return trips. He would be carrying a full backpack of provisions with fresh fanciful delights that his thoughtful brother had gathered to share with his family back home. Over the years, Tae's smoking habit had been one of the few luxuries, the only self-indulgent habit he allowed himself. He had rationalized that it was the little reward he granted himself. It was a more than a fair exchange, given the dangerous and physically demanding journey he risked traveling back and forth. As he reached the corner, he turned off his flashlight and waited. He let his eyes adjust to the darkness before he would look around the corner. Before he proceeded, he wanted to make sure that the tunnel diggers were nowhere near the collapsed section.

Tae crouched into a sitting position and waited. He had spent so many hours traveling through the underground dark environment that his eyes had adapted. The countless trips exposed him to hours upon hours of light deprivation. As a result, his eyes quickly adjusted to the darkness. He was capable of making out silhouettes where others saw nothing. This ability allowed him to walk in the darkness while maintaining his balance and keeping his sense of direction spatially oriented. This enhanced ability, combined with the internal road map image burned into his memory, helped Tae walk without the benefit of light.

After his eyes adjusted to the darkness, he stood and turned the corner. He held out his left arm. By touching the wall, it guided him. He had travelled this section of the tunnel so many times that he could literally have walked through it blindfolded. The path that ran against the wall was straight. He reached the location where the lava tubes joined together and opened into a large cavern. There was nothing but openness to his right. To his left was the common wall between the lava tube and the excavation tunnel. He could hear the trickling water and feel the cooler air cascade across his face.

With his eyes wide open and his left hand out, Tae proceeded along the pathway. The only sounds were the padding of his footsteps and the distinct trickling sound of the spring water ahead. He walked forward several more paces before stopping. He recalled that the collapsed section was in this general area. He paused. Freezing in an upright, rigid position, he waited motionless, listening. There were no sounds.

Tae leaned forward, peering into the darkness. He could just make out the opening in the wall and noticed that the opening had been closed from the other side. He took several steps forward. He could see that someone had backfilled the other side of the wall, in an attempt to disguise the opening. After a brief pause, he felt confident that the area was clear. He reached into his jacket and removed his flashlight. He turned it on and directed the light beam at the opening.

Tae leaned forward and studied the hole. It looked natural. If he hadn't passed through so many times and committed the trail to memory, he would never have noticed the difference. From a distance, Tae examined the opening before proceeding. As he walked in front of the hole, human curiosity got the best of him. He was like a commuter stuck in rush-hour traffic, with his attention drawn to the scene of an accident. As he paused in front of the hole, he leaned forward, sticking his head through the opening. He could see into the other side.

The excavation tunnel was much larger than he expected. He tilted his head forward just enough to see further down the tunnel. There were two sets of small railroad tracks. They appeared much narrower than those he saw leading into the capital. There were no lights coming from the other side. After a brief curious inspection, Tae turned away from the opening. Directing his flashlight back onto the path, he started walking to the opposite side, toward the pool of water near the underground spring. He turned left up one of the lava tubes and sat down. He pulled off the backpack straps and set the pack onto the ground. He glanced back toward the opening in the wall, confident that he was not in a direct line of sight. Thus assuming he was hidden from watchful eyes, Tae leaned back against the wall and slipped off his shoes. He eased his feet into the water and exhaled a sigh of relief. He was almost home.

*   *   *   *   *

When the man had peered through the opening, the supervisor looked up at his face. The man stared forward. The supervisor remained motionless, hidden below the opening. Had the man glanced down, he would have been surprised to see a face that stared back with eyes opened wide from shock and fear. To the supervisor's relief, the unknown man must have quenched his curiosity, for he then walked back toward the north along the pathway. The supervisor could hear footsteps as the man made his way into one of the lava tubes.

The supervisor assumed that the man had continued walking down the tunnel. Before standing, he waited until he couldn't hear any more noises. As he struggled up from his sitting position, his eyes peeked over the crest of the opening. He saw a light beam reflecting against the walls from inside the mouth of one of the lava tube openings. Mesmerized, he leaned forward through the opening. He watched the shadows dancing on the side of the lava tunnel wall. As his eyes adjusted to the darkness, he began to see things more clearly.

He could just make out a pool of water. There were distinct sounds of trickling water. He hadn't noticed that sound before. From his point of view, the supervisor could just see the man's feet above his ankle. They were submerged in the water. He hoped to get a good view of the man's face. Just as the unknown man leaned forward, the light from the flashlight turned off. The timing couldn't have been worse.

Disappointed, the supervisor pursed his lips. He continued waiting, afraid to move a muscle. As time passed, he was resolved to wait. He didn't want the unknown man to hear his footsteps. Until then, he hadn't appreciated how noise traveled in this underground environment. Sounds were amplified. He didn't want to spook the man. He wanted the man to think that his use of the tunnel was still a secret. The supervisor continued staring out into the darkness, waiting for something, anything. Then, it happened.

The man depressed a butane cigarette lighter. The supervisor could hear a distinct "chook" sound as the man thumbed the striker. As the flame caught, the supervisor saw the man's face. The bright flame was a double-edged sword. It increased his visibility, but also distorted his clear view. The lighter's flame stood dead center in the man's face. As he inhaled, the man wrinkled his nose and scrunched his mouth, which further exacerbated his appearance.

Once the cigarette was lit, the man released the toggle and the flame extinguished. The supervisor tried to recreate a clear full-facial memory. Unfortunately, the distorted images, the flame, and his facial contortions prevented him from reconstructing a clear image. He knew that he would be unable to make an accurate identification of the man.

Diligent, the supervisor hoped for another chance. After several minutes, he heard splashing of water as the man stepped out of the shallow pool. He could hear wrestling sounds as the man reached into his backpack to retrieve something. The supervisor's persistence paid off; the man turned on the flashlight again. Although the man's face never came into direct view, the light was directed at an unusual brown tote-style purse. It looked like a woman's leather shoulder strap purse, and it had strange exterior lettering. As the supervisor stared closer, he saw markings, like foreign letters. Not Korean Hangul script. He studied the letters, the color, and its shape. Because of his clear line of sight, he was certain he could identify the bag again. He guessed that this type of item was unique in the DPRK.

After the man adjusted the items in the backpack, he dried his feet. He put his tattered socks and shoes back on. Then he stood, adjusted the backpack straps, and began walking deeper into the lava tube. The supervisor saw a dim light appear from inside the lava tube tunnel and watched the shadows dance off the wall. He could hear the soft footfalls diminish as the man walked farther and farther into the tunnel. The supervisor remained standing motionless until the sounds and flickering dim light disappeared.

Reluctant to move, the supervisor waited several more moments. He wanted to make certain that the man had no intention of returning. Certain he was alone, the supervisor maneuvered through the makeshift covering. His mind wandered back to that unique purse with the foreign markings. He was certain that if he ever saw a similar purse, he would remember it.

Yes, he would remember it. Had he had access to the internet, he could have keyed up the search term "women's purse images." That term would have resulted in countless hits. He could scroll through hundreds of photos with detailed information about each one. He could have determined its name brand, model and price. He would learn that it was a woman's Louis Vuitton Neverfull tote copy. He would have been shocked that an authentic one sells for $1,260 US. But in the DPRK, there was no such thing as public internet access. None of that mattered. It was always the little details that made the difference.

14

For months, Kyle had been working in the DMZ. He hadn't received any additional instructions. The only advice Gibby gave was to "take it slow." He was still getting accustomed to his nighttime solo patrols. He was the new guy. They waited for human nature to takes its course. Soon, the others would become familiar with "the new guy." After they became accustomed to seeing him in the mess hall, walking in and out of the access barriers, and recognizing him based only on the way he walked, it would just happen. It was the human condition, magnified in the DMZ.

Many times, peoples' perceptions were influenced by the media. Unlike civilians, these soldiers patrolling the DMZ, aside from a few rare occasions, had predictable and mundane duties. So much so, that people inevitably became complacent.

On those rare occasions, when one sidestepped into the buffer area, doing something unusual or unexpected was when something dangerous happened. The time the South Koreans unexpectedly began cutting down cherry trees growing in the common DMZ area, for example. The DPRK soldiers had interpreted this as an act of aggression, a sign of disrespect. There had been no advance notice given. The DPRK guards watched in horror as the south began chopping them down with axes. The DPRK took this unexplained and unexpected destruction of the trees as an expression of dominance over the DMZ. In a kneejerk reaction, the DPRK soldiers present that day decided to enter the buffer area. Forcefully, they took away the axes and stopped the unnecessary destruction of the trees. The DPRK solders outnumbered the south. Things escalated. Two American soldiers were killed by an ax that was used to take down the trees. That very ax was still on display in a DPRK military museum, along with a description of the entire sordid event.

But those types of skirmishes were rare. On most days, it was nerve-wracking, face-to-face standoff. A nonstop game of flinch, each side waiting for the other side to blink. For decades, both sides had remained in a constant state of alert. Each side prepared to take it to the next level, should it come to that. The consequences of this never-ending state of emergency had a dulling affect. Like the movie *Groundhog Day*, the scene along the DMZ rarely changed. Its monotony was unavoidable.

Kyle was doing his best to blend in. He was ordered to avoid everyone. The troops assigned to patrol the DMZ had a feeling that he was up to something. The more senior guys commented on his unusual assignment. Solo night patrols were unheard of. The notoriety dwindled. From day to day and night to night, the same old routine at the DMZ took its toll. It had once been something that qualified as gossip of the day, providing others with a mental distraction. The newness of the situation resulted in constant over-analysis, idle gossip, and widespread speculation. But like everything over time, people's interest diminished to nothing. Been there, done that. Next.

Gibby watched the drama from a far. He had been using one of his available satellites. Over the years, he'd seen it time and time again. It was like clockwork. He had monitored Kyle's co-combatant patrol patterns through thermal imaging. Like circular dots on a game board, Gibby watched the other marines. Initially, he saw gossip-pods gather before and after his patrol. He could make out Kyle's solo heat signature dot walk by the other dots bundled together in close proximity to one another. As expected, Gibby watched the other group of dots reposition as Kyle's solo heat signature dot walked into the dark unknown. He could image their conversations. "Who is that guy?" "Is he crazy or what?"

As expected, as the nights marched on, this same group of men became less and less interested in the activities of Lt. Kyle Benjamin. The heat signature dots no longer grouped together watching him walk out on his solo patrols. As the weeks passed, the heat signature dots lost interest altogether. Just as Gibby knew would happen, by the thirtieth day, the infrared thermal imaging satellite showed only one heat signature dot coming into view. Kyle's presence in the DMZ had finally normalized. His presence was no longer a point of interest. It was old news.

Kyle had followed Gibby's instructions. He'd avoided the other guys, isolating himself by staying locked up in his room except when on patrols. The isolation gave him time to practice flying the metallic miniature drone inside of his room. He had been putting in between four and five hours of practice a day. He was more than proficient; he'd mastered it.

He could land it on the television, fly it into the closet or around the bathroom, and even have it land on the toilet lid. He could dive bomb and perform an abrupt landing on the bed or the couch. He could fly it under the coffee table, hover it in front of the door, and even steady it enough so that he could aim the drone's camera through the door's small peephole. He could run circles around the sink area and do stop-and-go landings and takeoffs from every chair in his room. He had perfected the ability to fly it inches off the ground and then inches from the ceiling. He had practiced so much that the plastic controller started to lose its new shine as the surface began to show wear and tear from his constant handling.

Out of boredom and to increase his efficiency and skill level, he created five different flight plans with different routes and landing spots. He had started timing each route with the goal of constant improvement each day. It was amazing how much he had improved over the last thirty days. Flying the drone had become an extension of himself. He had even started having dreams as if he were flying inside the mini drone. He felt like a fly in his dream, maneuvering around his room, practicing the routes over and over again.

As he concluded another practice route in the mini-drone, Kyle discovered a note that had been slipped under his door. He opened the plain unsealed white envelope and found a handwritten note. "Meet you at the BBQ shack at 3:00 p.m. today. What happened to the Scooby boxers?"

Kyle turned toward his bathroom and tore the note into pieces, flushing them down the toilet. As he locked his door and then made his way to catch a cab, he couldn't help but wonder how Gibby knew about the boxers. Then it finally hit him. He must be watching him flying the drone. The first time Kyle had used the mini drone, he had been sitting in those boxer shorts. After that day, out of embarrassment, he had tossed them in the trash.

After hailing the cab, he sat in the back seat. He began wondering what else they had seen him doing over the last thirty days. Suddenly embarrassed, Kyle broke the silence in the cab. "Shit!"

"Excuse me, sir?" asked the cab driver.

"Oh, nothing." Kyle replied. "To the Barbecue Shack, please." Mentally, he reminded himself to move those other personal activities into the shower, out of the view of wandering eyes.

*   *   *   *   *

Angelie sat comfortably in her airline seat. To pass time, she leafed through her carry-on bag and read her itinerary. It was a sixteen-hour, nonstop flight from LAX to Incheon International Airport in Seoul, South Korea. She closed her itinerary and opened her crisp new blue United States of America Passport. It was still empty; no stamps, at least until she got through customs in Seoul. For weeks, she had worried about reapplying for her passport. She had been required to secure one during her adoption and was too young to have any memory of the process back then. Her passport had never been used or renewed. It looked like it had never been opened, and it still had her baby picture inside. But this time was different. On the advice of her parents, she had waited forty-five days before submitting her application to the International English Teachers School. She agreed with her parents' reasoning, that avoiding scrutiny by the US government was a good idea. Their fears were unfounded. Even if a full-blown background check were performed, nothing would be revealed.

The only oddity that had taken place would never be discovered; it involved her parents' "jumping" over from China through Canada with officially forged documents. The DPRK had someone working on the inside of the Republic of Korea's immigration department who was able to legally conjure up identities for them that would stand up to any scrutiny. For all legal intents and purposes, they were citizens of the Republic of Korea, not the DPRK.

Since their arrival to the US, other than that single event, they had done everything legally. They had received green cards, gone through the citizenship process, and become full-fledged US citizens. In terms of Angelie, her adoption had been completely legal. The family paid its taxes and never had a single legal issue whatsoever. They were, from the government's and society's point of view, perfect citizens. However, their loyalties lay elsewhere.

They had never bought into the concept of the American culture. They hadn't adopted the lifestyle. They held no desire to chase the American dream. In a twist of fate, although they were free to choose their own path, they were psychologically trapped. It was as if they had been sentenced to a lifetime isolated from their homeland. There had been only one brief momentary lapse. It had taken place early, when their small business showed signs of growth. Angelie's parents were approached by a Korean immigrant.

He showed an interest in partnering with them to help each of them expand their businesses. He shared his vision and confirmed that he had access to enough money to make it happen. For a split second, Angelie's parents had forgotten why they were here; why they had been allowed to adopt a baby girl.

They had agreed to meet their newest and only real friend that evening. They had set their table and prepared an array of authentic Korean dishes. Their new friend explained he would bring his older brother along. His brother's money would be used to finance their partnership and expansion, and everything would be evenly divided. They would pay the money back through their profits. But from day one, all profits would be divided 50/50.

They looked forward to the meeting. Their excitement grew. They felt optimistic. They thought about making a good living and buying nice things. As they welcomed their new friend and his brother into their modest apartment, they were hopeful, flashing elated smiles. They bent forward from their waists at ninety-degree angles—their most honorific bow to express their sincere appreciation. It came as no surprise when the brother returned their bows with only a slight bend at the waist and dipping of his head. After all, he was the man contemplating the investment in this venture. He was the one who was in the position of financial power. As soon as he began to speak, everything changed.

His words were nonthreatening, outlining what his alleged brother had explained prior. But his accent was all they heard. The words no longer were important. They knew right away their mistake. Similar to the different regions in the United States, like the southern drawl of Texas and the other southern states; or the distinct pronunciation unique to the New England region where they dropped their r's as in "park your car in Harvard yard." This unique accent style was also present in Korea as a higher nasal tone with sharp vowel pitch phrasing. This distinction was obvious to people who lived in Korea. The accent would be detected immediately. The brother spoke with the unmistaken accent of a person from the north.

As the brother spoke about his time in the US, he seemed to overemphasize his accent. He made a conscious effort to accentuate rather than hide his northern accent. It was obvious that he wanted them to understand. He wanted them to ascertain their situation without his having to breathe a word of what was happening.

As he finished speaking, the table fell quiet. Angelie's parents' heads had been dropping. Their chins were now tucked down to the point of almost touching their chests. The mood had transformed from a happy, excited occasion to one dominated by fear and despair. They knew that there would be no investing, no expansion of their small family-owned business. With bowed heads, avoiding eye contact with the brother, they waited for him to speak directly, to discuss the real reason he was there.

"Comrades, I think you understand I'm not here to discuss any investments." He looked across the table and watched as they both nodded their heads acknowledging their understanding of the situation. Both parents remained still, avoiding eye contact.

"You must never forget why you are here. You must never think that we aren't watching your every move. You both have been loyal citizens of the Democratic People's Republic of Korea. You have sacrificed much to be here, separated from your families." He paused as he let the mentioning of their families sink in. The couple exchanged a brief sideways glance before returning to their downcast positions. The brother reached into the inside breast pocket of his wool jacket and extracted a thin envelope. He waved it in front of their faces before dropping it onto the center of their worn wooden table. Neither took their eyes off the sealed envelope.

"Inside you'll find recent photos and letter from your families. I know that it's been a long time, ten years since you heard from them."

The brother had no intention of staying any longer. Nor was he planning to eat the food. He stood, turned, and began walking out. Before he reached the front door, he stopped and glanced back to the other section of their apartment. He correctly guessed that their daughter was in that room, playing out of sight so the adults could "talk business." He waited for the couple to look up at him before he spoke.

"We understand that your sacrifice to be here takes its toll on your minds. For this reason, and only this one time will I overlook this digression. Keep in mind," He paused, waiting for their eyes to re-engage contact with his before continuing "having a child is a luxury. I would hate to have to remove her and send you both back."

He recognized the fear behind their blank emotionless expressions. He knew that they each had been surgically sterilized before coming to America. They were incapable of conceiving a child on their own. Although they had been granted the honor of raising a child, that child had a preordained future. If they remained faithful and devoted comrades, this honor remained theirs to achieve. This man was not their newest friend's brother. He was one of many DPRK monitors. He had read their files. This type of meeting was his job, his duty to the cause. He was very experienced and felt confident that these two would not cause him any problem. It was inevitable that sometime during an assignment, every agent was tempted. Only on rare occasions had anyone walked away; too many people back home depended upon their success and cooperation.

One common character flaw that Koreans seemed to possess was the habit of gambling. It had become a result of their isolation away from their homeland, and their fear of becoming culturally influenced by living in the west. As long as the gambling didn't attract unwanted attention, it was tolerated.

Angelie had no knowledge of that meeting so many years ago. Most issues that her parents faced were not discussed with her. Those obstacles had no bearing on Angelie's training. That knowledge could distract her from her objectives. As Angelie's handlers, her parents understood that their principal goal was beyond raising her to adulthood. Nonetheless, they were still human. They had watched over her, raised her, and celebrated her birthdays. Their attachment to her was much more than a decision to support the government and obey orders. They loved her in their own way, although the unique circumstance may have affected their ability to show emotions.

At an early age, her parents had been identified as strong candidates, and the DPRK had watched them each advance in their education. Unknown to them, each advancement in their educational progress had been orchestrated and supported by their government's Intelligence Department, where only the brightest of the bright were picked out of the public sector, while those less fortunate were abandoned, forced to fend for themselves, no longer receiving special governmental support. Most of these candidates found that prior deferrals from the mandatory ten-year military conscription requirements were no longer forthcoming, so that they were also subject to this military commitment.

Angelie stared out the of the porthole window of the wide body Boeing 747 Korean Airlines passenger jetliner, straining to see the large island of Hawaii that the pilot was describing over the loud speaker. She had already made her first connection from St. Louis to LAX, followed by a three-hour layover before boarding this flight. She had been reading one of the magazines that was stuffed inside the back seat pocket in front of her. An article detailed the prestigious awards that South Korea held, the first being that Incheon International Airport had been "Rated the World's Best Airport nine years running!"

As Angelie read the magazine, it seemed to suggest that South Korea in general was preoccupied with tallying up as many international honors as possible. She learned that South Korea possessed the tallest art gallery in the world; its Lott Cinema boasted the rights to the world's largest cinema screen; its COEX mall was the world's largest underground mall. As she continued reading, she couldn't help but smile as yet another article touted Seoul to be the world's most wired city, ranking it number one in technological readiness with vast interconnected wi-fi systems available throughout its entire railway and bus systems.

She closed the magazine. Reaching into the overhead compartment, she opened the folder detailing her new job. She had been accepted into the International English Teachers program. On her application, she'd explained she only understood limited Korean Hangul. Her proficient foreign languages were listed as French and German. This inability to speak Korean Hangul was a lie. Many countries wanted their children to be taught American English from an American-born-and-raised teacher; a person who was fluent in America's language and culture. These countries believe that having access to this type of education better prepared their children. Learning

English, with all of its unique slang, gave them an advantage. Being fluent in Korean Hangul was unimportant. Only Angelie's handlers, her legal adoptive parents, knew the truth. Angelie could read, write, and speak perfect Hangul. She also had been taught advanced Russian and Chinese Mandarin. At a very early age, it was decided that her skill set would be constructed so she could be assigned in many different regions around the globe.

The Korean organization she worked for arranged the flight and secured a one-year work permit. She had even received an extra bonus for accepting an assignment outside of the preferred metropolitan areas of Seoul, Busan, Incheon, and Daegu. Her assignment was to Daeseong-Dong, also called Tae Sung Dong, a small town that lay within the southern half of the DMZ, only 1.6 kilometers (1 mile) south of the bridge of no return. It sat less than one mile from the North Korean village Kijong-Dong. It was the only civilian population within the southern section of the DMZ.

The town's inhabitants had been assigned large plots of land. Their farming activities resulted in some of the best yields in the country. However, the proximity to the northern border with the DPRK made safety a big concern. There was an 11:00 p.m. curfew and a daily head count. The DPRK sometimes invaded the village, although these occurrences were rare. Everything about the assignment would be considered unattractive to most international teachers, but not to Angelie. She considered them a plus. She had actually fantasized what it would be like to cross over into the north. She yearned to meet her countrymen; to witness, firsthand, what it would be like to live there, to be with her people.

For the next year, Angelie would teach kindergarten through the sixth grade. The number of students varied from year to year. The total enrollment was around fifty students. The International Teachers School always assigned an interpreter and class assistant who lived in the community. The closest city was Paju, with a relatively large population of 400,000. However, the population was disproportionately military personnel occupying the area to defend the capital, Seoul. Paju housed numerous military bases and stood in great contrast to Daeseong-Dong village, which was home to some 225 people.

Angelie closed the folder, returning it to her carry-on bag stowed in the overhead compartment. She had just eaten and was feeling tired. Before she closed the compartment door, she grabbed a light acrylic blanket from within. The excitement of the trip, being on her first airplane ride, and now leaving the country by herself started to take its toll. As she contemplated what lay in store for her, she found herself exhausted. She curled up and reclined the seat to its full extension. For a brief moment, her thoughts returned to her parents. At that moment, she felt alone. Angelie pulled the soft thin blanket up to her chin. As she closed her eyes, a slight smile appeared across her face. She could over hear the flight attendants chatting in the back. They were speaking Korean Hangul, complaining about the obnoxious Americans on board. They had no idea she could understand their conversation. It was her best-kept secret, one that would save her life. She just didn't know it yet.

15

Carla sat on the plush armchair in the Incheon Airport terminal in Seoul. She was waiting for her ride. She stared at a large flat screen television mounted just inside the plate glass window. The airport was beautiful. The floor was marble, shined to an immaculate finish. Countless attendants scurried throughout the terminal with brooms and handled waste pans, retrieving every morsel of debris that fell to the floor. Large murals hung on the walls, and modern art was suspended from the tall, three-story ceilings. Carla Jo had travelled through Korea on one prior occasion. As before, she was reminded how different this airport looked compared to any she had flown through in the States.

A clear male voice boomed from the loud speakers, first in Korean Hangul and then in English. The voice reminded her of the Surveillance Tech's voice. She recalled being sure she would never see another day. As she mindlessly tapped her fingers against the armrest waiting for her ride, she relived that unforgettable day back at the Salton Sea safe house.

She was surprised to see the garage door open. As the door rattled upward, sliding along the automatic garage door tracking, Carla Jo placed her SUV into drive and pulled forward. She waited for the garage door to close before opening her car door. She was still in shock. She reached across to the passenger seat and grabbed the package before closing the car door. She then walked through the kitchen toward the living room area. A loud ringing telephone broke the silence. She'd been here several times before but had never considered that the safe house would have a telephone. She set the package on the countertop and answered the wall phone. Not knowing the protocol, she answered the phone using her code name.

"This is Spartan."

"I bet you're one happy lady right about now," said an authoritative male voice.

"You can say that again. What happened?"

"We had you on two cameras. Standard operating procedures. The above satellite image is always set on a large view just in case something like this happens. We saw the neighbor pushing the garbage can. We anticipated the possibility that his presence could distract you. Don't believe the rumors. The destruction sequence isn't automated. Too many unknown possibilities for that."

With a slight chuckle, Carla Jo replied, "Like some dumbass pushing a garbage can."

"Something like that."

"I owe you one."

"Just doin' my job. Out."

"Copy," replied Carla Jo before returning the telephone back to the wall receptacle.

Carla Jo glanced down at her briefcase. She had the memory stick formatted with Agency-encrypted software. All surveillance data had been transferred and date stamped, and it was ready for hand delivery. It was the only copy. The original was safely stored back in the

Salton Sea safe house. She knew that once the *Hummingbird* mission closed, a technological extraction team would be sent to clean the house. Those teams specialized in data storage and destruction.

She was wearing a wool business suit with a skirt cut just below the knee. Her hair was pulled back in a bun. She wore gold-rimmed glasses and looked nothing like she had while rowing out into the Oceanside Bay. GPS tracking devices were hidden in the heels of each of her shoes, inside her cell phone, and inside a small coated capsule that she had swallowed with an ice-cold Ginger Ale on the airplane just before landing. Covert Operations always flew commercial; traveling in a military plane was a dead giveaway. The odds of her being trailed were infinitesimal, but the Agency never took chances—especially when it came to these types of missions.

Carla Jo continued waiting. Under no circumstance was she to take an airport cab. She would receive a text message detailing what to look for. She knew that her ultimate destination was the Park Hyatt in downtown Seoul. It was centrally located inside the financial district and housed ten available rooms that the Agency had on constant reservation. These rooms were serviced by a specific set of housekeepers who were actually Agent operatives who specialized in video and audio surveillance. Not even their counterparts inside the Republic of Korea's NIS (National Intelligence Service) knew of this standing protocol. This was one of those occasions where a mission such as *Hummingbird* was beyond their purview.

The Agency had thought long and hard on how to handle this particular situation. To involve Korea's NIS would require its direct involvement, to include input in terms of the how to resolve the situation. The powers that be had already played out all of the scenarios and needed no additional input to make that decision. The Agency would proceed toward the destruction of the tunnel, period; end of story. The first step in the plan was to get Agency eyeballs down inside the tunnel. But before that could happen, the Agency required irrefutable evidence, and that physical evidence needed to be inside the Director's folder. The last thing anybody wanted was for some unforeseen event to hit the fan during the initial phase of the mission. The Agency appreciated the possibility that its actions could bring immediate attention to the situation, requiring the US to justify its actions to the world. If the situation required full disclosure of facts or some semblance of the truth, and if advanced intelligence data was not properly cataloged to justify the action taken, then, heads could literally roll.

It was part CYA (cover your ass) mindset, as well as mission protocol. Other than a snap decision that fell within the purview of the mission, everyone seemed to understand the bureaucratic likelihood that Monday-morning armchair quarterbacks would pile on the criticism. Careers were at stake. Lives could be ruined. There was little room for error.

Direct Valdez held the order to send in Lt. Benjamin. She waited for the proof that Carla Jo had in her possession. The proof had to be delivered and properly filed. Everything was almost ready. The pieces were falling into place.

Carla Jo scanned the airport terminal, studying everyone standing around. Most were Korean nationals, frantically searching their pockets for a cigarette before boarding their flights. Everyone else was shuffling along at a quick pace, en route to a connecting flight or rushing to claim checked baggage. Carl Jo was the only

Caucasian present. Her facial features, hair color, and height made her stand out.

Her cell phone began vibrating. She read the text message. Her ride was delayed and would be curbside in less than fifteen minutes. She was instructed to look for a white KIA 9000, plates ending in 1600. She couldn't help but smile. At the Agency, it was an inside joke. These numbers represented the street address for the White House on Pennsylvania Avenue. The driver would be wearing a Chicago Cubs baseball cap and chewing a big wad of bubble gum. He would wait curbside for no more than two minutes before taking one hot lap around the airport boulevard. If she missed her ride, there would be hell to pay, and she knew it.

Carla Jo replied to the text. "I'm just inside the curbside door waiting. Good to go." As she placed her cell phone back into her purse, she noticed a young Korean woman standing outside of the baggage claim area. For some reason, Carla Jo's prior military and Agency training tugged at her mind. Her inner senses recognized something was not right. There was something about the young lady that didn't add up. Without thinking, Carla Jo began analyzing the situation, reverting to her training in gathering data. She made a mental note that the young lady had a birth-marked hand. The LAX and STL stickers on her luggage confirmed that she had flown in from St. Louis Missouri. Attached to the handle of an oversized luggage was a red tag with the word HEAVY in all capital letters. Carla Jo began piecing together the information. She now knew that this person was coming in from the US and planned to stay awhile.

Carla Jo continued to watch the young woman with heightened interest. Tilting her head, she watched her open her passport to insert her boarding pass inside. As the passport was opened, Carla Jo could just make out a single stamped entry. As she closed the passport, Carla Jo could see the deep navy blue outside cover. In that brief moment, Carla Jo now knew that the woman was carrying an American passport. She was either an American or posing as an American. By the fact that there was only one stamp entry, this was most likely her first international trip. Although there was a chance that a trip could have been taken where the customs official had not entered a stamp, since 911 that was unlikely.

Carla Jo couldn't help herself. The years of training were something agents couldn't turn on or off. Their senses were always on high alert, their minds focused on everything, trying to glean as much as they could. There was a constant need to understand all players and potential players on the espionage chessboard. Most of the time, an agent's laser-focused analysis of a particular surrounding did not result in anything worthwhile. But when on the job, it was essential to constantly scan your surroundings and be obsessively critical about your environment. Analyzing a situation always paid off. And this was one of those random times. Carla Jo was picking up on something that investigators and intelligence agents the world over understood.

Like an unexplained déjà vu experience, investigative agents gradually developed the ability to be somewhat clairvoyant. When asked why or how a particular person had come under suspicion, most investigators stated that there was just something about the person that didn't fit. The investigative trained eye would catch some expression, some behavior, some peculiarity that just didn't match the situation.

As Carla Jo continued to study the young woman's behavior, something else stood out. With piqued curiosity, she watched the young lady make her way toward a small concession booth. While waiting in line, Carla Jo heard her speak. In perfect English, absent any hint at a foreign accent, she told the cashier that she spoke only basic Korean. She resorted to pointing at the menu pictures. However, while she stood waiting for her food, Carla Jo watched as the young lady glanced around the filled room. She looked to be enjoying the hustle and bustle of the other Koreans and their conversations. For some reason, Carla Jo could tell something was amiss. It was the young lady's facial expressions. Surrounded by strangers speaking a different language, why didn't she appear frustrated? It was a natural human tendency. This young lady's expressions didn't suggest that emotion at all. On the contrary, Carla Jo detected glee and enjoyment in the young woman's eyes.

Carla Jo noticed something else. The young woman was staring at two young children who were arguing. It was a verbal exchange with no physical movements or hand motions. So why was the young woman laughing? She appeared to understand what they were talking about. How was that possible? Why had she told the cashier that she didn't understood Korean, yet she was capable of listening to the children's conversation and finding it humorous? Carla Jo studied the other people gathered near the young woman. No one noticed. Everyone else was too busy with their own affairs.

All this got Carla Jo's attention. She couldn't help herself; her training always got the best of her. Although she had no concrete evidence, she trusted her intuition and was certain that the young woman had lied.

Without thinking, Carla Jo grabbed her cell phone from her purse. Pretending to check her email, she aimed the camera across the room. To magnify the view and get a closer shot, she pressed her thumb and index finger against the glass screen and pushed her fingers away from each other in quick successive motions. Based on a gut feeling, Carla Jo began taking multiple photos, followed by a brief video clip of this young woman. As the young woman gathered her food, Carla Jo's cell phone began vibrating. She pulled the cell phone closer and tapped the screen to retrieve the text message. It read, "Two minutes out." She typed her reply, "On my way to the curb now." She stood, gathered her things, and began walking to the automatic glass doors exiting the terminal.

Only moments before, she'd been surveying a young lady. Now, seconds later, she had already forgotten everything about her. It had been a brief moment. She detected an intellectual inconsistency. Spying on the young lady had only been a mental distraction. As she waited for her ride to arrive, it had occupied her time. Carla Jo had no reason to take the issue any further.

But for the young lady, it was different. She had literally just arrived. This was her first assignment. She hadn't even left the airport terminal. In that brief amount of time, she made her first mistake, a big one and one Angelie didn't even realize she'd made. She had attracted unwanted attention. This was no practice run. She was playing with grownups now, and there could be brutal consequences. The participants played for keeps. Things were different now. It happened because of a gut reaction. Carla Jo had acted upon intuition, as a result of years of experience. She recognized something "off," something "fishy." Angelie, on the other hand, had no experiences to build upon or tap into. She had a lot to learn.

Today was the beginning of her formal education. Unfortunately for Angelie, the school bell had already rung. As a covert operative, giving the other side information was a great sin. The information she had provided could lead her enemies back to her parents, her handlers, and their operation. The most devastating break had been the photographs and video clip. Now the Agency had her picture but didn't know it.

16

Director Valdez stared at the wall in her office. She had been checking in with the key handlers of the most important operation of her career, *Hummingbird*. The local asset, Gibby, confirmed that everything was on schedule. The newbie greenhorn, Lt. Kyle Benjamin, had settled into his evening solo patrol along the DMZ. He'd been accepted by the senior platoon jarheads, and they'd already forgotten about him.

These men weren't stupid. They knew something was up. No one, especially a new greenhorn, is assigned from the get-go to perform solo night patrols in the DMZ. They knew the drill: Don't ask, don't tell. That saying didn't apply just to a person's sexual orientation. Everyone recognized the signs. It had to be a clandestine black operation. It hadn't gone unnoticed that the fatigues he wore had no rank or name insignias. Some of the guys had even commented on the unusual impressions that the greenhorn's boots made in the dirt. In private whispers, many of the guys wondered if the newbie understood the significance. Probably not. It was better that way. When you're doing some crazy shit, sometimes too much information acted as a distraction. For those select few, the mission was simple. Stay focused, stay on task, do your job, and stay alive. If everyone did their job, the mission would succeed.

Director Valdez checked her wristwatch. It was time. The asset bringing in the satellite proof was en route to the Park Hyatt Hotel in downtown Seoul. They'd isolate her for thirty minutes to make sure everything checked out before she would meet Gibby and the Director. She had instructed Gibby to accompany her in the Agency bird. They would fly over together. She wanted to hear what he thought about their newest and most expendable newbie, Lt. Benjamin, and she wanted it straight from the source. She believed that more meaningful intel was gained by looking into a person's face. She could analyze their reactions firsthand. Those little indicators weren't available in a memo.

Director Valdez punched the intercom and spoke to her team. It was time. As she exited her office, she looked like a rock star surrounded by her entourage of bodyguards. The meet was set up in downtown Seoul's prestigious Park Hyatt Hotel. Her security detail were dressed in dark navy blue two-piece wool suits. They moved as a pack, two agents in front and two agents in back, each one protected with Kevlar body armor, flesh-tone earpieces, and patch-adhesive microphones stuck on their necks below the collar, hidden from view. As they stepped into the side bunker elevator, the highest-ranking member of the detail punched the elevator button up to the helicopter pad. Down would take them to the VIP bunker two hundred feet underground. As the doors slid closed, the Director couldn't help commenting on her detail's dress.

"Looking very GQ this evening, gentlemen."

The men smiled. They exchanged looks inside the rising elevator. "We try our best, ma'am," replied the most senior member.

*   *   *   *   *

Gibby sat in the Airwolf Bell 222 "Role Disguised" helicopter. The concept was that the helicopter could blend in, like a "wolf in sheep's clothing." The Airwolf was stealthy. It could travel at the speed of sound, fly upside down, and even into the stratosphere if needed. It possessed the most state-of-the-art weaponry to repel tanks and Triple-A fire. Its arsenal was capable of including Maverick, Hellfire, and Sidewinder missiles, all used with the Navy's F-14 Tomcats and F-18 Hornets of the Navy. To complement the technology, the Airwolf possessed an impressive communications system. It rivaled a standard land-based portable Agency Surveillance Station. It included stealth technology capable of rendering the helicopter undetectable by Triple-A radar systems.

The pilot leaned back through the front section of the vessel and instructed Gibby to remain seated in the back section. There, he would wait for the Director to arrive. It was obvious that the pilot didn't want Gibby touching anything.

This was Gibby's first ride in the Director's helo. As he waited, he examined the plush, soft leather-covered pads on the earphone headset. They matched the comfort of the Airwolf's expensive white leather interior. Gibby was dressed in his best suit, a dark blue wool two-piece pinstripe with his crimson power tie. He couldn't wipe the grin from his face. Back in the day, growing up in his small rural community in the outskirts of Northern California, he would never have guessed that one day, he, Michael Gibson, a.k.a. Gibby, would be hanging out with one of the most powerful and influential persons in Asia—let alone, catching a ride in a multimillion-dollar high-tech machine like the Airwolf Bell helicopter. The pilot smiled as he glanced back at Gibby, who looked like a kid waiting to meet Santa Claus, eager to explain that he'd been a good boy and deserved the gifts he'd scribbled on his list. It was a common reaction. The pilot turned forward to continue his preflight checklist.

This quick trip wasn't for a bunch of sightseeing tourists. They were on a mission in the DMZ. From time to time, the DPRK guys had taken potshots at the helicopter. The co-pilot was on high alert. His job was like the weapon systems officer, or "WSO," pronounced *wizzo,* as well as communications and radar. Although this Airwolf was painted to mimic a typical commercial helicopter used by the executives and news media, the fact that it was sitting at Camp Bonifas told a different story. Its flight plan was to travel to Incheon Airport for a touch and go before heading toward the Park Hill Hyatt's rooftop heliport. This maneuver would be less obvious than coming straight in from the north.

As the elevator door opened, the interior light cut through the dark night. The elevator had been built facing away from the north and was protected by a tall, solid, ten-foot-thick, reinforced-steel concrete barrier. It was battle tested, capable of withstanding direct hits from multiple RPGs and the kinetic energy of a penetrating tank round.

As the Director and her protection detail made their way to the helicopter pad, Gibby watched in awe. Their formation was impressive. Even inside the safety of the military base, her protection detail team remained on constant alert, scanning for anything out of the ordinary. They kept their principal hidden, surrounded by the four men. If the situation arose, they were prepared, ready, willing, and able to make the ultimate sacrifice. The lead agent reached out to open the door. Gibby noticed that he was wearing a suit similar to those worn by her detail. For some reason, their suits looked better on them than his did on him. The Director was practically lifted up by her elbows as her escorts helped her enter the Airwolf. Gibby rose as she entered.

"Good evening, Director."

"It's nice to see you again, Mr. Gibson. It's been awhile," she replied. As she entered, she grabbed a matching soft padded earphone headset that the co-pilot handed back. She had made similar trips countless times. Without thinking, she snapped the extension jack into the intercom system. She made some minor adjustments to assure that the earpieces fit snug against her head. She toggled a button on the cord attached to the headset and began speaking.

"Good evening, Captain Davies. I will need some alone time with Mr. Gibson as we fly over."

"Yes, ma'am."

The co-pilot waived the security detail into the center seating section. Gibby almost laughed as the four broad-shouldered men squeezed into the center bench seat. They rotated their chests so that everyone was facing the same direction. It was like stacking a cord of chopped firewood, making sure the heavy, thick pieces all fit together. The men seemed comfortable getting into this position. Gibby realized that they must have experienced this maneuver countless times. He was surprised how comfortable they looked being smashed together. As the guard slid the helicopter door closed, a thick Plexiglas barrier rose up from between the backside and middle row seats. The clear divider continued rising until it touched the ceiling. The

Director pointed to Gibby's headset as she removed hers. He followed her lead and removed his. As the helicopter began to rise, Gibby was surprised. The back sealed seating area was an airtight compartment. The outside noise of the rotating blades was reduced to a subtle distant hum. He felt like he was driving in a luxury soundproofed limousine. It was almost eerie. Gibby's trance was broken as the Director began speaking.

"So, Mr. Gibson, how is Lt. Benjamin doing?"

"As well as can be expected. I've been treating him like a mushroom, ma'am. Keeping him in the dark and feeding him shit." Gibby flashed his politician's smile. He'd always loved that line and had decided to use it today during their briefing.

The Director smirked, hearing Mr. Gibson's reply. "How much skill has he developed with the mini-drone?"

"He must have been a video-game freak as a kid. We've been tracking his maneuvers since day one. I'm going to have him run through the obstacle course starting tomorrow. Based on what I see, he'll probably score an 80 or better from the get-go."

"Is that good enough?" the Director asked as she leaned forward, studying Mr. Gibson's eyes.

"Well, he's been playing with the mini-drone as soon as he awakes and stays with it until he has to get ready for his DMZ patrol. He's already clocked in one hundred eighteen hours of real fly time. He's even watching TV while he flies it around. It's become second nature to him."

"Good. That's what I want to hear," she smiled. "Have you given any thought to how we're going to do this?"

And just like that, during a casual conversation, the two of them began plotting an invasion into the DPRK—

by definition, an act of war. Gibby paused before responding. During that pause, Gibby stared straight into Director Valdez's eyes, waiting for that inevitable twinkle, that moment when they both appreciated what they were doing. Gibby broke the silence.

"Yes ma'am, I have. I've got a couple of ideas."

"I'm all ears. We have twenty minutes. What do you have in mind?"

17

The supervisor had been called to a meeting with the military attaché. He dreaded those meetings. His boss had explained that this one would be different. They were both instructed to go to the capital, Pyongyang. They were scheduled to meet with the geologists and engineer teams, followed by another separate meeting with the logistics military transportation division. The transport division most likely wanted to discuss how much more time was needed to complete the tunnel. The supervisor had prior experience. He'd completed two other tunnels. He appreciated all the details involved to wrap things up. He was surprised how fast the time passed. It didn't seem like it had been that long ago from the construction onset, to its final completion.

The supervisor sat on the hard wooden bench seat. The constant vibration of the moving train seemed to mesmerize him into a calm trance, like a prolonged daydream. The train trip would take forty-five minutes to reach the outskirts of the capital. Using his tattered leather briefcase like a pillow, the supervisor hugged it to his chest. Although he had spent thousands of days underground digging this particular tunnel system, he rarely contemplated its purpose. Only during the final-stage meetings did those thoughts come up. He understood that creating these types of tunnels had but a single purpose. They were designed as a first-strike capability, to transport troops, military trucks, and other equipment under the DMZ and into the Republic of Korea. There was no doubt that such a plan was based on a sneak attack against not only South Korea, but also the United States. To contemplate such an event was beyond belief. To consider this type of decision carried dire consequences.

He could only hope that they would never be used. He wished that neither side would make that mistake. Things had changed. If there was another war, this one would end much differently. To escalate the conflict using a large-scale sneak invasion, even if initially successful, would result in a retaliation from the US that would be more powerful than their initial invasion. The US would exact a precise degree of devastation, punishing them for such an atrocity. Their dreams of reunification would forever cripple their culture. Damaging them and inflicting wounds which the Korea that once existed could never reemerge. It could be the end of their civilization as they know it.

The supervisor seemed to go through similar mental gymnastics during these meetings. Each time, he would ask himself the same list of rhetorical questions. But why? For what purpose? In his mind, there was no chance that the US would refrain from retaliation. Nor were they likely to stand by and allow their ally to be overwhelmed and occupied. As the interior of the train compartment passed through a large canopied section of track, a great shadow engulfed the interior. The supervisor closed his eyes and exhaled a deep sigh.

Building up the DPRK's Army, strengthening its naval forces, equipping its air force with new modern equipment. All of these decisions could be justified as defensive measures. But choosing to build these tunnels was different. The tunnels were strictly offensive. It wasn't like they were built leading out of the northern territory entering China as a secret and safe path of retreat. Over the years, he had concluded that it was the isolation and fear that Korea had endured. Having suffered for decades upon decades of the constant recurring theme of invasion, occupation, and then perseverance and survival had taken its toll on the Korean psyche. The diplomatic, rather than militaristic way in which Korea was divided further exacerbated its cultural norm.

The supervisor was old enough to recognize and wise enough to admit that the current state of his country, at least as it pertained to the DPRK, maintained an all-encompassing belief in self-reliance that, when taken to an extreme, prevented the powers from seeing things clearly. That belief was combined with the notion that Korea's continued survival depended upon and was predicated upon the fact that it remain a single unified country. Because of this ideology, there seemed to be an urgent desire to accelerate unification.

It was as if, each day Korea remained separated, anxiety within the DPRK increased. To understand their plight, the supervisor likened it to understanding parents whose child had been forcibly taken from them. The abduction was only part of the emotional turmoil. But in Korea's case, it was like forcing the parents to stare out across the physical separation and watch their child being raised and influenced by a different culture. If it were only a typical abduction, they would not be forced to endure watching their children change. Over time, they would begin to internalize anxiety over the influence that these foreigners had over their loved one. Over time, they watched a new culture born in which its citizens no longer identified with their relatives in the north. In fact, these two cultures had changed so drastically that not only were bloodlines ignored, but their common core belief in unity and self-reliance were demonized as unnecessary and evil. These underlying factors were at the center of the conflict. Staring out across the DMZ, yearning to live side by side with their now distant relatives, caused a degree of psychological turmoil. They recognized their relatives were now happily living in prosperity, having assimilated into another world.

As the supervisor's mind replayed the same broken record, contemplating separation and the need for reunification, he couldn't help but feel saddened at how everything was turning out. For decades, the USSR had ignored the DPRK. Its lack of participation during the 1952 Korean civil war created bad feelings throughout the DPRK, ultimately leading to the exodus of Soviet influence. Although China remained committed to supporting their cause, China seemed to view the DPRK's lack of natural resources as a constant bone of contention. Even with China's continued support for the north, like many of his comrades, he held a paranoid inferiority complex in the belief that China must feel somewhat unlucky to have been assigned the DPRK, as opposed to the Republic of Korea.

The Supervisor observed that the West had developed the misconception that the DPRK was somehow more similar to USSR and China, as opposed to the US and Great Britain. What most historians failed to point out was the fact that each side of the DMZ had evolved into different cultures based on the influence that their sponsors projected. It was the influence over the region that caused the differences, not the distinct characteristics that were hidden within the Korean people. It would make no sense to argue that these newly separated groups of Korean people had somehow possessed internal psychological and biological differences that shaped their new ideologies.

In fact, the entire Korean collective had shared a two-thousand-year history with a common culture, language, and ancestry. It was ridiculous to conclude that the DPRK and Republic of Korea were uniquely different by nature and that this difference had simply manifested itself after the separation along the 38th parallel. A better analogy would have been identical twins being adopted by different sets of parents and raised with diametrically opposing points of view, where each child was raised, nurtured, rewarded, and punished differently. Thus, it was no surprise that each side evolved to mirror the government that provided support and influence.

But that was then, and this was now. The clock couldn't be turned back. With another deep sigh, the supervisor forced himself to disengage from this type of thinking and forced his mind to focus on his current situation. He concentrated on his physical surroundings and tried to break this mental loop of contemplation. As his mind began to clear, he knew that most of his fellow comrades inside the DPRK , on a daily basis, did this same thing: a constant mental recitation and rehashing of their misfortune; dwelling on their blood relatives and fellow countrymen, and analyzing how they had become arch rivals; enemies that held opposing points of views from almost every ideological and philosophical perspective; a change that had taken less than fifty years, representing a sliver of time compared to the number of years that Korea had been in existence.

As the train continued to plod down the tracks, the supervisor remained entranced, trapped inside his own mind, dwelling on the same thoughts. Staring out of the windows, he watched the sparse landscape pass by. He watched his fellow comrades walking through the fields carrying and tending to their harvest. No one was operating large mechanical combine machines. He saw only a few modern buildings. In contrast, he'd seen photos of the south dominated by modern skyscrapers countless storefronts teaming with commerce. He turned away from the train windows, ignoring images that passed by his view, and slipped back into mental contemplation.

He considered the tragedy of the Korean separation. It had started by the creation of the physical barrier, each side capable of looking out across the divide to see a mirror image of itself while recognizing that they were nothing alike. Regardless of a shared bloodline, a common language, and an identical history, they no longer shared much in common. They were now true enemies. This was the conflict.

The biggest factors in the conflict stemmed from the lack of resources and perceived happiness in their new situations. The south had the benefit of financial prosperity and abundant resources, and its sponsoring countries encouraged innovation and growth. As a consequence, the south was able to look forward to its future with a sense of optimism. While the north, with its extreme temperatures and lack of natural resources, was restricted and challenged while simultaneously being forced to adapt to their sponsoring country that held a form of government that discouraged individualism and innovation. Rather, it taught the importance of communal compliance, emphasizing the importance of self-sacrifice for the betterment of the collective culture. The struggle placed on the DPRK as it learned this new culture, combined with the lack of resources, created a sense of loss. Its anger was misdirected at its geographical locations rather than the different ideologies of their sponsoring country. It could be argued that the biggest factor was the north's lack of natural resources; would the conflict still have existed if the northern side of the DMZ provided similar climate and possessed equal abundant resources? One could imagine that under such circumstances, those to the north would be better able to accept the separation. It was this inequality that created a constant yearning for reconciliation—or, more accurately, yearning to return to a time when, if nothing else, the Koreas shared an equal fate, where one side was no better off than the other.

It was the constant driving force in human existence, the battle between the haves and the have nots. If both sides of the DMZ possessed abundant resources, there might not be any conflict. But that wasn't the case. One needed only to look down from the night sky to recognize the obvious differences. The north was absent of lighting, while the south was lit up like a Christmas tree in all its splendor. The understanding of what the electrical grid and its usage screamed out to the world: that, to the south, a dense population existed, where there was enough wealth, commerce, and infrastructure to maintain such an engineering and sociological feat. As the supervisor's mind looped through the same issues, cycling through the same arguments, he once again dropped his head toward his chest. He knew his country's economy paled in comparison. In the 1990s, the North Korean GNP (Gross National Product) was one-tenth that of South Korea.

The train conductor's voice broke the silence, announcing their arrival to the capital downtown train station. The supervisor finally broke out of his trance.

The train was reliable and clean. There was no free wi-fi, no flat screen televisions, no colorful advertisements or graffiti. Still, even without the presence of these modern day things, it was reliable. The supervisor stood and adjusted his clothes, pressing his hands against them to remove the creases from his long ride. As the brake pads pressed into the heavy metal wheel casings, a loud screeching noise filled the air. The interior wooden-passenger-compartment area shimmied from the vibration. The train slowed, then came to a complete stop.

The supervisor looked out across the platform. Standing in front of the escalator, he saw the military attaché waiting for his train's arrival. The station was busy for a weekday, by North Korean standards. The supervisor and military attaché exchanged customary bows before climbing onto the escalator. The escalators carried passengers to the surface street. The rise was steep, climbing one hundred meters. In the DPRK, it was a feat of engineering.

The trains transitioned to a subway track. As they entered the capital, it gradually changed. Inside the city limits of the capital, the subway system doubled as a bomb shelter, having been constructed deep below the ground for added protection. As they held the moving handrails tight to keep their balance, the supervisor and military attaché exchanged brief smiles. In years past, he would have had to walk up a long flight of steep concrete stairs. As the escalator breached the top section, both men jumped off the moving steel stairway, practically jogging off to maintain their balance. With slight smiles, they both laughed. He felt like a child at the end of a carnival ride, but this brief pleasant moment evaporated as they began walking toward the governmental building. The supervisor was reminded that even military attachés were human.

"Do you have your data? Are your ready for your presentation?" asked the attaché.

Without saying a word, the supervisor raised his briefcase, patting the worn side with his free hand and nodding his head.

"Good," replied the attaché. "Keep it brief and to the point. It's not just you and your crew who are under scrutiny here."

They climbed the last step and the attaché pushed the front door open. As they entered the lobby, there was a huge mural of the Great Leader covering the entire wall. Without realizing it, the military attaché's eyes dilated and he wiped his forehead with his pressed cotton sleeve before letting out a deep exhale. The supervisor hadn't appreciated the stress that these meetings placed on others.

He knew it was going to be a long meeting. The supervisor fell in line following behind the military attaché. His shoulders sagged as the emotional and physical stress of his journey took its toll. In a brief instant, something caught his eye. Turning his head, the supervisor saw a middle-aged woman carrying an unusual brown purse over her shoulder. He had seen that purse before. He blinked his eyes and forced his brain to recall where he had seen that purse before. Then it hit him. It was the man! The man he had seen in the underground lava tubes. The supervisor remembered watching the man pull something out of his backpack. He had caught only a glimpse in a brief moment. Even still, he was certain. The bag had unusual foreign markings. As he collected his thoughts, he had no doubt it was the same. Before the supervisor could focus on the woman's face, she shuffled across the lobby and out of his view.

As the supervisor stood looking across the lobby area, the military attaché's voice caught his attention. "Hey, what are you doing? Hurry up!" he barked.

Regaining his composure, the supervisor turned and walked to the attaché who was holding open the door. As he passed through the doorway, he noticed the dark sweat stain seeping through the attaché's shirt. More drops of perspiration ran down his temple.

18

X.O. Newland grunted. "Moon Dog, we have a meeting with the Director in ninety minutes. Have you worked out the options we discussed?"

"Yes, sir. I have all four proposals ready to go. No one else has seen the final product. All pages have been stamped 'Top Secret.' Once the decision is made, I'll shred the unselected options. Then I'll scrub the laptop clean, destroying RAM and the hard drive. It was only prepared on one device. Standard operating protocol, sir."

"I'm gonna recommend the refueling plane scenario. It's ultimately the Director's call. But what do you think?"

"I'm in agreement, sir. It gives us the most control from a delivery and execution perspective," replied Lt. Elliott. "Is Gibby coming?"

"He should already be in with the Director now," replied the X.O. He grabbed one of the bound proposals from each stack and began flipping through the proposals. Direct force was the least favorable option. He knew that this option wasn't realistic, but it needed to be addressed. It always shocked him to think that the DPRK had an available manpower of 13 million, more than half their entire population of around 25 million. Of that number, 10 million were fit for service. At present, the DPRK had 700,000 personnel on the front line, with 4.5 million active reservists available if needed. They had 4,200 tanks, 4,100 armored fighting vehicles, 4,300 towed artillery, and 2,400 multi-launch rocket systems. To supplement that force, the DPRK had a total of 944 aircraft, of which 458 were fighter/interceptors and 222 helicopters. The coastal defense included 70 submarines.

In contrast, the Republic of Korea had a total population just shy of 50 million citizens. They kept 625,000 active personnel on the front line, with 2.9 million total reservists. Despite the south's superior population being twice the size of the DPRK, the number of active frontline personnel and active reserves was less than in the north. Contrary to what most people thought, the United States Forces Korea (USFK) maintained only 28,500 total personnel, consisting of soldiers, sailors, airmen, and marines. This group's main role was to train the Republic of Korea, as well as to develop plans to evacuate the noncombatants. The US also provided more than 2,000 tanks and hundreds of F-5, F-15, and F-16 fighter jets and bombers.

On paper, the DPRK's number made them more prepared for war. However, it had to be considered that much of the DPRK's equipment was older and not necessarily battle ready, whereas the US weapons and machines were state-of-the-art. Based on these different strengths, it was generally viewed by the international military community that, should another war break out, the DPRK would rely on its overwhelming numbers, opting for a swarm attack combined with the potential use of the estimated arsenal of twenty nuclear bombs.

The X.O. flipped through this folder. He reviewed the tables comparing both sides. He knew that direct force was not a realistic option. Looking at the remaining folders, he was intrigued about the viability of the other diversionary options offered. Whichever covert operation was selected, the most important aspect to consider, other than success, was the one most likely to remain a secret from the rest of the world. It was imperative that nothing come back to implicate the Agency or the United States. This mission was to be considered secret even inside the walls of the Agency and within military circles; it would never be subject to any congressional oversight committee.

The X.O. flipped through the Earthquake Scenario folder. The report pointed out that the main problem with this scenario was Korea's geological history. The Korean Peninsula was largely Precambrian rock, soils consisting of granite and gneiss. The area was considered geographically outside the Pacific Ring of Fire. Unlike nearby Japan, there were no active volcanoes nor moving tectonic plates. What further exacerbated the problem was the fact that in recent time there had only been four earthquakes that registered greater than 5.5 on the Richter scale.

The best way to fake an earthquake was to use heavy earth-boring bombs. The problem was the physics of using a missile. Inevitably, radar surveillance would detect it. There would also be a high likelihood that video surveillance of even common exterior security cameras could be gathered to support the fact that inbound missiles were involved. Even if bombs could be introduced manually, the explosions would leave physical evidence.

The X.O. glanced at the graphs. The locations of the prior earthquakes with their corresponding magnitudes were listed. He reviewed the various bomb options or alternative explosive systems that could be used. After closing the folder, he returned it to the stack and grabbed the next folder.

This option involved staging a natural gas explosion as the cover story. As he read the report, the X.O. adjusted his glasses. This option looked promising at first. Research had confirmed that, in search of natural gas and oil reserves, the DPRK and China had contacted a Singapore-based firm to survey North Korea. Based on the firm's preliminary findings, the DPRK had pursued outside investors. After more extensive research, the DPRK determined that large natural gas reserves were located in the Eastern Sea Regions. However, nothing had been found near the DMZ.

The X.O. continued reading. Although the Agency could stage an explosion, the existence of detailed research and reports with drill samples and other tests would force outsiders to perform an in-depth investigation. Given the prior efforts made by the international energy companies, they would certainly wonder why their research hadn't located these reserves. Those companies would want to know why they had missed locating it. If this error was proven to have taken place, their entire research results would come into question. These companies would have the technological resources and financial means to pursue the matter. Their reputation was at stake.

As the X.O. read the report, he shook his head. This gas leak option would result in a formal investigation. Even if their covert mission were initially successful, the cover-up would be found. Success required not only the destruction of the tunnel but also for the cover-up to remain a secret. The X.O. removed his reading glasses and pursed his lips. Lt. Elliott had been waiting for the X.O. to finish the three folders before interjecting. The X.O. set the folder down and spoke.

"Moon Dog, I'm guessing that you aren't too impressed with the first three options?"

"That's how I see it, sir."

"Has anything changed with our last option?"

"Nothing. It's the cleanest, most direct option. It's guaranteed to destroy the tunnel. From a collateral damage perspective, other than Lt. Benjamin, we would not be jeopardizing anyone from our side of the fence. It's unclear how many workers from the DPRK would be inside the tunnel. Once we get eyes inside there, we'll have a better understanding on those numbers."

Moon Dog paused, allowing the X.O. to process everything. Continuing, he said, "If their casualties are a concern, we could take down the tunnel in the middle of the night. You'd think that during that hour, the fewest workers would be present," explained Moon Dog.

The X.O. listened to Lt. Elliott. He couldn't help but think about Lt. Benjamin. With a deep sigh, the X.O. looked up from the table of reports and stared into Lt. Elliott's eyes as he spoke.

"What if Benjamin gets stuck down there?"

"He will not have any identifying patches or markings on his uniform. He probably hasn't noticed that all his gear, from his boots to his undershirt, have been eradicated. There are no manufacturing labels or size markings. Even the boot-sole patterns are uniquely designed and do not match any other US or Republic of Korea designs." Moon Dog could sense that X.O. Newland wasn't concerned with those matters. "Besides," Lt. Elliott continued. "with the amount of charges that will be used, if he gets stuck down there when it goes off, there won't be anything left. He wouldn't feel a thing."

A sense of guilt washed over their conversation as they discussed the potential demise of their newest agent. He was being treated like a disposable plastic utensil that could be tossed away after it had been used. Moon Dog broke the awkward silence.

"But that's not gonna happen, sir. He'll be playing a huge roll in this mission. The likelihood he'll get stuck down there is slim to none. My biggest concern is that he could be captured down there before we complete the mission. I'd hate to see what they'd do to him, trying to extract any information."

As if snapped out of his trance, the X.O. blurted, "Make sure he's got a cyanide capsule."

"When he started going out on his solo patrols, Gibby gave him two."

They both sat at the table in silence for several moments. Nothing needed to be said; it was the nature of the job. Lt. Benjamin was a vital key to their plan, but he was also their newest recruit. By design, he knew very little about anything. He had been isolated, assigned away from the Agency, embedded into a marine unit to patrol the DMZ. In theory, he was traveling alone. His only contact was Gibby, a civilian with no traceable connection to the Agency. Other than that, Kyle knew only fragments of the mission. Other than the solo patrols, he had no idea what was coming next. He had been isolated from the inner workings of the Agency and had never met the Director, X.O. Newland, or Lt. Elliott. Therefore, even if Kyle were to be captured, he couldn't hurt their operation. He was truly expendable.

The X.O. glanced at the wall clock and stood. "It's time. Let's make our way to the Director's sanctum." Moon Dog slid the folders into his briefcase. He let his hand slide down to his waist, checking to see if he was carrying a sidearm. He wasn't packing. He knew the drill.

*   *   *   *   *

Angelie arrived at the International Schools District Office earlier in the day. She had been introduced to the staff and, along with twenty-seven other first-time English teachers, had gone through the three-hour orientation course. Most of her colleagues were assigned to metropolitan schools. She was the only one heading into the DMZ community of Daeseong-Dong village. She had met with Human Resources, received her new Korean School–issued cell phone, timesheets, class materials, and a laptop with limited access to wi-fi, depending on each teacher's location. She had signed the authorization form acknowledging her understanding that all of the equipment was to be returned at the end of her tour, that any damaged or missing items would be her responsibility, and that any repair costs would be deducted from her last check.

She was taken to the school's main campus dormitory and assigned a room that was hers to use until she was to be driven out to her assignment. The room was located near the front door of the single-story dormitory. She had used her personal cell phone. Before she left the US, it had been programmed for international calls. Her parents explained that she was not to worry about the expense for the phone and was to use it as she saw fit. It was an essential tool in her limited box of tricks. As she sat on her bed, she looked across the small room and stared at the bright red "Heavy" tag that was tied to the handle of her oversized suitcase. Her thoughts drifted back to her first contact.

While in the LAX International terminal, waiting to catch her connecting nonstop flight to Korea, she was approached by a man who knew her parents well. He was one of their handlers. She sat in a low-profile chair that ran along the tall pane-glass window. While she looked out onto the dark night toward the runway, the middle-aged Korean man advanced. They were the only ones in the area. It was a mid-week flight, and few passengers were expected.

Rather than selecting one of the many empty seats, he chose one next to her. Angelie's sense of personal space had been temporarily altered during the busy day. Before boarding the plane, she had been herded through security and baggage check. During the four-hour flight from St. Louis, she had been cramped between two oversized Midwestern passengers. Thus, she was no longer overly sensitive about the infringement of her personal space. She was tired and the time zone changes weren't helping, so she barely noticed the man. When he spoke, he got her attention.

"How are your parents, Angelie?"

She tried to concentrate. How did this man know her parents?

"Excuse me. Do we know each other?" She replied, trying her best to appear calm. She stared back at the man. She hoped her voice hadn't given away the fear she felt.

"Technically, no. At your apartment, I've seen you many times. You were much too young back then to remember, though. Most of the time, you were playing games behind your bedroom door. Let's say that we've never been formally introduced."

"Can I help you with anything?" She began to realize that this must be her contact. Her mother told her that during her journey to Korea, she would be approached. Her mother explained that a man by the name of Mr. Hong would contact her, and he would give her an address. Before she started her assignment at the school, she needed to visit someone. He would give her a code name. She could hear her mother's voice, reminding her once again, as she'd been doing Angelie's entire life, "Do not speak Hangul." Angelie waited for the man to speak.

Looking around the gate area, he looked in both directions. It was clear. He started speaking in Korean. She waited for him to finish before replying. Although she understood everything he had said, she replied to the contrary.

"I'm sorry. I only speak basic conversational Korean; only pleasantries, really. Most of what you said, I didn't understand. Could you please repeat it in English? You do speak English, right?"

The man stared back, surprised. She was convincing, and he almost believed her. Processing what she'd said, he couldn't get over the idea that she was now alone on her first assignment, about to arrive in Korea; so how was it possible that she couldn't speak Hangul? His comrades most certainly had taught her the language.

After forcing a calm, relaxed expression, he blinked his eyes and turned toward Angelie. In a hushed whispering voice, he repeated himself in perfect English.

"My name is Mr. Hong. You need to go to the "Kimchi Market" on the first floor of the City Hall subway station across the street from Deoksu Palace. It's on the corner of Seosumunno and Taepyongno."

After hearing the words, now for the second time, Angelie reached into her purse and pulled out a map of downtown Seoul. After finding the location, she took a black Sharpie ink pen and circled the location on the map. She then wrote "Kimchi Market" above the dark black inked circle.

"Is there anything else?"

He glanced around the area again before speaking. "There will be a large unusual flower potted plant on the counter. An old woman is the only one who works the cash register. If anyone else is at the cash register, do not enter. Immediately turn and leave. Do not go inside. The odds of that happening are very unlikely. However, if that does happen, later someone will contact you. They will find you."

Angelie leaned forwarded listening to every word he said. She concentrated on each inflection and every syllable.

"When you approach the old woman, you must offer a deep ninety-degree angle bow. The most honorific one you've ever given. The one you save for funerals. When you rise up, point at the flower and explain to the old woman that you have one exactly like it back in the US. Tell her it's called a Country Jasmine."

The man paused, looking deep into Angelie's eyes, before continuing.

"Did you get that?"

"Yes, Country Jasmine."

"That's right. Country Jasmine." The man paused and glanced around the gate area one last time. He leaned closer to Angelie and began whispering into her ear.

"She will give you something. Don't say another word to her. Take whatever she gives you and leave. It will come with instructions. There is no need to pay her anything. Just leave. Do you understand?"

She nodded her head as she leaned back away from the man. Replying in a soft whisper, she said "Yes. I understand."

The man took a deep breath and exhaled as he stood. With an abrupt movement, he turned away from Angelie and walked away. As he walked, she could hear the snap of his black wing-tipped heels against the shiny floor.

A subdued knock on her dormitory door interrupted her thoughts.

"Yes?"

A soft female voice came from the other side of the door. "A cab is outside. The driver says you called?"

"Oh yes, right. Thank you." Angelie grabbed her purse and stuffed her personal cell phone inside. As she walked out the front door of the dormitory, she waved to the cabby and opened the back door of the cab. She sat down and closed the door.

"Could you take me to the City Hall subway station across from the Deoksu Palace? It's on the corner of Seosumunno and Taepyongno."

The cab driver sat frozen, staring back at Angelie as if she were speaking Martian. She reached into her purse and unfolded a street map. She raised it up to the driver and pointed to the location she had circled in black ink. The cab driver squinted as he looked at the folded map. With a big smile, the driver appeared to understand what she wanted. He nodded his head enthusiastically, to convey that he understood where she wanted him to go. He turned forward and drove away.

19

The supervisor was happy. At the capital meeting, things went as planned. Everyone was excited about the progress. They told him of their plans to provide a big celebration party. Everyone involved in the project, including his crew, was invited. He didn't mention having seen a man walking in the lava tube section next to their excavation tunnel. Besides, the man wasn't dressed in South Korean military clothing or some other official uniform. Likewise, it didn't appear that the man was defecting to the south because he was walking in the wrong direction carrying a fully loaded backpack. The supervisor concluded that the man was probably just a peasant using the tunnel to bring things back to sell on the black market.

The supervisor didn't want to spoil everything because of this smuggler, so he decided to keep it a secret. He didn't want to jeopardize the progress; an investigation would cause work in the tunnel to stop. In his judgment, none of that was necessary.

The tunnel was almost complete. The remaining construction would wait until spring. There were reservations about further excavating under the southern section. Given the amount of tunnel already cleared, the last thousand meters would be done as carefully as possible. The military had no immediate plans, so the crew didn't need to recklessly push forward. He also had suspicions that there might be some political motivation to keep this tunnel technically incomplete. None of that was of any consequence or concern to him.

The miniature tram tracks were being removed. Heavy trucks were driving up and down the completed sections to assure that the road was sufficiently compacted. Final touches were being done to install the air filtration substations along the entire length of the tunnel. The engineers were busy contouring the slope of the roadway. They needed to prevent the pooling of moisture and promote the drainage of subsurface water seepage. Once these last pieces were completed, the communications division would begin to lay miles of cable to support an underground surveillance camera system. Everything was going as planned and was on schedule.

*   *   *   *   *

Kyle was about to go out on his nightly solo patrol. His nerves were still rattled from yesterday's excursion. The day before, he made his first trip into the tunnel. Using his night-vision goggles, he had created a trail along a divergent stream that ran adjacent to a tall cliff formation. The cave opening was located high on the cliff, and the opening was protected from direct view by thick evergreen tree cover and untouched foliage below. The undergrowth stood chest high and hid the cave opening. He had been using deer trails that cut through the vegetation. He was still on the South Korean side of the DMZ, but due to its proximity to the northern border, it had been abandoned decades ago and had remained untouched ever since.

As the trail progressed, the ground began to incline steeply up a mountain and continued to rise for the next ten kilometers. Approximately one third of the way up the rise, Kyle located something. At an angle, the ravine fell off to the side, forming an abrupt drop-off cliff. There was a formation of rock that was smooth, as if it had been shaved off by a glacier's edge, tens of thousands of years ago. Hidden out of sight, the surveillance satellite images located an opening to a tunnel. Using the subterranean program, they could confirm that this opening led to a natural formation that ran parallel to the tunnel being excavated by the DPRK.

Using GPS tracking, Kyle worked his way through the thick underbrush and up the cliff face to reach this very spot. After he entered the tunnel, he noticed a worn trail that continued inside the tunnel. As he entered, he felt the cooler temperature and the increased moisture content in the air engulfed his face, and he deduced that there was an underground spring.

It was a lava tube. Kyle activated the chest-mounted body camera attached to his jacket. Gibby had explained that the information received from the camera was vital to their final mission planning. Before proceeding inside, Kyle dropped one of the many metallic spheres just outside the tunnel entrance. He had been instructed to deploy these metal devices every mile but not to activate them until he was at least one hundred meters away. Although the metallic spheres were designed to enhance communications that allowed underground use of the GPS and miniature drone, they could also remotely self-destruct. When discharged, they were lethal to anyone standing within five meters of the device.

With apprehension, Kyle continued forward. He had nothing to go on now but his own instincts. He was truly on his own. In the safety and comfort of his office, Gibby sat in his ergonomically adjustable leather armchair, wrapped with a thick cotton blanket and sipping hot tea, watching the image from Kyle's chest mounted camera. Like a fly on the wall, he had a clear, mint-green, night-vision view of what was taking place. There was no audio.

During Kyle's stroll into darkness, he continued to advance, dropping the metallic spheres, recording GPS locations, and video-documenting the entire maze of tunnel. After several hours, he came to a turn. From there, it opened into a huge cathedral space. As he approached this section, he could hear the soft trickle of water. He discerned several tube openings that met to create a large opening.

The opening was beautiful. Inside the massive cavity, he noticed something to the left of the worn pathway. His night-vision goggles had a way of exaggerating the texture, accentuating any differences in an objects composition. These contrasting textures stood out with the goggles. Kyle froze in his tracks. It was clear that he was staring at an opening in the wall. Was it some sort of secret passage? He leaned forward and stared more closely. Something looked out of place: the lines around the opening were too straight; it didn't look like something nature would have created. Kyle leaned down. Using his gloves, he gouged around the area. As the loose soil fell away, he saw deep straight lines as if they had been cut. He knew these markings were manmade.

He also noticed an abrupt texture and color change with distinct areas that seemed to be dripping down, as if the soil had been liquefied. Kyle removed a glove. Extending his index finger, he touched what seemed like dripping soil and realized it wasn't soil but dried concrete.

Kyle determined that he was next to the DPRK excavation tunnel. Turning his head, he craned his neck, looking up the trail in both directions. Confident that no one was present, he leaned up against the unusual concrete structure. Pressing his ear flat against the rough wall, Kyle raised his hand into a fist and rapped his knuckles against the wall. A soft echo resonated; it was hollow. He stepped back away from the wall and recorded the GPS reading.

At first, the GPS seemed frozen and unable to generate an accurate reading. Kyle realized that being underground and having traveled so far into this structure was affecting the device. He held the device as still as possible. He hoped that stabilizing it would allow the spherical communication relays down the tunnel a direct, unvarying signal location, which would increase its ability to transmit the signal up and down the line. He dropped to the ground. Taking a knee, he held the device against the cave wall. With his elbow perched onto the other kneecap, he stabilized the GPS, preventing it from moving. This seemed to do the trick. The device could communicate between two stable, constant positions and no longer had to demodulate between a moving, erratic location. Finally, the signal was now stable and clear. It passed between the GPS device and the last metallic sphere down the tunnel.

Like a miniature wireless network system, these spheres represented the next generation of communication technology, stand-alone devices that did not require huge, permanent towers. These mini-spherical relay communication stations boosted the transmission of both inbound and outbound signals. Each sphere housed a microscopic power supply that ran on the same principle of fusion, but on a much smaller scale. It was designed to be a temporary short-term communication conduit, with a lifespan of no more than 96 hours. After that, the intense heat and runaway energy source would destroy the spheres. At $1 million per sphere, the cost made their use impractical for the public; but even if the price could be scaled back, the health risks would certainly prevent them from ever entering the commercial market. These devices emitted electromagnetic energy waves that radiated well above what the US FCC deemed safe. During the boosting and transmission of information along the system, the RF energy was above the point of ionization for biological material. This exposure affected the eyes and external male reproductive organs.

The practical military application of this technology outweighed its risks. The entire network was designed to work with only a few devices, as opposed to typical commercial cell towers that exchanged data for thousands of users simultaneously. Nevertheless, Kyle received extensive one-on-one training with Gibby's tech team to get him up to speed on this essential technological tool. It would support the GPS and mini-drone system; it was vital and greatly increased the odds of a successful mission.

Kyle entered the GPS coordinates onto his notepad. He had documented the locations of every sphere. He returned the notepad into his hip pack and began nosing around the artificial barrier. From his crouched position, using his night-vision goggles, he saw a separation. This opening offered him a way to slip through to the other side. He turned his torso and found he could just fit inside. Rotating each shoulder in a rocking motion, Kyle squeezed through.

As Kyle turned his body, with his back pressed against the common wall, he stared out into the darkness. To evaluate the situation, he forced himself to remain relaxed and motionless for as long as necessary. He remained in a crouch, hidden from view, and glanced at his watch; it was 2:35 in the morning. He hoped the DPRK wasn't working around the clock.

As time passed, Kyle never heard a noise and never saw lights. What he did notice was the smell. This side of the wall had a dry sterile odor. It was in deep contrast to the moist, natural, cool quality on the other side. He was certain that this was no natural lava tube. It had to be what he was looking for.

He deposited another metallic sphere at the opening between these two tunnels. He wanted to make sure the signal would bounce through to this other side. Then Kyle opened the carrying case and pulled out the wireless mini-drone. This would be his first mini-drone flight outside of his room. Gibby had explained that without the benefit of a communication relay device, the mini-drone could maintain communication with the controller only for up to 1.5 miles. It was designed for covert missions. Once it reached the end of its communication tether distance, the programmers designed the mini-drone to stop, as opposed to barreling forward out of control, flying away without hope of recovery.

Heading north, Kyle sent the drone into the cave. He made sure that its night-vision camera was activated and the terabyte hard drive was recording. He loaded a fully charged battery, which assured him of at least five hours of nonstop flight time. After that point, he could still operate it, but it would be much less responsive; much slower and somewhat louder, given the reduced RPM of its rotor blades. From experience, he knew that if the mini-drone were in constant use, the battery would completely drain after six hours.

Like a kid given the opportunity to play his first regular season game, Kyle smiled as he began logging his first on-duty minutes of flight time. The outcome of this game was more than just bragging rights. This game came with dire consequences, where victory and failure were decided, as well as who lived or died.

Lt. Benjamin found the experience exhilarating. With his eyes glued to the miniature screen, Kyle felt like he was flying down the tunnel at 30 mph. As the drone flew down the tunnel it emitted a high-pitched, metallic whirling sound. It took the drone three minutes to reach the outer limits of the tether communication distance. The drone slowed and came to a soft controlled landing.

Kyle left the safety of his hidden alcove and walked forward and retrieved the drone. While watching the flyover through the drone's monitor, he knew what lay ahead. There were no buildings or guards. He almost forgot he was on a mission. The stress he'd felt outside had been greater, because he hadn't had the benefit of knowing what was ahead, whereas now the drone provided that advance information.

He proceeded down the tunnel. Every mile, he dropped a mini-communication relay. This process kept the distance between the relays within a five-mile distance, making certain that both the mini-drone and the GPS signals could bounce from their outside satellite to the relays deep inside this underground labyrinth.

*   *   *   *   *

Kyle's video documented ten miles into the excavated tunnel. He had also laid the relay devices. The communication line was tested and activated. It took him less than two hours to lay the relays and program the night-vision wireless cameras. Kyle wasted no time. Once he reached the ten-mile marker, he retrieved the mini-drone and started jogging back. In no time, he was back inside the opening where the DPRK tunnel and the natural lava tube met. He glanced at his watch. It was 5:40 a.m. Kyle depressed the stopwatch program. It had taken him a little over three hours.

Kyle crouched underneath the opening and tested the relay. He knew he was far enough away from the string of devices that the small amount of RF energy would not affect him. As the cameras came online, Gibby watched the monitor on his desk light up. With all the relays transmitting, Gibby could see the same view Kyle saw. Gibby configured his monitor to display the ground cameras inside the DPRK. All views displayed simultaneously on one screen. Gibby stood up from his reclining desk chair. Wearing only boxer shorts and white cotton socks, he threw up his right arm into a fist-pump celebration. He was alone in his office. There was no crowd present to go wild with excitement. Before returning to his seat, Gibby surveyed the quiet room. A smirk appeared on his face; he was pleased with their progress, and everything was proceeding as planned.

Using this newly activated communication relay, Gibby sent Kyle a text message. Instantaneously, Kyle's wrist device began vibrating. He toggled the switch and read Gibby's message.

"Perfect. 100% online. Now we need the rest of that tunnel."

Kyle pulled out an energy bar from his hip-pack and took a long swig of water. He loaded another fully charged battery into the drone. Then, he booted it back to life. In no time, the drone was traveling the other direction of the DPRK excavation tunnel. Right away,

Kyle noticed that this section of tunnel was different. It was less finished and looked rough. The floor hadn't been groomed and lacked the engineered, domed appearance. The obvious raw, unfinished look stood in stark contrast to the other side. He noticed the absence of the drainage and air filtration piping.

As the drone hummed along, Kyle saw a single set of fresh boot prints. Worried the drone might overtake someone walking, Kyle reduced its speed. As the drone reached its tether distance away from the controller, it went into an automatic landing mode. This time, Kyle sent Gibby a message:

"Watch my back. If you see anyone coming, let me know."

Within seconds, he received a reply. "OK."

Kyle knew his time was running short. It was almost morning, and he was certain that the DPRK workers would be showing up any time. He was right. The crew had already gathered at the entrance, preparing to climb onto the oversized compaction trucks. The underground excavation tunnel ran for fifteen kilometers. The convoy would travel slowly to reduce unnecessary vibrations. When they entered the southern border of the DMZ, they reduced their speed even more. Each day, the excavation crew's day started at 7:00 a.m. sharp. Kyle had twenty more minutes before they began their descent into the tunnel.

After collecting his thoughts, Kyle climbed out of the hidden opening and began jogging after the mini-drone. As he reached the drone, he set another relay device and positioned the miniature wireless camera. Once he was certain that everything was in order, he activated the drone and proceeded forward. This time, he chose to jog after the drone as it flew. This allowed the drone to travel farther, given that the tethering distance was also moving. Gibby was more concerned with the DPRK side of the tunnel. He explained that once the tunnel was destroyed, they could always excavate and fill the section that existed on the southern side of the DMZ. The discovery and presence of the tunnel would no longer need to be kept secret.

Kyle was young and in great physical condition. He showed no signs of exhaustion and bounded down the tunnel with ease. After dropping his third camera and communication relay, he received a message from Gibby. "The trucks are on their way. Let's wrap it up."

Kyle sent his reply and set off to recover the drone. As he continued down the tunnel, he saw a flash of bright light flickering from the drone's monitor. The unexpected color and movement caught his attention. He stopped running and stared at the monitor. A bright illumination burned on the mint green screen. At the extreme bottom of the monitor view, Kyle could see the outline of what appeared to be a man sitting over a fire warming his hands. He studied the image. It looked like the silhouette of the man's head. Kyle guessed he was smoking a cigarette. The images appeared to be a safe distance from the drone. Kyle hoped it had landed far enough away, and that the man couldn't see the drone.

Kyle looked up from the monitor. He began walking, careful not to make any noise. Through his night-vision goggles, he could see the drone sitting on the tunnel floor. Kyle installed the last communication relay device and night-vision camera. Once the devices were in place, he remained kneeling on the ground. Staring through the night-vision goggles, he contemplated his next move

20

The DPRK guard had been assigned to patrol the tunnel. It had taken several months before he became accustomed to the isolation and loneliness of this assignment. Like Kyle, he was a solo patrol. His assignment was to monitor and guard the farthest end of the excavation tunnel. In the event of its being discovered, he was ordered to retreat and report anything unusual. As expected, the last six months had been void of anything whatsoever that could be considered unusual, and the monotony and boredom had reduced his state of alertness. His routine now consisted of riding the last oversized compaction truck to the end of the line. As the trucks picked up the workers, he would be dropped off, and he walked the remaining distance down into the deserted, dark tunnel.

He always waited for all the excavators, engineers, and air filtration system technicians to leave. Then, after doubling back to make sure all the trucks were gone, the solo night guard would return to the far end of the tunnel, spread out a bedroll, set up a campfire, and drink several shots of strong rice wine. He no longer slept during his non-working hours. He did just the opposite. He was certain, after all these months, that nothing was going to happen. Now, while off duty, rather than sleep so he could be fresh during his night-shift patrol, he did all his personal domestic chores and errands. Once the rice wine had taken its effect, he would crawl under the blanket and fall asleep. Each morning, his worn plastic wristwatch alarm would sound so that, when the excavation crew returned in the morning, he would be wide awake. It was a boring assignment. Things could be worse. After all, he was dry, and he no longer had to endure the extreme winter winds and bone-chilling temperatures above ground.

As the night guard began organizing his bedroll, he was startled by an unusual metallic whirling sound. At first, he thought he had overslept and was hearing the noise from the oversized compaction trucks moving in the tunnel, but this sound was different, like nothing he had become accustomed to hearing.

The night guard stared out into the darkness. The whirling sound seemed to be getting louder. Unlike Kyle, though, he didn't have a pair of night-vision goggles. He relied on the small amount of light coming from the campfire. The night guard tilted his head from side to side. Concentrating, he tried to decipher this new sound. Using all his senses, he could swear that something had been hovering in the air and had landed just outside his field of vision. Like a deer able to detect the presence of a predator that hid beyond view, the night guard found himself changing positions. He placed the fire between himself and the unusual sounds. Staring out into the darkness, the night guard pressed his back against the tunnel wall.

Making a conscious effort to keep the flames between himself and the whirling sounds, the guard glanced down at his wristwatch. This was the first time he had been scared, and he couldn't wait for the oversized truck to arrive; he wanted to get out of the tunnel. The night guard continued to stare out into the darkness. His eyes darted from side to side, searching for any movement. He released a deep sigh as he waited for his comrades to arrive.

*   *   *   *   *

Kyle could see the drone. It had landed in the center of the tunnel. He contemplated his options. He was certain that the guard couldn't see him; still, he wasn't about to walk out there and pick it up. Kyle thought it unlikely that the guard had night-vision goggles. He probably had a flashlight. Kyle contemplated his options.

He watched the night guard stand and walk behind the campfire. Kyle was close enough that, as the guard walked, Kyle could hear the man's boots crunch on the ground. Hoping that the noise from the fire would camouflage the noise from the drone, Kyle opted to fly it back toward him. Kyle toggled the wireless controller and started the drone's rotor blades. He leaned the controller arm backwards. The drone rose and began to hover. Kyle reversed the drone and flew it back to him. Kyle stared at the monitor and watched the drone fly back in his direction.

*   *   *   *   *

The night guard's heartbeat increased and he felt the adrenaline surge through his body. Then, without warning, he once again heard the unusual metallic whirling sound. Whatever was making the sound appeared to flutter just outside of his field of vision. His pupils dilated. After all these months, he had become comfortable, and he almost forgot he had a flashlight. As the sounds increased, the guard chastised himself for not remembering to use his flashlight. It wasn't very powerful, but it could help. He reached into his bag and pulled out a small flashlight and depressed his thumb to turn it on.

Directing the weak beam into the darkness, the night guard caught a glimpse of something flying in the air. Unable to get a good view of what it was, his imagination got the best of him. He reasoned that because it was airborne, it was probably a bat or another winged creature. His fear continued to increase. Searching for a flying animal, he aimed the light beam up toward the ceiling. As his mind processed the information, he was doing everything to control his fear, holding back the urge to scream out into the darkness.

*   *   *   *   *

Kyle was caught off guard. Without warning, a weak flashlight beam cut through the dark tunnel, wreaking havoc with his night-vision goggles. And he was briefly blinded. For only a moment, the light beam shone directly on the drone, catching it mid-flight. Without thinking, Kyle increased the speed of the drone and accelerated its flight back down the tunnel, chasing it into the darkness. Kyle watched the flashlight beam searching in all directions as it moved about the upper section of the tunnel. As he glanced back, the beam hit him square in the face and found himself temporarily blinded as the night goggles further accentuated the light. Kyle pulled the goggles off his face and turned away from the light. Blinking, he tried to recover from the overstimulation. Kyle heard the drone fly by his head and continue down the tunnel.

His training had paid off. Controlling the drone had become second nature. Without the benefit of sight or watching the monitor, Kyle safely landed the drone. Then he lay down on the tunnel floor. He saw the light bouncing off the ceiling above. As his eyes began to recover, Kyle crawled backward, away from the night guard. With an outstretched hand, he could feel the sharp edges of the drone's rotor blades.

Kyle's eyes continued to recover. He pulled the goggles back into place and hugged the drone to his chest. In one smooth motion, Kyle stood and crept backward into the depth of the tunnel. He then turned and began running toward the safety of the opening between the tunnels. Without warning, he heard a blood curdling scream echo against the underground walls. The shriek ricocheted, bouncing through the tunnel chamber. Kyle's adrenaline kicked in. Like a racecar driver who had just pushed the nitrous oxide button on his engine, Kyle bolted down the tunnel at full speed and didn't stop until he was hidden inside the opening between the excavation tunnel and the natural lava tube.

*   *   *   *   *

Gibby froze. He watched the images from Kyle's chest-mounted camera. There was no audio. He saw the image of the guard sitting in front of the campfire, then a bright light, followed by Kyle's diving to the ground. Gibby stood up from his desk as Kyle's camera view smashed into the ground. As Kyle sprinted away, the image began to bounce violently up and down. Gibby watched everything unfold and remain frozen where he stood.

Things seemed to calm down. Kyle appeared to have stopped running and crouched down ducking into the alcove. Finally, the camera view from Kyle's chest-mounted camera stabilized. As Kyle caught his breath, Gibby saw the camera view rise up and down in a rhythmic motion. After Gibby was sure he was safe, he broke the silence. Alone in his empty office, he yelled, "Holy shit!"

* * * * *

Angelie had the taxi driver stop in front of the Kimchi Market. Not wanting to be stranded waiting for another taxi to arrive, before going inside she instructed the driver to wait. As she walked up to the door, she stared through the thick plate glass door. At first, she couldn't see anyone inside. Then, she noticed a white dishrag glide over the glass display case. Until she noticed the small wrinkled hand holding the rag, she thought her mind was playing tricks on her. Angelie's eyes followed the hand, tracing it back to a short old woman. She was spraying a cleaning solution onto the glass with her free hand. The old woman's eyes barely stood above the top of the display case.

Angelie looked up and down the street before pushing the heavy, commercial-grade glass door open. As the door opened inward, the top of the door swiped across the hollow metal tubes of a hanging door chime like a guitar player strumming its strings. A pleasing sound was created as the metal tubes bounced against one another. As the door closed, the chimes repeated. Alerted by the sound, the old woman glanced toward the door.

Angelie walked forward toward the counter. She saw a tiny set of eyes peering at her from the behind the glass display case. As Angelie approached, she noticed that the old woman was looking upward, staring into a large, angled mirror mounted to the ceiling. It had been installed to give this short woman a better view of people entering.

Without hesitating, Angelie walked to the counter. Just as Mr. Hong had explained, there was a large potted plant placed on top of the counter. During the flight trip to Korea and during the cab drive over, she had rehearsed her lines. Before speaking, she gave a deep, ninety-degree bow. In a clear, confident voice, Angelie pointed to the plant and said, "I have one exactly like that back in the US. It's called a Country Jasmine."

Angelie stood frozen with fear, waiting for the old woman's response. She never made direct eye contact. The woman continued staring at Angelie's reflection in the mirror. She studied Angelie's actions. After a brief pause, the old woman turned and walked into the back section of the store. Angelie wondered if she'd done something wrong. The old woman returned, carrying a plant and a gift-wrapped present. There was an envelope sealed with a large drop of melted wax that bore an embossed seal along the flap edge to protect the contents inside the envelope. Angelie's name was written on the outside. As she stared down at the envelope, she was caught in a dilemma. Her name was written in Korean Hangul script.

The old woman walked around the side of the display case. Finally, Angelie had a full view of her body and was shocked to see how thin and short she was. She couldn't have stood more than four feet six inches tall. Soaking wet, she probably weighed seventy pounds. Trying not to stare, Angelie stepped forward and took the items.

For a split second, Angelie was unsure how to proceed. She remembered her mother's advice; never admit having an in-depth knowledge of Korean Hangul. But how was she going to react, as the message was in Korean? She considered clarifying to the old woman that she didn't read Hangul. Did she really need to do anything now? In that moment, she thought back to her meeting with Mr. Hong. He gave her specific instructions. He told her not to say anything else to the old woman. He was adamant about it. He told her to take whatever she was given and to leave.

In an awkward pause, the old woman wondered why Angelie wasn't leaving. Tilting her head, the old woman began to analyze Angelie. Without saying another word, Angelie turned and left. Once outside, she walked straight to the waiting cab. After a slight struggle to balance the items in one hand, she opened the back door and climbed inside.

The cab driver turned on the interior dome light. Watching through the rearview mirror, he raised his eyebrows as if to ask Angelie for instructions. Now, she had an immediate dilemma. How was she going to handle the note? She sat motionless, running through her options. She had been warned repeatedly to speak only English. This warning had been constantly drilled into her mind, ingrained into her psyche. She had maintained the charade of possessing a limited understanding of Korean words and phrases. This lesson was so important that, to make the point, her parents administered physical beatings.

Waiting for instructions, the cab driver adjusted his rearview mirror. She raised her head and returned his stare. When their eyes met, she spoke.

"I'm sorry. The old woman has given me a note. I'm unable to read Korean. I may need your help reading it." Angelie kept her eyes focused on his. Through body language, she tried to communicate her meaning. It was essential that the cab driver believe her. This exchange was made more difficult, given that the driver apparently had only a limited understanding of English. As if by reflex, without thinking, the driver began to nod his head up and down; the universal sign for understanding. As if catching his mistake, he tried to disguise his physical faux pas and pretended to scratch his nose. It was too late. Angelie caught it. He had slipped up.

She averted her stare away from the cab driver. Looking down at the wax sealed letter, she tore it open and removed the contents. Inside, she found two separate pieces of paper. One had a street address. The other one had a person's name and room number. She handed the cab driver the first sheet of paper. He glanced at it. He turned off the interior light and began driving.

As the cab maneuvered through the surface streets, Angelie gloated. She tilted her head down so the driver couldn't see her facial expressions. She was certain that she'd outwitted him. This was her first game of cat and mouse. However, had inexperience caught up with her? Unknowingly, she had made a mistake. How was it that she knew which piece of paper to give the driver? The address was the second piece of paper. How did she plan to decipher the other message?

The longer he thought, he began to change his mind. As he continued driving, he considered the possibility that she had missed the other message. Maybe it had gotten stuck inside the envelope. He knew, once she was inside, she could ask someone to translate it for her. He was starting to believe that maybe she really didn't understand Korean.

After a brief drive, the cab driver pulled into Seoul National University Hospital. He turned on the interior dome light. When it came on, he turned and faced Angelie. He pointed his index finger to the hospital and handed back the piece of paper. Angelie raised her hand and padded the air, waving her hand downward several times. Using this sign language, she was trying to convey her desire to have him wait. While she made these gestures, she spoke in English.

"I need you to wait one more time." She feigned broken, purposely mispronounced Korean. "Chankomon" (wait). She again raised her eyebrows, attempting to communicate her intent visually.

The cab driver stared back and nodded his head replying in Korean, "Nay" (yes).

Angelie opened the door. As she exited, she balanced the plant and present in one hand. As she walked to the hospital entrance, he parked the cab at the curb and waited.

Angelie walked through the automatic doors and saw a receptionist desk ahead. She walked forward and handed the woman a piece of paper. Given the international appeal of South Korea, most of the public health and safety buildings in the major cities required that the receptionist be bilingual Korean and English. The receptionist looked up at Angelie and could tell, from her facial expressions, that the young woman had a limited understanding of Korean. Thus, she chose to lead Angelie back to the man's room rather than try to explain the route. There were two receptionists on duty. The woman holding the paper stood and replied, "Please, follow me."

Angelie followed the receptionist to an elevator. The receptionist punched the fifth-floor button and then turned and faced toward Angelie with a smile. Seeing the potted plant, she assumed that Angelie was a family member, probably visiting from America. The receptionist never asked who she was or how they were related, nor did she ask to see any identification. It was only by chance that Angelie's arrival coincided with the closing time for patient visitations. Her timing added to the apparent authenticity of the situation.

Within minutes of entering the hospital, Angelie was being led to the room. With a sincere and heartfelt smile, the receptionist opened the door. In a hushed whisper, she said, "You'll have about ten minutes before visitation time is over."

Before replying, Angelie looked back at the receptionist and bowed. "Thank you."

Angelie walked inside the room and closed the door. Lying on the bed sleeping was a middle-aged man. He had several IVs. Next to his bed, a respirator and life support monitors displayed his blood pressure, heartbeat, and pulse. The sound of the respirator forcing air into his lungs echoed through the private room. She stared at the sleeping man as he fought for his life.

There was an empty end table with a fresh circular water-spot stain on top. Angelie set the plant down on top of the stain. Then she sat in the chair next to his bed. She stared, wondering who he was, and why she was instructed to bring him the flower and present. She set the wrapped present next to the potted plant. It wasn't long before she could hear the overhead speaker announcement, first in Korean and then in English: Visiting hours were over.

Angelie stood. She glanced back at the man one last time. She walked out the door and backtracked her way to the elevator. From there, she walked back to the front hospital door. As she passed the receptionist area, another woman was there. Without stopping, Angelie continued out the automatic doors. At the curb, she saw the cab waiting. The cab driver saw her approaching and turned the interior dome light on. She opened the back door. Peering back, the driver was facing backward waiting for her next instructions.

She sat down in the back seat and slammed the door. Feigning poorly pronounced Korean, she spoke.

"Jeep (home)," followed by a more descriptive instruction spoken in perfect English. "Please take me back to the International School." The driver nodded his head and turned the interior dome light off. He put the car in drive and drove. He picked up his two-way taxi radio. Pretending to speak to the dispatcher, he reported in. He was really speaking to his DPRK handler. In code, he informed his handler that the plant and present had been delivered.

The agent receiving the message hit the enter key on his laptop computer, which activated a program. A smart phone buried deep inside the soil of the potted plant began transmitting. Unknown to any of the hospital personnel, from the hidden smart phone, a high-frequency transmission began emitting. The wireless phone began remotely reprograming the respirator and disabling the life-support monitors. Within seconds, the respirator ceased delivering oxygen to the sleeping man. It wasn't long before his vital signs began to show signs of distress. Using this hijacking program, the auditory and output signals that should have sent distress signals to the duty nurses were disabled. No warning signal of any kind was given. The program mimicked ten minutes of data transmitted prior. The commands and data transmitted in a constant unending loop, mirroring back this information to the nurses' station. When the sleeping man died, no alarms or digital announcements transmitted. Only later, when the night nurse made her rounds, was he found.

The investigators determined that the machines had malfunctioned. They failed to report the man's distress. The medical diagnosis was that the man had died of a cardiac arrest. Quietly, the hospital replaced all the equipment from the room. Nothing was ever mentioned in the man's medical notes about the equipment failure. The hospital didn't want to be involved in a potential lawsuit. The manufacturer was in total agreement. They replaced the equipment free of charge and destroyed the malfunctioning equipment. Weeks later, prompted by an outside investigation, they learned that an unknown woman saw the patient. The Korean National Intelligence Service concluded that something else probably took place. By then, it was too late.

By the time the cab approached the International School's dormitory, Angelie had already reinserted the note into the now opened envelope. She had been wearing leather gloves the entire time. Her bare hands had never touched the plant, gift-wrapped present, envelope, or notes. She was concerned about going out and had applied more makeup than usual. She had purposely distorted her facial appearance, pulling back her hair into a tight pony tail. She had also layered her clothes to give the impression she weighed more than she did. She had also worn nonprescription glasses.

As the cab pulled up to the front door, Angelie looked up at the meter. She opened her purse and struggled to retrieve the paper Korean Won currency note with her gloved fingers. When she handed the driver the bills over the back seat, she purposely dropped the envelope onto the floor of the back seat. She didn't want to risk having it in her possession.

After paying the driver, she stepped out of the cab. Before pulling away from the curb, the driver watched the young woman climb the stairs. As he made his way back toward his handler's house, he wondered whether she really couldn't understand Korean. Regardless, after tonight, the DPRK knew one thing for sure about

Angelie. This young woman was the real deal. She had proven her loyalty. She had demonstrated her ability to follow orders and remain calm in a very stressful, unrehearsed situation. Unknown to Angelie, she had played a major role in the assassination of a powerful South Korean politician. The DPRK wanted to make sure he never recovered.

Angelie had passed her first test. Her handlers were excited to have another covert operative who could roam freely inside South Korea. Better yet, she could travel anywhere in the world. She was an asset indeed. The handlers had no idea that their newest covert asset had already been video-recorded by a US Agent. In their rush to test and secure another covert operative, the DPRK had thrown her into an operation without giving her the opportunity to gain valuable experience. They had assumed that even if their target's death had come under suspicion, given that she had only recently been placed into play, her identity would still be a secret. They assumed that no one knew she existed. As far as anyone knew, it was just another American working abroad. They had no reason to believe that the US or the Republic of Korea would already have her information.

But life rarely played fair. Sometimes, things went against all the odds. In the Agency world, there were no such things as coincidences. What happened to Angelie was just one of those things—an unlucky break. She had made her second mistake. In this line of work, rarely could a covert operative survive such bad luck. Time would determine whether she was one of the survivors.

21

Tae stared out across the field. Over the last few weeks, there had been snow flurries only; it never snowed long enough to blanket the land, and only a few white patches dotted the landscape. He knew this would be his last trip until spring.

He had a ritual. Before leaving, he gave each person in his family a hug. For Koreans, outward signs of affection were uncommon; hugs were saved and extended only to loved ones. To Koreans, westerners appeared to hand out hugs like handshakes, giving them freely to practical strangers, as if hugs held no deep meaning. To Koreans, hugs were rare, intimate signs of affection that were rarely exchanged, even between family members. Each time Tae left, everyone understood his risk. If he were discovered by anyone, from either side of the DMZ, he could suffer great harm and probably death.

With his backpack filled with enough provisions for his journey south, Tae stepped off his porch. As he walked, he began thinking about the day he received a box. Those memories always brought a smile to his face. With a deep sigh, Tae stepped into the field near his home and began his long walk. The sun was still hidden below the horizon, but technically it was morning. His goal was to be deep inside the tunnel before the sun rose.

*   *   *   *   *

Lt. Benjamin had waited hidden inside the opening between the excavated tunnel and the natural lava tube. He had activated all the communication relay devices in the southernmost section of the tunnel. The night-vision cameras were installed and tested. Everything was working. It was time to get out of there. He gathered his equipment and then stowed the drone inside its carrying case and slid it into his backpack.

Kyle was about to crawl through the tight opening when he heard something inside the large cathedral opening. He'd grown accustomed to his night-vision goggles. They felt natural, almost like wearing prescription glasses except heavier. He craned his neck, allowing the goggles to clear the crest of the opening. He saw a man drying his feet. He must have just taken them out of the pond. Kyle watched the man put on his socks and shoes. The man glanced up and down the tunnel, in both directions, before standing. He seemed to be staring back, looking directly into the opening.

Kyle felt self-conscious, wondering if the man could see him. The man stood still several minutes, as if waiting to make sure everything was clear. As he waited, Kyle's pulse rose. What was he waiting for? To Kyle's relief, the man finally began walking and then, for some reason, ran by the opening. Kyle felt the air disturbance as the man rushed by. Kyle got the impression that the man knew the opening existed. Startled, Kyle froze in his crouched, kneeling position. He scanned the area. He wanted to make sure that no one else was following.

Without warning, several clumps of earth fell from above. He could hear the pebbles tumble down. Several small pieces landed on his head and settled in his hair. Straining to keep his composure, Kyle fought the urge to move and kept as still as possible. Frozen in an awkward position, he urged his calf and thigh muscles to cooperate as they began to tighten, on the verge of cramping.

After several minutes, sensing the coast was clear, Kyle typed a message to Gibby. "We have a walker heading your way."

*   *   *   *   *

When the message came through, Gibby was away from his computer desk, refilling his cup of coffee. He needed the caffeine to keep alert. It had been awhile since he'd pulled an all-nighter. The high-pitched electronic tone caught his attention. Gibby slid his sock covered feet across the floor and shuffled back to his desk. He read Kyle's message. He fought the urge to yawn and tried to kick-start his brain. He hadn't expected this. He was anxious to get a look at the walker. Gibby rebooted the program to display the cameras along the natural lava tube. Once they all came up live, he sent Kyle a message.

"Cameras are active. Don't get too close to the walker. I'll shut them down after he passes each camera. Double check your monitor before proceeding."

Kyle studied the controller's monitor and watched each camera come to life. All the cameras were now running. Knowing the location of each camera, he was comfortable following the walker. He slid out, squeezing through the opening. Before proceeding, Kyle glanced up and down and cautiously proceeded down the worn path. The last thing he wanted to do was get too close to the walker.

*   *   *   *   *

It took two hours for the walker to exit the tunnel. From his satellite camera above, Gibby watched the walker and was surprised when he took a sharp turn, following the ridgeline. It was obvious that the walker knew where he was going. He rarely used his flashlight. It almost looked like the walker could see in the dark. Amazing.

Gibby instructed Kyle to head back to camp and get some sleep. Gibby continued to monitor the walker from the satellite. Gibby instructed Carla Jo to anticipate where the walker was headed. She waited just on the outskirts of town. Gibby watched the walker sit on the bank of a drainage canal. It looked as if the man was staring at a building across a busy street. Gibby dispatched Carla Jo to that location. For the next twenty minutes, she watched him from afar. Having already taken dozens of pictures, she stowed her high-powered telephoto-lens camera away.

"So, what's he doing now?" asked Gibby over his encrypted secure Agency issued cell phone.

"Same thing. He's just sitting there waiting," replied Carla Jo.

Tae was waiting for his brother to open the drapes. He was grateful to see movement behind the window. Tae watched the curtains slide back. He felt a surge of energy pulse through his body. Following his routine, Tae stood and started walking away from his brother's house. After walking several blocks, he doubled back.

Carla Jo was sitting in the correct angle. Her attention was drawn away from the stationary, seated man and drawn toward the downstairs apartment. She couldn't miss the moving curtain as it opened. At that very moment, the man stood up and walked away. Her instincts were sharp. Before Tae meandered around, she had a good idea where he was heading.

"Gibby, the walker is on the move. I think he just got a signal. My money is on him ending up in front of the house that just opened its curtains." Carla Jo waited for Tae to cross the street before she started. "Leaving my car now. I'll follow the walker. Out," Carl Jo said into her cell phone.

She stayed back and kept the walker in her view. She was right. He wandered back several blocks then crossed the street. She could probably have stayed inside her car. She learned, years ago, nothing was taken for granted. Nothing should be assumed. She watched the walker double back. Quickly, she walked back to her car and hid inside.

As she predicted, the walker ended up back in front of the downstairs apartment. As the door opened, Carla Jo was ready. Before the door closed, she shot several close-up photos of the man who opened the door. She removed the camera's flash drive and inserted it into her laptop. In seconds, she sent Gibby encrypted images.

Wasting no time, Gibby downloaded the images and opened an Agency file on both men. He began cross-checking the apartment address with known DPRK agents. He then ran their images through a facial-recognition program. Within minutes, he had the apartment owner's name, date of birth, and his Republic of Korea driver license information. Within another five minutes, Tae's brother's file began growing. His financial records, voting records, and an asset search had been completed. Gibby began using one of Korea's most popular social media platforms, *Kakao*, to download more personal information.

Gibby's interest piqued as he uncovered another address. The property's title included the name of a female, presumably, the man's wife. Gibby placed several calls and retained the services of a local asset, a

Korean National with whom Gibby had worked on several prior occasions. In no time, Gibby received a text from the local asset, confirming that he was rolling to the other address. Gibby instructed the asset to tap the telephone and computer lines. He wanted eyes-on-target data, with photos of the house, inside and out. Gibby wanted to get up to speed on this new player.

For a career covert operative, Gibby felt blindsided. One of the most stressful times for agents is when they realize they have a blind spot. A successful career in this underworld required one to be obsessed with knowing all of the information. Access to all the facts usually resulted in well-informed decisions. Good decisions resulted in successful outcomes. This unknown player could change the game, and it was within Gibby's authority to make a snap decision.

His morning was taking on a different shape. Gibby's comfy king-sized bed with its goose-down comforter would have to wait. As Kyle crawled into his bed back on Camp Bonifas, Gibby was working his local asset and Carla Jo. Unaware of all the action behind the scenes, Tae and his brother relaxed, finishing up their meal.

*   *   *   *   *

The supervisor was adjusting to a new schedule. His most recent project was coming to an end. After the drainage, air filtration, and road compaction were completed, his regular crew would return to finish the last section, piercing the tunnel through the other side to create an opening into the southern section. During this schedule change, the supervisor began spending more time with his wife.

He learned that once every few weeks his wife traveled to the capital to meet her friend for lunch. Her friend worked at the public transportation department building downtown. It had become a special day, one she looked forward to. Her friend had recommended a great little restaurant, located on the first floor of the same building where she worked. Its location made it easier for her friend to get to. The public transportation building was a short walk from the train station. Its proximity to the train station also made it easy for his wife.

His wife grew accustomed to making the trip herself. Now, that her husband had spare time, she was hoping that he would come along.

"Chagia (honey), did you want to go with me to Pyongyang to meet my friend for lunch?"

He wanted to be supportive but honestly had no interest in sitting through a meal listening to the conversation between his wife and her friend. On the other hand, he knew that traveling back and forth would be better if he were there. He looked up into her eyes. He could tell she wanted him to come. She didn't want to appear too pushy. Either way, she would be fine. Without speaking a word, just by looking at each other, and conveying subtle gestures, their expressions told volumes. It was amazing how so much information could be exchanged without a single word's having been spoken. With one look, he knew she really wanted him to go. He blinked his eyes and nodded his head.

"Of course, it would be nice to see your friend. It's been a while." It was a little white lie. For a Korean, this act of kindness was remarkable. In the Korean culture, direct honest responses, especially between family members, was the norm. In most cases, the response would have been brutally honest without regard to the other person's feelings. He appreciated the fact that his job required him to be away for long periods. He thought it was the least he could do.

His wife was happy. She flashed a bright smile in return. "If you could wear your gray suit, I'll be wearing my white dress," she said over her shoulder as she turned and walked into their bedroom. "We have to catch the eleven o'clock train. We have an hour."

22

The night guard was still shaken. He couldn't stop thinking about what had taken place in the tunnel the previous night. Not only was he haunted by some unknown flying animal, but also he thought he saw what looked like a defector. He knew he should have told somebody. He was too surprised by everything. It happened all at once and he'd panicked. He was overwhelmed.

All day, he'd relived the events. His complacency had taken its toll on his psyche. He was no longer sharp. He blamed it on the constant boredom of this job. Everything became a routine. While waiting for the first compaction truck to arrive, he always stood in front of the opening, staring into the natural lava tube area. He was curious what lay beyond the walls. It helped him pass the time. He would point his flashlight beam into the opening, awestruck by the interior. The tranquil pool of water and the unique beauty of the underground sanctuary was calming. The unusual and exotic geological formations were mesmerizing. Last night, though, was something altogether different.

The night guard had approached the opening between the excavated tunnel and the natural lava tube. He was about to turn on his flashlight but was startled when something passed by the opening. He had flinched, pulling his arms back away from the opening. The flashlight touched the side of the hole. The impact caused pieces of soil to crumble off and tumble down. Without thinking, he automatically tilted his head to one side, directing his dominant ear toward the noise. Concentrating on his hearing, he listened to every sound coming from the other side. He was certain he heard feet slapping against the ground. The noise continued to echo in the adjacent lava tube cavity in a rhythmic repetition. There was no doubt in his mind: A person was running by on the other side.

The night guard's nerves were shot. He couldn't take any more. Sleeping alone in the suffocating darkness; the unexpected sounds; seeing some unknown flying creature; and now, a defector running through the adjacent lava tube. It was all just too much. The night guard turned and ran away in the direction where the compaction trucks would arrive.

It was a close call, like two ships passing in the night. The DPRK guard and Lt. Kyle Benjamin had been sharing the same space; they stood only inches away from each other without realizing it. Kyle had been in a crouched, kneeling position, peering over the bottom of the opening, while the night guard stood looking through the top section. This distraction, the sudden appearance of the running man, prevented them from noticing the presence of the other.

Lost in thought, the night guard stared back at his reflection in his bathroom mirror. He still felt guilty for not doing something, anything to stop the defector. He was disappointed in himself. He was hired to deal with this exact kind of event. It was his only purpose for being stationed in that precise location. His primary responsibility was to report exactly this type of thing.

He searched his mind, trying to come up with a viable excuse. He told himself that the problem was the limited training he received. He mentally rationalized that the succession of unexpected events was the cause of his inaction. He did not want to admit to himself that he froze from fear. From the safety of his room, no longer trapped underground, his mind was clearer. He could now accept the self-criticism for his inaction. After reliving that evening's events, replaying it over and over in his mind, he promised to redeem himself. He was committed to detain any future defectors he discovered, no matter what.

If he went to his superiors and told them what had transpired, he would not only open himself up to severe criticism but be reassigned and reprimanded for his ineptitude. Through his self-reflection, he was re-energized. He was a man on a mission, intent on redemption.

*   *   *   *   *

Kyle awoke from a deep sleep. The physical and emotional stress of the night before had drained his energy. He'd barely gotten his clothes off and had to muster all his resources to take a shower before diving into bed. Rubbing the crusty sleep out of his eyes, he saw an envelope that must have been slid under his door. Struggling out of his bed, Kyle shuffled across the floor, bent down and picked up the envelope. Tearing it open, he found another handwritten note. Kyle recognized the handwriting. It was from Gibby. The note instructed him to go to the BBQ Shack at 5:00 p.m.

*   *   *   *   *

The supervisor enjoyed the train ride with his wife. Traveling in a full-sized train in the open air was a nice change of pace. It took him time to adjust to the speed and loud noises. As the train approached the city, he noticed a gradual descent underground where the train connected with the capital subway system. A passenger manually opened the wooden sliding doors. The supervisor and his wife walked out onto the platform. Looking up, they stared at the steep incline of the escalator. This stop was familiar. It was the same one he'd taken with the military attaché. This time, he held his wife's hand, and helped her keep balance stepping off the escalator. In unison, they had jumped off the last escalator. Upon landing, they exchanged broad smiles.

He followed his wife. She knew the way and led them to the restaurant. Everything looked familiar. When they reached the building, he jogged ahead and opened the heavy door. As they crossed the lobby, they exchanged respectful smiles, admiring the mural of The Great Leader. After a brief pause, they continued walking across the lobby with its impressive mosaic tile floor. As she pointed to the restaurant door, she quickened her pace.

In her excitement to see her friend, she opened the door herself. She pushed it open and began searching for her friend. Remembering that her husband was following, she stopped, turned and waved him inside. As he entered, he saw her friend waving in their direction.

They walked to the table and exchanged bows before his wife made formal introductions. As the women sat, he watched her friend move a purse to an empty chair. His wife never saw the reaction on her husband's face. If she had, she would have immediately recognized something was wrong. When he saw the purse, it was like seeing a ghost. It was the last thing he'd expected. It took all his energy and concentration to remain calm. As casually as he could, he spoke.

"That's a very nice purse. Where did you get it?"

At first, his wife's friend's face lit up with excitement. She was happy that someone had noticed her purse. Receiving the compliment felt good. In an instant, her excitement faded. Her smile evaporated. Instinctively, she grabbed the purse. Without thinking, she picked it up and placed it under the table. He continued smiling as he watched. He tried to tame his extreme curiosity and interest.

"Thank you. It was a present," she replied flashing a forced insincere smile. His wife was unaware of the drama that was playing out before her eyes. She didn't notice her friend reach down and pull the purse close to her legs as if she were trying to hide it.

"It's so beautiful," interjected his wife. Her husband was thinking of what to say next. He wanted to pry more information about that purse. There was no doubt in his mind where he'd seen it before.

"I agree. It's unusual. What are those markings on the outside?" he asked his wife's friend.

The friend seemed to shrink back into her chair. As she contemplated her response, she began to mentally chastise herself for not listening to her husband. He had warned her about taking the purse out into public. It was obviously not made in the DPRK. He had reminded her that they didn't need to attract any unwanted attention.

She couldn't help herself. The purse was one of her most prized possessions. It was only human nature that she would want to show it off. She had justified her actions by bringing the purse out only during these lunch meetings with her friend, the only occasions she had to use it. As she thought about how she would respond, a sinking sense of dread began to dominate her mind. The attention she was receiving was more than she had bargained for. At that moment, she remembered that her friend's husband worked with the military. Her internal anxiety multiplied as that fact hit home. It was as if someone had just punched her in the stomach. But now, with her friend's husband so interested in it, she wished she'd never received the gift. She continued to chastise herself as she thought of what to say.

The supervisor watched her squirm in her chair. Her body language said it all. He had seen it all before. On occasion, he'd caught a crew member lying. Each time, they would avoid eye contact. Their shoulders would slump forward and their voices dropped in volume, almost to a whisper. Her posture removed any doubt he felt about the purse. He was certain it was the same one he'd seen in the underground natural lava tube. At the very least, she knew something about the black marketer.

* * * * *

Gibby knew what needed to be done. Things had changed. He was now faced with an evolving complication. How was he going to handle a North Korean? Was he receiving assistance from a South Korean? His myopic laser focus told him that the primary mission was to destroy the tunnel. With that being the goal, the answer seemed simple. He could eliminate these unexpected players. Although this type of narrow-minded thinking was justifiable, his years of experience demanded a more detailed analysis.

Other factors needed to be considered. Eliminating these men could create a ripple effect, complicating circumstances even more; who was the walker? Who was his handler? Was either man a part of the DPRK's plans? Was he entering the Republic of Korea to develop invasion plans? Which side was he working for? Could he be a double agent for the south?

Gibby had watched the satellite surveillance tape several times. He'd studied the still photos that Carla Jo had forwarded. The men looked similar. They had common facial features. Gibby was contemplating the possibility that the men were relatives who had been separated by the DMZ. Gibby also noticed that the walker did not appear to be carrying any weapons, nor was he using any high-tech devices. It almost seemed like these men were simply smugglers. It was difficult to ascertain exactly what they were doing; There were too many unknowns.

This would not be his call. Gibby contacted Director Valdez, and a meeting was scheduled. Gibby turned away from his computer screen and let out a deep sigh. He probably wouldn't get much sleep tonight.

*   *   *   *   *

Angelie had made it to the school without incident. She had been introduced to all the other teachers and administrators. There weren't many; with only fifty total students, the faculty consisted of five teachers, the headmaster, and the groundskeeper. No janitor was needed, as the children all took turns cleaning the floors, wiping the chalkboard, and cleaning the restrooms. Angelie would rotate between each class, spending one hour each day with each class. The teachers were all bilingual and could speak conversational English.

All her meals were included as part of her compensation package. During the week, breakfast and lunch were served at the school cafeteria. For living quarters, she was assigned a small house within walking distance of the school. It was the first time Angelie had seen a house with heated flooring. There was a hollow space under the wooden floor in which hot coals were placed on top of a stone-lined trough. The stones radiated heat upward, warming the flooring above.

The house had a small sleeping room, where, like other Koreans, she would sleep on the floor with thick blankets and pillows; an indoor bathroom with hot and cold running water; a small kitchen; and a living room. It was simple, cozy, and clean and provided a tranquil, relaxing atmosphere. Angelie looked out the back window over a field that continued to the horizon. The ground rose into the foothills. Patches of evergreen trees dotted the landscape. At higher elevations, the trees became more dense, And larger, more mature trees dominated the upper section of the slope. This section of the DMZ was off limits. The forest hadn't been touched for decades. No roads or structures of any kind existed. As Angelie admired the beauty, she imagined what lay over the ridgeline. She was so close to her true homeland, the Democratic People's Republic of Korea.

Angelie paused and then began thinking about her parents. She remembered the way they described their homeland. Although she had spent the first years of her life there, she had no clear memories of it, so she used her imagination to create her own version of North Korea. It was surreal. After all these years, she'd finally returned. Staring through the back window, she realized she was close to the border. If she wanted to, she could walk there in less than an hour.

She finished the dishes. She planned to go to sleep early, as she wanted to be rested for her first day as an English Teacher. Daeseong-Dong was the northernmost village in South Korea, and the only civilian-occupied area inside the DMZ. A mandatory curfew required everyone to be inside between 11:00 p.m. and 6:00 a.m. A designated security detail was available to escort people in and out of the village. In the past, the DPRK had sent invasion forces to pilfer, and on occasion villagers were killed.

23

Director Valdez had a meeting scheduled at an Agency owned and operated restaurant in downtown Seoul. She reserved a curtained-off booth in the back. The entire place was secure. Every booth had hidden cameras, but nothing was ever recorded. Each adjacent booth was occupied by one of her security detail guards watching over them. Every outside interaction involving the Director had risks. Her security team was always involved in the detailed planning, and this was no exception. As Gibby entered the restaurant, one of the Director's guards stood and waved him over. He was frisked and then escorted to the secure curtained booth.

Gibby glanced out the front plate glass window. He could tell it was bulletproof. It looked like the same setup he had at the BBQ Shack. However, this place had much more expensive fixtures and an expansive menu with appreciably higher prices. As Gibby ducked into the curtained booth, he was pleased to see Carla Jo and his local asset, Mr. Kim, already inside. The Director was casually dressed and could almost pass for a local.

"Evening, Director."

"Nice to see you, Mr. Gibson. I've had the liberty to speak to Carla Jo and Mr. Kim before you arrived. I'm up to speed on the walker and his contact at the apartment."

Without wasting time, the Director continued. "We've already ordered, so the food's on its way. Don't worry, your favorites are included. So, what have you got in mind about this new development?"

Gibby wasn't surprised. He'd worked with Director Valdez before. He knew she would be all business. Barely having had the chance to sit down, Gibby made sure to make direct eye contact with Carla Jo and Mr. Kim, and they exchanged quick head nods. Other than the Director and her security detail, everyone else, even the restaurant owners, worked for the Agency as independent-contractor professionals. Gibby had been thinking long and hard. He was the most senior independent contractor agent involved, which translated into his bearing the brunt of the blame if things went wrong. Although Kyle was the most expendable participant, Gibby figured that Carla Jo, Mr. Kim, and then he himself would be the next pawns to be sacrificed, and in that order. It was no surprise. It came with the territory. Their expendability was the reason they were paid so well.

"I've been thinking about this all day. The walker and his handler present too many variables. At this moment, I'm against any snap decisions. If either of them comes up missing before we take care of business, there is a high likelihood they'll be missed. And that would result in a potential search and rescue. The last thing we need are more bodies crawling through either of the areas.

"We've laid the COM lines. They've been tested and confirmed ready and operational. I don't want those devices to become accidentally damaged, misaligned, or, worse yet, discovered. If one device goes down, we could lose communications beyond that point. The technology is topnotch, but it's about physics. It's pretty dark down there; not much room for error. I'm concerned about them getting bumped out of sequence."

Before continuing, Gibby paused and surveyed the group. "Mr. Kim, what's the walker's handler's other location like? Have you been inside yet?"

"Yes. I got inside. The wife went to pick up the kids from school. They have two. Both attend a private academy. The boy is ten and the girl is twelve. I'm working on their school records and birth certificates. Wife stays at home. They attend a Christian church, they're Quakers. I've got surveillance in all rooms, even the bathrooms. Our cameras are rolling twenty-four/seven. My team will let me know if anything suspicious is going on. So far, looks pretty normal." Mr. Kim paused to see if anyone wanted more detail. He got his answer right away.

"Your thoughts, Mr. Kim?" asked the Director. "You've been doing this a long time. What does your gut tell you about them?"

Mr. Kim blinked his eyes in deep concentration. He'd had his targets under surveillance for less than four hours; not much time to make any real assessment. But because of the importance of this mission and the time sensitivity of matters, he accompanied the team and surveyed the location firsthand. Mr. Kim wanted to extract as much information as possible. There was no substitute for having boots on the ground and walking the scene.

"It's very early to make a full assessment. But from what I've learned so far about this guy, I think he's unaffiliated. There's nothing high tech about him. His life is out in the open, nothing suspicious. All his time seems to be accounted for. My gut says these guys are not professional. I'm guessing that they're probably just smugglers selling goods on the black market in North Korea.

"What's his occupation?" Carla Jo interjected.

"He's an insurance guy. A claims handler. My team has already hacked the guy's office. We've copied all internal security cameras for the last two months. Another team is hating life right now; they're fast-forwarding all that tape. Three hundred twenty hours for the last eight weeks. So far, the guy just comes in, does his job, takes a lunch, a few bathroom breaks throughout the day, and then goes home. We've synced up his time from the office to his home, and it looks like he goes straight home. The only anomaly is, once a month, he meets the walker at the apartment."

"Do they have any pattern as to when they meet? Same day of the month, what?" the Director asked.

"We've only got two accounts so far, but it appears to be based on the new moon. It makes sense, that would be the darkest night of the month. We've been looking at his computer too. Home and work. Nothing. No weird emails or vices. This guy looks pretty straight-laced, but you never know. It's always the small things that get people caught. We're on him; soon we'll know whether he's clean or not."

After a brief pause, Director Valdez turned her attention back to Gibby. "So, Mr. Gibson. What's your recommendation?"

"We've laid the groundwork. All we need is time to get Kyle back down there with the packages. My engineers are using the cameras to sync everything up. Kyle will just need to drop the packages at those camera locations, haul ass, and then we coordinate with the UAV (Unmanned Aerial Vehicle). Moon Dog hits the GPS location, and we're out of there. Easy, peasy.

Gibby continued. "I don't think there is any reason to vet the walker and his handler. We can do that later. My gut says we should proceed now, while all the pieces are in place. From our perspective, there has not been any breach. We're out of sight and under the radar. You say go, and we proceed as planned. We could make it happen within twenty-four hours." Gibby finished speaking and surveyed the room.

Everyone present had participated in countless prior missions, but this was different. It was the most important mission of their careers, and nothing prior compared. It would also be the Agency's first time to technically be invading the Democratic People's Republic of Korea. The final decision would be made by the Director.

Unlike the other members at the table, she had the benefit of the past forty-five days to have enlisted the enormous resources available through the Agency's network of consultants, historians, and tacticians. Her key players, Lt. Elliott and X.O. Newland, had been working the numbers and getting the necessary bureaucratic paperwork needed to proceed to the next phase of the game. To reach an unofficial collective decision, a subtle song and dance would need to take place.

She had her best people in place. It was time to take it up the ladder. This kind of decision had to be made face to face. She would meet with the National Director of the Agency, who in turn would meet with the National Security Advisor to POTUS (President of the United States). At no time would she have a direct one-on-one with POTUS; he was off limits, because he needed to have plausible deniability. By listening to the briefing of his advisors, they could pose a scenario in the "hypothetical," suggesting, for example, a training exercise. On the other hand, should POTUS and his advisors have reservations, they would put an immediate stop to the plan, hypothetical or otherwise. It was the Agency's job to provide options and the intelligence to make an informed decision. Although the decision would be made by these few, the accountability and consequences would fall to others.

After the facts were laid out, if the "powers that be" were in agreement, no alternative suggestions would be offered. Their silence would indicate that the plan was being approved. A face-to-face meeting required the director of that region to be back in the States, far away from the action. Putting as many miles between the Director and ground zero was part of the charade.

Director Valdez knew the drill. This was not her first dance. Only so many fall guys were available before the trail of crumbs led back up the food chain. With her position, she would be the last available player on the board. If the mission fell apart, she would be the last person to be thrown under the bus. If the plan failed, everyone knew the next order of business was damage control. Reputations would be laid to waste and creative narratives would be prepared, just in case things didn't turn out as expected.

In this line of work, it was never personal. It was always just part of the business of isolating and protecting their superiors. To be honored with the privilege and opportunity to sacrifice their careers, freedoms, and even their lives was part of a common goal. The ultimate sacrifice wasn't something that only battlefield combatants made. Many fighting soldiers in the field had no concept of the types of dangers that high-ranking superiors faced.

High-level bureaucrats and paper pushers—not the high-profile players whose names were well known by the public, but those influential, respected, and highly promoted superiors—could be the ones selected and held ultimately accountable. These faceless superiors would be asked to make the ultimate sacrifice. Their demise would not be quick and painless, nor would it take place on a glorious battlefield in some romantic faraway land while defending fellow soldiers during battle.

These select few brave men and women would accept their fate and take all their secrets with them. They would give preplanned narratives to the media, and the media would destroy their lives, reputations, and careers. Only the insiders would know the truth. Such loyalty and sacrifice would not go unnoticed. The elite knew the truth; yet, even with this knowledge, they were unable to throw their heroes a lifeline. Everyone had to watch them struggle to survive on their own.

Within this fraternity, the heroes never held any ill will toward their superiors. It was part of the rules of the real game. The sacrifice. An unspoken understandings between the players defined in this brotherhood.

Director Valdez glanced around the table. From inside the curtained-off booth, her eyes pierced through the darkness. She nodded her head in personal acknowledgment and appreciation for all their efforts.

"It's settled then. I'm heading to present the plan and get the approval. My guys have been working with Mr. Kim's team. We'll have the most efficient packages that Mr. Benjamin can manage alone." The Director stood. She toggled a button on her communication device attached to her belt loop. It signaled her security team, informing them that the meeting was about to conclude. Gibby stood and leaned forward, whispering to the Director. He made sure that the others couldn't hear.

"Ma'am, if you need face-time in DC, it will take you more than twenty-four hours to get there."

With a whimsical smile, Director Valdez replied in an upbeat, sarcastic yet playful manner. "Gibby, you've flown the triple connection before, haven't you?"

Gibby had never heard of such a route. Perplexed, he replied, "Sorry, no ma'am; I've never heard of it. What is it?"

"It's an F-15K Slam Eagle out of Osan Air Base to Kadena AFB in Japan. We switch jets there with the 36th Fighter Squadron on a two-seat trainer F-16 Eagle. Then off to Honolulu." Staring into Gibby's face, she enjoyed his disbelief. From his reaction on her Airwolf helicopter, she assumed he would appreciate the story. After a brief pause, she continued. "I know you're thinking that only gets me halfway, right?" She raised her eyebrows to confirm Gibby's suspicions.

Caught off guard, Gibby replied. "Yeah, exactly. Are you going to continue in the F-16 from there and do aerial refuels the rest of the way?"

She couldn't help but smile. She watched Gibby's facial expression revert to that of a young boy who just learned that his friend gets to ride the grown-up amusement-park ride without him. With a quick cadence, the Director explained. "No Gibby. We switch planes again. You have any idea which one this time?" she asked in a friendly, inquisitive manner.

"No, ma'am. Not at all. Which one?"

The Director smiled and started to walk away pretending to leave him in suspense. His face sank. He thought she was going to leave without telling him. When she reached the curtain, she stopped and turned back. She leaned forward to whisper in his ear. Carla Jo and Mr. Kim hadn't been paying attention. Even if they had, they wouldn't have cared. The Director knew Gibby's background and was certain he'd be jealous.

"We switch to an Agency modified British Airways Concorde jet for a straight shot to DC. No bags to check. Just a quick stop and go," she smiled.

"No shit. A Concorde huh?"

"Yup."

"Damn. Those things go Mach 2; about thirteen hundred miles per hour. You could get from Honolulu to DC in less than four hours," Gibby replied. He was amazed.

"Three hours and forty-five minutes," the Director corrected.

Gibby was shocked. If *green with envy* had been a single illustrated word found in the dictionary, it would have displayed Gibby's picture next to the definition. Before she ducked out of the curtained area, the Director couldn't help herself. She laughed and slapped his back.

Before the others exited the booth, the Director was surrounded by her security team. They marched her toward the exit. Outside, three black GMC Suburban sedans pulled up to the curb and stopped in front of the restaurant. The Director paused, allowing the guards time to form a protective circle; two guards on each side. In unison, like five people performing a well-choreographed maneuver, they crossed the sidewalk and slid into one of the armor-plated, bulletproof sedans. With ease, they slid into the center vehicle and surrounded the Director on all sides. The door closed, and in seconds the caravan speed away. Darting through the surface streets, they had several cars ahead to manage the traffic flow, making sure she had a fast, clear return to the safety of Camp Bonifas.

Gibby, Carla Jo, and Mr. Kim stood in the lobby of the deserted restaurant. Staring out the plate glass windows, they watched the caravan disappear into the night. Gibby finally broke the silence.

"I'm still hungry. We never got to eat."

"I think she was just kidding about dinner. They never even brought any food," Carla Jo replied.

"Do you want to stay and eat?" asked Mr. Kim.

"Are you kidding? I can't afford the food here. Let's go somewhere else," Gibby replied. As they were about to leave, a waiter scurried over.

"Excuse me. Your food is ready." They paused, unsure what to do. "It's already been paid for," said the waiter.

Gibby smiled. In a slow southern accent, in his best Matthew McConoughey impression, he said, "All right!"

24

"Moon Dog, did you read the encrypted message from the Director?" asked X.O. Newland.

"Yeah. Just read it. This is some crazy shit we're about to embark on, X.O."

"You got that right. She just met with the National Director. After her briefing, it was, well, not green-lighted, per se, but not rejected either. So for our purposes, it's a go."

"X.O.? Have our guys put their heads together on the schematic and package placements?"

"I've got it all right here," replied the X.O as he waved the folder. There will be a total of ten packages. They're lightweight, preprogrammed, and stable, just in case Kyle trips in the dark. We'll have his remote control configured within the hour. I want you to meet the techs and make sure you know how they work, inside and out. I need you to show Kyle how it works before he goes out tonight."

"That's weird," replied Moon Dog. "I thought we were supposed to keep away from Lt. Benjamin, you know, just in case."

"This part is too important. The techs don't have the clearance to be directly involved with the covert agents. You're good with that stuff, anyway," joked the X.O. "You need to go over it with him. Make one-hundred-percent sure he knows how to set them off. Once we activate the communication networks, if for any reason the detonation gets delayed, we'll only be able to delay the explosions for ninety-six hours."

"What's with the ninety-six-hour timeline again, X.O.?"

"We're using the communication relays to pump all of our data through the tunnels. To make sure we destroy them and the cameras, the program will trigger a max-delay self-destruct. Once any bomb goes off, it will override the delay settings and self-destruct. The cameras are located next to the communication relays, which maximizes the power and produces the clearest image. The proximity to the relays will assure us that all the equipment is destroyed. The last thing we want is for any of this technology to be found. If they're discovered, it would certainly lead them back to us."

As the X.O. finished speaking, Lt. Elliott continued staring at the X.O. with raised eyebrows. "And the ninety-six-hours?"

"Oh, yeah, right. If we must delay setting off the packages, we only have ninety-six hours. The spherical relays' self-destruction program cannot be shut off. Once they're activated, there's no turning back. No matter what, those devices will all blow up simultaneously, like a string of firecrackers. Once one goes, they'll all go. What about the UAV? Is it ready?"

"Yes, sir!" smiled Moon Dog. In preparation for the mission, he'd spent a lot of hours practicing flying the UAV. And ever since the mission had begun, he'd been practicing nonstop. Like Kyle, Moon Dog had been practicing for the last month. The biggest difference was that Moon Dog's drone was the biggest of its kind. It could be dressed out to look like any of several types of aircraft. For this mission, it was modified to look like Boeing KC-135 refueling Stratotanker.

The UAV had several challenges. One of the biggest concerns was making sure it carried enough real parts belonging to a refueling tanker. The Agency wanted to make sure the debris was consistent with what one would expect to find in such a crash. As such, two of the four turbofan engines and the special refueling booms would be placed on board the UAV. Much thought had been put into the deception, because the crash debris would need to convince investigators. The KC-135 tanker jet fuel capacity was eighty-three-thousand pounds of fuel. Upon impact, this quantity of fuel had an explosive force equivalent to several thousand-pound bombs.

Using a refueling tanker was a perfect disguise. A squadron of KC-135s supported the Pacific Force's 51st Fighter Wing and the ROK (Republic of Korea) Air Force located at Osan Air Base. To complete the charade, the Agency arranged to move the oldest KC-135 refueling tanker back stateside. First, the selected KC-135 would be sent to Vandenberg Air Force Base. There, its serial numbers would be swapped out. The tanker would then be flown to Fairchild AFB near Spokane, Washington, to join the 92nd Air Refueling wing, where it would be refitted to look like an EC-135 Looking Glass. Finally, it would be moved south to be mothballed at the Davis-Monthan AFB near Tucson, Arizona. That location had earned the nickname as the airplane graveyard. The refitted plane would then be prepped to withstand exposure to extreme desert temperatures and sand.

"We do have a technical problem, though, in terms of the credibility of this scenario. I'm afraid that, even with all of the efforts, it still will not stand up to strict scrutiny," explained Moon Dog. "The lack of large amounts of jet fuel at the crash site is a dead giveaway. Soil samples and the amount of burning would be easy to ascertain."

"Good catch!" said the X.O. "The analysis guys pointed the same thing out too. Last night, they offered their solution. It's ingenious, really. Just before you crash the UAV, we have another modified KC-135 refueling tanker designed with special outer skin and translucent emission systems. These changes will allow it to maintain a stealth profile and avoid detection by the DPRK radar systems. This tanker is also being modified to expel its fuel much faster through enlarged and modified openings through the emergency fuel dump. They've redirected the fuel pumps to force the fuel through a modified fuel-dump system, as opposed to the regular fuel transfer through the boom. The modified KC-135 could dump its entire load over the area. When you drive the UAV into the ground, the onboard explosion will ignite the jet-fuel–soaked ground."

The X.O. and Lt. Elliott thought about the mission. Everything was in place. Once Kyle was trained on the controller for the packages, the only thing left was for Kyle to deliver the packages back down in the tunnel and then use the controller to sync everything up. They would orchestrate the timing, literally counting down so everything would coincide with the UAV crash. A lot of moving parts needed to come together for this mission.

* * * * *

Gibby just woke up from an all-nighter. Because Carla Jo was part of the *Hummingbird* mission, Gibby had invited her to stay at his place. He was certain that as the mission progressed, there would be loose ends. With her skill set, she was perfect, and she was already cleared into the mission. Only a select few knew everything, and Gibby wanted to keep the number to a minimum.

"That food last night was awesome!" smiled Gibby. He stretched his arms and flashed a huge yawn with a gaping mouth. Carla Jo had taken his spare bedroom. She'd already had an early morning run. Like most military personnel, it was a habit. She sat on Gibby's couch doing leg stretches and squats. Between sets, she watched Gibby.

Gibby watched Carla Jo finish her morning PT (physical training). He walked over to his desk to check his laptop. He opened his email. He was surprised to have received a low-level assignment. An inquiry really. He glanced up at Carla Jo. He knew she was available, at least until he needed her for any cleanup work.

He opened the encrypted message, entered his agent code name, and deciphered the password. He peeled back the Sudoku maze and located the message. It was a lower level assignment and did not require any additional password protection entries. He began reading.

"Local high-level politician died in his hospital room while recovering at the Seoul National University Medical Center. A cell phone was found inside a potted plant. The plant had been delivered by a young Korean woman."

Several enlarged PDF security camera still shots had been pulled from the surveillance camera. They were grainy and in black and white. Several additional clear photos were included, and they had been computer enhanced.

Gibby downloaded the attachments. He printed the stills and started playing the surveillance camera footage. They had been taken from five separate video surveillance cameras from inside the hospital. As he sipped his coffee and ate a day-old bagel, he watched the footage in silence. On the clock with *Hummingbird*, he was unavailable. He wondered how to handle this new assignment. Then, he heard muffled grunts coming from the living room. He glanced away from his laptop and watched Carla Jo. With her toes tucked under the couch, she was busy doing stomach crunches.

"Hey, CJ! You want another job?"

Carla Jo stopped exercising. She got to her feet and walked over to Gibby's desk. With her hands on her hips, she replied, "Whatcha got?"

"Easy, peasy. Some local politician died, probably wacked. The Agency wants to see what may have happened."

Contemplating his request, they stared at each other. Other than the walker situation, she would be sitting around picking her nose. For now, she was on standby.

"Sure, why not?" she replied. "What's my share?"

"No cut. It's all yours. I want you nice and close in case I need your assistance with the walker, and with any loose ends. This new assignment probably isn't very exciting work, but work's work, right?"

"So. What have you got?"

"Later, I'll forward the encrypted package to your laptop. But here are the stills of the person. She appears to be of the female persuasion, and she appears to be delivering a potted plant. It allegedly held a cell phone. Pretty smart." As he pushed his glasses up to rest against his forehead, Gibby handed her a file.

Carla Jo grabbed the folder and studied the still shots. Something looked familiar, but the images were grainy. The enhanced images struck a chord, though. As it came to her, she tilted her head.

"It couldn't be," Carla Jo whispered to herself.

"What's up? You got something, CJ?" Gibby asked. He'd worked with Carla Jo on several other cases. She had that same highly attuned intuition that detectives had when piecing the facts together. As she gathered her thoughts, Gibby waited.

"When I landed, I was watching a young woman at the airport. There was something that got my attention. When she ordered her food, it was something she said. I don't know, there was something hinky about her. On a hunch, I snapped some pictures. Even took a short video clip." Carla Jo stared at Gibby but not really seeing him. She was mentally reliving the event. Breaking out of her trance, she walked to her room and retrieved her cell phone.

Gibby watched. He was amazed. It was interesting to see how different people react and perceive the same situation. She walked back from her room. Gibby wondered how many seasoned agents would have picked up on something, let alone had the foresight to get it on camera.

Carla Jo accessed the gallery feature on her Android cell phone. After locating the images, she walked toward Gibby.

"Here. Check them out. Not quite the same, but very similar," Carla Jo said as she handed Gibby the phone.

Gibby grabbed the phone. Before he spoke, he tilted his head back and forth examining the images from different angles. "Yeah, it could be. Her hair looks different, but the height looks about right." He turned his attention back to Carla Jo. "You said you have a video clip?"

She grabbed the phone back. She started the clip and handed the phone back. "Here."

Gibby stared at the clip. He replayed it several times. To get a better comparison, he held the phone screen next to his laptop. He watched the images side by side. He concentrated on the way the young woman walked. He studied the swing of her arms, the way she held her head, the length of her strides. Maybe?

"Run a biomechanical program and facial recognition against the surveillance tape compared to your stuff. Let's open a formal casefile on her," suggested Gibby.

"What should we call it?" thought Carla Jo.

After a brief pause, Gibby smiled and blurted out, "How about the Florist?" Carla Jo smiled.

"You know what was weird?" Carla Jo asked.

"What?"

"If it is the same person, we may have an even bigger problem."

"How so?"

"She is coming from the U.S. St Louis, Missouri, area."

"How do you know that?"

"I saw the tags on her luggage. And she appeared to be packed for a long visit in Korea." Before Gibby could reply, she turned and was walking back to her room. As Gibby watched her close the spare room door, he thought, *How did she know all that?*

25

Angelie's first day at the school was not what she had expected. Most of her life, she had focused on her covert assignment. She hadn't considered how she would react working with children. Unlike the other international English teachers, she hadn't been preparing to be a teacher. Her focus had always been about learning the skills of a covert operative. Being a teacher was a means to an end. Now, being surrounded by the children and interacting with South Koreans, she saw things differently. She was grateful to experience life in this small remote village.

Her hosts were sincere, warm, and friendly. She looked out across the classroom and saw the students' bright, smiling faces with the innocent honesty of youth. It was contagious. This was the first time in her life that she had allowed herself to see things from another person's point of view. Her years of training and the constant charade to feign an inability to speak or understand in-depth Korean Hangul, had paid off. Everyone there, even the children, believed her.

While pretending to read a lesson plan, she eavesdropped on the classroom teachers and the students. Each hour, she rotated to another classroom. At the top of the hour, she was given twenty minutes to speak to the class. For most students, it was their first time to meet an American. Most children had never been formally taught English. Angelie began class with "Hello" and the pronunciation of her American name. Outside of school, Angelie saw a boy wearing a Nike t-shirt. She guessed that he probably couldn't pronounce the word nor identify the products Nike sold. Regardless, someone in his household had been motivated to purchase it. Seeing several other name-brand shirts in the village, Angelie was surprised how far reaching the advertisers and marketing had penetrated this remote community.

At school, the dress code was different. All public schools in the Republic of Korea had a uniform dress code. The boys wore white, long sleeved shirts with blue neckties. They could wear either long pants or shorts, as long as they were light tan khaki. The girls wore white, short-sleeved blouses with blue scarf ties and skirt.

In the morning, once a week, the entire school assembled for an hour of Tae Kwan Do. It was their national sport. Every child was required to possess a basic proficiency. Angelie was amazed. Even the young kids possessed strong martial art skills. Following this tradition, her parents made sure that Angelie was trained in the U.S. She had attained a third-degree black belt. The children were coordinated. Their forms were controlled, fluid, and sharp. Their stances were wide and balanced. The shaping of their hands and feet throughout their punches and kicks were beautiful. She was impressed.

Although each student exhibited varying degrees of skill levels, everyone wore a white tti (belt). Each school used these special mornings to celebrate their national sport. Because Tae Kwan Do was required, it was a form of physical fitness as opposed to a means of recognizing individual skill levels. Like everyone, Angelie had been issued a basic white dobok (uniform). In the back row with the other teachers, Angelie followed along. The students were delighted to see her obvious prior training. The forms and one-step drills were universally taught. She found it refreshing and energizing to be included.

Standing in straight lines, the children and teachers gathered across the outside courtyard. The entire school worked out together. The muffled sound of the thick white cotton dobok arms and leggings reverberated in a loud unified cadence, as everyone's arms and legs snapped out: forward, down, and across, in a synchronized, thousands-of-years-old dance,. They walked through the most basic form, the one first taught to every Tae Kwan Do student. As a third-degree black belt, Angelie appreciated the children's skills. There was no doubt that several of the children, at the very least, were first-degree black belts.

The first kiap (yell) during the form drill that erupted was awe inspiring. The unified shout erupted. It was a display of cooperative energy and strength. Breaking down the root of the word, helps one understand the intent of yelling. "Ki" translated as energy power or force, while "hap" (the h being silent) meant to coordinate, gather, or concentrate. As Angelie heard the group's first kiap, she was mesmerized. The loud burst of voices created a simple, unified roar that cut through the mountain air and resonated against the mountain range. It brought an immediate rush of endorphins through her body. Even if she wanted, she couldn't have concealed the smile on her face. Angelie hadn't experienced anything like it.

As each day passed, she began to settle into a routine. The teaching experience had been transformative, and, engrossed in the newness of it all, she had become sidetracked and had briefly forgotten her real purpose for being there. She felt exhilarated and pushed herself to experience this new lifestyle. Somehow, she willed herself to accept this temporary indoctrination into the South Korean experience.

As Angelie joined the children in the Tae Kwan Do workout, the unified roar of their "kiaps" echoed across the field. She hadn't recognized that, at that very moment, she was experiencing her life—one she controlled. She was outside the physical control and proximity of her parents and handler.

Life was like a lake. In life, a person's actions sent ripples out across the lake's surface. If the impact of one's actions was big enough, the ripple generated could cross the body of water. The aftermath of decisions could result in either small disturbances or immense waves that devastated the opposite shoreline.

In Angelie's particular case, she participated in a very large, far-reaching event. That event sent out more than a ripple. It was more like a shockwave. Unwittingly, she participated in the assassination of a South Korean politician. Her actions could not be taken back, and that decision changed the direction of her life, moving her down a path that crossed country allegiances. Without realizing it, Angelie was following a path that could very well cost her everything.

Unlike the children who surrounded her, she no longer had the luxury of time. She was swimming with the big fish, and she needed all her wits to survive. Her first life-and-death decision was only days away; she just didn't know it.

*   *   *   *   *

Tae just finished a hot shower. He was full, ready for sleep. Before the shower, his brother showed him the large, oversized backpack and its contents. It was twice as heavy as normal. His family up north would be happy and appreciative.

As he began drying off, he used one of his brother's thick plush cotton towels. Tae pressed the towel against his face and smelled the fragrance from the fabric softener. It was a luxury most of his comrades in the north had never experienced. Tae glanced around his brother's bathroom and noticed many comforts of life he could only experience here when visiting his brother: disposable razors, deodorant stick, shampoo, hair conditioner, and shaving cream. In the DPRK, he used a solid bar of soap and liquid soap. He used a straight edge razor that he sharpened on a stone. He applied plain baking soda from the kitchen under his arms as deodorant. In South Korea, even the quality of toilet paper was thicker and softer. To Tae, it seemed like the south lived in the lap of luxury.

Tae appreciated that, over time, these luxuries came with a big price tag: They had made the south weak. Unlike his comrades in the north, the southerners would find it difficult to live without their electronics, fancy cars, shopping, varieties of food sources, reliable electricity and plumbing, entertainment, and the internet. If the Koreans ever unified, their challenge would be freedom of choice. How would they voice dissatisfaction about their government officials? If the southerners didn't adapt, they would face imprisonment or death. Tae believed his southern countrymen would have great difficulty adapting.

Few people in the north knew these luxuries existed in the south. The north had a different perspective. The north recognized the cost. Over the years, Tae saw the power that the imperialist United States had over the south. Most people outside of the Koreas had no idea that over seventeen-thousand South Koreans had been injured or killed during the Vietnam Conflict. South Korea sent to Vietnam more than three hundred thousand soldiers, more than another other country besides the US. In Tae's mind, the south was beholden to the imperialists; obligated to send their men to die in a war where South Korea had no direct national security interest justifying its involvement.

While Tae walked through the streets of the south, he noticed the way the US soldiers treated the South Koreans, as if the Koreans were an inferior race. Tae had been told many frightful stories while living in the north, and he came to accept that most of it was propaganda. He'd learned long ago to avoid talking politics with his brother. Tae focused on being grateful for the assistance his brother provided.

Tae's family was resolved that they would have to wait for their father to pass away. He knew that it was useless to plead with his father to defect south. Someday, though, Tae would bring his family across. Tae's dream was for the countries to unify so they could stay in the north. But, sadly, Tae knew his brother would never come back to the north.

For now, these infrequent visits would have to suffice. For the last decade, it had been working out just fine. No one knew about his visits. There was no rush.

Tae put on his pajamas and said goodnight to his brother. He had a long walk the next day and didn't look forward to carrying that double load. He climbed into an American style bed—not a heated blanket and pillow rolled out on the floor. Tae appreciated the soft cotton sheets, the thick goose-down comforter, and the electric portable heater fan in the corner. Tae curled up under the covers. He thought, *The southerners have all of life's luxuries.*

26

Kyle woke up late and glanced at his alarm clock. He was surprised to see that it was already 4:00 p.m.; he'd slept through the buzzer. Stretching his arms, he was overcome with an exaggerated yawn. Last night had been one of the most demanding in his life, and there was a moment when he feared being captured behind enemy lines. Kyle stared across the room and looked at his waist pack. Hidden inside were the cyanide capsules. This mission had serious consequences.

He climbed out of bed, showered, and dressed. As he was about to head to the mess hall, he heard a knock on his door. When Kyle opened it, he was greeted by a man.

"Good morning, Kyle."

Kyle was surprised by the informality of the introduction. Kyle searched the unknown man's uniform and immediately recognized the insignia: He was also a Lieutenant.

"Can I help you?" Kyle asked, studying the man. At that moment, Kyle realized that, aside from his first day when an unknown Agency person verified his identity, no one else had ever visited.

Before the man spoke, he glanced up and down the hallway. Confident they were alone, he leaned forward and, dropping his voice to the volume just above a whisper, replied, "My name is Elliott. Douglas Elliott. My friends call me Moon Dog. I'm here about *Hummingbird*."

Kyle nodded, stepped back into his room, and waved his arm toward the room's interior, inviting Moon Dog inside. Kyle noticed he was carrying a small brown bag that looked almost like a school lunch sack. After closing the door, Kyle retrieved a wooden chair from his kitchenette. He locked the door and wedged the chair under the doorknob. Kicking the chair legs, Kyle wiggled the chair, making sure it was tight.

"Bearing gifts, I see. So what can I do for you, Lt. Elliott?" replied Kyle, electing to remain formal. They weren't friends yet.

Moon Dog walked over to Kyle's sofa and sat down. Before speaking, he placed the small brown bag down on the cushion next to him. "Before you go back into the tunnel, I need to teach you how to operate the detonator. This device will trigger the explosives."

Lt. Elliott reached into the bag and pulled out a flat, black rectangular object that looked like a typical smart phone. It even had a plastic protective outer shell.

"A cell phone?"

"It was an easy crossover. We're already using a wireless system to communicate with cameras and other transmission sequences along the communication relays; it seemed like a no-brainer to continue along the same format and technology. It's based on the same concept as a cell phone. In this case, it's programmed to only communicate with the explosive packages that you'll be dropping off."

Kyle nodded his head. He didn't need to know the ins and outs of this technology. His only concern was that it worked the way it was intended. Moon Dog recognized the glazed stare. Lt. Benjamin wasn't an analyst or technician. Had he been interested, Moon Dog was prepared to explain every detail. The Agency had developed a hybrid mixture of 1MX-101. An explosive compound enhanced its already-efficient combination of intense energetic ingredients, yet was designed to be more stable. This hybrid could withstand various shockwaves and direct impact by gunfire. It could even withstand direct contact by flames. It was much safer to work with than traditional TNT, which was sensitive and vulnerable to common jolts and shocks.

Without going into specifics, Moon Dog explained that the bombs he would be using, if dropped, would not accidentally explode. Not even if they were struck by a projectile. Moon Dog had to remember that Kyle was a field agent. His main function was to do the heavy lifting. Avoiding the minute technological details, Moon Dog spent the next thirty minutes explaining how to program the detonator. It was simple and easy to use.

"Now, for the last, most important piece," explained Moon Dog. "I've programmed the detonation code as your birthday. March twenty-second, right?"

"Right," replied Kyle.

"Now, remember, it's only a four-digit code. It's 0322. Don't enter the year. Just the first four digits."

"Why not my full birthday?"

"The programmers wanted it as simple and straightforward as possible. So that's how they designed it. Again, it's 0322. Your birthday. Got it?"

"Got it."

"Okay, Kyle. We're counting on you. Get a good meal before you head out. The packages are already stored in your DMZ locker. Each bomb is numbered. You'll drop off number one package at the farthest camera and communication relay that you installed. Remember, when you set the package next to the cameras, enter the number into the controller. It will automatically sync up for you. It's almost as simple as walking inside the tunnel one last time and dropping the packages off. One minute to sync, then move to the next one down the line. Got it?"

"Got it. It sounds easy. There shouldn't be any problem."

"You won't need to hide them or bury them with dirt. You will be inside installing them when no one is present."

They paused and exchanged intense looks of determination.

"Gibby's gonna be watching you the entire time. If anything comes up, just text him. If everything goes as planned, I'll be speaking to you in about thirty -six hours. How do you feel? Did you sleep good?"

"Like a baby. I feel good. Rested. I'm surprised I'm not more nervous."

"Oh, when you get inside with the packages, you'll feel it. Believe me."

Moon Dog extended his right hand toward Kyle, and they exchanged a firm handshake.

"Good Luck, Kyle."

"Thanks."

*   *   *   *   *

Tae slept longer than normal. The winter was setting in. The temperature had dropped, making his journey above ground more challenging. The tunnels were much warmer, with no wind chill, no moisture in the air, and no falling snowflakes to contend with. He timed his departure to be sure to enter the tunnel after the engineers and technicians were gone.

During his last trip, Tae could tell the DPRK was still working on the tunnel. He was unaware that the excavation tunnel was almost complete. Later, they would finish the drainage and air filtration systems. For now, only the compaction trucks rolled back and forth inside the tunnel. Otherwise, it was quiet.

Tae ate an early dinner with his brother. This final celebratory meal before the onset of winter had become a tradition. They wouldn't see each other for at least three months. As always, Tae began his journey the day of the new moon, a date when no moon was present. Timing the trips based on the cycle of the moon did not require any communication back and forth. After all, tracking the moon was common within each country, so those dates were well known. Without a moon, no light reflected from the sun. The darkness helped Tae cross the DMZ, reducing the likelihood of his being seen by the DPRK soldiers. The day following the new moon was also absent any reflective sunlight off the moon. It was the perfect time to schedule the crossings.

With a full stomach, Tae and his brother said their final goodbyes. Tae struggled loading the heavy backpack onto his shoulders. Even before he left, he was looking forward to soaking his feet in the cool spring water near the cathedral area. He'd doubled up his socks, which helped offset the increased weight of the backpack.

With a large exhale, Tae set off into the early evening, unaware it would be the longest journey of his life, and one that would change his life forever.

Mr. Kim's crew had relieved Carla Jo. They were on watch, staking out the front of the apartment. They hadn't realized there was a back exit and that it led to a common area. Tae maneuvered through the back alley. Unaware of his departure, the crew waited on the other side. They discovered their mistake too late. It was the first of many things that would go wrong over the next twenty-four hours.

*   *   *   *   *

Kyle stared into his locker. The backpack looked too small to hold enough explosives to destroy the tunnel. He bent down to pull out the backpack, and as he held the straps in his hand, he paused. It hadn't occurred to him that for the next several hours, he would be carrying these explosives on his back. Lt. Elliott had explained that the bombs were extremely stable. With a long sigh, Kyle finished pulling the backpack from his locker. No need to dwell on the inevitable.

Kyle pushed an arm through the strap and adjusted the fittings. He wanted a tight fit. Taking a deep breath, he turned and walked out into the night and gazed into the night sky, seeing stars and clouds on the horizon. Because it was the first night of the new moon and also almost winter, this night would be one of the longest of the year. He adjusted his night-vision goggles and began walking.

*   *   *   *   *

"Moon Dog?"

"Yes, sir?"

"Director Valdez is going to be watching the live images feed from another satellite," X.O. Newland said. "They will not be seeing anything from inside the tunnels; just views from above. She'll be watching from a secure conference room back at the main office in DC. Technically, when this goes down, I'll be the highest-ranking officer in play." As he spoke, he stared at the palms of his hands. It hit Moon Dog and the X.O. at the same time: It was no coincidence that the Agency would extract the Director. It was probably standard operating procedure.

Moon Dog sat rigid in front of the large, full-wall projection images. During the mission, this wall would display the view from the UAV. The controller stick was positioned in the center of a desk, and operating it almost felt like a video game. Turning his gaze toward the X.O., in almost a whisper, Moon Dog replied, "What does that make me sir?"

After a brief pause, the X.O. replied, "Second in command. It's you and me, buddy. Our asses are flapping in the wind."

"Sir! Yes, sir! Right where we want 'em." Moon Dog barked back. They knew the score. In the very near future, the SAT INT unit stationed inside the DMZ was about to declare a *de facto* state of war with the Democratic People's Republic of Korea.

"Good to go, Moon Dog?"

"Sir! Yes, sir! Good to go!"

"Then roll-call the 18th Wing in Kadena. Get our KC-135 tanker in the air and on its way to the West Coast. I want status calls as it makes its way to Vandenberg. Also, what about our other KC-135 that's gonna rain jet fuel on our crash site? Status?"

"All prepped. It's one of our guys. Kadena's kinda pissed that we're pulling two strings at the same time, but they know the drill. He's fueled for the flight and his tanks are loaded to the brim. He's been briefed and has been running SIMS on his GPS target for the last month as well. His last sequence was ten for ten. I even had him run two out of the blue to test his readiness. They were unscheduled."

"And?" asked X.O. Newland.

"Two for two."

"I'm liking this guy. Who is he?"

"Davies. Mr. Peter Davies. He runs double duty as the Director's helo pilot. Given she knew she would be pulled stateside when this all went down, she allocated him to our team. "

"The Director's pilot?" asked the X.O. Moon Dog saw the color of the X.O.'s face drop a few shades.

"I thought you knew."

"We're good, we're good. If the Director's green-lighted it, I'm good," interjected X.O. Newland.

"Where's our good buddy, Kyle?"

Moon Dog minimized the screen. As the view changed, all the live satellite feeds appeared. They both stared at the mint green colored view of the steep mountain peak. Moon Dog increased the zoom. As the image changed, the bright dot on the screen was magnified, and they could just see the outline of Kyle's body. He was making his way up the mountain toward the tunnel opening.

"There he is. Let's check his chest camera view," instructed the X.O.

In seconds, another view flashed up on the screen. As Kyle walked, Moon Dog and the X.O. watched the camera view bouncing up and down.

"Perfect. Where's Gibby?"

Moon Dog sent Gibby a text that they needed some face time. Moon Dog waited to receive a reply before patching the call through. You never knew what Gibby was doing over there. At a time like this, there was no need to cause any unnecessary stress. Besides, Moon Dog and Gibby were longtime friends.

As the live feed connected, Moon Dog found Gibby alert and prepared.

"Good evening, Mr. Gibson," X.O. Newland said, calm and confident.

"It most certainly is, boss," Gibby replied. He stared at the screen with his mischievous smile.

"Are we good to go on your end, Gibby?" Moon Dog blurted before walking into view to stand next to the X.O.

"Hey, Moon Dog. We are done practicing our bleeding (military slang for wasting resources going through pain and suffering). Lt. Benjamin is en route. Everything is on schedule. The only hiccup is the night guard at the far end. I'm on it. We'll track him as soon as he arrives. I want to know where that guy is at all times. No soup sandwiches (more military slang for mistakes) today, guys. We are good to go!" Gibby replied. They could tell from his responses that he was a little amped up.

Moon Dog and X.O. Newland laughed. It was clear that Gibby had already ingested his share of strong coffee. He appeared to be riding a caffeine high.

"We've got the Director on standby," said the X.O. "They're ready to watch the live feed from a separate satellite view. I'm sure you're aware that she'll be sharing the room with God knows who. So it goes without saying, we keep it beyond professional. Moon Dog will announce when she will be patched through. They'll see it all from above. Remember, gentlemen, nothing is being taped," he clarified.

"I'm guessing that we'll be the only participants until it's show time. Are all the players on the clock?"

"Roger that. We'll check back in later. Good luck, Gibby."

"You too, Moon Dog. You as well, X.O."

Moon Dog diminished the face-to-face feed with Gibby. They would keep their lines open throughout the mission. As that view screen diminished, the satellite view of the bouncing images from Kyle's chest-mounted camera was projected up on the wall next to the image of the UAV in a split screen, side-by-side view. Everything got quiet. It was now a waiting game.

Gibby settled into his high-back, ergonomically adjustable chair. He felt the slow crawl of stress creep its way into his mind. He'd been on countless missions. Although many went off without a hitch, he knew there was a mathematical certainty of error; it was inevitable. The odds were even higher when a mission had too many moving parts. In this case, there were just too many things that had to go right. At the very least, they expected a few hiccups.

Most agents held small superstitions. Gibby had no intention of jinxing anything. He couldn't ignore what he felt. He had a feeling. So far, everything was falling into place. It was too easy. Such feelings were best kept to oneself. Like Carla Jo, Gibby had a sixth sense about things. Unlike Carla Jo, Gibby's gift wasn't based on an accumulation of the facts or evidence. For Gibby, it was pure intuition, a gut feeling that had never been wrong. He hoped his gut feeling was wrong this time, though.

Gibby took a deep breath. He finished off his fourth cup of strong black coffee. He wasn't feeling good about this one. He was right.

27

Tae was making his way through the lava tube. Every year, he forgot how difficult it was. It was much more difficult carrying that much weight. To take the load off his shoulders, he stopped more frequently. His feet were already sore, and he wasn't even halfway there. For the last ten years, he'd been making this journey. As he struggled to his feet, he wondered, *How many more years will I have the strength to make this walk?*

Tae adjusted the backpack straps, leaned forward, and continued walking. It wouldn't be long now. He fantasized about arriving at the pond near the cathedral opening. He was looking forward to having a smoke, a bite to eat, and a longer-than-normal rest. Soon his feet and legs would start to shows signs of cramping. He willed himself forward, concentrating on the halfway point, and chastised himself for dreaming about his arrival home. It was way too early to be thinking that way, and it was unproductive, especially when he was carrying a double load.

The last third of the trip was always the worst. Above ground, he would face the wind chill and winter temperatures. This trip was his most difficult one of the year. He dreaded it. Dwelling on the journey played havoc on his strength and motivation. Tae gathered his reserves and pushed forward. He was almost halfway there. It wouldn't be long now.

*   *   *   *   *

Gibby stared at the monitor, refusing to look away. Kyle had been walking through the lava tube and was making good time. He was fresh and determined. Kyle paused. He surveilled the area before he approached the final turn that ran along the common wall between the tunnel.

While Kyle walked, the compaction trucks ended their workday. Gibby informed Kyle that the night guard was there and had already walked past the opening. In the farthest southern section of the excavation tunnel, well past the opening, he was busy tending to his campfire.

Before Kyle entered the excavation tunnel, he wanted to check one more time. He sent Gibby a text. "Still clear?" Within seconds, he received the reply, "Good to go."

Confident it was clear, Kyle squeezed through the opening. Using night-vision goggles, he glanced up and down the tunnel.

*   *   *   *   *

The night guard was on edge and wide awake. He decided to forego the rice wine tonight, as he wanted to remain focused and alert. He was trying to psych himself up. He wanted to wait at the opening. He wanted to redeem himself by catching another smuggler or defector.

Throughout the day, the guard had fantasized about apprehending someone. Surprise was his advantage. He was trying to convince himself that it would be easy. He wanted to be a hero by catching a disloyal, weak-minded comrade. But now, alone, deep underground, his confidence and bravery waned. All he could think about were those flying creatures lurking about. He sat behind the fire, sipping hot tea. He clutched his flashlight with his free hand and scanned the ceiling. The flashlight had a fresh set of batteries.

He had all night. There was no hurry. As the minutes passed, he contemplated drinking the rice wine and considered hiding deep under his blankets and falling asleep. As those thoughts crossed his mind, he urged himself to be strong. He hunkered down, leaning his back against the tunnel wall. It was going to be a long night.

*　*　*　*　*

Tae relaxed in the lava tube. He pulled out some cold baked chicken. Even cold, it tasted great. He soaked his feet in the cool spring pond. Sipping on a bottle of water, he ate dried fruit. For some reason, this trip was proving more difficult. The weight of the backpack had sapped most of his energy. For a moment, he dozed off. He wasn't sure how long he'd slept. It felt like a while.

Still groggy, Tae urged his muscles to fire and to re-engage. He slid his feet out of the water. He dried them and pulled on his socks. He struggled to pull his winter boots onto his feet. Out of habit, he paused and listened. All he could hear was the soothing trickle of water seeping into the underground spring. The air was calm. Rather than standing, he pushed himself back away from the pool and leaned back against the cave wall. Without thinking, he pulled the backpack toward him and shoved it next to him against the wall.

Still sleepy and tired, he raised his legs up against his chest. His mind seemed foggy. He couldn't clear his thoughts. His eyes blinked several times. His eyelids were heavy, and he was unable to open them completely. As his body relaxed in this tucked position, with his feet now warm and comfortable inside the dry socks, it just happened. Without warning, Tae's eyes closed, and he drifted off into a deep slumber.

Fortune was on his side. He was tucked up against the cave wall. Unless he made a sound, someone could walk directly past him and never realize he was there.

* * * * *

Kyle was surprised. Staging the packages and syncing them up took no time at all. As he finished installing the last one, he was surprised how easy and smooth everything had gone. It felt like only minutes before he had started. As he paused in front of the opening, he texted Gibby.

"All Done." Within seconds, he received Gibby's reply. "Looks great. All clear. Start the sequence and start heading out."

Kyle took a deep breath. He activated the controller syncing the bombs. With that completed, he glanced up and down the tunnel. It struck him that it would be the last time he or anyone else would see the inside of the tunnel. Without delay, Kyle began squeezing back through the opening to the cathedral cavern. From that point on, everything began going downhill.

* * * * *

Gibby watched Kyle through his computer monitor. The only camera angle Gibby had was from Kyle's chest-mounted camera. As Kyle struggled to get through the opening, Gibby watched the images bounce around. Gibby almost got dizzy. In his excitement, Kyle was more forceful. As he turned his torso through the opening, his boot caught on something. A jagged rock was sticking out and caught the boot eyelet where the strings lace through. As he stepped through the opening, Kyle felt his boot catch onto something and tug backward. Without thinking, he increased the force of his leg and yanked his leg forward, hoping to dislodge it.

The jagged rock didn't budge. It kept a firm hold on the metal eyelet. Only a small portion of the rock was exposed; The rest was hidden beneath the dirt. Without realizing what was happening, Kyle exerted more than enough effort to dislodge the boot. With a strong tug, the small metal eyelet snapped under the stress and broke. Kyle tumbled forward and fell through the opening. He landed on the ground face first. His night vision goggles took the brunt of the fall and pushed the goggles back up into his face.

Kyle knew he'd made a big mistake. As he lay on the other side of the opening, he could hear the sharp metallic "ping" sound echoing on the other side of the wall. He froze, concentrating all his focus on his hearing. At the same time, he felt a sharp pain deep inside his right eye.

*   *   *   *   *

While Kyle was squeezing through the opening, Gibby's computer image seemed to freeze. With a puzzled look on his face, Gibby leaned back away from the monitor. "What the hell?" Gibby whispered staring at the screen. Carla Jo was in the other room on her laptop. She thought she heard Gibby speaking. She got up and walked into his office.

"What's up, Gibby?"

"I have no clue. The images just stopped!"

They both stood staring at the monitor and waited. After a few moments, the screen went blank. In complete shock, Gibby stood and started yelling at the blank screen. "Are you kidding me?!" After a brief pause, Gibby leaned forward. In a more elevated voice he yelled, "Are you kidding me?"

After several seconds, an automatic message prompt appeared on the monitor indicating that the satellite was undergoing a maintenance update. The message read: "The system is running its annual maintenance. Please be patient. Your work will be restored upon completion. It will take approximately ten minutes." The numbers 10:00 appeared under the message. It began counting backwards from ten minutes. As the seconds counted down, the numbers continued displaying.

As Carla Jo completed reading the message prompt, she couldn't help but raise an eyebrow and give Gibby a sideway glance. He was the senior agent on site, so she didn't dare say anything. But she couldn't help but think Gibby had just made a rookie mistake. In any satellite surveillance situation, it was Rule One. During the live mission, they must disable all automatic programming maintenance or software downloads. She tried to move past Gibby's mistake and broke the awkward silence.

"Was Kyle coming back through the opening? Nothing happened to him, right?" Unable to make eye contact, Gibby twisted his mouth and stared at the monitor before replying.

"Kyle was just squeezing through the opening. Nothing else was happening. It was all clear." Gibby's face said it all. He was disgusted with himself. How could he have made such a mistake? In a soft whisper, still facing the monitor, he said, "What a screw up. How could I have forgotten that?" Downtrodden, Gibby turned to face Carla Jo and, in a less-than-confident manner, asked her, "We're good, right? What could happen in ten minutes?"

Without speaking, Carla Jo lifted her eyebrows as if saying that ten minutes was a long time, and a lot could happen. She tilted her head. Through body language alone, she had asked Gibby what he thought. Not missing a beat, Gibby turned back to the monitor and watched the numbers counting down as the update continued. "Please God, don't let anything happen for the next ten minutes!"

They both continued standing. They watched the seconds pass as the timer displayed the remaining time. It would be a long ten minutes.

*   *   *   *   *

The night guard was startled as a sharp metallic ping sound came barreling down the tunnel. There was no doubt in his mind that this noise was manmade, not natural. The sudden onslaught to his senses was exactly what he needed. It jolted him to action.

He no longer worried about some unknown flying animal. The image of the middle-aged man he saw earlier came to mind and seemed to strengthen his resolve and increase his confidence. Without thinking, the guard stood. In that moment, it struck him that he was safer being the aggressor. Hiding in the cave hoping he wouldn't be discovered was more terrifying than being the pursuer. Each step he took toward the noise, his confidence grew. He knew where to look first—the opening to the cathedral cavity.

His pace quickened and he closed the distance. Without realizing it, he had turned on his flashlight with one hand and held his pistol in the other. Part of him recognized that using the flashlight would spoil his advantage of surprise, but the light allowed him to make better time. He began running toward the opening. Somewhere, deep down, he hoped that whoever had made the noise would see his flashlight beam and be frightened away, like a dog that chooses to bark as opposed to attacking first. Within seconds, the night guard was running at full sprint. He wasn't sure whether he was running toward or away from danger, but he had another advantage: The physical exertion had a real biological affect.

His body had produced adrenaline and his heart was disbursing it through his body. The use of his large muscles had kick-started his internal production of endorphins. This sudden increase in his natural chemicals seemed to give him courage. No longer fearing the unknown, the night guard pushed ahead. Now a different sound came echoing from the excavated side of the tunnel. Huffing and puffing, combined with the rhythmic piston-like stomping noises began to emerge and get louder and louder. The situation had changed. The night guard was transforming.

His decision to stand and face his fears was changing him. This new confidence appeared from nowhere. He had willed himself to be the person he'd always wanted to be. Courage had been inside him this entire time, and he was truly excited. He wanted to experience whatever lie ahead. He made a choice. He would no longer shrink back from a challenge. He was invigorated. He was determined never to be that weak, small person ever again. With all his energy, the guard ran down the tunnel.

*   *   *   *   *

"Moon Dog! What happened to the satellite feed?" asked the X.O. in disbelief. Standing in front of the projection screen, Kyle's chest-mounted camera displayed a grainy frozen image of Kyle squeezing through the opening. Within seconds, a message displayed. The screen notified them that an annual satellite maintenance download was in progress. As he read the message, Moon Dog's shoulders slumped. He stared in disbelief. The download timer began counting down from ten minutes.

Normally, on all prior live missions, he had been just one of technicians. He had never been in charge. He'd only been tasked with specific details of the mission. This was such a simple oversight. It was the precise moment of realization that "you don't know what you don't know."

Moon Dog recognized right away that this small crew of players was stretched too thin. Everyone was being asked to take on multiple duties, all vital to the mission. Moon Dog wanted to remind the X.O. that he had been so focused on flying the UAV that the distraction had certainly contributed to this mistake. He wanted to highlight the fact that his covert operative counterpart should have made sure that this was done. He found himself organizing all the reasons he could think of that would explain how this oversight could have happened.

However, Moon Dog, Lt. Douglas Elliott, was not about making excuses. He was a serious professional who took his duties and responsibilities seriously. In his early years, every time he and his other jarheads in the Corp had shouted "HUA!" it was more than some macho tradition. It was a promise to his unit, his brothers in arms, that everyone present had Heard, Understood and Acknowledged the orders. It was an oath, an affirmation that everything was accounted for. A verbal declaration that everyone present was good to go.

This was not one of those occasions. X.O. Newland stood by, watching Moon Dog. As Moon Dog processed what happened, he could almost feel his internal anguish grow. Personal growth comes from adversaries. To move forward, people must face challenges and learn from their mistakes.

X.O. Newland waited. Immediately, he recognized the problem. He'd ridden a similar pony before. He was confident the satellite would come back online. He'd seen it happen before. Satellites were different animals. They weren't like standalone PCs. PCs were much more sensitive than satellites. He'd learned from experience. The X.O. knew the satellite was still working. It was doing everything it was supposed to do. Those beasts were overbuilt. They were designed to hover over the earth, flying 22,300 miles above the equator, where most communication satellites parked. At that distance, the satellite was outside the force of gravity. These several-thousand-pound, high-tech wonders could survive in space for decades. They could withstand the extreme cold as well as impact from space debris. Through it all, they kept functioning.

During program maintenance, the scientists designed them to interrupt all downline communications. It was essential. They recognized the need for an immediate system change or upgrade. Any break or change needed to be able to take place immediately. These satellites controlled weapons and instructions that, although important in one context, could need to be diverted or immediately stopped in another. For this reason, they were programmed to stop or alter a task while in progress.

The current program change or maintenance issue being updated was unknown. The mission was only temporarily blinded; it would come back. X.O. Newland could only hope that nothing critical was taking place during the next ten minutes.

"Sir, it's all on me. I should have rescheduled the maintenance. There's no excuse. I dropped the ball. It was my responsibility, and it didn't happen." The words were clear, straightforward and direct. Moon Dog took it like a man. He didn't offer up a single justifiable reason for the miscue. He sat at attention with his eyes forward.

"You've sufficiently fallen on the sword, lieutenant. Your recommendation?"

"It's only a ten-minute wait, sir. It would take us longer to disrupt the maintenance program. If we tried to manually stop it, I'm afraid we could somehow alter the network relay in the tunnels. If that happened, we might be scrambling trying to resync everything. I hate being blind, sir. It should only be for ten minutes." Moon Dog stopped speaking and waited for the X.O.'s reply.

X.O. Newland looked. "And?"

"I suggest we wait it out. There are too many unknowns. Besides, Kyle's got the ball. It's on him. Even if we still had our visuals, we wouldn't be able to change anything. We're just voyeurs, sir."

"I agree, lieutenant. Let's wait it out."

Lt. Elliott and X.O. Newland stared at the projector monitor. With pained faces, they watched the counter time dwindle down. They had six minutes and twenty-three seconds to wait—an eternity.

28

Kyle was dazed. When he fell forward, his head hit the ground. The night-vision goggles moved out of place, pushing back against his right eye. Right away, Kyle knew something was wrong. He noticed his vision was distorted. It was like looking through a kaleidoscope. His vision was blurred, with multiple crosshatched images. The back area of his head, in the occipital region of his brain, felt different. It wasn't a piercing pain; it was more like a puffy, numb sensation.

Apparently, during the fall, the night-vision goggles had misaligned. As his weight fell forward, the edge of the goggle became misaligned over the center of his right eye. Upon impact with the ground, the goggle frame hit the ground sandwiching it between the ground and Kyle's face. Thankfully, his forehead took most of the weight. Even so, the frame pushed his eyeball backward, smashing it against his eggshell-thin eye-orbit bone. The good news was that it wasn't a full-on orbital blow-out fracture. Instead, the thin bone cracked, causing several spider-web fracture lines.

But then there was the bad news. In the short term, Kyle would struggle with temporary kaleidoscopic vision in his right eye, although eventually his brain would adapt. The best solution was for Kyle to close his injured eye. Otherwise, the blurred multiple vision would make it difficult to keep his balance.

Kyle struggled. For a moment, he saw stars. Lying on his back, he noticed a small beam of light dancing on the ceiling of the cave. Instinctively, Kyle closed his injured eye, and the motion seemed less pronounced. To catch his breath, Kyle remained lying on his back.

As Kyle began to regain his senses, he heard something. He turned his head, concentrating on his surroundings. Then, it came to him. The light was coming from the other side of the opening, and he could hear the impact of feet. Someone was running toward him. It had to be the night guard; he must have heard him fall.

Kyle got to his knees and struggled to his feet. He closed his injured right eye and backed away from the opening. In his condition, he couldn't risk running down the worn path. He didn't have enough time. Even if he was able to keep his balance, the night guard would see him wobbling along the path. Kyle searched for a place to hide. To buy time, Kyle moved toward the upper section of the cathedral cavity. He slipped into one of the openings and decided to wait there until it was clear.

With an outstretched arm, Kyle stumbled, leaning against the wall to keep his balance. He heard the night guard getting closer. Inside the cave, the rhythmic sound of feet pounding against the ground was amplified. Injured, Kyle found his confidence rattled by the unexpected appearance of the night guard. One minute he was about to return to the DMZ, and, in only seconds, he was now injured, unable to see or keep his balance. To top it off, he was being chased by a DPRK night guard.

Kyle's brain was on overload, and he was now in survival mode, his mind searching for options. Fight or flight? Given his physical limitations, flight was not his first choice.

Kyle backed into the lava opening and stared across the cathedral cavity area. He discovered that by closing his injured eye, he could see more clearly. He returned his night-vision goggles back into position. Safely hidden inside the far opening, he stared at the opening into the excavation tunnel. Kyle could just make out a face. It was the night guard peering through the opening.

Staring at the face, Kyle shuffled backward several steps. Kyle was in a predicament. He had his back up against the wall inside unfamiliar territory. He no longer had the benefit of the cameras. He had no idea what was inside this section of the natural lava tube.

The night guard poked his flashlight through the opening and aimed the beam into the exact area where Kyle was hiding. Afraid of being seen, Kyle took a quick step backward and was horrified as his boots splashed into a small pool of water. Inside the cave, the sound was loud and unmistakable. The distinct splashing sound echoed through the large cavern. Kyle lifted his foot out of the water and inched backward.

The night guard heard the noise. He aimed his flashlight in the direction of the sound. He saw a ripple on the surface of the water, so he steadied the light beam and watched small waves fan out. What had once been a perfect sheet of glass, was now disrupted by several ripples rolling across the pond. There was no other explanation for the disturbance. Something was there.

It hit him. The night guard mustered his courage. This was his opportunity to catch a smuggler or defector. For a brief second, his confidence waned. Without thinking, the guard spoke.

"Noo goo ya?" (Who's there?)

Kyle froze. After a moment, he stepped back and bumped into something he assumed was the side of the cave. Kyle's training kicked in. Enough time had passed since his fall. His mind began putting things back into their proper order. He calmed himself down and was better able to evaluate the situation. The answer was clear. He would wait for the night guard to step toward the cave opening. Then, he'd shoot him in the head with his Beretta M9 pistol.

Kyle lowered his right arm and reached for his weapon. He grabbed his black semiautomatic pistol and raised it up. In a modified "Weaver Stance," Kyle waited for the night guard to approach.

*   *   *   *   *

Tae felt a jolt against his leg. Until he heard the echo of a man's voice, he almost forgot where he was. The voice spoke Korean. Tae realized he must have fallen back to sleep, and opened his eyes. Just outside the lava tube cave, Tae saw a flashlight beam darting about. As the beam landed near the cave opening, Tae saw the figure of a man facing the opposite direction. He was aiming a pistol in the direction of the voice. There was just enough light present for Tae to see that the man was wearing military clothing. It wasn't a uniform he recognized. Tae studied the man's profile. He was wearing an unusual set of glasses. They distorted his appearance. Still, Tae could tell the soldier was American.

Listening from outside, in the cavern, Tae heard the Korean's boots scraping and shuffling. Sitting motionless, Tae watched the American soldier step forward and stumble. The American was having difficulty keeping his balance. Tae had to do something. Any moment, there was going to be shooting. His mind screamed at him, willing him into action. The last thing he wanted was a gunfight. Tae was concerned if there was one soldier, there might be others. He couldn't risk being discovered—worse yet, with an American soldier. The only advantage that Tae had was the element of surprise.

* * * * *

Tae slid forward, careful not to make a sound. The American was distracted. All his attention was focused on the night guard's movements. The American watched the night guard walking to the other side of the pond. Tae stepped behind the American and jabbed his cold metal flashlight into the middle of Kyle's back. Kyle froze.

Kyle knew that, somehow, he'd been caught. Without realizing it, another guard must have sneaked up behind him. In utter shock, and even with adrenaline rushing through his body, Kyle was devastated. His unexpected fall; his injured eye; hearing the DPRK soldier speaking to him in the darkness. Now his shoulders slumped. His chin fell to his chest. He'd sunk from one of the highest highs, where he thought he was about to finish his first covert operation, to now, just seconds later, facing the prospect of living the remainder of his life tortured and imprisoned in some isolated labor camp in North Korea.

Kyle stared across the pond and watched the other guard holding a flashlight in one hand and a pistol in the other. Kyle felt defeated. His life was over. It would never be the same. Still holding his Barretta M9, Kyle's arms dropped to his sides. He felt the person behind him tap his right elbow. With a deep exhale, overwhelmed at the sudden turn of events, Kyle contemplated his options.

Kyle, had no choice. The soldier behind him was holding a pistol or an AK 47 rifle to the square of his back. Fighting was futile. His first priority was to stay alive. To fight now, he faced certain death. He hated his options but accepted his fate. To have any realistic chance of seeing his family and friends again, he had to remain alive. For now, in order to live, he had to part with his weapon. There was no other option. For a split second, he thought about the capsule in his back pocket. If it came to that, he still had one more play. If he was going to go down, it would be on his terms. With that, Kyle let his Beretta fall to the ground.

*   *   *   *   *

The night guard stared out into the huge cavern. He aimed his flashlight around, surveying the area. Looking around, he became disoriented. There were many cave openings. He stepped forward, directing the flashlight beam onto the cavern floor. It took him a moment to realize that most of the area was a large pool of water. If he was going to inspect each cave, he would have to walk around the pond, staying close to the wall. Becoming familiar with the surroundings, he heard trickling water.

Out of nowhere, to the guard's far right, he heard a splash. It was, a falling boulder that dislodged from the wall. The combination of excavation-tunnel building and the increased activity inside the cathedral cavern—for at no time had there ever been three people inside the cavern at the same time—the tranquil environment had been awakened. As the boulder fell across a tunnel on the opposite side, Kyle was dropping his Berretta.

A hand grabbed Kyle's right elbow, gently pulling him backward. Kyle took several tentative backward steps. He glanced back over his shoulder, and his attention was drawn toward a large backpack on the ground. Then, Kyle was shoved in that direction, and Kyle saw an index finger pointing towards the large backpack.

Kyle understood. He reached out and grabbed the backpack, surprised at its weight. He could only imagine the size of the man who was carrying it. Kyle lifted the backpack and slid his arm through the strap, hoisting it onto his back. Kyle was pushed forward, unable to see who had captured him. There would be time enough for that later. Kyle's mind was racing. It took all his strength as he forced himself to relax. His mind needed time to take everything in.

The man kept pushing him forward. Still wearing his night-vision goggles, Kyle led the way. They continued down a narrow lava tube. There was only enough room to proceed in single file. Even if he wanted to turn around to see his captor, he couldn't.

They continued walking deeper toward the DPRK. After several minutes, the tunnel took an abrupt right turn before straightening out again. They continued, heading due north. The experience affected both men. Their bodies were flooded with adrenaline. Any prior preoccupations they had about their physical discomforts had vanished. Without thinking, Kyle kept his right eye closed. His vision was improving.

Tae no longer worried about the struggle he had faced carrying the heavy backpack. Tae knew of only one place they could go, a place only his brother and father knew existed. It wouldn't take long.

The green light on Kyle's chest-mounted camera dimmed. It was reaching the outer limits of the communication relays. As the signal weakened, the number of quality data packages transmitting along the relay decreased. Video data was processed in pieces of complete data bursts. When communication was interrupted, only completed data packages could be transmitted. The system would not dump corrupted pieces of data. As Kyle and Tae continued walking away, the number of complete data packages being sent were becoming smaller and smaller. The reception from the last relay became weaker and weaker. As the signal quality diminished, the green light began blinking off and on. Over time, the light blinked off altogether. Kyle was now too far from the last relay communication. No more data was being sent or received. When the satellite came back online, Kyle would no longer be in range. He was on his own.

29

Gibby and Carla Jo hadn't moved; they stood waiting in front of the monitor the entire time. When the counter reached zero, they turned to each other and took a deep breath. To their relief, the screen cleared and displayed the tunnel images. In celebration, Gibby raised both of his arms to the ceiling. "Yes, thank you, God!" Gibby said as he turned toward Carla Jo. They exchanged high-fives. But their excitement was short lived. Carla Jo noticed one of the image views was gone. Only a static, empty screen could be seen.

"We have a problem, Gibby."

"What do you mean?"

"Where's Kyle? Why is his chest camera transmitting static?"

Gibby turned his attention to the monitor. His face turned ashen gray. His blood drained away in disbelief. Gibby rushed to his desk and began clicking away on his keyboard. After a moment, he turned back to Carla Jo. With a sense of relief, he spoke. "We still have the packages on line. They're in sync."

After a brief moment in silence, he turned to Carla Jo. "The trigger's set. Regardless, we have less than ninety-six hours to find Kyle."

Carla Jo knew exactly what Gibby meant. The most important aspect of a covert operation is to guarantee, as best one could, that all covert devices used in the mission were destroyed. The Agency never left things up to chance. Even without additional precautions, the odds were very low that the communication relays and cameras would survive the explosion. However, in these situations, the Agency looked at the mathematical possibility that something could still go wrong. It was always possible that some unforeseen, unpredictable event could intervene. The destruction of physical evidence would not be left to chance. Every portion of the mission needed to succeed.

The Agency had untold resources at its disposal. It hired the brightest minds. It was committed to thinking through and analyzing every conceivable thing. When working through the "what if's," the Agency took the concept of planning to the next level. The Agency looked at statistical probabilities and also took possibilities to heart. The more important the mission, the more intense the scrutiny. For high-level missions, plans were based on possibilities, regardless of the probability. This mission was one of those occasions.

The Agency had been contemplating what would happen if the UAV, for whatever reason, were to miss its mark. In that scenario, the tunnel would still need to be destroyed, along with all the covert equipment. Everything needed to be destroyed. Everyone involved in *Hummingbird* appreciated that, just in case, other teams were hard at work dealing with other possible scenarios. Those teams had prepared for a hurricane, or typhoon as they're called in this part of the world; a mechanical problem with the UAV; the refueling tanker scenario; or a situation in which the UAV simply missed its target. The list of possibilities seemed endless.

Although *Hummingbird* represented the physical pieces of the mission, other teams were tasked with separate missions. One of the biggest projects was based on disinformation. Elaborate videos were created that would be strategically leaked through YouTube using cell phone clips. These clips would purport to be from multiple different "supposed" eye witnesses. These same witnesses would just happen to be present on that day. The release of these video clips would be distributed through a wide variety of social media platforms. The Agency was ready, regardless of what happened.

The only eventuality that they could not resolve was a scenario where physical evidence would not hold up to international scrutiny. If the communication relays or cameras somehow survived the explosion, they could not be explained away. Worse yet. What if the actual explosive packages themselves were videotaped? Those images could be used well after their destruction. The discovery of the explosive packages was the nightmare scenario. If that happened, it would be obvious what had taken place and who was to blame. For that reason, every effort was made to make sure that didn't happen.

The explosive packages were designed to avoid this problem. Once they were synchronized, there was no turning back. Regardless of the type of technology used, short of having the power to turn back time preventing deployment, nothing could be done to disarm them. Any attempt to tamper with any circuit to any individual package would set them all off.

Gibby stared at the screen. With this unexpected turn of events, more new decisions needed to be made. Gibby was certain that Moon Dog and X.O. Newland were watching the same, empty, static-filled images from Kyle's chest-mounted camera. Now what?

*   *   *   *   *

Moon Dog was relieved. As expected, the monitors came back on. He checked every camera in line and confirmed that the explosive synchronization was still good. Before he had a chance to review the last camera shot, though, the X.O. chimed in.

"What's up with Kyle's chest camera?"

Moon Dog's ear-to-ear grin vanished. Wasting no time, he began running diagnostics to see if there was a malfunction. Within seconds, he concluded that there were none. Moon Dog was confused. Everything was working properly. X.O. Newland watched Moon Dog pound away on the keyboard. After several minutes, Moon Dog looked up.

"I ran a report to check the frequency and strength signal history on Kyle's chest-mounted camera. Everything was fine until the maintenance download message came on. From that point, the amount of data coming through diminished," Moon Dog replied as he looked up at the X.O.

X.O. Newland stared back at Moon Dog. He knew Moon Dog was trying to make a point, but it was too technical; the X.O. wasn't getting it. A good leader was never embarrassed about not understanding something. The only dumb question was the one not asked. X.O. James Newland was no dummy. Not missing a beat, the X.O. asked, "What does that mean?"

Moon Dog realized he was speaking in techie speak. He paused as he reorganized his thoughts. He needed to explain this information more clearly, using easy-to-understand terms.

"Images are simply pieces of data. The more data that comes through, increases the detail of an image. When a transmission is impeded by some obstruction, like..." Moon Dog paused as he thought of a good example. As one came to mind, he continued speaking. "I got it. You know when you're on your cell phone and either you or the other person is speaking from a moving car?"

"Yes. Go on."

"What happens many times?" Not waiting for a reply, Moon Dog continued. "The signal is interrupted. Pieces of the conversation seem to be chopped out. The message is broken up, right?"

"Yes. I understand that. It's like the phone technology can't keep up with the moving car," replied the X.O.

"Exactly. Or when you're speaking to someone who is inside a large multistory building. The same thing happens there too! In that situation, the biggest problem is the signal. It's bouncing through openings in the building, traveling through glass windows, open doors, anything to keep the transmission signal traveling to and from the cell tower. As a person walks around inside a building, it becomes more difficult to provide a steady uninterrupted stream of data. The towers have a limited number of openings. Plus, it's dealing with a moving cell phone. When that happens, the cell phone signal temporarily breaks up. It's caused by incomplete data being received and transmitted through the tower.

"The conversation becomes clearer each time the person inside the building stops walking around. By eliminating the motion of the cell phone, the tower is better able to receive and relay the stream of data."

"I get the cell phone part. But I still don't see how that applies to our situation," said X.O. Newland, pleading for Moon Dog to explain further.

"The information I just ran on Kyle's chest-mounted camera shows the quantity of data being exchanged through the communication relay was diminishing. Yet every other device remained strong and constant. They never changed. I'm inferring—" Moon Dog paused and changed his vocabulary, "—guessing at the reason." Moon Dog stopped. Before continuing, he wanted to see if the X.O. understood what he was saying. "The only reason the data from Kyle's chest-mounted camera would become weaker and weaker is—"

The X.O. cut off Moon Dog. The X.O. understood and completed Moon Dog's sentence for him. "—is if Kyle was traveling farther and farther away from the communication relay, right? If Kyle were walking back toward the opening of the cave, he would be passing right by one of the communication devices. The signal wouldn't be getting weaker. It would remain strong. Okay, okay; I got it."

"Exactly. If there was a malfunction on his camera, and he were walking back toward us, we should see him on one of the other cameras. But nothing," Moon Dog added.

As the X.O. and Moon Dog paused, it finally struck the X.O. Kyle had been walking away from the opening and heading north. Kyle was heading deeper into the DPRK. It was the only thing that made sense. But why?

* * * * *

Kyle walked nonstop for over an hour. As he followed the trail, he noticed a slight incline. They made no direction changes and walked almost in a straight line. He was surprised that he wasn't tiring. He was so focused on thinking through his situation that he wasn't distracted by the pain from his injured eye. It had become almost second nature. Kyle just kept his right eye closed to avoid blurred vision.

Kyle benefited from the silence. After he had calmed down, no longer in immediate danger, Kyle focused on the sounds around him; the footfall noise; the breathing. He was one hundred percent sure that it was just him and the one soldier who had shoved the gun into the middle of his back. It was possible that others were walking farther back, but he doubted it. The entire time, he hadn't heard an echo, a cough, rocks being kicked, another set of feet dragging—nothing.

Also, Kyle wondered why they walked away from the other guard. At no time had his captor attempted to call out to the other soldier. Why not? While walking, Kyle replayed the scenario over and over. Something else stood out. His capturer was doing everything in his power to defuse the situation. It was as if he had been extracted to avoid a shootout. Kyle entertained the possibility that the man wasn't necessarily intent on turning him over to the DPRK.

If this were true, Kyle tried to remain as calm as possible. Up until this point, he hadn't resisted or tried to escape. He didn't want to place too much hope on this theory. Even so, this sliver of hope kept his spirits up and his mind clear. He needed to control his fear. Hope was better than nothing. He continued to mull over what he knew. He needed to make good decisions. If he was going to do something, he may only have one chance. Kyle wanted to make sure he was making his best possible move.

For now, he was alive and breathing. That was step one.

*   *   *   *   *

The night guard had returned to his campfire at the end of the excavation tunnel. His feet were in front of the fire. He was mesmerized by Kyle's Beretta M9. It was much heavier than his Russian Makarov pistol. He thought about what had happened.

After he had walked around the pond, he started inspecting the caves. Inside the first one, he saw two sets of footprints. One was much smaller than the other. The impression left by the larger prints were unique. He'd never seen boot mark impressions like these. The guard placed his boot next to the larger impression. In comparison, he deduced that the person that belonged to these impressions was much bigger than himself.

As he had been about to walk out of the cave, his foot had kicked something. He aimed the flashlight down, found Kyle's pistol, and picked it up. Without examining it, he shoved it into his jacket pocket and had continued searching the other caves. No other footprints had been found.

Confident that the men had traveled down into the first tunnel, the guard re-entered the first cave and followed the footprints. After traveling down several hundred meters, the tunnel split. This section of cave was made of solid rock. There was no loose sediment or dirt anywhere. The absence of pooling water or runoff prevented any unusual accumulation of loose earth on the ground. The guard had no way of knowing which way to go. The solid rock took away his ability to see any tracks.

The guard aimed the flashlight beam down each section of tunnel. Uncertain which one to choose, he wisely chose to return to the opening between the excavation and the natural lava tubes. The last thing he wanted to do was get lost deep inside these unknown tunnels. After waiting an hour, he returned to his campfire.

The guard sipped another cup of hot tea. Holding Kyle's Beretta felt good. He was finally doing his job. He held one pistol in each hand. He stared out over the excavated tunnel area. His confidence was growing by the minute. He no longer felt afraid. He was becoming a changed man.

*   *   *   *   *

Gibby and Carla Jo were in a secure teleconference with the X.O. and Moon Dog. It had been four hours since they'd lost contact with Kyle. It was a little after two in the morning. Their timeline had been pushed back, and everyone was on standby.

"Any news?" Gibby asked the X.O.

"We just received word from the Director. They teamed up with Gamboa's team out in California. They've moved a specialized satellite into the area just in case. To determine if anything was being broadcast about someone being captured, they dumped all cell and landlines monitoring the DPRK around the clock. All known detention facilities are also being watched. It's all quiet. Nothing," replied X.O. Newland.

"What's our new final drop-dead timeline?" Gibby asked.

Moon Dog and the X.O. exchanged glances. The X.O. cleared his throat before speaking. "We're giving Kyle until 7:00 a.m. local Seoul time. The Director and others are worried about the compaction truck crew. As they drive up and down the tunnel, even if they don't spot the packages, the vibrations could adversely affect the communication line. If that goes down, we'll be relying on the ninety-six-hour self-destruct.

"Without being able to coordinate the detonation with a visual timing when the drone hits, we stand a greater chance of other aerial footage documenting the inconsistent double explosion. You know the drill, Gibby," X.O. Newland concluded.

Carla Jo and Gibby looked at each other. Gibby had been prepared for that answer. He entered a countdown timer to track the time leading up to the 7:00am deadline. Kyle had less than five hours. Gibby converted the countdown to minutes. Seeing the result, Gibby stared at Carla Jo. They both realized Kyle had less than three hundred minutes to show his face.

*   *   *   *   *

Kyle was in a daze. With so much going on, his mind ignored his pain. Physically, he was on autopilot. He contemplated his options. Without warning, the cave tunnel they'd traveled took a severe right turn. Kyle felt a tap on his shoulder and stopped.

Kyle focused his attention on the man's hand. The Korean searched with his hand along the wall. Finding a crack in the wall, he bent his fingertips and, using his arm, pulled backwards. To Kyle's surprise, a small section of wall gave way. Like a sliding-glass patio door, it rolled away and disappeared behind a portion of the tunnel wall. For the first time, Kyle got a clear full view of his abductor. He was shocked to see a small, middle-aged Korean who stood no more than five-feet, four inches tall and couldn't weigh more than a hundred forty pounds.

Kyle watched the man walk through the opening. He then turned to face Kyle. In a pleasant, friendly smile, the man waved his hand forward as if inviting Kyle inside. Kyle looked down the narrow tunnel in both directions. There was no one else present. Unsure what to do, Kyle followed the Korean inside.

As Kyle entered, he saw the cave was fairly large and it had a dirt floor. There was a wooden table and several oil lamps. The Korean struck a wooden match and lit one of the lamps. The sudden presence of light momentarily blinded Kyle. Covering his eyes, Kyle turned away from the light and then removed his night-vision goggles.

The Korean walked toward Kyle and helped him remove the backpack. He set the backpack on the dirt floor and opened it. Sticking his arm inside, he pulled out several bags. He kept one bag, and handed Kyle one. Again, the Korean reached back inside the backpack. This time, he pulled out two plastic bottles of water.

Kyle watched the Korean take a long drink from his bottle and wipe his forehead with the sleeve of his jacket. The Korean nodded his head and smiled, before walking back to the opening. He slid what appeared to be a large flat rock back into place, hiding the opening. As the large heavy stone fell into place, Kyle heard the sound of stones scraping against each other.

The Korean stepped toward the far corner of the cave. He came back carrying two wooden stools. He sat one in front of Kyle and sat down on the other. Reaching into his breast pocket, the Korean pulled out a pack of Marlboro Reds. He pulled a cigarette out and popped it into his mouth. After yanking out a plastic butane lighter, the man flicked his thumb and sparked a tall flame. With a deep inhale, he lit the cigarette. As he exhaled, the Korean handed the pack of cigarettes to Kyle.

Kyle wasn't a regular smoker. But hanging around a bunch of marines, it was something he indulged in from time to time. Smoking had become a bonding ritual, as opposed to a habit. Kyle laid down his night-vision goggles and grabbed the pack of cigarettes. As Kyle pulled one out, the Korean extended his arm and lit Kyle's cigarette. He then placed the lighter back into his breast pocket. Kyle took a long drag from the strong cigarette. Almost immediately, Kyle could feel the nicotine jolt.

As the smoke cleared, the Korean smiled. He chuckled and pointed at Kyle's face. The Korean could tell that the American didn't understand. Pointing to his own face, the Korean used his index finger and drew imaginary circles around both of his eyes. He then opened his eyes in an exaggerated fashion and pointed back toward Kyle. Kyle realized that the man was commenting on the indentations that the night-vision goggles must have left on his face. Once he understood the meaning, Kyle laughed.

"Oh, right. The goggles," Kyle said softly.

The Korean smiled. He pulled out a piece of meat from the bag. He stuck it in his mouth and tore off a section. It looked like pale beef-jerky. As Kyle watched the man chew, he realized he was also hungry. Following suit, Kyle took a piece of meat. After staring at it, he raised it to his nose. It had a salty and slight fishy smell. It wasn't bad. He had no clue what it was. Kyle stuck a chunk of meat in his mouth and began chewing. He was hungry.

It was meat, some type of dried seafood. It had a slight fishy taste and was delicious. Kyle stuffed another piece into his mouth. He looked back at the Korean and smiled. Without thinking, he said "Thank you for the food" and nodded his head.

The Korean wasn't sure what the American had said. He was guessing that the American had thanked him for the food. In response, the Korean said "Chun muneyo" (you're welcome). The Korean then took one of his hands and patted his chest, saying "Tae." The Korean paused and tapped his hand onto his chest again, repeating himself: "Tae. Tae."

Kyle pointed his finger at the Korean and repeated "Tae." The Korean smiled and nodded his head. He pointed his finger at the American and raised his eyebrows.

Kyle responded in kind by mimicking the Korean by tapping his chest with his hand and said "Kyle. Kyle."

Tae reached out to the backpack and pulled out a persimmon. Persimmons were considered a delicacy in Korea. Tae continued eating until he finished off the bag of dried squid and bag of dried persimmons. Tae threw back the last drops of water inside of the bottle before standing and walking toward Kyle.

Tae raised his wrist, pointed his finger at his wristwatch, and spoke.

"Hanna" (one), "tool" (two). As Tae spoke, he raised his index finger and then his middle finger as if he were counting. Staring into Kyle's face, he repeated it again. This time, Tae pointed his index finger toward his own chest, then pointed forward. He nodded his head as he pointed at his wrist watch and counted again. "Hanna, tool."

"One? Two? So what are you trying to say?" Kyle replied. As Tae pointed at his watch the second time, Kyle thought he understood. Sticking up two fingers, Kyle responded "Two hours? Two hours, is that what you mean?"

Tae smiled back. With a polite bow, Tae turned and walked to the opposite side of the cave. Without his night-vision goggles on, Kyle couldn't see where Tae was going. He heard a familiar scraping of rock on rock sound, followed by a low rumble. Then, Kyle could feel a rush of fresh cold breeze enter the cave, followed by the scraping of rock against rock before a thud. It sounded like a large heavy object falling into place.

Kyle sat and listened. He guessed that Tae had left him alone in the cave. Kyle sat in silence. He could tell that Tae meant him no harm. Kyle considered running away. Running blindly was more dangerous than staying put. It was possible that other guards were waiting outside. Tae left the backpack. It was full of supplies. Nor had Kyle been tied up. For a fleeting moment, Kyle thought about the cyanide capsule hidden in his pocket. He pushed those thoughts out of his mind.

Kyle glanced down at his chest camera. The green light was no longer lit. He was not surprised. It was a long distance from the last communication relay near the opening to the excavation tunnel. Even if there was enough power pumping through the tunnel, they had made several turns. Kyle was certain that no signals could be sent or received this far away. Just in case, leaving nothing to chance, Kyle typed a text message.

"I've been captured. Walked two hours north. Still underground. I'm alone in a room. Injured my right eye."

Kyle sent the message. Unlike a typical cell phone, this relay communication system used unique video data transmission for everything, even texts. Video data only uploaded once and didn't re-transmit. Text messages were different. The agency understood that missions depended on sending and receiving data. Unlike video transmissions, text data would not disrupt overlaid information. The text program was designed to hold, in queue, every text. Once a clear solid frequency was re-established, all text transmissions would be sent until they were received. Gibby had been sending countless messages. They were being held in queue.

After Kyle finished sending the text message, he resumed eating the meat.

As Kyle ate the last piece of meat and finished his bottled water, his body started to feel the effects of the ordeal. The physical demands of walking such a long distance, combined with his fall and injured eye socket, were compounded by the stress of being captured and taken north to this unknown location. Now alone and in relative safety, Kyle's body no longer pumped adrenaline and he began to relax. He couldn't fight the sudden onset of exhaustion. He sat down and curled up on the dirt floor, resting his head against the backpack. Within seconds, Kyle closed his eyes, falling to sleep immediately from exhaustion.

Kyle would need as much rest as he could get; his life depended on it. Kyle had less than five hours to show up. After that, the tunnel would be destroyed, trapping him behind enemy lines.

30

Tae's wife was up early. Sitting alone at the dining table, she sipped hot tea and ate rice soup. The sun wouldn't rise for several more hours. She wanted to be awake when Tae arrived home; she needed to let him know what had happened.

She thought about the unexpected visit from her friend's husband. The memory brought a single tear that rolled down her cheek. It was all her fault. She had put her entire family in danger. With the back of her hand, she wiped the tear away. She lifted the porcelain teacup to her mouth and recalled that meeting.

When he arrived, she was the only person in the house. It was her day off work. Tae had already started his journey south. The children were at school. Tae's parents were in the backyard in the garden. She had been organizing the pantry, making room for the food that Tae would bring back. At first, she hadn't heard the knock at the door.

When she opened the door, she was surprised to see her friend's husband. The same man that had shown so much interest in her purse. She wondered why he was standing on her front porch. She glanced around to locate her friend. He waited for her to make eye contact before speaking.

"Annyong haseayo" (Hello).

"Nay, annyong haseyo" (Yes, hello).

"I'm alone." The man said in a cold, unemotional manner. "My wife isn't here."

In a shaky, weak voice, she asked, "Can I help you with something?"

He replied in a calm controlled matter-of-fact manner. "Yes. I need you to give your husband a message." Tae's wife pursed her lips and averted her eyes. Avoiding eye contact, she waited for him to speak.

"We have an opening in my... crew. I wanted to let your husband know that if he wants, I could put a recommendation on his behalf. The working conditions might be better suited to his liking," said the supervisor. He raised his eyebrows in an exaggerated manner, as if trying to convey a more subtle, alternative meaning.

Catching his unusual voice inflection, she stared up into his face. "What type of job is it?" she inquired.

"I'm sure my wife told you I work for the government."

When her friend informed her of their move to the outskirts of the capital Pyongyang, she guessed as much. It was a well-known fact that only important government employees were moved closer to the capital. Only high officials and military personnel were permitted to reside in the actual city. It was a form of reward, a privilege that the government extended to the elite. She just nodded her head and didn't speak.

"Protocol requires that I refrain from disclosing exactly what I do. However..." The supervisor paused for effect and waited for her to look up before proceeding. "In this case, I feel it is essential that I let you know. But before I do, I must ask that you swear upon your life and the lives of your entire family that you will never utter a word of this, only to your husband. Do I have your word?"

She stared back into the man's serious face. In the Democratic People's Republic of Korea, such a promise was never made halfheartedly. Such an oath came with a sincere, absolute consequence. These words were spoken only in times of utmost importance.

"Yes, I promise."

"I need to hear you say it," he urged.

She paused and peered into his eyes. They never blinked. In a careful, calculated response, she said, "I promise to tell only my husband. I promise not to tell anyone else. I promise on my life and on the lives of my family."

With a slight nod of his head, the supervisor continued. "I work for the military. I supervise a crew that excavates tunnels along the DMZ." He made a point of emphasizing the word "tunnels."

His words were like a long, hot knife, piercing her chest. Without directly accusing her husband, he was, at the very least, letting her know that he had some suspicion that her husband had been using the underground tunnels.

The supervisor waited for her reaction. Her face turned pale and her mouth gaped open. Based on her reaction, he was certain she got the message.

"Discuss my offer with him. There is no need to contact me. If I can justify hiring him, I'll be back." The supervisor waited for her to nod her head. This time, she couldn't look him in the eye. During the conversation, her posture had become progressively weaker, to the point that she no longer stood upright. Without realizing it, she was frozen in a slightly bent fashion, leaning forward from the waist. As the supervisor turned to leave, he paused and spoke over his shoulder without looking back. "By the way, that is a lovely purse you have. Your husband

has good taste." Before she closed the front door, she watched him climb down the stairs.

A river of tears spilled down her face. She sobbed uncontrollably.

She remained sitting with slumped shoulders at the table and stared out the window into the dark winter sky. There was no moon. The clouds hid the stars. She continued to wait for Tae's return.

*   *   *   *   *

Deep inside the Agency's Main DC Office, Director Valdez sat in an isolated room. She'd always liked her visits to Washington with its monuments and Smithsonian Museums, but this trip was different. Until the mission concluded, she was ordered stateside. Like anything secret and important, everybody knew something was up. Too many Agency VIPs had been called to Washington. It had become one of those "tells," like a poker player who unconsciously played with his chips when bluffing.

It was SOP (standard operating procedure). The Agency pulled the Director out of the theatre of play. If things didn't go as planned, the Director would be available to explain, face to face, what had happened. No middlemen. No misinterpretations. No vaguely drafted memos.

All missions inevitably had setbacks. Pulling the directors out of the mission kept them out of the immediate loop of information. Directors dealt better with the big picture, rather than the intricate, microscopic details. Director Valdez had been told only that the detonation had been pushed back until around 7:00 a.m. local Seoul time, which translated to 5:00 p.m. EST.

It was Friday, a normal workday. The hustle and bustle of Washington would soon overflow the DC beltway. With so many legitimate VIPs about, when Director Valdez changed the direct feed teleconference meeting from 10:00 a.m. to 5:00 p.m., in other regions of the globe no one gave it much attention. Eight other Agency covert operations were underway. The bureaucratic machine that orchestrated and controlled the biggest covert organization on the globe was flexible and experienced. Such setbacks were expected. Without missing a beat, schedules were tweaked, calls were made, and secure satellite conference rooms were moved to accommodate the schedule change.

She was grateful that the satellite conference hadn't originally been scheduled zero dark thirty Washington time. Otherwise, the VIPs would have to await the seven-hour pushback during the quiet, inactive dead of night. Out of boredom, the VIP's would have demanded answers, not out of necessity but rather out of irritability, because they had wasted valuable sleep time for no good reason. It was okay for the service men and women in the armed forces to hurry up and wait, but delays never went over well with upper management.

Unknown to the other Agency bigwigs, Director Valdez knew something was up. Short of a technological malfunction, the only reason she could imagine pushing back the satellite conference call was some human element. It hadn't gone unnoticed that a deadline had been set for 7:00 a.m. local time. She recognized the significance. The deadline was set at the exact time the compaction trucks were scheduled to begin another day's work.

It was Agency protocol. Once all the major pieces of a mission were in play, very few things could push the time schedule back. Most of the time, even losing personnel wasn't a justifiable reason. Extending the start time a few minutes would be tolerated. Other than that, the X.O.'s hands were tied. He couldn't extend the deadline much further. He had a small degree of flexibility at his disposal. The Director had already checked the weather in Korea. It was overcast with some snow. There was no mention of extreme weather that could influence the mission.

Going against protocol, the Director texted X.O. Newland on her secure phone. "What's up?" Within seconds, she received a reply. "Bird's gone missing. Everything ready. Waiting until last minute for his return before proceeding."

The Director set her phone down on the table. She stared up at the reprinted framed painting on the conference room wall. She realized that she hadn't even met Lt. Benjamin. The Director glanced at the clock. It was 1:08 p.m. Washington DC time. Kyle had less than four hours.

*　*　*　*　*

"Gibby, I've got Mr. Davies waiting at Kadena. Even if Kyle comes back into contact, it would still take him at least two hours to hump it out. We need time. Mr. Davies is to arrive no later than 7:00 a.m. local time. He's waiting now on standby," explained Carla Jo.

Gibby heard her. He knew it was time. They need to start planning to proceed without Kyle. Staring at the monitors, he checked each camera feed. Nothing. The only good news was that there was no chatter about capturing anyone inside the DPRK. Gibby was thinking that, even though it was very early in the morning, if an

American had been captured. Such an event would be considered big news. Huge news. If that happened, the information would be sent up the line, probably straight to the Exalted Leader. Gibby figured if things got bad, Kyle still had the capsule. For a second, Gibby considered whether he'd already used one.

To clear his thoughts, Gibby shook his head. "Poor kid," he said, while looking at Carla Jo. Gibby checked the clock. Kyle had less than four hours. Gibby turned his head and looked out the office window. It was still the dead of night. Kyle still had a chance.

"Have you checked in with Moon Dog? Make sure he keeps tabs with Kadena." As he spoke, Gibby kept his eyes glued to the monitors. The fact that the night guard had returned to the fire gave him hope. If Kyle had been captured, the guard would most likely be part of it. He wouldn't have returned to the fire. Gibby continued to watch the guard. Then, he saw it.

The guard appeared to be holding up two guns, one in each hand. One of the guns got his attention. Gibby zoomed the camera in for a closer look. There was no doubt what he was looking at. Everyone carried one. It was a standard issued Beretta M9. Gibby froze. In a defeated voice, he spoke.

"CJ, take a look."

Carla Jo turned her attention to the monitor. Without missing a beat, she said "That's a Beretta M9."

They both stared at the screen. Neither spoke. What else could they be thinking? Kyle's chest-mounted camera had been off line for nine hours. An analysis of the chest-mounted camera confirmed that it was working. By all indications, he was moving away from the communication relay, which prevented them from getting a clear reception. By all accounts, Kyle was taken deeper into the DPRK. And now the night guard was carrying two pistols. Before now, he had carried only one pistol. Now he also had the exact type of sidearm Kyle had.

Gibby and Carla Jo stared at the night guard. Although the night-vision camera couldn't pick up his facial expressions, his actions said it all. He looked like a kid playing with new toy. He held the pistol up close to his face. He was preoccupied and fascinated by his find. It was unmistakable. The guard was holding the pistol in one hand, trying to guess its weight.

Gibby was a professional. When faced with hard physical evidence, he had to make his best-informed decision. With a stern look and clenched jaw, Gibby finally spoke. "At the very least, Kyle is somehow incapacitated. How else can we interpret the guard holding Kyle's weapon? At worst, he's already dead. If he's captured, he might as well be. They'll keep him in prison to interrogate him. If they torture him, or if he's worried about being tortured, he would have eaten the capsule."

With his decision made, Gibby turned off the countdown tracker. In Gibby's mind, the mission needed to move on.

"CJ, my concern now, regardless of Kyle's situation, is this: If the guard has Kyle's weapon, he might start nosing around the tunnel and stumble onto the packages. Let's get Mr. Davies in the air. It will take him awhile to get over the drop location anyway."

Carla Jo nodded her head. She contacted Mr. Davies and gave him the green light. Mr. Davies confirmed the tanks were full. Just in case, he could stay up flying standby well past the drop-dead time. As the KC-135's wheels lifted off the tarmac, Mr. Davies realized this would be his first trip directly over into the DMZ. So far, he'd only flown the Director between Camp Bonifas and

Seoul, well south of the DMZ. Mr. Davies hoped like hell those DPRK guys didn't have trigger fingers. Carrying so much fuel, if he took a round, his aircraft would light up like a Roman candle.

31

Tae walked up onto his front porch. It felt weird to be returning without the oversized backpack. As he opened the front door, he was surprised to see his wife awake, sitting at the dining table. She heard him enter the room. With her head bent down facing the floor, she stood. She couldn't make eye contact. She walked toward their bedroom before turning back. In a calm, sad voice, she said, "We need to talk."

Tae followed her into their bedroom. She sat down on the wood floor. Tae knew something was wrong. She hadn't even asked him where the supplies were. Tae pulled out a pack of cigarettes. He lit one and sat down beside her. Handing him an ashtray, she told him about the visit.

Without interrupting, Tae listened. She was surprised. He showed no signs of anger over the purse. She had explained how her friend's husband revealed that he worked for the government and excavated tunnels in the DMZ. As he absorbed the words, Tae thought back to the first time he saw the digging crew. He stumbled across an opening into the natural lava tube. He was certain now: He had been seen.

Tae waited for his wife to finish. He knew she needed to retell the entire event. Tae was patient and waited. He patted the back of her hands. While she spoke, tears pooled in corners of her eyes, periodically sliding down her checks. Before she finished, Tae knew that their lives were about to change.

While walking the remainder of the way home, he'd contemplated killing the American soldier. Before sliding the boulder back into place concealing the opening, he stared at the sword. It was safe, wrapped and protected hanging on the wall. During his last visit, he had pulled it down and sharpened it. It gave him something to pass the time while regaining his energy for the trip home. Tae was sure the American soldier was injured. He'd purposely forced him to carry the backpack, hoping to further weaken and exhaust him. He couldn't bring himself to kill the American, though. Tae had never killed anyone before. After listening to his wife, Tae was glad he hadn't. Helping the American soldier might be their only hope.

The purpose of the man's visit was clear. He wanted to warn Tae. He had to know that he was using the tunnels to travel back and forth from South Korea. It was no longer a secret. He probably thought Tae was a smuggler. It was the man's way of giving him a second chance. If the man had followed protocol, he would have contacted his superiors. The visit should have resulted in his being taken to the authorities, while everyone else would be taken to a Labor Camp.

Tae knew they had no choice. Tonight, they would leave under the cover of darkness. They had to leave now, while they still had time. How was he going to tell his father? His father would be devastated. This time it was different. If they didn't all go, it was only a matter of time before someone came to take him away. He needed to explain how an Imperialist American soldier, came to be hiding inside their family shrine.

For most of the day, Tae's wife thought about what had to be done. The visit from the government man made the choice clear. She knew what needed to happen. Dwelling on their options, she came to the same conclusion. She pointed her index finger toward the corner of the room. She had already packed the children's belongings. She'd also packed a bag for her and her husband. Her children's backpacks would no longer be filled with school books, folders, pens, and pencils. Now they carried extra clothes, food, and water. She'd sent the children to sleep early and dressed them both in long thermal underwear. She hoped that once they were awake, they could just slip into their pants, shirts and jackets. With as little a delay as possible, they could be on their way. They were prepared to go.

She was most concerned about her daughter. How would she react? She was the oldest and had been singled out for strong language skills. She had been accepted into the Junior Language Academy and was excited about the opportunity. She hoped to enter the mandatory ten-year conscription requirement in the DPRK military to compete for a slot as an English translator. She knew this experience would assure her of a bright future.

"What did you tell our daughter?" Tae asked.

"I told them both that we were taking a family trip." Tae and his wife remained seated, mustering their courage and energy. Tae felt more refreshed than he had anticipated. His extended nap at the pond and forcing the American to carry the heavy backpack saved his strength. He would need all his wits to convince his father to leave. If his father refused to go, Tae wasn't sure what to do.

Their attention was drawn to the sounds coming from behind their closed bedroom door. They heard the distinct shuffling of two sets of slippers against the wood floor. They'd heard it every day for years. It was Tae's parents. They were awake, earlier than normal. His conversation with his wife must have awakened them. Tae could see his father's slipper-covered feet appear from under the crack of the door. As the door opened, his father stuck his head inside. In a soft, crackled smoker's voice, Tae's father spoke.

"What happened?"

*   *   *   *   *

With a blank shocked expression on his face, Tae's father stared back. Everything was coming without warning. How could he leave his home? How could he abandon the cause, the national dream that someday Korea would reunite? He had never held any desire to run away in search of selfish comforts. If they left, there would be no chance of returning. As Tae's father processed what had happened, he wasn't leaving without a fight.

"Why don't we just kill the American soldier? The government man was just sending a warning. If they had plans of taking you, we wouldn't be having this conversation," he pleaded.

No one spoke. The grandchildren were still sleeping. It was just the four grownups. Unable to speak, the other three kept their heads down. Tae's father searched their faces for support. It finally struck him. He was the only one who had been to war. He was the only one who had fought and killed another person. The invading Japanese soldiers had been ruthless. It was something he'd hated doing. The circumstances forced his hand. The Japanese had been the aggressors. They had invaded their homeland. While the eldest son stayed home to take care of his mother, he had gone out and fought. Tae's father mistakenly interpreted their silence for fear. Without looking up, Tae spoke.

"What if something goes wrong? What if his body is found in our possession?" Tae paused before continuing. "What if they come for me anyway? The only reason the government man came at all was to send a message. Someday, they will come back. And it may not be just for me."

As Tae spoke these last words, his father looked at his wife. He scanned the room and knew Tae was right. If they came for Tae, then everyone, even the children, would pay the price. Tae's father had no qualms about staying and being sent to die in the labor camps. At least he would die in his homeland. But what about his eldest son, his daughter-in-law, his grandchildren? They had most of their lives yet to live.

Years ago, they urged him to go south. He'd refused. If it hadn't been for his physical ailments, his son wouldn't have been making the trips south. So in a way it was his fault that they were in this situation. Tae had told him their plan. When he passed away, Tae would take the entire family south. He doubted that Tae's mother would leave, even after his death. Tae's father knew that if he refused to go, his wife wouldn't leave either. She would stay by his side, no matter what.

Tae's father exhaled. The weight of the situation was heavy. The question was no longer some intellectual possibility that he could argue. Tae watched as his father struggled, deciding.

Tae said, "Until now, we had no leverage going south. Maybe, if we help return the American to safety, they will offer us asylum?"

Hearing Tae's words, he studied the sad faces of his wife and daughter-in-law. It was his turn to repay the favor. He could no longer allow them to sacrifice for his benefit. Resolved and determined, his father spoke.

"You're right. Get the children ready."

They all stared at him with shocked faces. With a sense of urgency, the women gathered the children. They fed them hot rice soup and then bundled them in warm clothes. They helped them put on their winter jackets and mittens. Each child struggled, pulling their backpacks on over their thick layered clothes. Their mother covered their heads with wool hats and ear muffs. Within minutes, their small group was ready.

They walked out onto the front porch. Tae and his father took one last look inside of the open front door. Their house had served them well. Tae and his two children had been born and raised there. It was the only home they had ever known. Before meeting up with everyone across the dirt road, Tae's father closed the door and bowed. Tae led them across the empty field and then stopped on the rising slope. He turned back and took a final peek over his shoulder. He could just make out the roofline of their home. Tae turned on his flashlight and walked into the night. They would never see their home again. While they marched through the field, it began snowing.

*　　*　　*　　*　　*

Angelie awoke earlier than normal. It was Saturday, and there was no school. She poured a hot cup of tea. It had become her ritual. Each morning, she stared out the back window of her little house to watch the sun rise from behind the mountain range.

Over the last few days, just before the sun rose, she noticed dim lights cutting through the night air. Tonight was different. It was the second day of the new moon, and it was one of the darkest nights of the year. Winter was coming. For some reason, she awoke several hours early. The sky was pitch black, and a blanket of thick clouds hid the stars. During the night, it snowed off and on. Soon, it would snow in earnest.

As Angelie stared out into the mountain range, she saw several bright flickering dots of light. It brought a smile to her face. As she studied the lights, she saw several large embers rise and float into the sky. The lights were campfires. In her excitement, Angelie went to her bedroom. She pulled out the introductory packet provided by the International School. The packet included several maps. One map detailed the area surrounding the village. She held it in the air, repositioning it. Finally, she found her location on the map.

She hurried back to the window, and held the map up to the window. She compared the map's location to what she saw outside. She was certain she was looking at the northern border of the Republic of Korea. The map showed a dotted line running across the mountain range. She turned her attention to the campfire lights. She realized that the campfires must be from DPRK soldiers, probably guarding the southern border along the DMZ. It brought tears of joy. She let her imagination run wild, thinking about meeting her fellow countrymen.

Without realizing it, Angelie began rubbing a small birthmark on her right hand. The birthmark was located just above her wrist. For years, she hadn't thought about the connection and significance of the birth mark. Seeing the campfires stirred memories that she had long since suppressed. At that moment, a vivid memory came storming out of her subconscious. She had a brother. She began recalling small pieces of incomplete memories.

She remembered that her parents had died. She couldn't remember what they looked like. Yet she could somehow sense, even at that very young age, that they were gone. Her mind flashed images of being a young girl. She and her brother were taken to an orphanage. She could sense that they wanted to hold onto each other, but at night they were separated. The boys were placed on one side of a large room filled with small bunkbeds lined up in neat rows.

Each night, she made sure she slept across from her brother so they could see each other's faces. As those images seeped from her subconscious, she found herself raising her hand to her eyebrow and stroking the small hairs. As she became conscious of the feelings that this memory stirred, she realized it was their secret signal.

On numerous occasions, they had been warned about speaking across the room. At night, their conversations disturbed the other children. After threats of separation, they created this secret sign. When feeling lonely, they looked at each other and ran their index finger across an eyebrow. This gesture was their way of communicating across the divide, a sign they used to comfort each other without anyone else's knowing.

Angelie had suppressed these memories. She had somehow forgotten having a brother. As tears flowed, she realized that it was her subconscious mind tugging on her emotions. The memory of her brother had more to do with her deep emotional desire to return to Korea than all the years of training. She just hadn't realized it.

With the back of her hand, Angelie wiped the tears away from her face. Then, another image appeared. It was her brother's face. He had a gentle, calm expression, with big round eyes; much more oval than a typical Korean. His most distinguishing trait was his birthmark. While her birthmark was on her hand, his was on his cheek. It was almost a perfect circle, about the size of an American quarter. They were twins. Until her adoption, they were inseparable.

Angelie stared out across the field. Her eyes were drawn upward toward the mountain. She paused on the campfires. Then, she continued gazing at the mountain range. She urged her mind to complete the image of what she would find on the other side. This time, her imagination included an image of a young man who looked about her age and had a small birthmark on his right cheek. As Angelie brought the cup of tea to her mouth, more tears slid down her shiny cheek.

*　　*　　*　　*　　*

Tae was worried his children would have difficulty walking. To his surprise, they seemed full of energy, distracted and amazed by the beauty of this untouched wilderness. Doting over the children's safety, his wife and mother were just as distracted. The women hadn't noticed the physical strain their bodies were enduring. As the snow continued falling, Tae paused. He glanced back, making sure everyone was keeping up. With each small hill they climbed, his father fell farther and farther behind. His father was the last one in line.

Despite the cold temperature, he was grateful for the snowflakes. He reminded everyone to cast their flashlight beams down toward the ground. The snowfall provided an extra element of cover. As they marched along, the falling snow broke up the outlines of their figures. Using flashlights was necessary. Although Tae could have done without them, this was everyone else's first trip along this route. Only his father had a general idea where they were headed. The darkness of night and falling snow had confused his father enough that he no longer was certain where they were.

After walking thirty minutes, Tae stopped along a dry creek bed. He glanced up and down the creek. Confident it was clear, he led them across. Then they struggled climbing a steep slope. Tae helped pull each person up. Walking along another trail that ran along the mountain ridge, Tae urged everyone to use their hands to balance themselves against the side of the mountain. They worked their way along the ridge. Finally, they came to an overgrown area. Tae looked inside the vegetation. He made sure no animals were hiding inside and then waited for everyone to gather before proceeding.

Tae's father was confused. He'd never seen this area before. Tae pointed his flashlight into the corner of the mountainside. Hidden by the bushes was a cave opening. After everyone was inside, multiple dancing light-beams wouldn't draw unwanted attention from soldiers or predators. The temperature seemed to be warmer. Inside, there were no cross breezes or falling snow to create wind chill. Tae glanced back toward the cave opening. He watched the snowfall cover their tracks with fresh flakes.

Tae led the group through the cave. Unaffected by the maze of lava tubes, Tae walked through the tunnels with speed and confidence. Finally, Tae's father recognized the area. He'd used an alternative route to the family shrine. Using the tunnels, he cut through the mountain and saved over an hour's time.

Tae glanced back, making eye contact with his father, and his father flashed a smile. He recognized where they were. It had taken Tae three hours to walk home, explain the situation, pack, and then lead his family back. He was late. He wondered how Kyle was doing.

Tae slid the heavy stone door away. He heard an unusual sound. At first, he thought there was an animal inside. The noise was a deep guttural sound. Tae peeked around the corner of the shrine wall. The oil lamps were still on. To his relief, he found the American soldier sound asleep, curled up against the backpack. Kyle was snoring.

Tae waited for everyone to enter. He slid the rock covering back into place. Everyone looked down at the sleeping soldier. Tae's son was curious. He tiptoed toward Kyle. Everyone aimed their flashlight beams down at Kyle's face. Tae's son leaned down for a closer look. It was the first time he'd been this close to an American.

Fascinated by his features, Tae's son studied Kyle's face. Compared to a typical North Korean, Kyle was huge. He was six feet two inches tall, and weighed two hundred ten pounds. Given that the average North Korean was five feet five inches tall and weighed less than one hundred fifty pounds, by comparison, this man was a giant. Unexpectedly, Kyle inhaled, creating another loud snore. The noise scared Tae's son, causing him to flinch backward and fall onto his backside. He wasn't injured, just startled. In unison, everyone laughed.

Hearing the sudden outburst of noise, combined with the concentration of light pointing into Kyle's face, he awoke. Opening his eyes, Kyle was surprised to see two children, their faces red from the outside cold. Behind the children, Kyle saw two women, an old man, and Tae. Kyle shook his head, struggling to get his bearings. After an awkward moment of silence, Kyle managed to get to his knees and stand. With seven people bunched inside, the shrine seemed much smaller. Kyle wondered how to proceed.

In a soft voice, Tae's daughter said, "Hello."

Kyle turned his head toward the sound. At first, he couldn't comprehend why he was hearing a child's voice. As he glanced around, he realized that it was the young girl who was speaking.

"You speak English?"

"Some. A little."

Kyle couldn't help himself. Just hearing someone speaking English restored his sense of optimism. For the first time since his capture, he felt there was a chance of getting out of this thing alive. Unable to hide his joy, Kyle flashed a huge, ear-to-ear grin. Without understanding Kyle's words, they could see he was happy. In an exhilarated display of excitement, Kyle spoke, "All right!"

For the second time, their family shrine was filled with laughter. Everyone needed a release from all the stress. It seemed they were all on the same team, working together. Wasting no time, Tae pointed at his watch. He spoke to his daughter, who became the official translator.

"My father says not much time. Trucks coming soon. We need go now before they come back," she explained in choppy, yet understandable English. The meaning was clear enough. Kyle had been listening to every syllable.

He could feel his confidence wane as he considered the possibility that he was going to be taken deeper into the DPRK. He needed to know. Without considering the potential consequences of his inquiry, he spoke.

"Where are we going?"

As the young girl translated, Kyle's nerves were frazzled. He was on the brink of panic. He waited for the response. As he listened to her translation, he couldn't believe his ears.

"Back south, where my father found you."

32

"X.O., We may have a problem," Moon Dog explained.

"What is it?"

"It's starting to snow." He could tell that the X.O. didn't see the significance, so he explained. "I'm concerned that if the snow gets too deep, there's a chance that the first fuel dump could be minimized by the presence of the snow."

"What are you thinking?"

"Just an observation. I just want to make sure that we consider all variables."

"I see your point. But we'll be dropping more than eighty thousand pounds of jet fuel to prep the area. We could fill a hotel swimming pool with that much fuel," X.O. Newland replied. "Besides, there isn't that much snow. We're good to go."

Moon Dog nodded, agreeing. The delay caused by Kyle's disappearance was taking its toll. They'd delayed exploding the tunnel over six hours. They'd pushed back all the time schedules and had been monitoring the communication lines. The cameras inside the tunnel were working. The images were clear. They all showed empty sections of tunnel. The only movement came from the night guard. He had returned to his campfire. No new information about Kyle was received from their

Agency counterparts. They were eavesdropping on all phone activity. Nothing. It was the middle of the night. Unlike the US, people weren't ordering pizza or cruising night clubs. This was the DPRK. Probably the only place in the world where even small insignificant rules were obeyed. Everything was quiet.

"Where is Mr. Davies?"

"It takes two hours and fifteen minutes to get from Kadena AFB, Japan. He'll be taking the scenic route. The Agency wanted him coming in low." Fully loaded, Mr. Davies had the ability to fly over fifteen hundred miles. He had a top speed of five hundred eighty miles per hour. The KC-135 Stratotanker could throttle it if they needed to push the drop time up. For now, slow and steady was the name of the game; he had to avoid any unwanted attention. Moon Dog checked his screens and confirmed that Mr. Davies was inside South Korean airspace. Using the scenic route, he could stay in flight well past the 7:00 a.m. deadline.

"Mr. Davies is in the theatre. He's just circling, waiting for the word," Moon Dog replied.

"What about the UAV?" the X.O. asked.

"It's been prepped and hidden in a hanger. All the markings have been completed and essential gear stowed for the impact scenario."

The X.O. stood and walked out of the secure room where he and Moon Dog would spend the remainder of the mission. He needed to go to his office and make sure everything was in order. It was the final step before dropping the tunnel. He needed to make sure that all the indirect plans were ready. Once it started, there would be no time to fill in any missing gaps.

X.O. Newland entered his office and locked the door behind him. He checked his hidden monitor. He was confident no one had entered his office. He unlocked his desk and began reading his checklist. The presence of the specialty tanker gear was supposed to support the illusion that a real KC-135 had crashed. Specialized replacement engine and refueling arms parts had been taken from the real one that was getting prepped to be sent to Arizona's mothball fleet. The serial numbers would match up perfectly. The Agency had been in the espionage business for decades and had it down to a science. They had fictitious personnel records with each person's family histories, ready to go.

For years, agents had been recruited for their acting skills. If "fact checkers" began digging into the pasts of these illusionary casualties, home addresses, pictures of family members and deep paper-trail documents would be needed. The Agency no longer scurried about patching together credible cover stories for these ICs (Imaginary Citizens). Depending on the complexity of a mission, the Agency created profiles with storylines from birth.

Before leaving to Washington DC, Director Valdez had made sure all the FIC files were ready. The only foreseeable casualties were the KC-135 Tanker's three-person crew. Their profiles had been conjured up years before. Computer programs were being utilized to initiate real telephone conversations between agents assigned to the FIC Unit. These agents used real phone numbers and real phone lines. The agency wanted to create actual paper trails; real billing statements for utility bills, credit cards, even car loans. The Agency purchased real cars, using specific controlled addresses simply to build the paper trail that would stand up to scrutiny. Bills were paid with real checking accounts and mailed from real post offices.

One of the most dreaded assignments was inside this section of the FIC. Every active agent that came through FIC spent six months making fictitious calls, writing checks, and otherwise acting like one of the imaginary citizens or ICs. Each agent was assigned twenty-five ICs. Over the next six months, specific profiles were created or expanded upon. This unit spent all its time building paper trails. With the advent of the internet, even emails were created and messages crafted to support the type of person the Agency needed.

The depth of the deception was almost beyond comprehension. Certain profiles called for obsessive-compulsive personalities. The agents followed the psychological profiles of these ICs, making sure that automatic bill pays were utilized, bank accounts were never overdrawn, and email communications were clean and straightforward. All efforts were made to support the characteristics of each imaginary citizen. His grades were good, attendance was perfect, and job evaluations consistently reflect high marks. While other ICs were designed to appear erratic, unreliable, unkempt, and disorganized. These ICs would have bad credit scores, lack personal relationships or other social attachments, possess a criminal history, and have had repossessions, foreclosures, demotions, reprimands. The Agency spent hundreds of thousands of hours a year conjuring up these imaginary citizens.

The Agency could cross-reference the needs of a mission and peruse its massive database and hand-pick its IC's. It was like taking a book off a shelf. Small armies could be conjured out of thin air. The government controlled various types of bureaucracies and independent contractor firms across the globe. All the tax and payroll records for these IC's could be funneled through these legitimate companies. Each entity provided much of the necessary background for the deception. Telephone and computer lines could be redirected through untraceable means, landing back at the Agency's FIC unit.

Director Valdez had handpicked the ICs for this mission. Their profiles were selected and the FIC Unit had been enhancing current relevant communications and documents that would support their actions. Calls were made, dry cleaning had been picked up, mail had been allowed to pile up in post office boxes. Agents had been assigned to recreate entire families, co-workers, and neighbors. The Agency would typically assign at least twenty acting agents to rehearse and supplement these paper and electronic back stories with real conversations, real Facebook streams, emails, and Instagram postings. It was like a Broadway play rehearsal as they prepared for the mission.

Hummingbird had elected to go with only three deep IC scenarios—the crew of the KC-135 tanker. The Director had pulled ten additional ICs with only paper and electronic cover stories in place, just in case. X.O. Newland kept all IC files in his desk. He'd looked at them several times just to familiarize himself with their names and basic bios. Once the drone crashed, the cover story would be sold to the local media and through Asian geographically specific social media, news briefings were ready to be released to all major American news media outlets later in the afternoon. That is, assuming everything went as planned.

As the X.O. was about to close and lock his desk drawer, he saw Kyle's folder. Inside were four scenario folders, each manipulated and falsified to support a specific background that the Agency wanted to portray. The X.O. had placed Kyle's original authentic personnel record folder on the bottom. He now had other versions in case he was captured or killed during the mission. X.O.

Newland released a deep sigh. He was convinced it wasn't going to end well for Lt. Benjamin.

Lt. Kyle Benjamin wasn't an IC, he was real flesh and blood. Most agents recognized the advantages of never being found. It was best on family members. There would be no need to use false deceptive storylines designed to protect the mission. Otherwise, reputations would be ruined. It was part of the job. It didn't take agents long to learn that you never believed what was being said by the media. Inside the Agency, there was an unwritten rule: For those in search of the truth, answers were confined to successful missions, where answers could be exchanged only between those with long professional relationships.

The X.O. locked his desk and reset the hidden security camera. The camera had been designed to begin recording when motion was detected. He was inside a top-secret building that required secure pass cards and other strict identity-verification protocols. This additional level of security inside his office was standard operating procedure, necessary in case a team member had been compromised. At some level, every Agency had to trust its personnel. In most cases, double agents appeared to be completely trustworthy loyal agents, above reproach. Catching them making a mistake was many times based on a simple, low-level security measure like this.

The X.O. left his office. The door automatically locked and required a pass card to re-enter. He began walking back to the secure conference room. This was his last chance to alter the plans. Once it started, there would be no turning back. The X.O. slid his pass card into the magnetic reader and pushed the doors open. As the heavy doors closed behind him, he glanced up at the clock.

It was time. They couldn't wait any longer. As he approached Moon Dog, the X.O. quickened his pace. With a nod of his head, he spoke.

"Lieutenant. Is Mr. Davies ready?"

"Yes, sir."

"Is your UAV fueled, all items loaded and good to go?"

"Yes, sir. Just waiting for your orders. It's tarped to avoid unwanted attention."

"Word has been given. Let's uncover the UAV and make your way to the tarmac," ordered the X.O.

"Sir! Yes, sir!" With the official order given, Moon Dog radioed to the ground crew. Within minutes, Moon Dog had the UAV taxiing through the falling snow toward the runway. Moon Dog stopped the UAV on the runway and checked his readings. Typically, he would pause only for a moment before proceeding. However, just as he was about to push the accelerator, a loud electronic tone broke the silence. Moon Dog's face recoiled as the noise broke his concentration. He turned away from the large image projected on the wall and stared into the X.O.'s eyes. In an elevated voice, Moon Dog responded.

"Oh, my God!"

"What is it? What's that noise? Is there a problem with the UAV?" X.O. Newland asked in rapid-fire succession.

"No. That's the data feed inside the tunnel."

"What does it mean?"

Moon Dog's face tilted as if trying to make sense of what had just happened. "The data feed. I've been monitoring it the entire time, ever since Kyle went missing. It's the first data we've received from his chest-mounted camera in the last eight hours!"

X.O. Newland jogged to his computer. He had all the live camera feeds displaying. The X.O. studied each monitor and couldn't see any movement. Even the night guard was out of view. He located Kyle's chest-mounted camera view. Nothing but static. Moon Dog was stuck at the UAV controls and couldn't abandon them to follow the X.O. Eager to learn what the X.O. was seeing, Moon Dog turned his head toward the X.O. "Can you see anything? Is the image changing? Are we receiving an image?"

The X.O. stared intensely at the monitor. After a few seconds, he saw nothing new. Everything was the same. The X.O. appeared confused, reluctant to proceed. "Do you think it could just be the snow interfering with the satellite transmission?"

"It's possible," Moon Dog replied. "If we start getting more data-spike notifications, and if they begin to happen with greater frequency, I'd bet that Kyle is walking back this direction."

"What if he's not walking?" asked the X.O.

"What do you mean?"

"What if he's being led? Or worse. What if only his body is being carried this direction? Unless we can get a visual confirmation, we're still just guessing," explained the X.O.

For a moment, they sat motionless without speaking. They each contemplated how to proceed. The UAV sat at the end of the runway. The maintenance crew had been scraping the runway clear of snow with several snowplow vehicles. The airfield's maintenance crew were accustomed to winter weather maintenance. This airfield location was selected based on its ability to handle such a large plane. It needed to make sense. However, this airfield was not located inside an American military base. The Agency decided to use a joint task force location that utilized Republic of Korea and civilian personnel.

The Agency knew that all aspects of the mission needed to be able to stand up to international scrutiny. It also knew that enemy spy satellites were permanently watching their installations. To reduce the likelihood of tipping anyone off about *Hummingbird*, it was decided that it would be safer to send the airplanes out from different locations that were not under constant surveillance. Although the UAV could have taken off from many different airfields, this one was selected because it had a long enough runway and provided refueling ground facilities that had serviced these types of KC-135 refueling tankers in the past. For the cover story to appear realistic, the UAV had to take off from a location that could handle this type of plane and provide these types of services. The Agency knew that others were always watching.

On this particular evening, one of the regular maintenance crew members was unavailable. He had been granted leave for the weekend. As the unexpected snowstorm rolled in, the specialized maintenance crew was hurried onto the airfield to begin their work. It could be a busy day, keeping the runway clear.

It was early morning. The substitute snowplow operator had received a call from his controller. Arrangements had been made. He was going to be assigned as the substitute maintenance crew member. For quite some time, the DPRK had been waiting for an opportunity to get a look at the types of planes serviced at this location. Although the substitute crew member had hundreds of hours in winter airfield maintenance, his real specialization was in military aircraft recognition.

As the snow continued to fall, he waited for the KC-135 refueling tanker to take off. For some reason, the plane was stopped, sitting on the runway. As he continued waiting, he watched the snowfall begin to accumulate on the windshield. He wondered why the pilot hadn't turned on the windshield wipers. As an expert in aircrafts, he knew that in this weather, the pilot would be flying by instruments. But even so, it was human nature to clear the windshield. Why wait, he wondered? The snowplow operator became more curious. As he continued waiting, he noticed something unusual. There was no movement in the cockpit. He couldn't see any glow from the interior instruments. Nothing.

Moon Dog glanced up at the projection wall image that was coming from the UAV. He had been so distracted about the alarm sounding that he almost forgot he was manning the UAV. The UAV's camera view had become blurred by the accumulating snow. Moon Dog activated the windshield wipers. The cameras had been installed inside the front-mounted lights. The wipers began clearing the glass, protecting the camera lenses. The designers of this UAV chose the headlights, as it provided additional protection from impact by flying objects. The glass used was designed to remain crystal clear and to easily shed moisture. Even so, the Agency designers understood that rain, dust, and snow would still cause a problem. To account for these possibilities, the engineers had worked hard to design a retractable windshield wiper system that could withstand the high inflight speeds and still include aerodynamic properties too.

The engineers were too focused on the functionality of the wiper system. They had tunnel vision. All their efforts concentrated on enhancing the design; they forgot to step out of their analytical minds to recognize the oddity it would present if someone saw the wiper system being used. No other KC-135 had such a device. It wouldn't take long to reason that the only purpose for such an elaborate miniature wiper system would be installed over the exterior surface of these lights. Upon closer examination, it would lead others to logically conclude that something inside the light required a clear exterior surface. The next obvious reason would be to deduce that there must be a camera inside of the light fixtures.

To the engineers' credit, most UAVs were designed to provide unmanned missions. They were not designed to appear as if they were manned aircraft. That inconsistency hadn't crossed their minds. Other than the obvious exterior markings, the designers were most concerned with the UAV's functionality. To them, those other issues were of no consequence. It was a detail that another department needed to consider and account for. It would be left up to the entity that chose to use the UAV for a covert mission to account for those inconsistencies.

The Agency ground team in charge of staging the UAV were diligent. The had recreated all the proper exterior markings and revamped the UAV's cosmetic appearance. During all prior practice runs, the UAV had never stopped after exiting the hanger. Moon Dog would maneuver the UAV straight to the runway and throttle up for an immediate take off without pausing.

Tonight, things were different. The UAV had been sitting at a complete standstill on the runway. On all prior runs, there were no runway maintenance crew members present waiting for the UAV to proceed so they could continue to remove the snow on the runway. The substitute crew member sat atop his snow plow, only meters away. His location was to the side of the UAV. He was out of Moon Dog's view. Inside his blind spot. The substitute crew member was getting an unobstructed close-up view of the UAV. It was never designed to stand up against such scrutiny.

Something caught the snowplow operator's attention. He could see what looked like two sets of miniature wiper arms pushing the snow and moisture away from the front fuselage lights. He was taken aback. He'd never seen anything like it before. He glanced up to the main cabin windows. He waited, expecting to see those wipers begin to clear the main windshield. Nothing happened.

In earnest, the substitute crew member began to study the large plane. The maintenance crew had been rushed through security as one group rather than individually. The security guard had recognized the crew leader and many of the other crew members. In favor of expediency, the security guard ignored protocol. His main priority was to whisk the maintenance crew through so they could begin to clear the runway. In his haste, the guard missed seeing the substitute crew member. With the turn in the weather and falling snow, combined with each crew member's wearing thick winter jackets, hats, and gloves, it was easy to understand how he was missed.

The substitute crew member took advantage of the situation. He was surprised that he hadn't been searched, and that he hadn't been instructed to remove his cell phone. Before acting, he glanced around the tarmac. Once he was sure no one was watching, he pulled out the phone and began recording a video clip. He made sure to keep the phone down, hiding it from view.

The video cameras installed in most commercially sold cell phones were high quality. There was no need to carry anything else. The clip he took lasted two minutes and forty-nine seconds, and he was beyond excited at securing such a find. Finished recording, he hid his cell phone back in his pocket. Elated, he couldn't imagine a better feeling. Only later that day would he learn the importance of what he had documented; of what that clip proved. It was one of the most devastating pieces of evidence the Agency would have to face.

"We can't return the UAV back to the hanger. It will draw too much attention," explained the X.O.

Without further delay, Moon Dog checked the instruments. Confident everything was in order, he pushed the remote throttle arm forward and accelerated the UAV to takeoff speed. He'd rehearsed this takeoff hundreds of times. This time, it was for real. As the wheels retracted back into the UAV, Moon Dog maneuvered it into the night sky. As the UAV climbed, another alarm blared. Moon Dog turned his attention away from the projection monitor, searching for X.O. Newland.

"It's Lt. Benjamin's chest-mounted camera again. X.O., check my desk. The monitor on the right side shows the data transfer from the camera. Has the value increased?" Moon dog asked, practically yelling over his shoulder at the X.O. Flying the UAV and thinking about Kyle's camera monitor were requiring all his concentration.

X.O. Newland scurried over to the monitor. "Yes, it shows a considerable increase. About twice as large. What does that mean?"

"I'm guessing that Kyle, or his body, or just the camera, is moving closer to the last communication relay. If the camera continues to move in this direction, the signal will become stronger and stronger. He is still some ways away. Otherwise, we'd be getting some video too. Check his monitor view. Is it still just static?"

The X.O. leaned across scanning the other monitors. All the cameras were broadcasting clear images inside the tunnel. Kyle's was still static. "Nope, nothing on Kyle's. Just static."

Moon Dog took a quick glance away from the wall projection image and looked at the X.O., as if asking what he thought.

The X.O. was deep in concentration. For the last eight hours, they had heard nothing from Lt. Benjamin's chest-mounted camera. Now there were two small receptions. The last one had been twice as strong. As much as he wanted to give Lt. Benjamin more time, they had no more time to give.

The UAV was up, and Mr. Davies was in the neighborhood. It was snowing and it would be sunrise soon. They needed more information to warrant any more delays. Regardless of what happened, Kyle had less than thirty minutes to show his face. Short of video confirmation of his existence, Lt. Benjamin would become part of the collateral damage.

"It's not enough Moon Dog. Get synced up with a piggy back ride with Mr. Davies. We're out of time. Unless we get conclusive video evidence of Kyle's whereabouts and condition, we proceed. If he's being escorted by DPRK soldiers, we have no choice. You understand, right?"

"Sir! Yes, sir!" replied Lt. Elliott. He didn't like it. But he understood. Moon Dog concentrated on flying the UAV toward an intercept course with Mr. Davies.

33

Gibby and Carla Jo had been watching through their live feed. They shared views identical to those of Moon Dog and X.O. Newland. Gibby had also been monitoring Kyle's chest-mounted camera. There was no need to place a text or call the X.O. It was standard operating procedure. The Agency had given Kyle as much time as they could without jeopardizing the mission. Without visual confirmation of his condition, they couldn't alter the plans any further.

Gibby had been watching the data that was being pushed between the last communication relay and Kyle's chest mounted camera. The data that would eventually provide images was coming through with greater frequency and detail. However, it was still too sparse to provide an image. It was more like random bursts of partial data packages. It would take a definite solid non-varying signal burst to allow a large bundle of data to be transmitted before any visual image could be seen in the monitors. Both Carla Jo and Gibby remained hopeful that their newest buddy, Lt. Kyle Benjamin, still had a chance. It wasn't much of one, but it wasn't over yet.

With the stress of another all-nighter, and the last-minute changes, Gibby was getting frazzled. Staring at the monitors, Gibby broke the silence as he yelled at the static filled monitor.

"Come on, Kyle, get your ass in gear! Move it, son. Move it!"

*   *   *   *   *

Tae was in the lead. Kyle put his night-vision goggles back on and followed him. The others followed Kyle, placing the children between them. Tae's father was the last in line. Tae was anxious to try to get through the tunnel as quickly as possible and his fear pushed them forward. He had to get his family to safety. He was hopeful that their good will would count for something with the Americans. Tae no longer walked at a tentative pace; in fact, he would have run if it were an option. But his limitation now was the speed at which his family could travel. They continued pushing along through the narrow tunnel. Without realizing it, Tae and Kyle began to distance themselves from the others.

Tae glanced around. They were approaching the opening to the excavation tunnel. Peering around Kyle, he could see in the distance the flashlight beams from the rest of his family. Wanting to reach the spring pond near the cathedral cavern, Tae decided to push forward. They could stop there and rest. They wanted to make sure the night guard wasn't around before his family moved forward. He gave Kyle a brief smile. They were almost there.

*   *   *   *   *

Gibby had been going crazy. Kyle's monitor was a constant chatter. As the communication relays began picking up Kyle's signal, it was getting stronger, coming through with much more frequency. Ever since the break following the eight hours of silence, the signals began to trickle in every twenty minutes. Now, it was almost a constant bombardment of incomplete data transmissions. Unfortunately, there wasn't enough data to see a complete image. Just intermittent flashes of images.

Gibby and Carla Jo were mesmerized at their static-filled monitor screens. They refused to give up hope of seeing something, anything. Kyle was running out of time. Unable to take it any longer, Carla Jo was first to break the silence.

"We've got to wait. He's so close. It's obvious. What if he's alive and unharmed? Maybe he escaped. We just can't kill him! Can you imagine what he's gone through? What if that were you or me, Gibby, huh?"

Gibby returned Carla Jo's intense stare. Everything she said was what he had been thinking. But she was still young. He'd been down this rabbit hole before. He'd lost other colleagues under similar conditions. He recalled feeling the same way. It hadn't done any good then, either. Besides, it wasn't his call. It was all up to X.O. Newland now.

"I hear you, CJ But, we need visual confirmation. If we pull back and something goes wrong and we can't drop the tunnel, there'll be hell to pay. And even if Kyle is alive—and I hope to God he is—even if the X.O. decides to delay the mission, there's no guarantee he'll make it out alive. We need more," Gibby explained. "I wish we could, but we can't."

As Gibby stopped speaking, it happened. Kyle's chest mounted camera reception was strong enough to receive and transmit. The constant erratic static image of the monitor now was transmitting clear images. In the blink of an eye, they could see through Kyle's camera. But what they saw wasn't good. Stopping in mid-sentence, Gibby pointed to the monitor.

"Damn!" he shouted, pounding his fist on the top of his desk. "They have him, CJ. Look!" he said as he pointed his index finger at the monitor. "It's a soldier!" They both gasped, stunned by this new revelation. From their point of view, they had no other way to interpret what they saw. Tae was a DPRK citizen, and he was leading Kyle back.

If only the designers of Kyle's text device had programmed the unit differently. All the prior text messages were still piled up in queue. They were being held as a single data stream. However, because the images took precedence, the sequence to release the messages needed to be reinitiated by either party. Only then would the text messages stream through and transmit. As Kyle followed Tae, he was focused on walking out. It hadn't occurred to him to try to send a text. He had assumed that he was still too far away from the last communication relay for him to be back online. If he had only glanced down at his chest-mounted camera, he would have seen the strong, bright green glow that indicated a good signal.

*　　*　　*　　*　　*

"I see you, Mr. Davies. Before we descend to our target, I want to be right on top of your tail fins. I don't want the radar to show us as two separate aircrafts. When we go in, I want there to be one dot," Moon Dog explained. The X.O. had muted the program that had been monitoring Kyle's chest-mounted camera, because the constant blaring had become a distraction. The X.O. and Moon Dog were unaware that Kyle's camera had come back online. Even if they had known, what they saw wouldn't have changed their minds. The images would have confirmed that they didn't need to wait any longer. Kyle was lost. They would be forced to proceed.

"We're about five minutes from the target," Mr. Davies explained. "When I drop the fuel, the loss of my load will cause my plane to rise up. After it's empty, I'll pull left. Be sure to rise up when I drop the load."

"Copy that," Moon Dog replied.

*   *   *   *   *

Tae had made it to the pond. He glanced back and could see Kyle waiting for the others. As Tae turned his head, all he could see was the end of the barrel of the night guard's Russian-made pistol. Before Tae could yell out to warn the others, the guard hit Tae with the butt of the pistol grip across Tae's forehead. Had it been any harder, Tae would have died. As it was, Tae was knocked unconscious and fell to the ground.

The night guard glanced down the tunnel. He could see several flashlight beams. He grabbed Tae's arm and dragged him toward the opening, leaving him between the lava tube and the excavation tunnel. The night guard crouched down next to Tae and waited.

As the others approached, Kyle removed his night-vision goggles. The flashlights were playing havoc on his vision. His headache had slowly dissipated to just a numb irritation. For some reason, Kyle glanced down at the chest camera, and his eyes were drawn to the bright green light that cut through the otherwise dark tunnel. "At last," he thought. They can see me. They should know that I'm safe. As he watched the women and children proceed past, Kyle paused, searching the tunnel for the old man. After a moment, he heard the old man's shuffling feet and saw another flashlight beam bobbing up and down reflecting its light against the tunnel walls. Confident that the old man was still coming, Kyle turned back the other direction and began walking to catch up with the others. Kyle could barely see the others. He put his night-vision goggles back on and began moving.

Tae's wife was first to emerge into the large cathedral cavern. The beauty was breathtaking. She glanced around, aiming her flashlight beam about. Her attention was drawn to the underground pond. The top of the water shimmered like reflective glass. Hearing movement to her right, she aimed her flashlight toward the sound. At first, she assumed it was her husband, but she froze in place when she recognized the military uniform and saw a man aiming a pistol at her.

Her children came up from behind, her daughter reaching for her hand. The others could see only some of the area and, distracted by the awesome spectacle of the cathedral cavity, neither child noticed the soldier. Tae's wife stretched out her arms, gathering the children closer to try to protect them from this unknown threat.

The night guard saw a woman and two children enter and stared in disbelief. He waved his free hand, wanting them to move in closer. Nobody moved. He directed his flashlight beam down toward the ground, where Tae was recovering from being pistol whipped. Tae, now conscious, struggled to his knees. Seeing their father, the children moved forward. Tae's mother hadn't noticed what had taken place. The others blocked her view of the soldier. When Tae's mother heard the soldier speak, she realized there was a problem.

"Are there any more?" the soldier asked, as he counted all the bodies. He was now responsible for the capture of five defectors. Tae's family couldn't help themselves. They had been raised in the DPRK with the constant intimidation and had a clear understanding what happened to people who disobeyed orders. The years of fear-based conditioning created an obedient group of citizens. Without thinking, they replied in unison, "Yes," nodding their heads. The guard turned his attention to the lava tube opening. Aiming his pistol at the entrance, he waited.

*   *   *   *   *

Mr. Davies was a retired Navy pilot. He was one of the lucky few who had been cross-trained under a special task force, so that he was qualified to fly every aircraft available to the Navy. For a brief period, the Navy flirted with the idea of creating several groups of these unique pilots to disburse throughout the globe. Having the ability to utilize all different types of aircraft gave them a unique advantage. These units could be flexible and multidimensional; they could react quickly without being limited by the absence of certain skill sets. It was no wonder, then, that not one of these specially trained pilots had ever made it to the private sector. Instead, they each had been tapped for the opportunity to be assigned to an Agency director.

Out of respect for the uniform, Mr. Davies refused to go by an official rank. In his mind, he no longer held the military authority that his prior official rank demanded. As such, he asked that people referred to him as Mr. Davies. That title was more accurate.

Mr. Davies had flown a similar version of this modified KC-135 Stratotanker, but never under these conditions. Keeping these heavy planes under control was bad enough. Having a UAV hitching a ride above his tail, with snow falling, added to the difficulty. Then, factoring in the dumping of eighty thousand pounds of jet fuel over the most dangerous place on earth took his mission to a completely new level. If he pulled this one off, Mr. Davies would become a living legend within the U.S. covert society.

"We're approaching the target. My call sign will be Tanker One Six." He couldn't help but perpetuate the use of the double meaning codes. Call signs for aircraft typically used only two numbers, and anyone from the Agency who heard his call sign numbers would understand. The numbers one six were the first numbers of the White House address. As he confirmed his call sign numbers, Mr. Davies couldn't help but smile.

Moon Dog was concentrating, keeping a safe distance behind and above the modified KC-135 tanker. Mr. Davies disengaged his stealth program.

"I'm initiating the prerecorded distress signal," explained Mr. Davies.

Moon Dog could hear the recording playing out over their intercom. They were ninety seconds from releasing the fuel. Just in case, the Agency had used Mr. Davies' voice on the prerecorded message. If they needed to modify their plans, Mr. Davies could interject a real-time message. If something went wrong, this decision gave them more flexibility. The recording was designed to build upon the cover story.

"Osan Tower, this is Tanker One Six Heavy. There seems to be a malfunction. Over." The recording was on a continuous play and built upon the idea that their communications failed which prevented them from having a two-way conversation with the tower. After only a short pause, the recording continued. "Osan Tower, I'm having communication issues. I'm not sure you can hear me. I've lost all control. I'm near the DMZ and can't climb. Osan Tower, this is Tanker One Six Heavy. Mayday, Mayday, Osan Tower. This is Tanker One Six Heavy calling to report a complete malfunction. My locations is—" The recording cut out. Unless there were any changes to the mission now, any future communications would be transmitted by Mr. Davies live. Otherwise, no more communications would be broadcast. Almost immediately, the Osan Tower began transmitting relies.

"Tanker One Six Heavy, this is Osan Tower. We see you on radar. Where did you come from? You are entering the DMZ, over. Tanker One Six Heavy, this is Osan Tower. Can you hear me? Over."

As Osan Tower continued to broadcast, Mr. Davies turned off the communications radio. It was distracting him. Mr. Davies brought the modified tanker in low. If he emptied the fuel while flying too high in the air, the jet fuel liquid would be churned into a thin mist, almost transforming the fuel into a gaseous aerosol vapor. The mission called for a liquid deposit, like a fire-suppression tanker dumping water onto a forest fire.

*   *   *   *   *

Gibby and Carla Jo were glued to Kyle's chest-mounted images. They could see him approaching the opening to one of the tubes that emptied into the large cathedral cave. He stepped through the opening, and it was their worst nightmare: Standing dead center in the camera was a DPRK soldier, aiming a pistol at Kyle.

Wasting no time, Gibby speed-dialed X.O. Newland on their secure line. It was answered immediately, and the X.O.'s number was forwarded to this conference room. Only a select few people had his number. If a call came through, it could only have been Gibby or Director Valdez.

"This is X.O. Newland."

"Are you getting this?!" asked Gibby, his voice hysterical.

"What are you talking about, Gibby? What's happening?"

"It's Kyle's monitor. He's alive. He's back online. His monitor shows him approaching the opening. And he's got some serious company."

The X.O. had turned off the volume on the warning signal for Kyle. He'd already decided to proceed with the mission regardless. But hearing Gibby, he glanced over at Kyle's monitor. What he saw wasn't good. It seemed clear that Kyle was in some serious trouble.

The X.O. glanced up at the UAV's view on the projected wall images. As he watched the images, it felt like he was flying above Mr. Davies and the KC-135 tanker. The UAV's camera was clear. It looked almost like a video game played in high definition. Moon Dog was deep in concentration, waiting for the refueling tanker to dump its load. He was so focused on controlling the UAV, he didn't even hear the X.O.

The X.O. knew it would take about thirty seconds from the time the tanker pulled its modified emergency fuel dump to the time all the fuel would be pumped out. Everything was in play: The recorded emergency message had played, the tower had responded, both the tanker and the UAV were being tracked, and the fuel was only seconds from being dumped. During all this confusion, the X.O. remained composed as he turned toward Lt. Benjamin's chest-mounted camera display.

*   *   *   *   *

The night guard couldn't believe his eyes. There was no doubt in his mind that this was an American soldier. The uniform, the size of the soldier's body, the high-tech night-vision goggles. It was a dream come true. He couldn't help but think about how his supervisors would reward him for such a find. The excitement flashed across his face. His eyes dilated and his eyelids stretched opened wide. He could barely control himself, bouncing up on the balls of his feet. He began shouting in Korean at the American. Kyle couldn't understand him. Kyle raised both his hands up over his head. He glanced at Tae's daughter, hoping she would translate. The DPRK soldier was waving his pistol toward the others as if directing Kyle to join them.

The girl spoke, explaining what the DPRK soldier wanted. "He wants you to move over and join us." She said without emotion. Like a robot parroting the words.

Kyle was careful to avoid any quick movements. He took his time walking over and joined the others, pausing briefly before he stepped up shoulder to shoulder with them. Tae had regained consciousness and was leaning against his wife. In a single-file line, with their backs against the wall between the lava tube tunnel and the excavation tunnel, the six of them waited to see what the DPRK soldier was going to do next.

34

Gibby and Carla Jo were mesmerized at the images coming from Kyle's camera. The X.O. had kept the telephone call connected and had placed it on speaker. The X.O. was watching the same images on his monitor. As Kyle began walking toward the group of people against the wall, Carla Jo was the first one to make the connection.

"Hey, that guy! He's the one that was leading Kyle. If he has his hands raised too, he can't be with the North Korean soldier. It's the walker!" Carla Jo had been following Tae for hours the day before, and she was certain.

Both the X.O. and Gibby processed what Carla Jo had just said. They each turned their attention to Tae. CJ was right. Why else would the walker be lined up with his hands raised in the air? As Kyle turned his body, the camera panned across the others in line. The images on the monitor showed the walker holding his head with his hand. Upon seeing the images, Gibby spoke up.

"X.O., we had it all wrong. They were helping Lt. Benjamin. They weren't detaining him. We need to give him more time."

The X.O. processed what Gibby said. He agreed that they had misinterpreted what was happening, but none of what he was seeing would justify delaying the mission. Although they now knew what had happened and where Lt. Benjamin was located, delaying the mission did not guarantee that giving Kyle additional time would change the situation. He was being detained by a DPRK soldier. Even if the X.O. ordered a pause, giving Lt. Benjamin more time, that didn't guarantee Kyle would be saved. In fact, pausing now only increased the odds that the mission would fail. With only seconds to decide, X.O. Newland chose what he saw as his only option.

"What I'm seeing doesn't change anything, Gibby. We can't help Kyle out of this one. I'm sorry."

Gibby and Carla Jo knew the X.O. was making the right decision. Without delay, the X.O. sent Director Valdez the text. She had been waiting all day. They had the principals in the room. Delaying the live satellite feed had increased the tension in the conference room. It was almost five o'clock in Washington DC, and their weekends were about to begin. This conference satellite viewing was the last thing that stood between the viewers and their weekend.

Unlike the images that the X.O., Gibby, and Carla Jo had been watching, the ones that the Director's group would see were being transmitted from an independent satellite feed looking down twenty-three thousand miles above the target site. Three images were being broadcast: a large overview of the area, a more magnified view of the anticipated crash site, and one that was tracking the KC-135 tanker and the UAV.

The meeting had started at 4:30 p.m., giving the Assistant Director of the entire Agency organization time to brief the principals about the circumstances leading up to this mission. These people were not interested in the gory details, or all the work everyone had performed. For this mission to have led to this point in time, it was understood that much work had been accomplished. The people in the room dealt only in broad brushstrokes. They didn't need or want to know the names of the participants. Like some family members who arrive late to see a family member's newborn baby, they only wanted to see the baby from behind the safety of the glass window. They didn't need to be in the delivery room. They just wanted to see the fruits of so much labor.

Director Valdez sat down. She, like all the other principals, were just observers. No one expected to hear any oohs or ahs. They were all professionals waiting to make sure what needed to be done was done.

The other directors present glanced in her direction, exchanging professional nods of their heads. For those directors lucky enough to be granted the privilege of leadership in this elite covert organization, such matters always came to pass. Even though they disliked the unavoidable scrutiny such situations warranted, it was an opportunity for others to evaluate the type of people a director had selected, to evaluate what kind of leadership the director provided. It was the ultimate chance to display what a director could accomplish with the immense resources available. Those who succeeded here would be tapped with other opportunities.

Everyone present understood directors relied on their personnel. Regardless, responsibility had to fall to someone; it came with the territory of the job. Such missions showcased how effectively a Director, under unprecedented circumstances, could be relied upon.

The lights were dimmed; no previews of coming attractions, and no popcorn. Without fanfare, the satellite images began displaying against a twelve-foot-high by sixty-foot-wide wall. The close-up images of the

KC-135 and the UAV were in the center position. No cameras were allowed inside the room; it wasn't being taped. Forty very important people in total were present. The room was quiet as they watched the mission unfold.

*   *   *   *   *

"Once I start to offload the fuel, I'll begin to count down. I'll continue to count down until I have no more fuel to dump. When I get to five, slow your speed. You should be able to line up the UAV dead center into the fuel dump area. As I move out of your way, I will pull left. When I'm clear, you take the UAV down," repeated Mr. Davies. They each knew the drill. They'd been rehearsing it for the last month. The repetition during their training increased the likelihood of success. And part of their routine was to verbalize this timing. Moon Dog and Mr. Davies were sticking to their drill, just like they'd rehearsed it. "Confirm back."

"At five, I slow down. At zero, you'll pull left. Once you're clear, I take it down," repeated Moon Dog.

"Copy that. Here we go!" replied Mr. Davies. The countdown began.

"Moon Dog, we're almost over the area. On my count, rise up twenty feet and reduce your speed. As I drop my load, the tanker will naturally rise because of its loss in weight," Mr. Davies explained for the last time. This was no longer a rehearsal.

"Copy that," Moon Dog replied.

Everyone watching the mission live, waited with bated breath.

In a calm controlled voice, without any raised inflection, Mr. Davies began speaking.

"Three, ... two, ...one, ..now."

At that very instant, Mr. Davies released the emergency fuel dump. The modified pumping system began forcing out the fuel through the enlarged openings. There were four times as many openings as a regular fuel tanker, and all were much bigger than normal. The fuel gushed out of the plane in huge volumes. All the engineering on this KC-135 tanker was designed to offload the fuel as quickly as possible. Even with all these changes, it would still take thirty seconds to empty its load.

Moon Dog elevated and reduced his speed. As the tanker began dumping the jet fuel, he saw the modified KC-135 slowly rise. Moon Dog watched the plane below him. It created an illusion, like the plane was landing in a body of water. As the fuel fell, the liquid disbursed downward and the gravity and forward motion sent the liquid downward and out away from the plane. From Moon Dog's viewpoint above, it created an optical illusion. It appeared as if the refueling tanker were landing on a snow-covered lake and the body of water below was splashing up as it pushed down against the water, creating a wake from the heavy tanker.

*   *   *   *   *

Kyle was still wearing the night-vision goggles. He had been exposed to such a constant amount of stress that his mind had somehow grown accustomed to his predicament. He had adapted. He no longer felt pangs of apprehension and fear. His mind remained relatively calm. With his arms raised into the air, he contemplated his next move.

The women began speaking to the DPRK soldier. It sounded as if they were pleading with him. Urging him to let them go. The DPRK soldier became distracted by the women's voices. Watching through his night-vision goggles, Kyle could see that the soldier wasn't looking his direction. Kyle was still on a mission. He had been out of the loop unable to send or receive any text messages. He didn't realize that all the prior texts had been held in queue. Kyle reached up to his wrist and hit the resend button on the communication device.

Instantly, all the text messages he'd sent while being held captive were transmitted. Simultaneously, over forty-three text messages came barreling down to Kyle's wrist communication device. The programmers who designed the device had intended the recipient to be notified by a quick vibrating burst. This type of notification would allow the agent to be aware that a message had been received without alerting others.

While Kyle's arms were raised, he could feel the device begin to vibrate his wrist nonstop. Unknown to him, the device was individually acknowledging the receipt of forty-three messages. The developers hadn't considered the scenario that Kyle had just endured. Kyle didn't understand why the text device seemed to be vibrating nonstop. Afraid of alarming the soldier, Kyle was unable to lower his hand to read the messages. He glanced down at his chest. What caught his attention was the bright green light emitting from his chest-mounted camera. He realized that the others could see everything.

Kyle assumed that the constant vibrations were messages from Gibby or Moon Dog. They must be ordering him to do something. As the constant vibration pinged away on the device, it shook nonstop on his wrist. Unable to read the messages, Kyle could only interpret the vibration to mean one thing: They must be ordering him to detonate the packages before it was too late.

Kyle's mind seemed to clear. This was it. He had never considered knowing the exact moment when his life would end. He'd always imagined dying in an accident or during a shootout on the battlefield. When he left last night and began walking toward this tunnel, he hadn't really considered that this would be his last day. Not like this. Time seemed to slow down. He felt relaxed. At peace.

After a deep exhale, Kyle slowly dropped the arm that was located away from the soldier. In a calm, smooth manner, he reached into his pocket and located the detonation mechanism. He took one more breath, then glanced at the soldier. Kyle could feel his courage begin to wane. Before he could change his mind, he looked down. Without thinking, he pushed all doubt from his mind. In a decisive motion, he dropped his other arm so he could use both his hands. Holding the device level with one hand, Kyle entered the code.

The DPRK soldier caught the sudden movement by Kyle. The soldier glanced at Kyle and realized that the American had dropped his arms. The DPRK soldier had been too distracted to think things through. He hadn't expected so many people to exit the cave, nor the presence of the American soldier, and now the women's screeching voices. He now realized he hadn't checked the American for weapons. As fast as he could, he sidestepped in front of the line of others until he stood in front of the American. He raised the pistol, pointing it into Kyle's face.

Kyle didn't see the soldier move. He had been concentrating on entering the code. The night-vision goggle plastic frames were wide. They were designed to reduce the amount of light entering from the user's peripheral vision. It was probably better that Kyle didn't see what was coming. Using his right thumb, he punched the numbers. First his birth month, "03." Then, the day he was born, "22." Followed by his birth year. He didn't want to change his mind. He placed his thumb over the enter button. With closed eyes, he pushed the enter button.

* * * * *

Moon Dog was in deep concentration, trying to keep the UAV above the modified KC-135 tanker's tailfin. His face displayed an intense steely focus with a clenched jaw. The KC-135 continued rising as the jet fuel pumped out over the target area. Moon Dog continued listening to Mr. Davies count down. It was surreal. The UAV display screen was in high-definition color. Moon Dog could see the wing markings on the tanker below, and the falling snow crossing his field of vision.

"... eight, ...seven, ...six, ...prepare to reduce your speed more," instructed Mr. Davies.

Moon Dog took a deep breath. This was it. All his training was coming down to this. All he needed to do was wait for the tanker to clear left. Then, he would barrel the UAV into the ground aiming for the center of the fuel soaked ground. The X.O. would time the impact of the UAV and then detonate the packages inside the tunnel.

"Copy that. I'm ready to reduce speed," replied Moon Dog while glancing up at the X.O. Moon Dog was taken by surprise, the X.O. wasn't' paying attention. He was staring at Kyle's monitor. The X.O. appeared distracted and unprepared to detonate the packages. The UAV's impact into the ground needed to occur simultaneous with the detonation of the explosion. Unable to take his attention away from flying the UAV, Moon Dog practically shouted.

"X.O.! We're coming down now!"

"...five—reduce your speed, Moon Dog," said Mr. Davies, who was still speaking in a calm, relaxed voice.

"Copy that, reducing speed now," replied Moon Dog. He was shaky, distracted.

"—four, ...three, ...two, ...one, ... breaking left," announced Mr. Davies over the secure line.

Moon Dog watched the tanker pull ahead and bank left. With one last inhale, Moon Dog began to squeeze the stick that controlled the UAV.

*　*　*　*　*

Director Valdez and the other VIPs had been watching the live feeds. The room had remained perfectly quiet and still. Once the images began to broadcast, no one had spoken a single word. Not even in a whisper.

She could see by some of the facial expressions that her team was certainly making an impression. Other than the time-schedule change, everything was proceeding as planned. Later, the Director would learn all the details that had caused the delay. She couldn't help but feel a sense of pride and admiration for her team's efforts and execution.

As the modified refueling tanker pulled to the left, everyone in attendance seemed to inch up and lean forward in their seats. Everyone was anticipating what would come next.

*　*　*　*　*

Gibby's and Carla Jo's eyes darted back and forth as they tried to watch the views from both the UAV and chest-mounted cameras. They noticed that Kyle's arms had dropped. At that very instant, they watched the DPRK soldier move in front of Kyle, pointing his pistol directly into the camera. Carla Jo and Gibby exchanged knowing glances, each thinking the same thing: that it might be better this way. It seemed certain that Kyle would, at the very least be held captive and probably tortured. Better to end it all right here and now. This way, Kyle wouldn't feel a thing.

They continued glancing back and forth. Then it happened. Gibby and Carla Jo froze, staring at the images displayed through Kyle's chest-mounted camera.

*   *   *   *   *

"Sir." Waiting a second without a reply, Moon Dog continued. "X.O. Newland. I'm preparing to crash the UAV," urged Moon Dog. Still not hearing a reply, Moon Dog took a quick glance toward Executive Officer Newland. He was staring at Kyle's camera monitor. When the X.O. finally turned his head, making direct eye contact, Moon Dog couldn't believe what he heard him say.

"Pull up! Pull up! That's an order. Pull up!"

"Sir?" replied Moon Dog. Now staring at the X.O. Incredulous, Lt. Elliott asked for confirmation "What? Are you sure X.O.? Pull Up?"

"Yes, pull up. Then reactivate your stealth programs and bank left. Make a one-eighty turn and then return to this exact location. I need ten minutes."

"Sir. Yes, sir." Unsure what had just happened, Moon Dog banked the UAV left and reactivated the stealth technology.

35

Kyle's eyes were still closed. He'd thought that the packages would have detonated by now. When he opened his eyes, he could see the DPRK soldier waving a pistol at his chest. The young girl began translating what the guard was yelling at Kyle.

"He wants you to raise your hands," she said in a frightened, shaky voice.

Slowly, Kyle raised his hands above his head. The DPRK soldier seemed to relax, pleased that the American hadn't pulled a gun. The DPRK soldier looked up and down the row, wondering how he was going to get them all through the opening without one of them running away. They could only go through the narrow opening one at a time.

Suddenly, the soldier froze and then his posture became distorted. For some reason, he stumbled forward. To everyone's surprise, the DPRK soldier's face winced in obvious pain. His fingers that held the pistol grip loosened. The gun began falling from his hand. Through the soldier's open jacket, a dark spot appeared on the front of his shirt. Through the center of that spot, a pointed metal object pierced through the shirt fabric. Everyone stared at the soldier's chest. The protruding pointed metal object suddenly twisted clockwise, causing large amounts of blood to flow freely out of the enlarged opening. The blood flow increased as the soldier's heart continued to pump his life's blood out of the wound. As the dying soldier fell forward toward them, they saw an old man posed in a deep lunging position, like a fencer, holding out his sword. It was Tae's father, frozen, in his pose, as if honoring his victim in a silent coup de grâce.

In all the commotion, everyone forgot about Tae's father. He had been trailing everyone, the last one in line. Carrying the family heirloom, he was shocked to find his entire family held at gunpoint. He knew there was no choice. If he didn't react now, other soldiers could arrive. He had the advantage of surprise.

In a calm exacting motion, Tae's father pulled the sword out of the bundle and walked out into the cathedral cavern. No one noticed as he walked up behind the night guard. He forced his mind to ignore the empathy he felt toward his fellow comrade; a countryman, a common Korean doing his job. None of that mattered. this was necessary, unavoidable.

Tae's father could just make out the soldier's shoulder blade. Aiming below that mark, he stepped forward and thrust the sword forward. He leaned out and extended his arm and knew he'd hit his mark. As the sword pierced through the night guard's flesh, Tae's father felt the sword slide past and in between the man's ribs. As the blade continued forward, Tae's father waited until it traveled through the soldier before twisting the weapon.

As the night guard fell away and tumbled to the ground, Tae's father felt deep sadness and shame at what he'd done. He'd killed another Korean, a man just doing his job. Tae's father closed his eyes and remained frozen in his lunging position. Things would never be the same.

* * * * *

Tae saw the flashlight beam reflect off the metal sword. It was his father. He was holding the ancient family heirloom. The sword that had been passed down from generation to generation. The sword was his father's responsibility. He had been entrusted with its safety. In all the distractions, no one had noticed that he wasn't present.

The large cathedral cavity fell silent. Only the soft trickle of spring water could be heard. Tae's daughter was the first person to break the silence. She ran toward her grandfather. Everyone followed. They rushed forward and surrounded him. They squeezed the old man, trapping him in a group hug. Tae's father had saved everyone, including Kyle.

Kyle watched the family huddle together, exchanging kisses. At that moment, another vibration from his texting device got his attention. The nonstop vibrations signaling the receipt of prior message had long since stopped. Kyle realized that this must be a new message.

No longer concerned about the DPRK soldier, Kyle was free to read the message. It was from Gibby, and it read:

"Go now! Hump it! You have less than 10 minutes. We're about to drop the tunnel."

Wasting no time, Kyle looked up at Tae's daughter. "We have no time. We must go now! Run! Everyone, Follow me!" shouted Kyle. He waited for her to translate. When everyone's face snapped up, Kyle turned toward the tunnel and started running.

* * * * *

"Yes! He did it. Way to go, Newland!" yelled Gibby as he and Carla Jo watched the UAV pull to the left. Exchanging high fives, Gibby wasted no time. He typed Kyle a text message.

"I wonder who those other people are?" asked Carla Jo, still smiling from the unexpected turn of events.

"Whoever they are, they're apparently good guys. For now, anyway," Gibby replied. "We may have some new problems."

Carla Jo looked puzzled. Until she followed Gibby's index finger pointing at the other satellite feed over the entrance to the excavation tunnel. The compaction truck and crew had entered the tunnel and were driving toward the first package.

The sun had just started to rise. Moon Dog and the X.O. still needed to get the UAV back on target. Now the appearance of the compaction crew gave them something else to worry about. Their only hope was that the crew didn't notice the packages. Even so, there were concerns about whether the vibration from the heavy trucks would jostle the packages out of synchronization. Worse yet, what if they were found and the crew called it in?

Gibby and Carla Jo looked back toward Kyle's camera view. The images were bouncing rhythmically up and down. There was no doubt where Kyle was now: He was at a full sprint running down the natural lava tube. It ran away from the excavation tunnel. It wouldn't take long to reach a safe distance from the blast. Kyle wasn't taking any chances. He'd been briefed on the destructive force yet to come. Just the thought of being anywhere near the excavation tunnel when the devices exploded provided more than enough motivation to keep moving. Kyle was still a good distance away from the cliff-side entrance. Using common sense, He didn't want to be underground inside the natural lava tube structure when it collapsed. Kyle's main goal was to put as much distance as possible between himself and the explosion.

Well behind Kyle, Tae and his family were running as fast as they could go. Tae knew this section of the natural lava tube by heart and led the way. As they ran, four sets of flashlight beams bounced along the tunnel as they ran. The sound from seven sets of feet pounding through the cave sent shockwaves that echoed off the tunnel walls.

*   *   *   *   *

As the UAV pulled away from the crash target, the audience of VIPs inside the secure conference room exchanged worried glances. Something had happened. No one in the room could fathom what could possibly have happened to warrant a change of plans. They were only seconds away from completing the mission. The UAV had been directly over the target. Short of another country's calling them to acknowledge that the details of the mission had been leaked, nothing came to mind that would justify the decision to postpone the explosion.

All the VIPs in the conference room came to the same conclusion. Heads began to turn, searching for Director Valdez. She couldn't miss their wandering eyes but did her best to remain stoic and confident. For the first time in her career, she was grateful not to have been the person in charge of this aspect of the mission. Naturally, she felt ashamed of this cowardly thought, but, after this digression, she wasn't too hard on herself. After all, she was only human.

Turning her attention back to the mission, Director Valdez focused on the live satellite images tracking the

UAV. It appeared to be making a U-turn. She could be a Monday morning quarterback later. Right now, she could only hope that the mission sustained a minor setback and there was still a chance of success. She refused to show any signs of weakness. Her mouth had become very dry. She fought the urge to reach for her glass of water. As she regained composure, she knew all was not lost. The mission could still be completed.

As the UAV continued its redirection, the VIPs redirected their attention to the live satellite images. It was anyone's guess what would happen next.

*   *   *   *   *

Moon Dog turned his full attention toward X.O. Newland. "What happened? Why did you order me to abort?" The stress of the moment had been replaced by confusion.

"It was Lt. Benjamin. One of them somehow killed the DPRK soldier," the X.O. explained. "I know I'll take heat for that decision. I felt I needed to give him a chance."

Mr. Davies' voice came through the radio. Moon Dog turned away to focus on controlling the UAV. Moon Dog was shocked that the X.O.'s decision.

"This is Davies. What happened?"

"The agent and the others killed the DPRK guard. Given everything they've gone through to get to this point, I felt like I had to give them a chance to clear out before the explosion. The UAV is returning to the drop zone now. No more changes. Straight in," the X.O. said. Judging by his expressions, he seemed to be second guessing his decision.

As Mr. Davies processed the information, he felt compelled to share his thoughts. "Sir, may I suggest that we fly the UAV back in an erratic fashion. This would support the idea that the KC-135 tanker had a malfunction. I also suggest we start broadcasting some disinformation about the so-called problems. I could explain to the tower that I chose to dump the fuel in preparation for a controlled crash landing."

The X.O. and Moon Dog considered his recommendation. Mr. Davies broke the silence again, "Sir, with all due respect, I never liked the idea of having the UAV go straight down. It would suggest that the pilot was knocked out cold. Or the pilot had absolutely no control over the plane and lost control. Ordering the change could be explained away. You could take the position that you changed the scenario because this makes more sense."

X.O. Newland agreed. He knew Mr. Davies was right.

"Moon Dog, do as Mr. Davies suggests. We'll need to turn off our stealth systems too."

Moon Dog nodded his head in agreement. He disabled the stealth programs and began jerking the navigation stick forcing the UAV to move erratically, up, down, right and left.

"Mr. Davies, we need your assistance. Please broadcast a live announcement to Osan Tower," ordered X.O. Newland.

"Right away, sir," Mr. Davies said as he turned his normal communication radio back on. He could hear the Osan Tower still calling out to him, trying to get a response.

"Osan Tower. This is Tanker One-Six Heavy. I have lost all controls. I've been forced to dump my fuel and will attempt a controlled crash landing." The X.O. was surprised that Mr. Davies' voice was still steady and calm. Osan Tower immediately responded.

"Tanker One-Six Heavy. We see you now on radar. We copy. Understand you're trying a controlled crash landing. Good luck, Tanker One-Six Heavy."

"Ten-Four, Osan Tower. This is Tanker One-Six Heavy. I repeat, I will be trying to make a controlled crash landing. Thanks. I'm going to need all the help I can." This time, for effect, Mr. Davies forced his voice to rise just slightly, yet still very much in control. Controlling the tone of their voice during a broadcast was just something pilots did.

"Okay, Moon Dog. Now, it's all on you. Take it in," ordered the X.O.

"Yes, sir."

*   *   *   *   *

Because the entrance to the excavation tunnel area was already completed, the compaction trucks could roll faster in this section. The four heavy compaction trucks were loaded down, ready for another day's work. It was still dark as the convoy drove into the tunnel. The crew were fresh, rested from a good night's sleep. Each truck turned on its headlights. As the trucks entered, the tunnel lit up.

The drivers had become accustomed to this unusual work environment. Like commuters driving the same route to work every day, these men had come to expect the same landscape. The trucks motored along deeper into the tunnel. After traveling a third of the way inside, something caught the lead driver's eyes. He thought he saw an unexpected object along the road. He slowed down, then lost sight of it. At first, he thought his eyes were playing tricks on him. As the lead truck maneuvered around a soft bend in the road, the driver needed to be alert. This time, he was certain that he had seen something.

He slowed down and coasted through the turn. The drivers were always more careful in this section of tunnel. Several weeks back, it had been filled with workers and engineers. Now that the tunnel was empty, slowing down through the curve had become a habit. The lead driver checked his side mirrors. He made sure the other trucks cleared the turn. Being the most senior driver, he was responsible for everyone's safety. Watching the other trucks come around the bend, he noticed the headlights from one of the trucks reflect off something. This time, the lead driver stopped the truck. Leaving the headlights on, he stepped out.

The other drivers saw the lead truck stop. The cave was filled with red lights as they each depressed their brake pedals. Each truck parked in the center of the road. Leaving his headlights on, the lead driver waved up the other drivers while pointing to side of the road. With a tilt of his head, he studied the object.

He'd never seen anything like it. As he walked over to the side of the road, he stayed well back from the object, waiting for the others to join him. Like four tentative biologists who'd just discovered a new species of animal, the drivers approached the unusual object and looked perplexed. Keeping a safe distance, they encircled it. Squatting next to the package, they leaned down for a closer look.

"What is that?" asked the lead driver.

*   *   *   *   *

Gibby and Carla Jo stared at the image. The images transmitted from package two's camera were dominated by the compaction truck driver's faces. Wasting no time, Gibby contacted the X.O.

"X.O. We've got visitors. Check out package two."

X.O. Newland turned his attention away from the UAV wall projection images. He located the monitor that Gibby mentioned and saw the live feed from inside the excavation tunnel.

"We have company," the X.O. explained to Moon Dog, who was busy flying the UAV back to the target. Too occupied controlling the UAV, he couldn't look away from the monitor. Moon Dog nodded his head. "Not too much longer, sir. I'm almost back on track."

The rising sun was peaking over the horizon. The sunbeams reflected off the crystal snowflakes below, looking like a blanket of diamonds. The clouds had disbursed. The morning dawn signaled the beginning of a new day. The sky had cleared, and blue sky dominated the UAV's field of vision. Moon Dog maneuvered the UAV back onto the correct approach line. He noticed that the jet fuel stood out against the frozen snow below. Unlike water, the jet fuel wasn't freezing. It had pooled on top of the snow. The jet fuel was a pale lavender color. The scene below looked like a painting, in which the jet fuel stood out like brushstrokes of watercolor painted across a white, snow-covered landscape.

"In a calm and controlled voice, Moon Dog spoke. "X.O. I am descending toward the target. I will count down from ten. On my mark, trigger the explosion."

"Copy that," replied X.O. Newland. "I'm awaiting your countdown."

"Ten,... nine,... eight,..."

*   *   *   *   *

Kyle had been running nonstop. He was certain that he'd traveled a safe distance. He stopped and turned around looking for the others. It sounded like a herd of footsteps pounding through the tunnel. After a few seconds, he saw six separate flashlight beams reflecting off the ceiling and tunnel walls. As he caught his breath, the children approached first, then Tae, his wife, and his mother, in that order. Pulling up the rear, was the old man. He was moving much slower than the rest of the group. His flashlight beam was still, without any erratic movements. He had resorted to walking.

Kyle was calculating how far they had traveled. He estimated they had travelled over a mile from the excavation opening. This distance should be far enough away. Kyle waited for the children to catch up. They jogged up next to him, then stopped. He was surprised how well conditioned they were. They weren't breathing that hard. The adults weren't fending as well. Kyle placed his hands on his hips and continued to catch his breath.

Kyle glanced down at the text device on his wrist. He tapped the receive button and began reading Gibby's message.

"Run, Forrest! Run!"

Kyle turned to the young girl. "We're almost there. Tell everyone to hurry up, keep running."

The little girl nodded her head and began yelling to her family in Korean. Kyle took off. This time, he urged himself not to stop until he saw sunlight. He knew they had less than two miles to go to reach the cliff opening. As he sprinted away, he could hear the young girl's high-pitched voice echoing behind him urging her family to move faster.

*　　*　　*　　*　　*

The lead driver was the oldest and had the most experience. It was his decision. He wasn't certain what to do. He knew the tunnel hadn't been completed yet. He'd been told that the drainage and air filtration systems were still being installed. Maybe this strange object was part of that equipment. But what if it wasn't? The DPRK played by different rules. Failing to make the correct decision, many times, cost one's life. Unwilling to assume anything, the lead driver stood up and walked back to his truck. His decision had been made. He was going to call it in. The other drivers stayed, behind staring at the object. While waiting, they took a smoke break.

*   *   *   *   *

Carla Jo had been fixated on the truck drivers. She watched one stand and walk back to a truck. The others waited. She assumed he was going to call it in.

"Not good, Gibby. He's calling it in. They found package two."

Gibby had just sent Kyle a text message. With a funny smirk on his face, he turned his attention to the monitor for package two. He saw a close-up of three Korean men's faces. They were leaning down, staring directly into the camera. The hot cigarette embers stood in deep contrast to the otherwise dark tunnel. The mint green night-vision images looked like a strange cartoon.

"There's no time. Moon Dog's coming in with the UAV now," replied Gibby. Besides, what could they do now anyway? Carla Jo leaned forward and watched the images from the UAV's camera.

*   *   *   *   *

"...three, ...two, ...one, ...mark!" Moon Dog pushed the controller stick forward and drove the Unmanned Aerial Vehicle into the pool of jet fuel. As the nose of the UAV plowed into the ground, the metal frame collapsed downward. The momentum of the aircraft collapsing drove the wings and tail section forward. The image displayed on the wall vanished and was immediately replaced by static.

X.O. Newland had been counting down with Moon Dog. At the exact moment Moon Dog had said "mark," the X.O. had pushed his index finger down on the enter button on his keyboard, triggering the explosion of all the packages. Everything worked as planned. The packages had remained in synchronization. In milliseconds, the data transmitted up to the satellite. It then traveled back down to the first communication relay near at the cave entrance.

That first communication relay was designed the strongest, as it was tasked with transmitting and receiving every piece of data that was sent. It acted like a gatekeeper, responsible for everything going in and coming out. Everything worked perfectly. The signal traveled wirelessly, passed along the airwave through the natural lava tube, through the narrow opening at the cathedral cavity, and then into the excavation tunnel. As the signal passed through each explosive package, a few microsecond pauses allowed each package time to arm and to detonate together. The explosion was synchronized, maximizing the damage and accentuating the reaction. They exploded in concert as one unified explosion, instead of multiple individual ones.

Everyone waited: Moon Dog and X.O. Newland, hidden inside an isolated conference room inside Camp Bonifas; Gibby and Carla Jo inside Gibby's office; the VIPs in a secure conference room inside the Agency Headquarters back in Washington DC; Mr. Davies, still flying under the cover of stealth technology in the modified KC-135 Tanker back toward Kaneda AFB; and Lt. Benjamin, running at an all-out sprint somewhere deep underground along the DMZ.

*   *   *   *   *

The driver grabbed his onboard two-way radio, similar to those used by taxi services. Grasping the handheld microphone, the driver spoke.

"Headquarters, this is Truck One." After a brief delay, the driver heard a response.

"Yes, Truck One. Go ahead."

"We may have found something down here."

The three other truck drivers could hear the conversation. They were still squatting, staring at the device. At the same time, they all saw it. A green light turned on. For a microsecond, they were curious what the green light meant. It was the last thought any of them ever had.

A millisecond after the light turned green, each package synced up. In one unified moment, each package detonated. The energy released upward. The destructive power of each explosion had the destructive force of a surface-to-air missile. Unlike those weapons, these special packages had no wasted mass. The packages were stationary objects. No effort was wasted on launch or delivery. No programming, design or fuel was needed to deliver them to their targets. One hundred percent of the effort and design was dedicated to maximizing their explosive properties.

The truck drivers felt nothing. Their bodies had been vaporized, reduced to their cellular components and dispersed. The tunnel provided a perfect environment in which to deliver the explosives. The energy was released into the earth above the excavated tunnel, pushing the soil and rock upward. Everything became superheated. Above ground, the bomb inside the UAV detonated upon impact. The friction, flames, and scraping metal from the colliding aircraft would have been sufficient to ignite the jet-fuel-soaked ground, but the bomb made sure it did. As the UAV pummeled into the ground, the natural forces of the crash, together with the bomb and the eighty thousand pounds of jet fuel, lit up the morning sky.

An intense mixture of orange and blue colors flashed into the air. While the initial flash heat evaporated some of the snow, much of it melted. Like a flash flood, water poured through the cracks of the soil and saturated the earth below. The simultaneous explosion below caused the hundred feet of earth above the excavation tunnel to be attacked from two directions. The water that had melted and seeped into the soil below added to the overall explosive reaction. The superheated molecules below, combined with the newly trapped water inside the earth, accentuated both explosions. Like a water boiler exploding, the heated water was reduced to its gaseous form of hydrogen and oxygen, each volatile in its pure state. The pressure from above and below created another natural explosion of the gaseous atoms trapped between the UAV bomb and the explosive packages underground.

The explosive force was much greater than the Agency engineers had anticipated. They hadn't accounted for the presence of water that the melted snow created. In one moment, the explosion churned the earth, jet fuel, and gaseous H_2O into a huge unrestrained chemical reaction. The devastating force pulverized the earth, collapsing an entire stretch of excavated tunnel extending fifteen kilometers, a little over nine miles in length. From above, the section of earth looked like a newly formed underground fissure caused by an earthquake.

The explosion rocked the area and could be felt throughout the region. The Agency later learned that seismic devices in Seoul and Pyongyang registered, leading both countries to believe they had just sustained a mild earthquake.

*   *   *   *   *

Watching the most important aspect of *Hummingbird*, Director Valdez had been glued to her seat. Given the results, people in the room began to wonder if the initial delay could have been part of the intended scenario. The Agency directors in attendance had all faced similar situations. They expected missions to be fluid and flexible. They had all encountered last-minute changes.

With a sigh of relief, Director Valdez could feel her confidence return. In Washington, she was just another mid-level important person lost in an ocean of authentic VIPs. She closed her notebook and was preparing to exit the conference room when a man approached her. The lights inside the conference room were still down. The other attendees were starting to stir.

An unknown man tapped her on the shoulder. "Excuse me, Director. Someone needs to speak to you."

With a puzzled expression, she glanced up from her chair. She assumed the National Agency Director wanted to get some face time.

She stood and followed the man. They exited the conference room just before the lights turned back on. Those still inside searched for Director Valdez. They wanted to extend their congratulations. Many were surprised to find her chair vacant. Without fanfare, the room emptied. The participants began making their way out of the building.

The unknown man led Director Valdez to a nondescript area adjacent to the conference room. It had no room number nor was there a doorknob. As the Director stood next to the man, she saw him look up toward the ceiling. Within seconds, she heard a soft click as a door opened out from the wall. The man turned back toward the Director.

"This way, ma'am."

She followed him through a dark hallway. It led to a huge oversized elevator that could easily have held thirty people. After the man depressed the elevator button and they entered, she watched the large elevator doors closing and wondered where she was being taken. When the doors opened, she was surprised to see bright neon lights coming from an outer corridor. As they walked toward the large double doors, she was taken aback. It was an underground roadway. A black GMC Suburban sedan waited at the curb.

The man led her to the vehicle and opened the back door. As the Director climbed inside, the man spoke. "They'll take you from here, Director." Distracted by his comments, she glanced back while ducking into the vehicle.

It was dark inside the sedan. It took her eyes a few moments to adjust. As the vehicle began moving, the interior dome light turned on. To her surprise, she was face to face with the President.

"Mr. President?" she said in a shocked manner.

He turned his head. Reaching out, they exchanged a firm handshake.

"Congratulations, Nena. I know I'm not supposed to know anything about this mission, but," he said with a warm, knowing smile, "this mission has so many implications. It could have ended badly." He paused. He understood that he shouldn't say too much. It was his idea to break protocol and meet her. "I just wanted to thank you in person. Be sure to pass my gratitude on to your team. All of your efforts will be remembered.."

Nena listened to POTUS. She was surprised he knew her first name. She looked into his eyes and didn't know what to say. "Thank you, Mr. President."

The President turned back toward the driver. He nodded his head signaling him to stop. Nena glanced out the window as a soldier approached the back door. While the door was being opened, POTUS spoke.

The President flashed his politician's smile. "It goes without saying, Director, that outside of the small circle comprising your team, this conversation never took place, and I was never here."

"Of course, sir."

Director Valdez stepped out of the vehicle. As the vehicle drove away, the soldier who closed the back door remained standing at attention. Her underground ride took them only a few hundred yards. She understood the need for secrecy. No one could ever know that the President knew about *Hummingbird*.

The soldier pointed to another oversized elevator door. Everything had happened so quickly. The elevator chime rang out, waking her from her trance. As the elevator doors opened, she raised her hand to block the incoming sunshine. She stepped forward and found herself on the surface sidewalk along Pennsylvania Avenue. The street was filled with cars chauffeuring legislators, lobbyists, and their staff out of the city. They were all looking forward to the weekend.

Her attention was drawn to a man standing curbside, waving his arms to get her attention. She recognized him: It was her assigned attaché. The elevator doors disappeared as a concrete panel slid in front, disguising its presence. If she hadn't seen it for herself, she would have never believed that an elevator was hidden there.

The Director approached her attaché. He opened the back door of his vehicle, and she climbed inside and waited for him to enter.

"It's been a long day, Major. If you could get me back to JBAB (Joint Base Anacostia-Bolling), I'll just catch some sleep on the flight back."

"Not the hotel?"

"No. I've decided I need to get back."

"Yes ma'am."

As they drove away, Director Valdez wanted to know what had happened. On the secure phone on the plane ride back, she'd get the story. She was curious: Why the change in plans?

36

Kyle felt the explosion through his feet first. As he ran, he could feel the vibration of the tunnel floor and struggled to keep his balance. Without warning, a tremendous blast of hot air picked him up off the ground, and he was thrown forward. The explosive forces pushed the air down the tunnel, away from the blast. It had the force of hurricane winds topping two hundred miles per hour. Like a tennis ball being shot out of a machine, Kyle and the others were tossed through the inside of the lava tube. The thick winter jackets, boots, and gloves prevented them from being seriously injured.

The blast force carried them forward for some distance until gravity brought them tumbling back to the ground. They each hunkered down on the tunnel floor, covering their heads and closing their eyes. Dust and small granular pebbles pelted their bodies and ricocheted off their clothes. A windstorm churned through the tunnel. They all readjusted their body positions so their head was pointing away from the direction of the blasting wind. It took several moments before they could uncover their mouths and noses. Then, as suddenly as it had started, the wind stopped.

Kyle was the first one in the group to struggle to his knees. He stood up and regained his balance on wobbling legs. Throughout the ordeal, his night-vision goggles had somehow remained strapped to his head, and Kyle adjusted the fittings back into place. Through the goggles, Kyle stared down the lava tube, searching for the others. Under a layer of dust and debris on the tunnel floor, he saw small movements that looked like insects climbing out of the ground. He counted six moving mounds of debris. He walked back and started helping everyone stand. It was a miracle that no one had been seriously injured.

*　　*　　*　　*　　*

"Oh my God," whispered Carla Jo. They had watched the scene unfold. Kyle's chest-mounted camera and the overhead satellite images were the only camera views still operational. All others displayed blank, static-filled screens.

"That was completely insane," replied Gibby. He turned toward Carla Jo before continuing. "That was beyond crazy. Unbelievable."

"Yup. Beyond words," she replied. "Now what?"

Gibby knew she was right. They needed to get going. But what were they going to do about the others? Carla Jo studied Gibby's face. She knew what he was thinking.

"Killing them is not an option. If it hadn't been for them, Kyle would never have made it out."

Gibby nodded. "You're right." He paused and walked back to his desk. He picked up his secure landline and punched the numbers to his local go-to guy.

"Mr. Kim? It's Gibby. Can you get your hands on a large van or truck? I need one ASAP. Preferably a dark-colored one with dark tinted windows."

Mr. Kim was used to calls like this from Gibby. They were in luck. He had a large extended cargo van that he'd modified for another job. "I've got one. But I may have to tweak it."

"Why?"

"We added bench seating to handle nine adults. Did you need me to remove the seats?"

"No, no, the seats are perfect. I need you to disable the interior locks, though. I don't expect any runners, but you never know," Gibby added.

"Oh, oh. A snatch and grab?"

"Not exactly. We're facilitating six DPRK defectors. Two are children. You never know. Sometimes people change their minds," Gibby clarified. "Oh, and I want you to pick them up with me. I need a trusted translator available. Our boy Kyle will be there to assist."

Gibby looked at Carla Jo and raised his eyebrows as he explained further. "Carla Jo will text you the pickup coordinates. It will be out in the boonies along the DMZ, so come prepared." Carla Jo nodded her head, understanding her role.

"Okay, no problem. By the way, did you feel that small earthquake earlier?" Mr. Kim asked.

"Nope. Didn't feel a thing," Gibby replied. He thought, *My friend, that was no earthquake.* Instead, Gibby said, "Okay, I'll talk to you later" and hung up the phone.

Gibby had another issue to worry about. What was he going to do about the walker's handler? First things first. Gibby and Carla Jo needed to make some plans. Where were they going to take the North Koreans?

* * * * *

The field maintenance crew had long since finished clearing the snow. The snowstorm had ended, and air traffic was running smoothly. The steady north wind had made the sky a bright, pastel blue. One would never have guessed that just hours before, a full-blown winter storm had passed through. There was no longer a need for the extra personnel. Continued efforts to remove the snow were no longer necessary. As a substitute worker, he was the first one approached to be asked to turn in for the day.

The substitute worker was excited to report his findings. After leaving the airfield, he went to a small outside restaurant tent and ordered a hot soup. He called his handler and waited. As he ate his food, he glanced around, making sure he hadn't been followed. As other tables became available, he switched locations. After several such moves, he was confident that no one could approach him without being seen. He couldn't help feeling excited. While waiting, he replayed the video clip images. The longer he watched the clip, the more he was convinced that what he had filmed was a drone; an unmanned vehicle. The other thing that stood out as unusual was the exterior skin covering; he hadn't noticed it before.

The substitute worker continued to eat his early lunch, waiting for his contact to arrive.

*   *   *   *   *

The two-way operator had been trying to re-establish contact with the truck all morning. He finally gave up and decided to bring it to his supervisor's attention.

"Sir, something happened to the trucks."

The officer's morning smile disappeared. The last thing he wanted to hear was that there was a problem. One problem leads to more problems, and those turned into decisions made by his superiors. Involving them certainly left him open to criticism. If something went wrong, he would be blamed for having created the problem in the first place. What started out as a beautiful morning just turned into a very bad one.

"What happened?"

"Early this morning, I received a call from Truck One. The driver mentioned locating something unusual inside the tunnel."

"What did he find?" asked the supervisor.

"That's just it. The transmission stopped. I tried calling him back, but he never picked back up. I even tried calling the other three trucks. No one is picking up."

The supervisor knew better than to assume anything. "Get me a car and a driver. I need to get back to the site right away," he ordered. His mind began churning through different scenarios. He'd learned long ago that many hours could be wasted speculating on countless possibilities. He needed to know facts. The supervisor grabbed his winter jacket and his lucky hard hat. He walked outside and met his driver, and they jumped into a vehicle and started off. It would take him less than an hour to get to the tunnel.

*   *   *   *   *

Kyle led the others out of the lava tube. Only one flashlight had survived. The Koreans were grouped close together, with Tae leading the way. To Kyle's surprise, Tae's father and mother had made it out alive. As he had watched them compose themselves, he noticed a certain intensity and internal drive. Kyle was a professional combatant. Even for him, the ordeal was horrific. The others exhibited a unique ability to persevere. Facing the soldier and then the collapsing tunnel had been just another obstacle they had to overcome. They never complained. Even the children picked themselves up and helped dust off the others. No tears were shed. No drama needed to be played out. With a sense of determination, they had gathered themselves and pressed forward. If it hadn't been for them, he would have died. Kyle was impressed beyond words.

The vibration on his wrist broke his trance. Kyle paused and read the message.

"We'll pick everyone up at the trail entrance. You're almost home. :)" The message ended with a colon and right parenthesis. It brought a smile to his face. Of course, the message was from Gibby; who else would have included the smiley face. He was almost home.

*　*　*　*　*

The substitute worker received a text from his handler. He walked to the street and jumped into the parked car. The handler replayed the video clip. His handler hooked up the smart phone to his laptop computer. Then he began transferring the clip to his laptop. When done, he pulled out a flash drive and made an encrypted copy. The handler returned the man his cell phone. He didn't need to remind him not to mention this to anyone. The man exited the car and watched his handler drive away.

The handler made a call on his cell phone.

"I have the clip. I think he was right. It looks like a drone to me too."

The voice on the other line sounded like a very old woman. "Do you have the copy?" she asked in a frail voice.

"Yes. Do you want me to drop it off?"

"Yes, right now. I'll be waiting." She replied. Without waiting for his reply, she ended the call. She walked to the front lobby and pulled on a metal chain that hung from a neon sign. With a solid metallic click, the open sign lights switched to red lights and displayed the

Korean word for closed. The old woman shuffled across the cold, linoleum-covered floor. She glanced up at the mirror mounted near the ceiling, high above the front glass display case. She turned the corner, hiding in the back section of her shop. She sat down, looking up at the mirror, and waited for the man to arrive.

*   *   *   *   *

Angelie had been daydreaming, staring out the back window, when she saw a huge ball of fire shoot up into the sky. Several seconds later, she felt a shock wave. After a brief delay, she heard the explosion. For a split second, she wondered if war had just broken out. Her mind seemed to be piecing together everything that had been happening. Earlier, she had heard the engines of a big plane fly overhead. She had grown accustomed to hearing the high-pitched noise of the fighter jets that patrolled the DMZ. But the sound she had heard was much deeper. It sounded more like a low rumble. She didn't realize it was Mr. Davies flying overhead.

Angelie stood on her tiptoes, trying to get a better view into the valley. She heard a knock on her door. When she opened it, she realized that this was her first guest. It was still early in the morning. The sun was just beginning to rise. She opened the door and recognized the school principal. He could speak broken English.

"Good morning. I want explain. Plane crash, over hill. Small earthquake also. Okay, you?"

"Yes, yes. I'm fine," replied Angelie. She smiled back as she returned the obligatory bow.

"Good. Making sure," he replied. Without waiting for a response, the principal hurried off her front porch to warn the other villagers. Angelie understood their concern. Living inside the DMZ, they were all on a constant state of alert. She couldn't imagine how the elders were feeling. The explosion and crashed plane were unsettling. She watched the principal jog down the street.

Others were darting back and forth. This village would put every neighborhood watch group in the US to shame. They had no choice. Being aware and prepared was an essential prerequisite for all citizens living here.

She saw four older buses drive past her house. They looked like old, decommissioned city buses. The exterior paint was faded, but the engines still ran fine. Angelie noticed them parked along the school grounds. She knew all the children walked to school. She'd wondered what purpose the buses served.

Curious, Angelie stepped off her small front porch. The buses were being parked on the main dirt road down the center of the village. She watched them being parked one behind the other in the center of the road. As the bus drivers exited, they left the doors open. Angelie was standing on the road when a middle-aged woman approached.

"It looks like they're getting ready to evacuate, just in case," she said in a quiet, concerned voice.

"I'm sorry, I don't speak much Korean." Even though she had understood every word, she replied in English. Angelie did this her entire life. She maintained the charade and feigned poor Hangul mal. "Chaso hamnida, Hangul mal chogum amnida." (I'm sorry, I don't speak much Korean language.)

The woman looked at Angelie. Unable to hide her displeasure that Angelie, who was clearly of Korean blood, couldn't speak Korean. The woman nodded her head and replied, "Mi gook saram?" (American?)

"Nay" (Yes), Angelie replied.

The woman looked into Angelie's eyes. With great concern, she said "Jo shi maseyo" (Be careful.). Angelie nodded her head and offered a deep honorific bow as she replied, "Nay, kamsa hamnida" (Yes, thank you).

The woman paused just a moment. She was taken aback at how fluidly Angelie had replied. With a knowing smile, the woman walked toward the buses.

Angelie had been too distracted to notice. After the crashed plane, the earthquake, the early morning visit from the principal, and now the village buses being staged to prepare for an evacuation, Angelie had been disarmed by the woman. It may have been something in the way she spoke, or the cadence of her words. Somehow, she had a calming effect. In some way, she reminded Angelie of her mother back in Missouri. She hadn't spoken to her mother, face to face, for weeks.

Angelie noticed the bus drivers milling about. She could sense that this morning's events had everyone on edge. Without an immediate threat on the horizon, Angelie returned to her home.

The woman waited near the buses. Her intuition told her that something else was going to happen. Just in case, she chose to remain near the buses. From the center of the village, the woman sat down on a bench. She watched Angelie walk up the porch and into her house. For some reason, the woman had the feeling that the American could speak and understand more Hangul mal than she let on.

On both counts, the woman was correct. Some people had a sixth sense; a strong connection to some natural intuition. This unique ability had served her well. The woman turned her gaze toward the mountains. Everyone in the village knew about the campfires in the hills. It was a game of cat and mouse. The DPRK soldiers were always nearby.

37

The DPRK unit had been startled by the explosion. They had been camped along the ridge only a few kilometers from the crash site. The men could feel the temperature change from the heat blast. Several soldiers had covered their faces, unsure what to expect. Like spectators at a rock concert that experienced the pyrotechnic explosions close enough to the stage to feel the heat against their faces. Like every soldier assigned to the DMZ, regardless of their loyalty, the men from this DPRK patrol had frozen from fear. Hearing the explosion, they contemplated the possibility of a surprise military attack by their enemies. Every man clutched his weapon and steadied his nerves. When it had passed, a sense of relief passed through the unit.

This patrol unit consisted of first- and second-year infantry. The only officer among them had received a field promotion. He knew that being promoted to an officer had its privileges. He also recognized that most officers had no desire to accept a promotion to night patrol along the DMZ. Those from the capital Pyongyang avoided the DMZ at all costs. Those lucky ones born into the elite class could guarantee that their children would be assigned to more appealing locations.

This officer had accepted with open arms his mandatory ten-year conscription into the DPRK military. His parents had passed away when he and his twin sister were very young. Not long after entering the orphanage, he had been separated from his sibling. Alone, he struggled to establish his own personality. He grew up isolated in the government orphanage.

He found this assignment refreshing. The stale, multilevel brick government building he had been raised in stood in stark contrast to the beautiful trees, wildlife, and running rivers and streams. While other officers looked forward to another assignment, he knew he would miss being in the DMZ. The prospect of staying inside the DMZ his entire ten years would suit him nicely. A voice brought him back from his thoughts.

"Sir, you have a call."

"Yes. I'll be right there."

The two-way radio technician handed the young officer the mic. "Yes, this is Captain Hong."

"Hong, how close are you to the explosion?" the Major asked.

"We're looking down at the flames as we speak."

"Get down there and call me back. I want to know what you find out."

"Yes, sir. Right away."

As the young Captain ended the call, he ordered his men to move out. With their interests piqued, the patrol of young men, boys really, practically ran down the mountain toward the steaming trees and burning debris. Captain Hong wasn't far behind.

*　*　*　*　*

Ten kilometers away, the supervisor was standing on the last section of undamaged underground tunnel road. He and his driver had to struggle over the earth that was piled up and blocking their way. After climbing out of the tunnel, they stood on top of a mound, looking down at the terrain ahead. What had once been a flat and level stretch of land covered by trees and shrubs had been reduced to a continuous mixture of pulverized soil. As far as the eye could see, the ground had sunk, leaving a long trough.

They slid down into the underground section of tunnel, back to their parked military jeep. The consistency of the soil was very unusual. It was as if the ground had been pulverized into small grains of round balls. As they slid down, a fine powder drifted upward, covering them from head to toe. This section of tunnel was where the first package had detonated. It was located well inside the DPRK border, approximately ten kilometers from the DMZ border.

As the supervisor dusted the powder off his uniform, he was certain that this damage could not have resulted from an earthquake. He grabbed a cup out of the back of the jeep and filled it with soil. He wanted to show his supervisor what it looked like. He rubbed the soil between his fingers. He'd seen powdered and pulverized soil many years ago when they used explosives to make the tunnels.

"Take me back now. I need to speak to the Colonel."

* * * * *

As she heard the metallic chimes ring, the old woman lifted her head. The front door opened and closed. She stared at the image reflecting off the ceiling-mounted mirror.

"Hello," said a man as he entered. He knew the drill. The man walked up to the display case and pointed to the potted plant. "I have one exactly like that at home.

It's called a Country Jasmine." After a brief pause, he heard what sounded like an old woman's voice.

"Leave it on the counter and go."

He could tell that the voice was from another room behind the counter. He followed her instructions. He placed the flash drive on the glass display case. As he turned to leave, a reflection in the ceiling-mounted mirror caught his attention. He could see two small piercing eyes staring back. She was aiming a gun at him over the counter. Abruptly, the man turned around and practically ran out. As the door opened and closed, the metallic chimes played their melody.

Certain that the man had left, the old woman returned the pistol to the top drawer. She walked out of the side room and retrieved the flash drive. She carried it to the back of the shop, where her teenage grandson waited. She put the flash drive into a brown paper bag and folded it several times before taping it shut. She handed the bag to her grandson. He walked outside, climbed onto his bicycle, and rode off.

Using several trusted associates, the brown bag was handed over to several people in turn. The grandson transferred the bag to a taxi driver. The driver hand-delivered it to a small mail delivery service. The owner took the bag and personally drove it up into the DMZ area. He arrived at the center of a small village. The village was in the DMZ, only one mile away from the DPRK border.

The driver entered the only postal building in the village. He walked over to the counter and rang the bell on top of the counter. The postal manager's head snapped up at the sound. In less than an hour, the package was about to go across the DMZ.

"Special delivery," the driver said as he handed the postal manager the brown bag. Without waiting for a reply, the driver turned and walked out and drove away.

The postal manager placed a closed sign on the front door and walked outside to the back. A tattered South Korean flag hung at half-staff from a pole attached to the back wall of the postal building, visible only from the back side of the building. The postal manager glanced around. Confident that he was alone, he untethered the rope and raised the tattered flag up to the top of the pole. After tying off the rope, he grabbed the fishing pole that leaned against the side shed.

Carrying the fishing pole, he walked away from the village, toward the river. This area was one of the most dangerous places in the world, not because of wild animals, but because the river was literally a stone's through away from the North Korean border. The postal manager continued walking deep into the forest.

He approached a large boulder next to the river and looked about several times before bending down and digging through the fresh snow. He located a flat paver stone. He struggled as he slid the heavy stone aside to uncover a deep hole. Inside the hole was a rusted metal container with a lid that could be unscrewed. The postal manager untightened the lid and removed the top. He slid the brown bag inside the metal container, retightened the lid, and then placed the container back into the hole. Before sliding the paver stone in place, he glanced about to make sure that the area was clear. After covering the paver stone with snow, he turned and walked back to the village.

It had taken only ninety minutes to complete the entire process. The village had only two hundred fifty total permanent residents, and there were very few packages arriving or departing. In his absence, he hadn't missed a single customer.

Other than the DPRK agent who saw the flag raise up the pole, no one else had seen a thing. By the time the bag had been retrieved from the hole, the postal manager had already forgotten about it. It was human nature. Eventually, repetitious tasks transformed into meaningless job functions. While the DPRK agent was carrying the flash drive hidden inside the bag across the DMZ, the postal manager was glancing at the wall clock. He was counting down the minutes until he could close for the day.

*   *   *   *   *

Since the American refueling tanker crash along the DMZ, the DPRK's Head of National Security Office had been busy. They'd received a surprise call from the US Military on a landline through the main switchboard. The General who took the call was, under these situations, unclear about the protocol. The US caller spoke fluent Korean Hangul mal. No translators were needed.

"General, we need to inform your country about an accident. This morning, the pilot of a KC-135 refueling tanker was forced to dump his fuel before attempting a controlled crash landing. The tanker had mechanical and communication malfunctions. After circling the area, it never regained control. The attempt failed and all the crew members are believed to have been killed."

The General didn't know what to say. Given the direct, straightforward conversation, he felt compelled to offer condolences.

"We are sorry for your loss."

"For our pilot's unintentional and unauthorized entry into your airspace, the US is prepared to make an appropriate financial restitution for damages. Based on satellite data, it appears that no DPRK structures were damaged. Nor, were there any injuries to your personnel. Soon, the US will prepare a proposed reimbursement schedule for the market value of the damaged trees.

The General was surprised at how reasonable the US was being. This time, because no interpreter was being used, there was no miscommunication.

"Could you please provide a fax number. We'd like to confirm everything we've discussed in writing."

To the General's surprise, five minutes from the end of the telephone conversation, a letter from the Department of Defense was received extending a formal apology for the accident. It repeated in writing everything that had been discussed. Not a single detail was missing.

The accident was confirmed through DPRK's media intercepts. All the local Seoul news on SBS and MBC, as well as other Asian networks, were broadcasting the story. Images of the crash site were going out, and social media was showing a few comments as well. In fact, the US Military was refuting the rumor of a small earthquake. During a news conference, the US spokesman was going into detail about the crashed refueling tanker. The spokesman went into detail about how the concentration of fuel dumped over the area accentuated the explosion.

As the day progressed, the DPRK National Security Agency was considering the matter a simple accident. That all changed when two separate calls came through.

"General, we just received a call from our excavation division. One of our tunnels was destroyed."

"What happened?" asked the General.

"It was the US refueling tanker accident. It crashed directly on top of the tunnel. The supervisor just called it in. And there's something else. The supervisor believes there was an explosion that caused the cave-in. At the time of his call, the supervisor had no knowledge of the crashed tanker. We had to tell him."

"Hmm, that's strange." The General paused as he processed the information. "Given the fact that the large refueling tanker crashed above the tunnel, it seems consistent with what caused the tunnel to fail, as well as the explosion."

The other officers in the room listened and contemplated the information. One of the senior colonels spoke up.

"General, maybe we should pull up anything we have on the radio chatter during and after the crash. May I also suggest we contact Beijing and request any satellite images that they may be able to share." Everyone listening began nodding their heads in agreement.

Another colonel added, "I find it a little coincidental that the tunnel so happened to be located directly under the crash site. A little too convenient, don't you think?"

It was a funny thing how, once the seeds of doubt were planted, other theories emerged. Paranoia was finding a way of creeping into their thinking. Earlier, the General was about to write it off as a mere accident. Now, everything that was being said was changing his mind.

"You all have good points. I agree. Reach out to Beijing and your contacts south. Let's see what we find out." He was just about to conclude the meeting when a high-ranking officer from the State Security Department (aka The Ministry of State Security) asked to be admitted into the briefing.

As a military attaché announced his title, the officers in attendance exchanged nervous glances. Even with their military rank, they feared any dealings with the Ministry. The Ministry Officer was dressed in his formal uniform. He was either coming from or about to go see the Great Leader.

"Comrades, we have uncovered some vital photographs and video. I will pass them around for your viewing. Obviously, you may not take any of the pictures nor mention what we discuss here, yes?" He asked in an arrogant manner. He stared down each person in attendance.

After everyone nodded their agreement, the Ministry Officer passed two folders around the room. The General held one folder and studied a still photo. It was extracted from a video clip. Puzzled, he looked at the Ministry Officer.

In a steady, confident, and controlled voice, the Ministry Office explained, "If you look at the aircraft's windshield, you'll notice that a thin layer of snow has accumulated." He waited for the men to turn their attention back to the photos. Because the General had kept the folder in front of him, the other officers scrambled around the only other available folder of photos and peered over each other's shoulders to get a look. "Now look at the headlights. You'll notice the small wipers."

Each officer, seeing this detail, said, "Ahh," before the Ministry Officer continued. "Also, notice the outer skin covering of the plane. Both very unusual."

"For those of you wondering, no, these are not common features on other KC-135 refueling tankers. We checked. This was a one-of-a-kind unique tanker. Coincidentally"—here he paused for effect—"it was the same one that crashed this morning along the DMZ."

On hearing the words, the General's and his officers' eyes opened wide. The General wasn't the only one in the room who was missing the deeper meaning of what they were being told. Having the highest rank in the room, though, the General was the only one in a position to save face and ask for clarification. While the other officers remained quiet, contemplating the significance of what the Ministry Officer was pointing out, the General pushed forward, breaking the silence.

"Ministry Officer, if you would forgive my ignorance, could you please explain the significance of this tanker's unique attributes. I'm not seeing the importance."

The other officers were grateful to hear the General's question. Without delay, the Ministry Officer explained.

"General, the reason there were no windshield wipers on the tanker is because there are no pilots inside flying the plane. The reason that the lights have their own wiper blade system is because cameras most certainly are installed inside. The wipers are designed to keep the view clear for the camera inside."

"Comrades, we got a break. For some reason, the plane had been delayed. It stopped on the runway long enough for us to get these images. If it had proceeded directly to takeoff, we would never have noticed." As he studied the men's faces, he could tell that they still weren't getting it. Frustrated, he explained further.

"The tanker wasn't a regular plane. It was an Unmanned Aerial Vehicle. It was a drone." The Ministry Officer was grateful to finally see recognition appear on their faces. The other officers began to recognize the situation for what it really was.

"Furthermore, comrades, this was no accident. If the tanker had accidentally crashed as we are being led to believe, it would be a physical impossibility for the crash alone to have caused our tunnel to collapse."

"Comrades, the Imperialists are trying to deceive us. Those bastards invaded our sovereign country!"

The room fell quiet. Faces froze in shock. The air left the room. Each officer began regretting ever being promoted to his current position. No one wanted to be there. As the gravity of the situation became clear, they all turned their attention toward the General. He was in charge; it was his call.

The General, unlike the other officers, had decades of experience dealing with such matters. He knew that the Ministry of State Security never attended these meetings without also having a recommendation. The General, paused contemplating his response. His officers watched in awe at how he handled himself. He appeared calm and collected. Their confidence grew as they watched him absorb and process the information.

The General had learned the skill of diplomacy. He was an extremely capable decision maker. He'd also learned how to incorporate recommendations into orders. He could maneuver around and avoid being boxed into a situation that left him solely responsible for the outcome; acting that way would be a rookie move.

With the utmost tact, the General avoided the landmines. One misstep spelled disaster. His goal was to avoid making a direct recommendation. He couldn't become the single source of reason. Should things fall apart, he would be vulnerable to direct criticism. In a controlled and confident voice, utilizing all the wisdom he'd accumulated, he spoke.

"This type of tactic is nothing new. With the presence of new advanced technology, only the means of the deception have changed. History has taught both sides about this timeless dance between ourselves and our enemies. We have developed a predictable, yet acceptable retaliatory response to these types of covert acts of aggression."

The General paused, studying the officers' faces and giving them time to absorb his every word and gesture. Without hesitation, the General continued his eloquent, unscripted monologue. His poise and delivery caught the Ministry Officer by surprise.

"Comrades, for years in advance, we have planned and developed myriad retaliatory responses. I could literally pull one off the shelf. It would be as simple as reaching out my hand and extracting a scenario. All the political concerns and necessary issues have already been regurgitated. All of the minute details have been pondered and debated."

"However, before I give my orders, I would be remiss if I didn't ask for any input from the Ministry of State Security. Does the Ministry wish to inject anything into our plans? We could, as our Imperialist enemies say, 'kill two birds with one stone.'" Turning his head, the General eloquently looked at the Ministry Officer, awaiting his input.

Just like that, the General opened the door. Even the Ministry Officer failed to see the brilliance in which the General offhandedly offered to accommodate the Ministry of State Security's agenda. It was as if the General were offering to take care of the Ministry's problems in conjunction with a predetermined National Security response. In truth, the General knew the shelf he had referred to was empty. Other than dropping another South Korean civilian passenger airliner or the bombardment of some local village, the General had nothing.

"General, I am very appreciative that you are willing to consider our goals into your response. In fact, we did have something in mind. It is simple and direct, and it would send a message to the Americans without fear of escalating the matter," the Ministry Officer explained.

"What did you have in mind?"

"It involves an American school teacher. She is teaching near the border inside the Village of Daeseong-Dong in the DMZ."

*   *   *   *   *

Captain Hong was standing just outside the crash site. The fires were still smoldering. The remnants of the jet-fuel-soaked ground and vegetation burned under rubble. He could see several large jet engines and a mangled object that was what remained of the refueling arm. Pieces of jagged metal were strewn across a ten-kilometer stretch of land. The debris field left no doubt that there could be no survivors.

Captain Hong's men had used their personal cellphones, a recent phenomenon that had even reached this hermit country of the DPRK. Unlike the West, selfies had yet to become part of their culture and probably never would.

"Excuse me, Captain Hong, you have a call."

As the Captain took the two-way radio receiver, he received new orders. Unflinching, he acknowledged his understanding and got his platoon on the move.

"Comrades! Let's lock and load. We're going to be paying our southern brothers and sisters a little visit!" the Captain yelled.

For many of the younger soldiers, this would be their first visit across the DMZ into the southern territory. Captain Hong had been across before. This would be his fifth visit. This time, he had specific orders.

It would be his responsibility to locate and kill the American school teacher. She was just across the valley in the small village of Daeseong-Dong.

*   *   *   *   *

Angelie had been nervous. The entire morning, the other villagers had been scurrying about. In an abundance of caution, all the children were gathered and loaded into the first bus. The buses had been topped off with diesel. Not having a typical gas station, by hand they tilted metal canisters to fill the buses. The mayor had called into the next largest adjacent city and secured enough temporary housing for the entire village population.

With the arrangements secured, the decision was made to set out now, before nightfall. It would be easier to go now under an organized, calm evacuation than to attempt a frantic nighttime escape. Angelie was impressed at the adaptability of the villagers. Although fearful, they remained calm, even encouraging the children to sing songs to keep them preoccupied. An escort from the Republic of Korea military was present. Several military vehicles were prepared to escort the entire convoy of buses out. The villagers were reluctant to hold up the evacuations and chose to move the kids out first. As the first loaded bus of children and their mothers pulled out, Angelie could see the relief wash over the remaining villagers faces. The military trucks were in front of and behind the bus as it left.

In an organized fashion, the second bus was filled with the older children and their parents. As this second bus pulled out, the singing could be heard, but with less enthusiasm and excitement than the youngsters had shown. These older children understood what was happening and were less easily distracted than the younger ones. The military trucks again surrounded the bus and escorted it out.

Angelie waited with the remaining villagers. The third bus had been filled with the very elderly and other miscellaneous food and beddings for their brief trip. As Angelie climbed onto the last bus, she was impressed. She observed that the third bus also left under military escort. The entire village had been mobilized and evacuated in a quick orderly fashion. As she was walking through the center aisle of the bus, it happened.

Without warning, several DPRK soldiers entered the main street. The soldiers were carrying automatic rifles and began running toward the bus. The villagers were surprised, unprepared for a full-out assault. Their military escorts were overrun. Their escort trucks were stopped. The drivers and soldiers were shot and killed. Prior invasions had taken place during the dead of night. On those occasions, no one had been killed. Only cash, jewelry, alcohol, and cigarettes been taken. It had been years since anyone had been murdered.

The villagers screamed at the driver, urging him to pull away before it was too late. Amid the screams, the driver cranked up the diesel engine and tried to speed away. For a moment, it looked like they would make it. The driver stomped on the accelerator and the bus lurched forward, but as the bus approached the end of the street, the sense of elation evaporated.

In the center of the road stood five DPRK soldiers. The tallest appeared to be the one in charge. In contrast to the frightened faces of the other armed soldiers, boys in uniforms really, stood a DPRK Captain with the face of a hardened combat veteran. In one swift sweep of his arm, he raised his automatic Russian made rifle and aimed it into the air while depressing the trigger. The rapid-fire chatter of the bullets cut through the silence of this country valley and echoed out and reverberated inside through the open bus windows. The officer stepped in front of the bus and aimed his weapon into the driver's face, daring the driver to proceed.

The driver slammed on the brakes, bringing the loaded bus to an abrupt halt. Dust rushed forward in a cloud that engulfed the soldiers. As the dust cleared, the villagers gasped in disbelief. The soldier walked toward the doors and began tapping the end of his machine gun against the glass doors. The driver could see by the grimace on his face that he would not ask twice. Deflated, the driver put the bus into park, opened the doors, and turned off the ignition. There was no doubt in his mind that if he didn't, the soldier would have killed him and others.

Unlike the other buses, this bus held the working men and women in the village. There were no frantic children or hysterical old ladies. No one screamed or cried. Angelie heard the distinct sound of heavy, boot-covered feet striding up the bus steps. She froze in fear. Looking toward the other passengers, Angelie was surprised at the other passengers' facial expressions. They were stern and defiant. In that split second, Angelie realized that these villagers had chosen to remain. This part of the DMZ was their home. It had been where their parents and grandparents were born. Those who remained could retrace their heritage back hundreds of years. Nothing was going to take away what was rightfully theirs.

Not everyone born here had the same burning desire, that unwavering commitment to protect and defend this stretch of land. Not everyone born here needed to call this place their home. Those less dedicated, those unable to cope with the harsh circumstances, had left. Only those with the same unyielding feelings had stayed. Based on the meager population of two hundred fifty residents, most had chosen to leave. Angelie was the only one on the bus who had no stake in this fight. Unfortunately, she was the one the soldiers were looking for.

As Captain Hong climbed the stairs, he studied their faces. He was surprised to see the looks and stares. He could tell that they weren't afraid. In fact, it was just the opposite; it was as if they were defiant, practically daring him to do something. To deflect their animosity, he began speaking.

"Comrades, I mean Imperialistic sympathizing Koreans who eagerly accept the influence of the Americans in exchange for the comforts of luxury; in pursuit of things, selling out your daughters and future generations to fill the pockets of international bankers."

As Captain Hong continued his rant, he scanned the passengers' faces, looking for the American. He looked at each face. Unable to locate who he was looking for, he became frustrated. He shouted, "Where is the American?"

The woman heard the soldier's words. It was an innocent reaction. She hadn't intentionally tried to point Angelie out, but, hearing the soldier's question, she reacted unconsciously and, to her own dismay, she glanced back toward Angelie.

Captain Hong saw the woman's reaction. As he followed her eyes, he located a young lady who appeared to be about his age, staring back at him. Her eyes were wide open, like a deer caught in the headlights. He glared into Angelie's eyes. To his surprise, she was obviously Korean. The distinct facial features; her eyes, nose, even her skin color. There was no doubt in his mind that she had Korean blood.

Captain Hong stepped down the aisle. To everyone's shock, the young woman stood. She had a puzzled expression on her face. What had originally been fear had now softened, and she looked confused and bewildered. Captain Hong stepped directly in front of Angelie. With a soft knowing smile, Angelie's head tilted sideways. The universal sign when a person realizes that some unknown answer snaps into place; like correctly placing a piece of jigsaw puzzle.

Angelie's eyes focused on the Captain's face. Her eyes were fixated on his cheek. As long as he could remember, it was a personal flaw, a physical trait, that had haunted him. He had treated it like a deformity and was traumatized by its presence. It was a birthmark in a perfect circle, about the size of a quarter. It had been the subject of many cruel jokes and comments.

In hindsight, though, he had come to appreciate his birthmark. Its presence had hardened him. The cruelty it attracted forced him to overcome the ridicule of others. He'd been forced to grow up early and had developed a strong self-image because of it. At a very early age, it forced him to deal with the criticisms of others. It was as if the discriminatory treatment he had endured had helped sculpt his character, helped instill the drive to prove others wrong. It was a cornerstone to his internal determination to succeed.

Captain Hong studied this young woman's face. He could tell that her attention to his cheek was not in malice. It was in recognition. As he stared at Angelie's face, a single tear drop slid down her cheek. He watched it fall to her lip, and he was surprised to see her smiling. As the Captain contemplated what to do, Angelie extended her right arm. She turned her wrist over. With her opposite hand, she pointed her index finger at the birthmark on her hand. Her birthmark was a perfect circle about the size of a quarter.

Captain Hong's eyes followed Angelie's finger and it was as if time stood still. Without warning, old hidden childhood memories came flooding to his conscious mind. He remembered having a sister. He'd forgotten. His sister had a birthmark similar to the one he saw on the young lady's hand.

Angelie could see something change in the soldier's face, like a frozen plant that was coming back to life as its branches began to thaw. Sensing his discomfort, without thinking she raised her index finger to her eyebrow and slowly stroked the hair along the ridge of her brow line. Until that moment, she had forgotten about its meaning. It had been their secret sign, and it had served them well. It was the only way they could communicate across the empty space between their beds separated on opposite sides of the orphanage dormitory. It all came flooding back. It was her brother.

She gazed into his eyes. She could no longer hold her emotions in check and, without reservation, extended both arms toward her brother and hugged him around the shoulders. She began to sob uncontrollably. Tremendous rivers of tears cascaded down her face, and her shoulders shook.

Captain Hong's mind flooded with warm, loving memories that he now recalled. At that moment, he forgot who he was and why he was sent. He had no recollection that he was on a military mission. It was as if he had been given a rare, unbelievable gift, the gift of knowing he wasn't alone; that he hadn't been by himself all this time; that he had family; that there was another person in the world who remembered him, cared about him, and truly loved him.

Captain Hong slid his rifle over his shoulder and adjusted the strap. He let the weapon slide around and settle against his back. He returned his sister's embrace and patted her back, comforting her as her tears subsided.

The passengers sat staring at the two. In disbelief, they watched the drama unfold, uncertain what was happening. Many of the passengers wondered if the American was pleading for her life. The driver was unaware of what was taking place. He was preoccupied watching the soldiers outside surrounding the bus.

Captain Hong waited. He was in no hurry. He appreciated the moment, knowing this would be the only opportunity to see her. He held her close. He inhaled, trying to mentally record this moment. He wanted to remember everything that was happening. For several uninterrupted minutes, they stood in a deep, loving embrace. Angelie's breath returned to normal. They both sensed it was time.

She released his shoulders and stepped back. With one final look into each other's eyes, they both exchanged a warm, soft, sincere smile. With the back of his hand, he wiped his tears away. Angelie dropped her head and sat down. To everyone's amazement, the soldier turned around and walked off the bus. He never looked back. From outside the open bus door, he turned around and yelled at the bus driver.

"Close the doors and go. No Americans here. Just Koreans."

As the bus doors closed, he turned toward his men. "Let's go. No Americans, just Koreans." His soldiers agreed. They watched everything from outside. They hadn't seen any Americans either. None of his men dared ask him who the girl was. As the bus sped away, the platoon set off across the creek toward the mountain range.

* * * * *

As Kyle led the group through the underbrush, he lanced through the small group of shrubs. They'd been walking nonstop since exiting the cliff opening. It was a slow go, and they were exhausted. It took them most of the day to reach the trail entrance.

Kyle crouched down and slid under the branches. With a clear view, he saw Gibby, sitting in the passenger seat of a van and tapping his fingers against the dashboard.

Kyle stepped around the shrubbery and waved. Then, with slumped, exhausted shoulders, Kyle motioned the others forward. He opened the van's back door and helped everyone climb inside. Tae's father was the last one to enter. While walking, Tae's father had rewrapped the long sword. Carrying it in one hand, the old man looked back one last time, gazing at the mountain. This had been the only home he had ever known.

As the van doors closed, Tae's father stared out the dark tinted windows. He looked at the sword laying across his lap, and a single tear rolled down his cheek. He had chosen life over his country. He'd killed a fellow countryman, a Korean. The night guard was only doing his job. He hadn't hurt anyone, really. All he was trying to do was take them back home. Back where he wanted to go. Where they all belonged.

As the van drove away, the mountain range slipped farther and farther out of view. He stared out the window until the mountain disappeared from view completely. As he turned away, he knew he'd never be coming back. He would never see his homeland again.

38

Gibby and Mr. Kim paid a visit to Tae's brother, who soon understood the dilemma. Gibby pointed out that his family had been cooperating with North Korea. Technically, his country was still in an open military standoff, an ongoing conflict with no apparent resolution or reconciliation in sight. Through Mr. Kim's translations, Gibby made it clear that staying in South Korea was impossible. Things had changed.

The north would never believe that Tae hadn't, at the very least, been an Imperialist sympathizer. Even if they did believe it, he was still at the wrong place at the wrong time. While no one would ever need to know about the killing of the DPRK soldier or helping Kyle, there would still be the question of how he and his family came to be living in South Korea. Nor would they be able to satisfactorily explain why they had abandoned their home at the exact time of a plane crash that, coincidentally, landed on and destroyed their tunnel. The DPRK would never accept them back; if they returned, they would all face imprisonment or, more likely, death.

Similarly, the South Koreans would have deep reservations about what to do with the North Koreans. It complicated matters, given that they had no desire to live in South Korea. Rumors were spreading that the Americans had destroyed a tunnel. Although the Republic of Korea was feeling grateful, it wouldn't take long for people to recognize that Tae's family were from the north. In the end, their accents would give them away.

This would cause South Korea's National Intelligence Service to begin nosing around and open an investigation. It would require only one interrogation of the parents; discussing the safety of the children would do the trick. Within seconds, each adult would cave in. None of them were professional operatives. Once the South Koreans learned what really happened, it wouldn't be long before everyone in the intelligence community would be piecing everything together.

Tae's brother had been picked up and taken to a safe house. It took the brother less than twenty minutes to work it out in his own mind. He knew he was being told the truth. The Agency, out of gratitude for saving Lt. Benjamin, was willing to turn its head and close its eyes. If they chose to stay in South Korea, it would prove difficult to remain neutral. Gibby knew that, if they stayed, over time, loose lips would sink ships. The Agency couldn't let that happen, kids or no kids.

Through indirect channels, Gibby received reassurances that all additional costs associated with permanently relocating everyone would be considered a reimbursable expense. No receipt would be required. The Agency was unconcerned about the money.

The Agency saw this small expenditure as an investment. The return on investment wouldn't come from the parents and grandparents. The Agency had its eyes on the four young children—Tae's two and their newly discovered cousins, his brother's children—all of whom were old enough to have learned Korean Hangul mal and who were the perfect age to assimilate into a new culture. In terms of future covert assets, it was a potential jackpot. Over time, the Agency knew the children would come around. They would finish their education in the US, growing up watching YouTube and celebrating holidays. The girls would attend slumber parties, while the boys would join Little League baseball or soccer. All four would apply to colleges. It was inevitable.

The Agency always took the long view. It planned decades into the future. This was no small gesture of goodwill; the Agency had ulterior motives.

What choice did the Korean families have? To stay, both countries would hate them. Their lives and the lives of their loved ones would remain in constant jeopardy. The Agency would extend this offer one time. Now. Today. If it was rejected, they would be left to fend for themselves. There would be no second chances. It was a take-it-or-leave-it proposition.

Gibby made all the arrangements, and Mr. Kim accompanied him. As both families were reunited, it was painful and awkward to watch. Tae's brother embraced his parents. It had been too many years since they'd seen each other in person. As he explained who the woman and two children were, elation was soon replaced by sadness and shame for having hidden the fact that he had been married and had children. It was equally sad to watch the brother explain to his wife and children who the others were. They had no idea of their existence. Everything they knew about Tae's brother had been a lie. The magnitude of the deception cut deep. The brother felt distrusted and hated by everyone at the same time.

The awkward reunion was short lived. Hastily, all ten Koreans were transported to Pusan in two separate

Agency GMC Suburbans. Listening to those conversations, it would have been easy to determine which family came from where. In the southern family, the children were arguing about which game to play on the onboard gaming station, and they sometimes complained of being tired or hungry. The children from the north were complete opposites. They never complained; they seemed content just to be together, to occupy the same vehicle.

Regardless of their different behaviors, one look at their clothing would have been enough. There were no designer pants, shirts or shoes on anyone from the north. The clothes worn by the northerners had been custom hand-sewn by Tae's wife and mother. Their shoes were issued by the government, available to anyone who wanted a pair; although the shoes weren't stylish or colorful and bore no logo, they were comfortable, durable, and practical.

The Agency delivered the group to the dock. Their destination was a large cargo ship anchored offshore. Accompanied by four very large and capable Agency operatives, Gibby crossed over first. The Director wanted a safe transfer and had insisted that the Agency participate. The additional Agency presence reduced the likelihood of a double cross by the Chinese smugglers. Gibby was certain that his Agency chaperones would plant tracking devices onboard the ship. The Agency wanted to protect its future assets.

Gibby handed over a large duffle bag. One look at its contents and the Chinese smuggler knew he was dealing with American cargo. The money was stacked in bundles of ten-thousand US dollars each. The bills were crisp, uncirculated hundred-dollar bills, still wrapped in their bands. Unintimidated by the four large escorts, the smuggler randomly selected a bundle from the middle of ten separate bundles. The smuggler handed the bills to one of his men. In front of the others, he scanned the bills. To no one's surprise, they were authentic. In perfect Mandarin, Gibby asked, "Are you going to count it out while we wait?" The sarcasm in his voice was obvious. Gibby was disgusted and irritated by these smugglers. He didn't trust them and hated having to deal with them, but it was the Agency's call, not his.

Surprised, the smuggler looked up and shook his head, calmly saying, "That won't be necessary. We can count it out later. There are ten total passengers, yes?" the smuggler asked in perfect English, with no trace of an accent. Two could play the I-speak-your-language game.

Not to be outdone, Gibby replied in Cantonese, the other prominent Chinese dialect reserved for the nobility. "Yes, ten. And don't get any ideas," he replied as he pointed into the sky. Switching to English, he warned the smugglers in a menacing voice. "If anything happens to any one of these people, our people, we'll blow up your goddamned ship!" Gibby didn't flinch. He glared intensely into the smuggler's eyes.

The American had just delivered five-hundred-thousand US dollars. The rate had not been negotiated. They paid the full freight. Fifty thousand per person, regardless of the person's age. No senior, child or group discounts offered or requested. A life was a life. Same price for each person.

Regardless of this payday, the smuggler couldn't wait to get underway; the sooner the Americans left his ship, the better. Gibby watched the skiff transport the Koreans to the ship. No one appeared nervous. In fact, they appeared resigned. There was no excitement about moving to a new country. It was a journey neither group of Koreans wanted to make. After all these years, the Koreans were still caught between the power struggle of others. Again, these Koreans found themselves being forced to live, move, and exist as best they could under the control and direction of others.

After arriving at the cargo ship and boarding, the families were shuffled across the deck. Gibby waved goodbye, and the children waved back. With slumped shoulders, a defeated Tae led the way. As the last person ducked into the metal doorway, the smuggler closed the heavy metal door. The sound of creaking steel echoed onto the deck. Gibby waited until the smuggler turned around.

"Remember, we'll be watching the entire way." Right on cue, he pointed into the sky. Mr. Davies came roaring overhead with an unannounced flyby and looked down from the cockpit of a two-seat trainer F-18 Hornet. It had been a while since he'd piloted one. He'd called in a favor and made all the arrangements. Of course, Mr. Davies had control of the stick as it screamed over the cargo ship. For good measure, he rocked the tailfins as he passed by, the universal sign from pilots to acknowledge that they had been seen.

Watching the F-18 fighter jet disappear over the horizon, the Chinese smuggler nodded. He knew these Americans meant business, and he couldn't wait for Gibby and his entourage to leave his ship. When they finally did, he released a deep exhale of cigarette smoke and watched the small dingy carry Gibby and the other men back to shore. In perfect English, he spoke out loud to himself and an otherwise empty deck.

"I hate dealing with the Americans. Always so much drama."

*   *   *   *   *

Kyle had been hidden away out of sight. He slept uninterrupted twenty-four hours. His vision had returned to normal, although for several months he would feel a dull pain in the back of his head. After a thorough medical exam, complete with blood and urine lab work and full battery of x-rays, it was determined that he had sustained a spider-web fracture to his right eye-orbit. He was lucky the fragile thin layer of bone hadn't given way. If he had sustained a full blow-out fracture of the bone, reconstructive surgery would have been required. Through it all, he had sustained only a concussion and was expected to make a full recovery.

Kyle was told to avoid swimming or any physical activities that could aggravate the eye. That meant no surfing, flying, or scuba diving for a while. Any increased pressure to his eyes could cause the thin eggshell bone to give way. He was advised to refrain from such activities over the next three months, and if he could make it for six months, all the better. He'd earned a break and was placed on paid leave for the next thirty days.

"Lt. Benjamin," said X.O. Newland.

"Yes, sir."

"It's nice to see you again. You look much better than the last time I saw you," he smiled.

"Thank you, sir."

"I've been asked to escort you to the Director's office. You've earned the privilege."

Surprised, Kyle smiled. They walked through the main road inside Camp Bonifas. As they approached the restricted area of the Agency, the X.O. slid his security card to open the door. As they were about to enter, Lt. Elliott approached.

"Kyle. How are you feeling?" Moon Dog asked.

"Much better, Lieutenant."

Moon Dog stared down at Kyle's sidearm. For a brief second, just for fun, Moon Dog reconsidered letting Kyle walk through the Director's inner sanctum with his firearm strapped to his hip. But Kyle had been through enough. Moon Dog gestured toward Kyle's new Beretta M9 as he spoke.

"Better stow your piece before we see the Director."

"You think so?" Kyle asked with an unknowing glance.

"You'll see why later," Moon Dog replied.

They waited for Kyle. Inside the Agency Building, Kyle placed his weapon inside a secure locker and the trio set off toward the Director's office. As they went through the security drill, Moon Dog enjoyed being the spectator. Even for a hero like Lt. Benjamin, rules were rules. Everyone who entered was subjected to the full body scan, followed by a single-file walk through the descending cinderblock corridor.

Although Moon Dog and X.O. Newland were accustomed to this environment, it was very different from what Kyle had been exposed to so far during his South Korean Agency assignment. Other than his living quarters and brief stay at the medical facility following the conclusion of *Hummingbird*, Kyle had spent his entire time wandering around the DMZ.

As the men entered the Director's wing, Kyle was given the honor. He led the group inside her office. Before stepping inside, Kyle was curious about something.

"Moon Dog, why didn't the bombs detonate when I entered the code?"

Moon Dog and the X.O. exchanged knowing glances. With a big smile, Moon Dog replied.

"At first, we hadn't realized you tried to detonate the packages. During the follow up and briefing phase, I discovered what you did. Lucky for everyone you made a mistake. You included your birth year. The code was four digits, not six. You were supposed to enter only the month and day."

The X.O. and Moon Dog watched Kyle's facial expression as it sank in. The X.O. broke the silence.

"It's all good, though, Lieutenant. I'll let it slide this time."

They laughed it off. As Kyle walked through the Director's door, he was struck by his good fortune. It was the best mistake he'd ever made.

"Gentlemen," Director Valdez said as she raised her eyes from a four-inch-thick folder. "Please, take a seat."

There were three strategically placed chairs in front of her large desk. As they sat down, they saw the Director press her right thumb into a spherical ink blot, saturating her thumb in red ink. She placed her ink-covered thumb over the top page of a thick folder and pressed down, leaving her thumbprint impression next to a blank signature line. She dated, signed, and glanced at the wall clock before scribbling the time onto the page.

"Lt. Benjamin. We finally meet," the Director said with a full confident smile. "I've heard a lot about you. And it's all been good," she added as she glanced at the other two.

"Thank you, ma'am," Kyle replied. Moon Dog and X.O. Newland smiled as they watched the introductions.

"For your first assignment, you pulled off a doozy. We've decided that, given the sensitive nature of this mission, it's best to get you out of Asia for a while. You did a great job! You've been cleared by medical, but they want you stay off planes for a while. You've been assigned to our Office in Germany. You'll be catching a ride with the Atlantic Fleet's Aircraft Carrier *USS George H. W. Bush* CVN-77."

As Moon Dog heard Kyle's orders, to be transported on the CVN-77, he couldn't help but see the irony of it all. The Director noticed Moon Dog's reaction.

"Lt. Elliott? You seem to approve of the assignment," the Director asked.

"Yes ma'am. It just seems fitting that Kyle, I mean, Lt. Benjamin, would be catching a ride on that particular aircraft carrier," Moon Dog clarified.

"How so?" she asked.

"Well, ma'am. The *USS George H. W. Bush* was the first aircraft carrier to launch UCAVs. (unmanned combat air vehicles). The X-47Bs are drones designed specifically for aircraft carriers," Moon Dog replied.

She smiled at Moon Dog. She knew that Moon Dog was going to be a perfect fit. She already knew the significance. She just wanted to see how informed Lt. Elliott was. The Director switched her attention from the X.O. back to Moon Dog. She continued in an offhanded manner. "It's no coincidence, Lt. Elliott. We thought, given your recent level of experience, you could travel along. Don't worry, you're just going to babysit Lt. Benjamin to the Mediterranean. To make sure he doesn't get lost." She glanced back at Kyle with a friendly smirk. "Then, Moon Dog, you'll be brought back here. We're thinking it would be a good opportunity to discuss the use of Unmanned Aerial Vehicles as a standard deployment force for all permanent Agency locations throughout the globe."

Not missing a beat, Moon Dog replied, "I look forward to the opportunity. When do we go, ma'am?"

"Start packing, gentlemen," she said.

Surprised, the X.O. chimed in. "Me too?" By his facial expression and tone, everyone could see that the X.O.

was just kidding. He had no desire to go on another trip. He had far too many hours on his resume already.

"Sorry, X.O. You're staying here with me," the Director replied. She stood and shook Lt. Benjamin's hand. "Again, my congratulations to each one of you. Job well done."

In unison, they saluted and stood at attention. Even though they were technically in a civilian capacity, their military backgrounds made it almost impossible to change their protocol. Director Valdez nodded her head and returned their salutes. "Visit Mr. Davies outside. He'll fill you in on the time schedule."

As the three men exited her office, she saw an email pop up from Agency Director Gamboa in California. It looked like something was up. At the Agency, the excitement never stopped for long.

*   *   *   *   *

The smugglers were used to these trips. They did it four times a year, and it was a business they'd enjoyed for several decades. The human cargo was always hidden deep inside the bowels of the cargo ship. As the ship inched across the Pacific Ocean, no one was allowed up top. As they approached Canada, they were moved inside a large steel cargo-freight-train boxcar. The boxcar was later unloaded and dropped along the US-Canadian border.

The smugglers promised to return within two days. They supplied enough food, water, sleeping bags, pillows, and bedding for everyone. The boxcar's occupants were forced to share two large plastic buckets to relieve themselves. Spare batteries and flashlights were handed out. There would be no fires or electric heaters. They didn't want any chance of a fire.

The following evening, as promised, the smugglers returned. Everyone inside was grateful to hear the heavy metal doors open and breathe fresh Canadian air. The smugglers helped the passengers climb the snow-covered bank near the railroad tracks and climb into the waiting van. The smugglers noticed that this shipment was a mixed group. Some appeared tough as nails, unaffected by the difficult journey, while others, seemed to be physically and emotionally drained by the ordeal. Concealed beneath the night sky, the van bumped along a dirt road. In no time, the van entered a paved road and led them undetected into the US. It was an uneventful and quiet crossing, the kind the smugglers and their customers preferred.

One of their last obligations was to get the passengers a hot meal. The smugglers' final responsibility was to deliver them to the bus station and purchase each passenger a one-way ticket to Los Angeles. As the smugglers surveyed the passengers' faces, they found it difficult to guess which ten were the special passengers. The oldest couple, and the family of four, seemed to fit the bill. These six seemed better equipped to face the journey ahead. There was no doubt in the smugglers' minds these six passengers were from the Democratic People's Republic of Korea. The other stowaways were probably South Koreans. They watched the passengers stuff their faces and down hot coffee.

Within an hour, the group had completed their meals. For some, this was their first introduction to an American restroom, hot running water, tall stall-surrounded toilets, and motion-sensor paper-towel dispensers. The North Koreans were amazed; the South Koreans weren't. They'd seen it all before. In fact, the restrooms in South Korea were more modern and cleaner.

After a quick freshening up, the ragtag bunch re-boarded the van. From there, they were transported to the Seattle Greyhound bus station. To the smugglers' surprise, a tall Korean man dressed in a suit and tie was waiting for their arrival. He pulled ten of his passengers out of line, and they all seemed to recognize him. He led them toward two black GMC Suburban sedans. Without looking back, the ten stowaways separated into two groups and climbed inside. Within minutes, the two vehicles pulled away heading toward the Interstate 5 onramp heading south.

As the remaining stowaways watched, one of the smugglers stuffed the money he was going to use to pay for those ten passengers' bus fare back into his pocket. He was glad to be rid of them. Ever since he had taken possession of them, he'd been worried and fearful that something would happen to one of them. Before turning back to the bus station ticket line, he looked up into the sky, wondering if the Americans were still watching him from above.

*   *   *   *   *

Angelie had been recalled by the International School. Given the killings in the village, they didn't feel comfortable sending her back. All of the other teaching slots had been filled. She was given the option of staying in the dormitory for the next month in hopes of filling a vacancy for a teacher with some unexpected emergency, an illness, or a change of heart.

While Angelie waited in the dorm, she received a call on her personal cell phone. She was instructed to wait outside of the dorm and told that a cab would pick her up.

She wasn't surprised to see the same driver from her last visit. Without any drama or speaking, she entered the cab. He took her to the Kimchi House to meet the old woman. After parking in front, he turned back toward Angelie. In perfect English, he spoke.

"She's waiting for you inside."

Angelie guessed the cat and mouse game was over. The driver no longer pretended to be just the cab driver. As she pushed open the heavy door with the plate-glass window, the metal door chimes announced her arrival. Glancing up at the large ceiling-mounted mirror, Angelie saw the reflection of the old woman's face. She was hiding behind the display case, waiting in an adjacent room. Angelie was surprised to hear the old woman speak. In a clear, confident, powerful voice, and without any hint of a Korean accent, she spoke.

"Angelie, come back behind the counter."

Reluctantly, Angelie dropped her head. What choice did she have? Without delay, she walked around the glass display case and approached the woman, who was sitting on a wooden stool with her elbows on the small wooden desk. There was no other chair. Angelie avoided eye contact and stared at the floor. She stood in front of the old woman and waited.

"You've done well. Don't be scared."

Hearing her words, Angelie glanced up. To her surprise, the old woman was actually smiling. There was something powerful about her. Despite her size and age, she demanded respect. Angelie was certain that the woman could handle herself.

"For now, we're going to send you back to the US. I need you to go back to the International School. Let them know that you've changed your mind."

"Where will you send me, home?" Angelie asked.

"Not yet. For now, we're sending you to Los Angeles. There is a huge Korean population there. The man you met at LAX will escort you to your new assignment. We have several apartments along Wilshire Blvd. He'll explain everything."

"When do I leave?"

"Tonight. Here are your tickets."

The old woman opened the top drawer of the desk. She grabbed the tickets, which were lying next to a handgun.

"You'll be working in a restaurant for a while. Be careful," said the old woman as she handed Angelie the tickets. "One more thing," said the old woman. "I need you to learn to speak fluent Korean while you're there."

Angelie glanced down and read the ticket and itinerary. They were in her name. When she looked up, the old woman had already stood and was walking toward another room. The old woman never looked back. She walked into the next room and closed the door. Their meeting was over.

*   *   *   *   *

Carla Jo had made all the arrangements. Their apartment was deep inside of LA's Koreatown. Mr. Kim had made the trip back to the US and was chaperoning their guests from Seattle to LA. During the drive down the West Coast, Mr. Kim switched back and forth between the two vehicles. It gave him an opportunity to speak to each group. They stopped sixteen hours later in a Holiday Inn along I-5 in Redding, California. Each family had their own room. After everyone showered, the group was treated to a hot authentic Korean meal. Mr. Kim kept the room keys and emphasized that they could not leave their rooms. He needn't have been concerned; no one had any intention of running away.

They had no idea where they were, but they felt safe and taken care of. For the first time in decades, Tae's family was together. They were soon fast asleep.

The next morning, the families had another round of Korean takeout before the vehicles were back on I-5 heading south. Other than two more gas and restroom stops, they kept moving. It had been a boring, ten-hour drive down the center of California, through the barren section along I-5, but that all changed as they climbed the Grapevine pass and entered Los Angeles County. All the passengers pressed their faces up to the windows, as the size of the freeway expanded with additional lanes. When they reached Highway 101, they turned east and continued toward downtown Los Angeles.

Awestruck, they began passing places they'd seen only on television. Like tourists, they pointed at the Sunset Strip exit, signs for Dodger Stadium, and the famous Hollywood sign. They seemed disappointed to learn that Disneyland wasn't in LA County but further south in the city of Anaheim in Orange County. Finally, the vehicles exited Highway 101 on Vermont Avenue and began entering Koreatown.

They began seeing store signs and billboards written in Korean Hangul script. Their faces lit up. For the first time, smiles flashed across their faces, especially the children's. The farther the vehicles drove into Koreatown, the denser the Korean neon lights and advertisements seemed to be. The sedans turned right onto Wilshire Boulevard, and they drove down a busy street in the center of K-Town's financial district for a distance before turning into an underground parking structure.

Mr. Kim led the family through the parking garage and into the lobby of their new apartment building. They all squeezed into the elevator and rode it up to the eleventh floor. The Agency would be picking up the tab for everything. They wanted to keep a tight watch over them. Every room was bugged. Hidden cameras were staged throughout their apartment.

The apartment had five bedrooms and four bathrooms. Outside of Korea, Los Angeles's Koreatown had the biggest concentration of Koreans on the globe. Koreatown was located just outside of Beverly Hills and was home to some of the wealthiest people in Southern California. The goal was for Tae's family to adapt into the Americanized Korean culture. It was a chance to start a new life together. They would no longer be separated.

The Agency had ulterior motives. Nothing came for free. For now, nothing would be asked of them. Paybacks would come much later. The four children were the perfect age. One day, the children would be approached, probably while they were still in high school. Scholarships would be extended. Teachers, who had shown special interest in their educations would make subtle suggestions. Tae and his brother would also be given jobs. It would start out subtle. No direct quid pro quo would be mentioned. They would wait for Tae's parents to pass away; it would be easier. The Agency would wait and do anything in their power to help Tae's family accept their new lives. They would wait until Tae's family considered themselves to be Americans, both legally and emotionally. If they cooperated and adapted, the Agency would help them gain citizenship. Then the Agency would make its move. It was the Agency way. They always took the long view. The Agency thought in terms of decades.

Tae and his family opened the door to their new apartment. They couldn't believe this was where they would be living. Unlike Tae's brother's family, this level of luxury was unimaginable. While his brother's children ran through the apartment, exploring through every room, the others walked tentatively, careful not to touch anything. It took a while for them to find the formal dining room. They all were awestruck to see the table full of Korean food.

Mr. Kim watched it all unfold. During their trip south, he watched Tae's wife and children as they saved all of their empty plastic utensils, disposable wood chopsticks, and drink containers, keeping them organized in a plastic bag. Tae's wife carried that same bag into the kitchen and washed them all in hot soapy water. To dry, she set them on the countertop.

Carla Jo had made sure that their first night was special. When she picked up the takeout food, she noticed a young lady server. There was something familiar about her. If Carla Jo hadn't been so preoccupied with organizing the apartment for Tae's family, she might have noticed similarities. This time, Angelie's hair had been colored and cut short. She was no longer pretending to be unable to speak Korean. Neither woman noticed the other.

Carla Jo had taken the liberty of mounting Tae's family's heirloom high on the dining room wall. It had been shined and fully restored. Tae saw it first. As his father entered, he pointed it out. Tae's father's eyes filled with tears of joy. He thought that the Americans had taken it away. He was certain he would never see it again.

Mr. Kim explained that, for their own safety, they could not leave the apartment. If they needed anything, he was in the apartment across the hallway. Carla Jo watched the scene unfold on the Agency monitors. She and Mr. Kim would babysit Tae's family for the next few months. Mr. Kim left. He walked across the hall and opened the door. Carla Jo turned away from the monitor and waved Mr. Kim in. They had converted the dining area into a surveillance room.

Like a television sitcom, Carla Jo and Mr. Kim were mesmerized by what they saw. It was more like a reality show. They watched Tae's father start an unplanned impromptu family ceremony. Mr. Kim translated as Carla Jo watched the family kneel down on the carpeted floor and bow to the ground. They all faced the wall-mounted sword. After paying their respects to their ancestors, they stood and took positions around the large table. The northern family members seemed to feel uncomfortable sitting in the chairs around the table. Their previous dining room table had been a low table where they sat on the floor. His brother's family had no adjustments to make. It was just like their home back in Seoul.

Each wife scurried off to the kitchen in search of utensils, chopsticks, and glasses of water. Mr. Kim noticed it first.

"Tae's family is sitting on the same side as his father," Mr. Kim pointed out. Carla Jo tilted her head as she studied their positions around the table. Tae's father was seated facing the wall mounted sword. Carla Jo had been adamant that the sword was to be centered around their table. At first, Carla Jo assumed that out of habit, Tae's wife and children were accustomed to eating sitting next to Tae's father and mother.

But Carla Jo noticed something else. Tae's wife had placed the freshly washed and clean used plastic containers and chop sticks on their side of the table. Tae and the children were busy drying off the disposable wooden chopsticks and plastic spoons, and placing them down on top of paper napkins. In contrast, his brother's wife had located the new silverware inside the kitchen. She placed the new, never-before-used metal chopsticks and long silver serving spoons on top of cloth napkins. They were all so happy to be able to sit down, together as a family that they hadn't noticed what each group was doing. Each side of the family behaved the way they been taught. Neither group noticed the differences.

As they sat down to eat, Mr. Kim made a final observation. He noticed the family still appeared separated. Divided by their differences of habit. Then it struck him. Tae's wife and children were gathered on the northern side of the dining table, while his brother's wife and children were on the southern side. Even now, after traveling thousands of miles away from their homeland, without being forced apart by those in power, it had become an unconscious reality. What lay between them and brought them together, was the presence of their father, a person who still paid tribute to and acknowledged the sacrifices of his ancestors and fellow Koreans.

It was the sword. It was a symbol that represented the struggle that Korea had endured for thousands of years. Yet the sword was still there, a modern reminder of the ongoing struggle where two Koreas tried to coexist. Some people still hoped that someday Korea would reunify. The struggle continued, played out along the 38th parallel; a struggle that also played out on the eleventh floor inside an apartment complex in the heart of Los Angeles's Koreatown.

THE END

Afterword

The idea for this book started following a conversation with a friend. She explained that the North Koreans dug invasion tunnels under the DMZ. During the Korean War, the tunnels were used to infiltrate South Korea. I'd never heard the story and thought it was an urban legend. I was intrigued.

As I researched the topic, I was surprised to learn that these tunnels really do exist. Based on what was available over the internet, YouTube documentaries, and reliable national news media reports, three tunnels were found in the 1970s, one in 1990, and the most recent one in 2014. The Republic of Korea's Defense Minister believes that as many as twenty infiltration tunnels could still be in existence.

As recent as October 2, 2014, CNN interviewed a retired two-star General from The Republic of Korea's Army, Major General Hahn Sung Chu. Chu is now considered a "tunnel hunter." He claims to have uncovered three new tunnels below an apartment complex in Seoul, South Korea.

The current South Korean budget allocated to search for these tunnels was dramatically reduced. The Republic of Korea believes, given the DPRK's pursuit of nuclear weapons, that the effort to continue to build these tunnels is no longer a priority. Even so, recent defectors maintain that the tunnels previously dug are protected. Should a war break out, they will be used.

As I developed the story around these tunnels, it was impossible to remain true to any accurate historical timeline. Don't become distracted trying to determine the age of Tae and his family members. I wanted to incorporate modern technology into the plot, but this would be problematic if I had become too caught up in the true historical dates of the Korean War; for, in order to keep an accurate timeline, the Korean family members would be too old to engage in the physical demands of the storyline. Therefore, I avoided stating a specific date. I also avoided specifying an age for any of the adult Korean family members. Consequently, the story needs to be appreciated as pure fiction.

My girlfriend is Korean, born and raised in Seoul. Through our relationship, I've learned about the Korean culture; their food, attitudes, and beliefs. I find Koreans fascinating. As I wrote the story, I tried to avoid clichés and prejudicial beliefs about North Koreans. I tried to describe the plight of the situation, exploring the tragedy when families are artificially separated. I wanted the story to focus on the human and personal emotions of the situation, rather than their ideological differences.

I hope the story was enjoyable. Much effort was spent to depict the characters' human side. My goal was to convey the consequences of artificial and forced separation as a universal phenomenon. People from the West, when comparing other societies, tend to focus on others' deficiencies; their lack of freedoms and opportunities while facing extreme hardships. Given a choice, based on these differences, one would assume that its citizens would choose to abandon their culture and their community. However, a society's worth should be based on other factors.

Affiliation is a powerful influence. A group that bands together forms a collective. This bond is created through their commonality. It is this affiliation, the existence of common goals, as opposed to the quality of the landscape, the weather, or the amount of riches that the land possesses, that creates the concept of home.

"Home" is intangible. It conjures up feelings that every human understands. The term isn't reserved only for direct family blood relatives. Nor does it pertain just to physical structures and buildings. To these people, as well as orphans, single individuals, or the abandoned, home could represent a phenomenon in which people share common interests held together by mutual affection. *Home* is a word that describes feelings associated with a specific location. It is why the term "homeland" stirs up similar emotions.

When this type of personal connection happens, and it takes place in a general geographic area, time becomes another element. Time enhances one's emotional attachment. The longer a people, or groups of people, coexist while overcoming challenges through their shared perseverance and commitment to each other, the more they begin to identify as a group, a team, a family, a community, a culture, a country. It is through this collective identification where the emotional term is born. It is this human process conveyed through one simple word: *home*.

Tunnels attempts to convey emotions common to any community. It requires viewing things from another person's perspective. My hope is that, through experiencing the journey of these fictional characters, we come to appreciate the views of others. We can begin to refrain from placing value judgments over which side is right, wrong, or superior. Rather, we can begin to see the beauty of another culture, regardless of its possessions.

Tunnels attempts to explain why most cultures deserve respect. When we see life through the lenses of the human experience, we begin to imagine how different our own lives would be if we were forced or had the misfortune of being born into another set of circumstances. If individually we could identify with the plight of others, maybe collectively we would be less likely to categorize people, dividing humanity into *us* and *them*.

Made in the USA
San Bernardino, CA
19 October 2017